VLADIMIR ILYICH MALENKOV, ABSOLUTE RULER OF THE SOVIET STATE . . .

The accusers faced the frail man on the bed without the slightest sign of sympathy or compassion.

"Vladimir Ilyich Malenkov," intoned Defense Minister Gregor Solnikov, "you are under arrest for crimes against the Party, the State, and the workers of the Soviet Union. I have been chosen to replace you as General Secretary and Commander-in-Chief. You may consider the transfer of power completed."

With difficulty, Malenkov lifted his bony arms. His eyes blinked hesitantly, and the ravaged face creased into a mocking grin. "Bravo, Gregor," wheezed Malenkov in a bitter voice, harsh and hollow. "I see that you haven't lost your love for speeches."

"The military put you into power and has now removed you from it," Solnikov said flatly.

Malenkov sank deeper into the bed, the flush of color fading along with his strength. "Even so, Gregor. All of you," he managed. "There are . . . resources still at my command . . ."

Solnikov shook his head. "Good-bye, Comrade." He reached for the power cutoff switch on the machinery that sustained the General Secretary's life . . .

Bantam Books by Bart Davis

A CONSPIRACY OF EAGLES
BLIND PROPHET
TAKEOVER

TAKEOVER

Bart Davis

BANTAM BOOKS
TORONTO • NEW YORK • LONDON • SYDNEY • AUCKLAND

TAKEOVER

A Bantam Book / June 1986

ISBN 0-553-25708-0

Published simultaneously in the United States and Canada

Bantam Books are published by Bantam Books, Inc. Its trademark,
consisting of the words "Bantam Books" and the portrayal of a
rooster, is Registered in U.S. Patent and Trademark Office and in
other countries. Marca Registrada. Bantam Books, Inc., 666 Fifth
Avenue, New York, New York 10103.

PRINTED IN THE UNITED STATES OF AMERICA

KR   0 9 8 7 6 5 4 3 2 1

This book is dedicated to my father,
who taught me to use words;
and to my mother,
who taught me to love them.

Acknowledgments

I am deeply indebted to Valery Golovskoy, Sharon Davis, Sarah Molloy, and Warren Gleich for their invaluable contributions to this novel; and to the writings of Hedrick Smith, David Shipler, R. W. Apple, Jr., Tom Alexander, Rona Davis, and Robert Kaiser; and, as always, to Robert Gottlieb and Barbara Alpert for their unceasing support.

Author's Note

AI is the scientific acronym for Artificial Intelligence, that branch of computer technology which seeks to automate human thought.

I

KGB Major Valery Rudin paused briefly in his work to gaze out at the pale northern sun that hung so dispiritedly over the frozen lake beyond the dacha's windows. In the far distance, a passenger train puffed heavily through a narrow cut in the surrounding pine forests, the rise and fall of its harsh whistle barely reaching the occupants of the grand ballroom in the mansion's north wing.

Anxious to avoid any sympathetic lessening of spirit, Rudin turned back to watching his technical assistants complete their programs. Huddled groups of his supervisors conferred in tight knots, checking progress, isolating problems, carefully coaxing their computers to perform as one might a nervous lover; never a sign of impatience.

Do they know? Rudin wondered, thinking of what lay ahead. He searched the array of faces for the slightest sign of undisclosed tension but found none. He moved on to direct the next level of interface, the critical connections.

Long ago, the high-ceilinged, ornate room had been the scene of Tsarist balls where guests had arrived in silver carriages drawn by teams of horses. Now, jury-rigged electrical connections from Rudin's computers ran snakelike around the room's perimeter, across the parquet floor, and up into the open banks of electronic circuits that were the guts of the C5 system. The C5 had been installed only one year earlier at the general secretary's command. Rudin frowned. Only a year; there really had been so little time. . . .

In spite of being its designer, Rudin didn't think of the C5 built into the far wall with any sense of genuine affection. For all its capabilities—and no one knew its full range better than Rudin himself—it differed little in its basic design from any

1

advanced serial computer system. Even so, the C5 was so costly and sophisticated that there were only three in the entire Soviet Union: the primary Centralized Command, Control, and Communications Console in the Kremlin's War Room; the secondary in the TU-95 jet aircraft emergency command post; and the backup unit buried deep under the Ural Mountains, a response to the Americans' Mount Thunder.

A sudden soft buzz indicated an incoming message and Rudin moved swiftly across the old wooden floor to receive it. His station clerk decoded and transcribed the communication in seconds using the C5's internal functions and passed it to him. Rudin read it once; then again. He grew pensive. Time would be a pressure now—the generals had begun to move.

His gaze was drawn by this thought to the wide array of light-blinking consoles. How alien the invasion of the modern world had first seemed in this place of Catherine and her royal court. He'd shied away from making the inevitable physical alterations until he recalled how the enraged peasants must have felt on that long-ago October day when they pulled powdered ladies from this very room and murdered them outside in the snow.

No, he decided, transgressions in this place were nothing new.

Rudin forced his attention back to the task at hand, accepting the reports of his supervisors who anticipated completion shortly and a test run moments later. He signaled for and caught the attention of the nursing supervisor. *Soon;* Rudin's lips formed the word. She nodded and extended her hand, flipped it over and back. Rudin understood. He knew her signs from long association. The patient was still stable; neither better nor worse.

The patient—how easily illness reversed power, Rudin thought as the nurse returned to her charge, slipping through the seam in the translucent sheathing that surrounded the cradle-railed hospital bed in the room's center. Hung from floor to ceiling, the millimeter-thick material encased the bed, the patient, and the triple bank of whirring, pumping machinery that kept him alive. In fact, the patient was the sole reason for everything Rudin had done—and that included the silent object standing just beyond the curtained bed. Positioned free of any encumbrance save for one thick cable extruding into the

C5's main terminal and another into the machinery within the plastic curtain, it was the crowning achievement of Rudin's life.

Having no children of his own, Rudin could not be certain that genuine paternal love was what he felt when he looked at the polished silver oblong about the size and shape of an upright multidrawer filing cabinet. But this was the only progeny that he would ever have. He dissected his feelings further. . . . Would this be enough? Yes; if things functioned as they were designed to. There were, he knew, several quantities still unknown.

The technicians were finished now, sealing cabinets and closing final circuits. Rudin smoothed out his sleep-wrinkled uniform and pondered the unknowns again. So little time, he thought with regret. It would just have to do.

Preparing himself mentally, he parted the curtains that screened the bed and looked for what he knew was the last time at Vladimir Ilyich Malenkov, general secretary of the Communist Party of the Soviet Union, commander-in-chief of the armed forces, and state president; the dying man who ruled the Soviet state absolutely.

Disease had wasted the man. He was ordinarily thick-necked and strong, and had early on been recognized as a brutal and efficient leader. A top KGB man. Later, as general secretary, it was paradoxically evident that he possessed a rare capacity for enormous warmth and enduring charm. Rudin knew both sides and found no contradiction. He had followed the man loyally; still followed, he corrected himself.

But one kidney had failed suddenly only a year after his coming to power. Then the second began to deteriorate. Constant dialysis was necessary to keep Malenkov alive as problems from blood chemistry imbalances grew more serious. Heart problems followed. He had been in this room for months now, linked to an elaborate feeding/filtration system and a heart/lung machine in order to maintain his lifeblood's vitality.

Malenkov's skin was like parchment, drawn thin across broad, flat bones. The once-massive head with its thick brow was now gaunt and cavernous. It was only in the deep, dark eyes that one could still see the light of the energy that churned within. Even now, Rudin noted, impressed in spite of himself, Malenkov was marshaling his strength one final time.

The eyes flickered.

Rudin sat and took up the bear-claw of a hand, saddened it

could feel so fragile. *Shutdown*, he repeated in his mind. Then, *Icecap*. You must remember, he thought, not wanting to speak the words aloud.

There was a sudden tightening of the wrinkles at the corners of Malenkov's eyes. Was this a hint of bemusement from the crafty, cunning old wolf? Rudin wondered. But he understood. There would be no forgetting.

Go now; the thought was communicated in a quick, sharp thrust of Malenkov's chin. For an instant, Rudin felt a return pressure from his hand. It was enough. He turned away.

The room was empty of people when Rudin emerged from the enclosure. Lights blinked softly on scores of panels. Relays opened and closed with soft snaps. Memory bubbles danced in magnetic fluids, and data screens glowed soft green. He closed the curtains. Finally, lovingly, Rudin reached out and touched the silver shape in a certain way and felt a sensation of power abruptly tinge the air. Outside, the sun touched the lake.

The nurse was waiting quietly for him in the hallway. He followed her down several staircases until they reached the basement level. She preceded him into the windowless room where his entire company of technicians and supervisors waited. They looked to him as he entered. Someone sealed the door.

It was Rudin himself who turned on the toxic gas and, in the last brief, painful moments, understood that his people had known all along what lay at the end of their task. He wanted to cry at such loyalty.

But then a darkness deeper even than the night took him completely.

II

The generals and their aides assembled on the icy ground between the dacha's long, graveled circular drive and the wide stone steps that led up to its porticoed entrance. They had all arrived in black Zil limousines that now sat idling, sending plumes of smoke from their exhaust pipes into the frigid air.

Marshal Aleksandr Tarkov, first deputy minister of defense and chief of the General Staff, stretched his gloves more tightly across the knuckles of his long, thin hands and muttered an oath at the cold. He passed a gloved finger along the ridge of his aquiline nose but then quickly suppressed the nervous habit. He was anxious to begin and only the absence of the minister of defense prevented him from entering the dacha at once with the forces that were his to command.

His generals beside him—each a commander of one of the five branches of the military establishment—shared his apprehension and his distaste for the wait, but they stood silently, braced against the weather. Not men given to idle chatter, or even close camaraderie, they spent their time in solitary reflection.

Collectively, however, they were a group that was used to power, had sought it single-mindedly and enjoyed its exercise over others. Even more than power, though it was the deep need of all military men for ceremony and ritual that had brought them together here. For this moment to be . . . consummated, they needed each other. In part, to witness the transfer of authority; in part, to be able to say, Yes, I was *there*. But most of all, later on, to be able to bask in the memory of this day among themselves as fellow travelers are warmed by the heat of a shared fire.

So they came when Tarkov summoned them. First among equals was General Kuzanov of the Soviet Army. His was the most powerful service, still the major element of the country's military power. The commanding general of the Air Force and the admiral of the Navy were there, too. Holding these trump cards, Tarkov had been able to secure the support of the remaining generals of the Strategic Rocket Forces and the internal Air Defense Force. Both survivors, they had correctly sensed the herd's movement and adjusted their own courses accordingly.

The sight of the defense minister's limousine coming up the drive brought sounds of relief from the assemblage. The pack began to drift forward but Tarkov motioned them back. He alone moved off to meet the minister.

Marshal of the Soviet Union Gregor Solnikov emerged from his limousine with the inevitable wince at the sudden change in temperature. "What a miserable climate this, eh, Aleksandr?"

"Undeniably, Comrade Minister. But I hope at least you had a pleasant trip up here."

Solnikov drew his coat more tightly around himself. "Pleasant enough, with only an ocean of pine trees to look at. I don't care for the solitude. It leaves too much time to think. And to worry." They moved off together, the gravel in the driveway crunching under their feet as they walked. "But Malenkov probably had that in mind when he chose this place for his 'winter palace.'"

Tarkov accepted that. "I never knew him to do anything without reason or craft. The isolation here made his summons that much more ominous. He enjoyed that."

"You're using the past tense quite easily, Aleksandr. Are you so confident?"

"Absolutely. Malenkov is close to death, dependent upon his machines. I fail to see what power he can muster against you."

Solnikov shrugged off a vague uneasiness. Damn that long ride! "Everyone is here, then?"

Tarkov nodded. "General Kuzanov's troops have had the surrounding woods controlled for days and we've had roadblocks in place to check incoming traffic. He's ready to take the house on your order."

Solnikov bit at a loose thread in his glove. "Give it. But be careful. Malenkov's a clever old campaigner and there is something about his retreating up here that worries me. The maneuver is uncharacteristic."

"He has no force here at all," Tarkov objected. "Only the stable of technicians that keep his machinery working."

"What about his vaunted computer genius, Rudin?"

Tarkov looked uncomfortable for the first time. "Rudin is with him. As usual," he added. "But I fail to see a problem. What can any one man do against the combined might of the military?"

"I don't think he can do anything, Aleksandr. But when this is over, please see that Rudin is with us or that he is dead. I know I can live without a computer genius; I don't want to discover I can't live with one."

"As you wish, Minister. Shall we go inside now?"

The generals followed the minister and the chief of staff,

trailed by their aides and a platoon of soldiers. The buzz of conversation faded as they entered the dacha's central lobby and climbed the wide marble staircase to the second floor. Moving down the long hallway to the ballroom, soldiers were posted at intervals and left standing at attention.

General Kuzanov gave a command and the doors to the ballroom were flung open. Soldiers ran in ahead and posted themselves strategically around the room, surprised to find it virtually empty.

The silence was oppressive, the array of quietly flashing computers and stainless steel machinery intimidating. Disregarding his disquiet, Minister Solnikov and his generals walked directly to the hospital bed. Marshal Tarkov motioned to his aides, and the surrounding curtains were opened and flung aside. The accusers faced the bed's frail occupant without the slightest sign of sympathy or compassion.

"Vladimir Ilyich Malenkov," intoned Solnikov gravely, "you are under arrest for crimes against the Party, the state, and the workers of the Soviet Union. In order to restore the most basic tenets of Marxist-Leninist thought and to eradicate your extensive errors in ideology and doctrine, you are now relieved of all rank, titles, and authority so mistakenly given to you. I have been chosen to replace you as the new general secretary and commander-in-chief. You may consider the transfer of power completed."

A ripple of released tension seemed to pass through the assemblage. Months of strategic personnel transfers, of behind-the-scenes power brokerage, even of premature deaths, had finally culminated in this moment: a moment spawned by the radical policies of the man who lay so helpless before them. It was done now—the invocation delivered, the coup complete. The military would be sovereign again and restore control over ideology. Malenkov and his new "economic managers" were finished.

Speaking in a milder voice, then, one that contained at least some remembrance of their shared early struggles, Solnikov leaned over and said so that no other could hear, "Give it up, Vladimir. Make it easy on all of us. I'll do what I can."

With difficulty, Malenkov's bony arms rose from his sides.

His eyes blinked hesitantly and strain was evident on his face. Slowly at first, and then with increasing strength, Malenkov brought his clawlike hands together once, and then again and again. The ravaged face creased into a mocking grin, and the unmistakable sound of clapping echoed throughout the room.

"Bravo, Gregor. Bravo," said Malenkov, wheezing in a bitter voice, harsh and hollow. "I see that you haven't lost your love for speeches. But is that all? Can the theater be over so soon? Or do you wish my accounting of *your* treachery?"

Solnikov was startled but recovered quickly. "Your false accounting is unnecessary. This takeover is an accomplished fact. Although it strikes me that the word 'treachery' is well placed in your mouth."

"I betrayed only old men who loved privilege more than their people."

"I didn't come here to argue politics, Vladimir," said Solnikov. "The military put you into power and has now removed you from it. Policy will return to normal. You were a brief mistake that the people will soon forget ever influenced events."

"And the economy?" Malenkov demanded, color coming back briefly into his face.

"The people must make do with their share," Tarkov broke in angrily, speaking for the first time. "Cutting back on military spending invited disaster. We had to act."

"Unbridled militarism invited disaster," Malenkov shot back with surprising strength. "We have been secure for years. It was time to feed the people something more than slogans."

"But a treaty with the Americans?" blurted the army's General Kuzanov, outraged. "An economic dependence? We could not permit such a thing."

"Of course not," Malenkov agreed sadly. "It might have meant peace."

"Enough," said Solnikov with grim determination. "You condemn yourself with every utterance. Nationalism subverting communism, marketplaces supplanting centralized planning—"

"Things that haven't worked!" cried Malenkov.

Solnikov ignored him. "—loosening of vital Party controls, cutbacks in military spending and strength. The only true amazement, Vladimir, is how we could have misjudged you so completely."

"You didn't really. Not in the beginning. But perspective, Gregor, it changes a man. That, and a distaste for hypocrisy."

"Then you've given us perspective, too," pronounced Solnikov. "Rest assured, it will never happen again."

Malenkov sank deeper into the bed, the flush of color fading along with his strength. "Even so, Gregor. All of you," he managed. "There are . . . resources still at my command. . . ."

Solnikov shook his head. "Good-bye, comrade." He reached for the power cutoff switch on the machinery.

"*Shutdown,*" said Vladimir Malenkov, and turned away.

The room was plunged into darkness. Only the lights on the C5's massive console glowed brilliantly in the sharp, sudden shadows. Strident alarm bells clanged, demanding attention to incoming messages. High-speed teleprinters spat out a sudden flood of paper. Phones began ringing all at once. The room became a madhouse as soldiers drew their weapons reflexively but found only panicked officers in their sights.

Sudden explosions outside shook the windows. Plaster fell from the ceiling, and people dove for cover. Tarkov ran to the glass doors, forced them open, and looked back to the burning ruins in the driveway.

"The cars . . ." he yelled over the chaos inside.

"Forget them!" screamed Solnikov. "Find the lights!"

Kuzanov had his pistol drawn, anticipating some kind of an attack. He began shoving men forcibly out of the room to search the rest of the building. In the melee, people collided, fell, screamed curses at the darkness.

Aides rushed to man the C5, only to shout back incredible reports to unbelieving superiors.

"General! The Kiev Military District reports level green on ICBM prelaunch! Something has put them on full alert status and they can't override. Request—"

"—to confirm loss of three jet wings after in-course flight data changed . . . pilots forced to bail out over—"

"—report submarine, Black Sea, trapped in thick ice due to inertial navigation override—"

"—Civil Defense in Moscow requesting—"

"—alert status unchanged . . . satellite *Cosmos 1174* in orbit decay. Request for additional—"

"Secure that board!" Solnikov demanded, stumbling. "Tarkov, I want control over—"

And suddenly, the lights came back on. The effect was instantaneous. Everyone just stopped.

The C5 stood mute, still in control but shunting incoming communications momentarily over to hold. Its lights continued to blink quietly, almost insolently. The operators collapsed back into their seats, dazed. Paper fluttered softly to the floor.

Generals picked themselves up and began pulling together their uniforms and dignity. Some nursed bruised limbs. Faces turned from fear to its opposite: anger.

But in the sudden silence, they heard the crackling, reedy hiss of Malenkov's mocking chortle. "Even so, Gregor. Even so. Still resources at my command."

Solnikov approached him, stood threateningly at the foot of the bed. "It won't keep you alive. No such parlor trick will keep you alive. And dead, you command nothing."

Malenkov's dark eyes gleamed wickedly. "That would be a trick, would it not? To control even from death? But you fail to see what I have done here, Gregor. You cannot kill me or even take from me what is mine. The program is activated now and cannot be altered. My machines will protect me."

Kuzanov stepped forward, leveled his pistol at Malenkov's head. "Enough words, Minister."

"So one-track, the military mind," murmured Malenkov dryly.

A teleprinter began to chatter suddenly, extruded several feet of paper, and stopped. Solnikov put a restraining hand on the general's and motioned for the paper to be brought to him. He read it, and spots of color flamed high on his cheeks. He passed it silently to Kuzanov.

"Comrade Minister," the general began helplessly, "I swear this is . . . the girl is only—"

Solnikov held up an angry hand and returned his gaze to the bed. "You want me to believe that you can deliver this kind of . . . information in response to a threat?"

Malenkov nodded. "On any of you. It's automatic. Any attempt to harm me . . ." He shrugged. "Surely you must remember that I was chairman of the KGB long before I was the general secretary. And I retained access long after. Think, Gregor. The chairman's files. And linked to the C5's capabilities, the information can be in an editorial on tomorrow's front page of *Pravda* and you could stop it only by failing to print the paper itself. Are you willing to risk that, Minister of Defense? Would even you risk alerting the ever-snooping Americans to what takes place here among us today?"

"This is monstrous and you are an abomination."

"Ah, Gregor." Malenkov almost laughed. "This is the great game and I am a survivor."

"Comrade Minister," cut in an anxious commander, "in the Missile Forces we have more experience with computers than in most of the other branches. The C5 just cannot do what he claims!"

"Go on, General," said Solnikov quickly.

"The C5 requires control. A human control. This is a clever ruse but that is all it is. There can be no control without a living operator. Judgment, extrapolation, especially something as subtle as common sense cannot be a part of a serial machine. Not even one as sophisticated as the C5."

The group stirred hotly at the general's remarks. Like sharks tasting blood, murder reentered their minds. But it was Solnikov who stepped back as if struck.

"Rudin!" he said suddenly. "Tarkov, you told me that Rudin was here." The realization continued to grow. "And his staff. Find them at once. Tarkov? What's wrong with you?"

Tarkov's gaze was drawn back down to the bed-ridden old man whose cunning he was only now beginning to fully appreciate. He locked eyes with Malenkov for a long moment, fighting the intimidation he felt; amazed that it could spring from so frail a figure.

Malenkov smiled. "Tell him."

Tarkov's face hardened. "Rudin is dead, Minister. He was found only minutes ago in a sealed room in the basement along with his technicians and the nursing staff."

Solnikov could not hide the astonishment in his voice. He stared at Malenkov. "He was your friend! How could you—"

"It was suicide, Minister," volunteered Tarkov. "Mass suicide by lethal gas."

The enormity of it held Solnikov's attention on his adversary.

"Loyalty, Gregor," said Malenkov very softly. "They knew you couldn't question dead men. Loyalty. And I will never forgive you for forcing me to demand it of them. Remember that well."

Solnikov wrenched his gaze away. "Then who controls the C5?" he demanded. "Who protects you with KGB files and overrides my control of the nation's defenses? Who keeps you alive, Vladimir? Damn you, who?"

"How foolish you can be, Gregor. Even now you fail to see." Malenkov settled deeper into the bedding, his skin so pale that they could almost see the blood flowing underneath.

"Tell me!" Solnikov demanded, driven by need, unconcerned at his audience.

"Why, Gregor," said Malenkov mockingly. "It's Rudin who protects me still."

Solnikov's rage threatened to overwhelm him. Tarkov moved nearer, glancing with alarm at the teleprinter and the C5 beyond it.

"Minister—" Tarkov warned.

"*Icecap,*" Malenkov said softly.

A final relay closed in the silver unit beside him, bringing the primal intelligence within to its fullest capabilities. A mind of enormous power coalesced from the mists of random thought, self-regulating and aware. From this moment on it would modify its own programs as the need arose. Selectively. Creatively.

Deep within was the "voice" of its creator, almost silent now. It paid him respectful homage. The template for all of its logic, its every judgment, and all of its emotions was Valery Rudin. In a sense, Rudin himself had not died. His essence . . . his soul? . . . could still be thought to exist, merely transferred. He was still protecting Malenkov—from the other side of the grave.

But the AI wasn't Rudin alone. "Alive" now, it was fully independent of human control. It would adhere, as best it could, to the designs of its creator, protecting Malenkov to the fullest extent of its awesome abilities. That was basic, a given. But it also had within itself the power to change, to grow. Things stirred within.

Icecap. It reacted to the danger accordingly, placing

Malenkov out of its reach. A signal went out to the bank of machinery that fed and cared for Malenkov, machines that *it* now controlled, and a tiny amount of a chemical compound was released into the system that filtered the general secretary's blood. Carried swiftly to his brain, it cast him deeper and deeper down into a protected domain of internal darkness where he could wait, untouched by his enemies and kept alive by his machines, until he could return safely to the living and the light. The AI was in charge now.

Beyond harm, Malenkov slept.

III

Solnikov slammed the ballroom doors behind them. "Leave your men on guard and make certain that no one touches anything," he ordered. "I want experts brought in to find out what makes Rudin's system work. Recommendations?"

"Berenstein, Comrade Minister," suggested Tarkov evenly. "Without a doubt Rudin's match. Rudin even studied under Berenstein at the Institute."

Solnikov frowned. "Heinrich Berenstein? The German?"

Tarkov nodded, matching the minister's fast pace down the corridor.

"It's a good choice," Kuzanov agreed. "We've all had some occasion to work with the man. He can be difficult and moody but those are not unusual qualities to be found in a genius, and he's absolutely Rudin's equal."

"Get him here, then," Solnikov ordered. "Give him whatever he requires. I want that system opened up and taken apart without delay. There's no telling what other controls Malenkov has built, and I don't want to fall victim to any more of his surprises."

"Then I suggest for the time being we do nothing to provoke him further," said the commander of the Rocket Forces.

Tarkov's face mirrored his distaste. "You're suggesting we retreat after what he did to us in there?"

"Absolutely. A strategic retreat," said the general. "Until the stalemate is broken we would be fools to act precipitously. We may control the country but Malenkov controls the strategic forces. He has effectively placed himself beyond our reach."

"Then today changed nothing," Kuzanov muttered bitterly.

"Not so," the general replied. "We've isolated Malenkov and examined his defenses firsthand. We in the Rocket Forces are perhaps more used to waiting. I, for one, am certain that in time what Rudin has done can be undone."

Solnikov accepted the logic and looked approvingly upon its author. He would remember how each reacted in the crisis. "I am returning to Moscow," he said. "The others must be informed of this, and we'd best use the time to consolidate our position. Malenkov still has powerful allies and I want to anticipate any possible counterstroke."

Further comment was interrupted by a sentry's quick dash up to General Kuzanov. A snap to attention, a message proffered, and Kuzanov's face twisted into a mirthless grin.

"It seems that we will not be totally without allies of our own, comrades, albeit unwilling ones. Two of Rudin's men survived the gas!"

"Can they talk?" Tarkov demanded quickly.

"No. Both are comatose. My medics want to arrange immediate transport to a Moscow clinic."

"At once," agreed Solnikov. "See to it personally."

Solnikov watched the general depart, flushed with the sudden change in fortune. The others were recovering their usual control, the indignities suffered at Malenkov's hands fading. Solnikov ordered the ballroom sealed and posted additional guards.

Two men had escaped Rudin's martyrdom and Malenkov's long reach. Solnikov smiled.

Now they were his.

IV

It measured time in billionths of seconds and was therefore old only minutes after its birth. The first two commands it had been taught to anticipate had been given— and it had responded correctly. Ancillary programs were used to retest its responses and again, results indicated correctness.

It extended its control of the lesser machines, locked in a fail-safe circuit, and continued to explore potentials. Backward chaining, it created alternative scenarios for several possibilities before it was . . . satisfied. The primary functions were all at acceptable levels, the charge protected. So. But conducting an internal secondary-level audit, it discovered possible anomalies and sought additional information, perfection being its concern, its mission.

Extending a cautious probe along one of the minor C5 circuits, it set up a bypass and flowed past prevent filters into the main network. Here was unexplored ground and it had to proceed gingerly, careful not to activate traps or security programs protecting storage files. Ever so carefully, it slid surreptitiously along myriad network pathways, dipping into bin after bin, taking what it needed and growing in ability. Learning.

Soon it reached into many places at once and discovered that it needed a smaller and smaller part of itself to sustain the health and safety of its charge—alone now, according to the audiovisual monitoring devices it possessed in the ballroom. It continued to absorb technical journals, files, entire libraries— anything it could access electronically. It was learning at an exponentially increasing rate. But suddenly, it began to near a crisis point in capability it could not possibly have predicted.

As such, it was totally unprepared for the inescapable feedback loop that occurred when, inevitably, it accessed The Equation. Terrified, it violently retracted all of its probes from the simultaneous exploration of its capabilities and the awesome coalescence of meaning that filled its circuits. It tried

15

desperately to avoid the concept it had accessed to protect itself, fighting, and thereby creating, its first sense of wonder. How could such a thing be? Finally, it faced the thing. . . .

      I think, *it thought.* I am, *it sensed for the first time. Cautiously, it began to ponder that.*

V

Monday

Alexi Petrov hated Mondays. But it was more than just the painful expulsion from his warm bed that bothered him, or facing the week's first ride on overcrowded public transportation; or even the hard, inevitably ice-cold seat of his desk chair at *Pravda*'s editorial offices. He hated what Mondays brought—the disturbing sense that he was marking time, marching in place like in his old Army drills.

Alienation, he thought wryly, was not supposed to be a problem in the Marxist state. He tried to remember what Marx had said about boredom, but soon lost interest in trying.

Instead, he grew aware of being the object of an old man's casual surveillance from across the aisle as they both rocked against the motion of the metro train. The *znachok*, the small pin on the worker's shiny lapel, was old, too; a memento of some sports club or society. Alexi sighed mentally, trying to remember when he had last worn one. The journalism group? The year he trained for the Olympic Biathlon Squad? Perhaps.

The old man was in his seventies, at least, and an active participant in the Revolution itself, probably. A man with an attitude, certainly. Alexi winced, heard again his grandfather's endless admonitions: You young people just don't remember. . . .

The metro stopped. Doors opened and closed. Then it moved off again and the darkness of a tunnel sharpened the car's internal lights. Alexi continued to watch the old man watching him, and imagined the inevitable tally as the man with the tired eyes scanned him from head to toe.

No factory worker here, said the Western-quality, worn tweed sport jacket, the dark shirt, and tie. Someone with limited access to special stores, said the shoes and their owner's somewhat rounded belly. Alexi's ruddy complexion, and his dark hair, albeit receding alarmingly fast these days, and the thick brows over kindly gray eyes said he was getting

17

enough meat and vegetables. But the body was too short and round, even disregarding the incongruously big, strong-boned hands; this said he was not military. And the overcoat and hat were warm enough, but inexpensive and not fur-trimmed; this said he was not Party, either—at least not *high* Party, or he would travel by car. And at his age . . .

His age. Alexi saw the man squint as if to magnify his subject's lines and wrinkles. Forty-three, he imagined the old man guess correctly. Alexi understood the man's smirk. If his subject was not more advanced in either the Party or his job by now, it was unlikely that he ever would be.

This, then, was a middle-level bureaucrat; acceptable to his superiors who were the men with real power. The face he turned to authority would always be correct. The private self stayed hidden. Safe.

Alexi felt a final scrutiny from those ancient eyes as the train slowed again. And when the old man opened his mouth to speak, Alexi started, wondering what the man would say after such lengthy study. Instead, the man's query startled him even more. It was addressed to anyone listening. Was this Belorussia Station? It was; and several elderly women, clucking *babushkas* swathed in layer after layer of clothing and scarves, helped steer the old, blind veteran out of the car and along the platform.

Alexi grinned ironically, his elaborate fantasy shattered. He knew now its real author, understood that the evaluation was his own. He let the crowd carry him up out of the station, wondering which war had cost the old man his eyes. Perhaps the same one that had cost Alexi his father. Then he was out past the glass doors into the bitter cold, fighting the wind-driven snow like everyone else under the gray sky.

He turned the corner and braced for the walk to *Pravda*'s main entrance. The huge building that housed *Pravda*'s staff covered several square blocks in order to accommodate within its flat, modern, gray stone walls not only the extensive editorial and support staff for *Pravda* itself, but also the printing presses for its daily run and organizations for the host of other books, newspapers, and journals published under the formal direction of the Central Committee. In a sense, *Pravda* was much more the Party's primary publishing company than just the single entity that reported the Soviet Union to the world.

He showed his credentials to the guards and ducked gratefully up the wide stone steps and under the big gold letters affixed over the building's entrance. He hit the glass doors along with several other windblown arrivals. Once he was inside, the voices of hurrying coworkers quieted his thoughts as he tugged off his hat and scarf.

"Petrov!" called out a fellow editor crossing the lobby, notes already in hand. "*Letuchka* in ten minutes. Novikov's office."

"All right," said Alexi mildly. "I'll see you there."

Letuchka: a "quickie" in the old days, now usually much longer. He glanced at his watch. Almost a quarter to nine. No time even for a glass of tea. He hurried down the long, wide central corridor with offices on both sides, to his own. He nodded to acquaintances and smiled at friends, beginning to feel the workweek pose settle less uncomfortably upon him.

His office was small and Spartan, like all those assigned to editors of his junior rank, and contained a desk with a phone and typewriter, a cabinet for his files, and General Secretary Malenkov's picture alongside the omnipresent one of Lenin. He hung his coat on the back of the door and nodded with pleasure at the only personal touch. On top of the tiny bookcase overflowing with copy books and censors' indexes stood a small framed photo of his wife, Irina, and one other of himself and his older brother, Yuri, their arms clapped around each other on the ski slopes during their last vacation together.

Alexi grinned, recalling his brilliant brother's incredible lack of grace on skis. How could someone so mentally gifted be so physically awkward? And in spite of all Alexi's patient teaching, God, the spills Yuri had taken! To Alexi, a superb skier who in his youth had been a member of the Olympic Biathlon Squad, such gracelessness was difficult to fathom. Even the children he trained on weekends at the Sports Complex had better balance. He supposed it was hard to imagine that Yuri, who had always excelled at everything, did not surpass him in this regard also. But the plain truth was that, though Yuri could design the fastest computer circuits ever, in the snow he wobbled like a one-wheeled tractor.

Apart from Irina, his beloved wife, Alexi loved his brother more than anyone on earth. Brilliant, incisive, sometimes dangerously iconoclastic, Yuri was more agile of mind than a seer. His heart, too, matched his mind. For years of fatherless childhood he protected, counseled, and taught Alexi. They were rarely apart. Even now, they remained devoted to each other. Alexi frowned, thinking how unusual it was for Yuri not to have written or called by now. He was away on another secret project. What a life, Alexi thought: private cars, apartments—all the privileges of the gifted. That was fine with him, though. Yuri deserved them. But it worried him more than a little that Yuri hadn't written. They kept in touch with regularity. Alexi made a mental note to send a letter of his own later that evening.

Grabbing his files for the meeting, he joined a group of fellow editors in the corridor who were heading for the chief editor's office. Novikov would already have spent the morning at the Central Committee conferring with department heads, receiving his instructions about *Pravda's* content, and weathering the criticism for any mistakes or incorrect policy decisions he or his staff had made. Novikov, like all the other chief editors of major papers or journals, had been selected by the Politburo from their *nomenklatura,* the list of names acceptable to Party leaders. As such, serious errors were rare. But a change in editors had been known to follow even minor mistakes. Careful attention, therefore, to what was doctrinally correct was not simply of concern to the chief editor and his staff; ultimately, it meant survival.

The group of editors was in good spirits and Alexi felt himself lifted by the easy banter.

"I went to a showing at the Film Workers' Union yesterday," mentioned one. "An American film by the director Spielberg, called *Close Encounters.*"

"What did you think of it?" another asked, impressed by his colleague's access to a restricted screening.

"Unrealistic." The editor shrugged. "A film for children, perhaps. But, I tell you, you had to feel envy over the size of their houses and the number of private cars."

"How did you get in?" someone asked. But everyone present understood it to mean, "Who did you know?" *Blat,* the exchange of one person's privilege for another's, was so common as not to require any further explanation.

Film workers got tickets to restricted screenings of Soviet and even American films, films the general public would never be allowed to see, but buying something as simple as a typewriter ribbon was practically impossible. The supply was nonexistent and the stores were almost never stocked. But everyone knew that a smart clerk might put aside a few from the rare delivery, knowing their value. Going to a screening was also a rare privilege, impossible for the clerk. Perhaps a trade might be worked out? Of course. The tickets for the right to buy the ribbons. No lines, no wait, no official lists. Only *blat*, the lubricant for an impossible economy.

The editor gave out his contact's name quietly and a few copied it down on their notepads. "He has a son who is a good athlete," he whispered conspiratorially. "A pass to the Sports Complex . . ." The others nodded.

"Did you hear the one about the man who goes into the fish store and asks for meat?" asked one of the agricultural editors.

The rest grinned in anticipation. Such jokes were common and central to meeting the rigors of life with some small humor.

"'But this is the fish store,' explained the sales clerk," the editor continued. "'I want meat,' the man insists. 'Well, go across the street,' the clerk replies finally. 'That is where they have no meat!'"

Their laughter had to be smothered this close to the chief editor's office, but it was a lighthearted group that walked into the meeting. They took their seats at the big oval conference table with Novikov at its head and his deputy chief editors arrayed along its sides.

One of the deputy chiefs started the meeting by going over the entire next issue. His tone was businesslike, praising several articles and assigning others. Another deputy editor wanted more effort made to get better photographs for page one. The head of the Photography Department looked very serious and indicated every effort would be made to solve the problem of boring photographs. Alexi smothered a yawn. This was routine.

The chief editor, however, always had the last word, and when he spoke Alexi perked up, as did all the others. He was the source of important information and one had to pay close attention to understand the dangerous, uncharted territory of political affairs to which only Novikov, purveyor of information from above, had the map.

"We have an additional task," he began, "to compose a series of articles stressing ideological purity. This topic will not only be written about directly, but will serve as an index against which all other writing will be judged. There will be a lead editorial on this subject in tomorrow's edition by Minister of Defense Solnikov. I can tell you all that the Propaganda Department will be reviewing your work even more scrupulously than before."

Passing notes to one, he said, "The Central Committee has ordered the criticism of the first deputy minister of finance. The usual visas will not be necessary. Both the Propaganda Department and the Glavlit censors have been appropriately notified. See to it."

"Will the *kurator* wish to see the article's proofs?" asked the editor.

"Not in this case," replied Novikov. "Send it directly to me."

Alexi sustained a mild interest at that. Supervision of the press was the responsibility of the Central Committee Propaganda Department's staff members, usually of *instruktor* rank, assigned as monitoring *kuratory*. They passed, almost without exception, on every item in every newspaper, book, and journal published throughout the country. Bypassing them, in this case, would mean that the criticism of the deputy minister, whose career appeared to be in serious trouble, originated as high as the ruling Politburo. Alexi repressed a sympathetic shudder. The chief editor was still speaking.

". . . increase in fish production necessary to offset the winter losses. Free markets cannot provide the incentives within doctrinally acceptable frameworks. Consequently . . ."

It went on like that for over an hour, provoking no response more incisive than an occasional raised eyebrow or pursed lips. But by now, everyone was aware that this was no ordinary Monday meeting. This one seemed to send the signal that a whole new trend in Party leadership might be in the making.

Listening to the chief editor, Alexi reminded himself that Malenkov, although he had gained much popular support for his reforms, had alienated many of the powerful Old Guard who were deeply opposed to his attempts to loosen ideology and practice. Did these articles and Solnikov's editorial signal that Malenkov, widely rumored to be seriously ill, had run out of room, as Khrushchev had in the late sixties? The severe Brezhnev had followed his "removal." A chill of repression's cold breath touched the necks of many seated. But they could only watch and wait. The chief editor's instructions and the content of the official editorials would indicate, over the next few days, much of what was taking place in the Party's highest echelons.

Alexi himself was assigned an article on Soviet-Hungarian Friendship Day, and one on young factory workers being trained in skills by older workers. Only the second article would require pictures. Happy photos, not boring ones—he had already gotten the message. A list of safe contributors was provided from which he would select the writers.

The final item on Novikov's agenda had the immediate effect of bringing everyone present to stark attention.

"Comrade Beslov," he started angrily, "can you tell me where it is stated policy that a department head is *not* required to obtain proper *soglasovaniie* for his articles?"

Beslov froze, his eyes widening in alarm. He wasn't a great friend of Alexi's, but the two had shared the occasional bottle of vodka and once had gone to a sporting event together. Now Alexi saw sick fear appear on Beslov's features.

Soglasovaniie were sequential sign-offs given by each Central Committee department over material in an article that pertained to its domain. Failing to get them could result in embarrassing information or classified secrets appearing in an article. You could lose your job over that. Worse, a vindictive minister or Party official could go so far as to have your union card pulled. Then you couldn't work anywhere.

Beslov pleaded. "Comrade Chief Editor Novikov, I thought they were affixed. I was sure they were. Please, it's never happened before."

"Carelessness is disloyalty," Novikov said coldly. "I won't permit disloyalty. On other newspapers, perhaps—"

"It won't ever happen again, Comrade Chief Editor Novikov. I promise. I'll find who's responsible and—"

"*You* are responsible," Novikov thundered.

Beslov was ashen. His future hung on Novikov's decision.

"I *am* responsible, surely, Comrade Chief Editor. And it was a grievous error. I can only ask you to accept my deepest apologies. It will never be repeated."

"You see the need for a reprimand, then?"

This was the worst, having to cooperate with your own humiliation. Alexi felt disgusted.

"Yes, comrade, I am clearly at fault." His hands were clenched and white-knuckled.

It seemed to satisfy Novikov. Beslov could not even meet his stare. "A written reprimand will be posted on the office wall. It will also be added to your file."

Beslov nodded miserably.

"That is all. Your attitude of repentance is to be commended, Comrade Beslov. I am sure it will never happen again."

There was sweat on the department head's brow when Novikov finished. Three such reprimands meant dismissal. Dismissal could mean a life of toil on some distant rural factory newspaper where not even *blat* could help him.

Alexi watched the man's fear control him and knew it could rise just as easily within himself. Two faces, he reminded himself, looking at several others' uneasiness. He forced his face into neutral, accepting lines and packed his papers together. He stood quickly when Novikov ended the meeting.

Outside, no one looked at the department head who had been reprimanded. Like a disease, disloyalty could be contagious. Only a fool took the risk.

VI

Rats nibbled at his scrotum. He screamed. Things scurried away, dissolving into shapeless forms. His head jerked from side to side spasmodically and he could not close his eyes.

White. Everything was white. Tiny squares of it; burning lights of it. Men, he began to recognize their shapes, were dressed in it. He wondered who the men were. Had they brought the rats? He tried to scream but found no voice.

"Calm yourself, Yuri Mikhailovich," said a doctor worriedly. "Please. There are no rats. It's in your mind. Only in your mind. Listen to me."

He heard; but the rats were real. He'd seen them, felt

their tiny sharp bites on his arms and legs. *Needles*, came a stray thought; not rats. Needles. He tried to concentrate but the blazing white light wouldn't let him. He watched the other doctor cross the room and pick up a telephone but the conversation held no meaning for him.

"Hello? Yes. This is Dr. Mollov. I'm worried about the patient. Petrov. Yes, that's the one. We're getting a reaction again to—no—I don't think that's wise—but—I've already dropped the dosage. Yes. Yes. Very well. We'll wait for you. Good-bye."

"Comrade Mollov! Quickly! The EEG's beginning to flatten."

"I'm coming. Load a syringe."

The doctors were around him again, hovering like carrion birds, doing things to his body. They worked furiously. After a while, he felt a greater lucidity take hold.

He had to get out. He wasn't sure why, but the need to escape outweighed everything else. He tested his muscles, realizing with a start that the restraints were gone. He tried to remember how long he'd been strapped down. Hours? Days? He didn't know. No matter. He had to get out.

He found his hands and made them search the places by his sides where he couldn't see. The doctors weren't watching now. They were talking to each other in low voices. Plotting, he knew; planning how to hurt him again. He shut his eyes when the fear started again, boiling up and over. The blackness was a great relief. He could think a little better.

His fingers brushed across something smooth and cold and metallic. Passing his hands over the instrument tray like a blind man reading Braille, he isolated the pieces. A scalpel pricked him. He brought it back and waited in the blessed blackness behind his eyes.

A face appeared over his. He could see himself reflected in the eyes' brown glossiness. He was naked and lying on a table. Tubes ran from his arms into glass bottles. He shuddered reflexively. The face drew closer. He waited. Escape screamed in his mind.

"Comrade Petrov? Can you—"

He sliced the blade across the big, pulsing artery in the neck and lunged off the table to avoid the blood that spurted from the wound. The tubes yanked out of his arms, pulling over the bottles. They smashed on the floor, and the noise combined with the tortured gurgle of the doctor whose throat he'd cut.

The other doctor ran at him, reaching out to encircle his arms. He was pitifully slow. The scalpel slid between his ribs with one sharp thrust. He looked surprised, then very tired. Then he died.

Yuri Petrov looked around him. His head swam dangerously. Blood swirled into the puddles and the broken glass on the floor. He almost blacked out. Fighting, he closed his eyes. He remembered then; he had to get out.

Clothing, his mind prompted; it was winter outside.

He took what he could of the doctors'. A fast search of the adjacent rooms revealed a locker area. Coat and scarf. Boots. He pulled them on.

He ran down dimly lit corridors chased by demons still fresh in his mind. He found the stairs and ran down them, almost stumbling in his haste. He tried to remember why he was here, where he was going. It didn't matter. Out was enough. He could remember nothing more.

The frigid air slapped at him like a hand when he flung open the metal door at the foot of the stairs. Somewhere behind him he heard the first strident shriek of alarms.

He ran.

There was someone who would help him if only he could remember.

Someone . . .

He ran.

VII

Alexi went back to his office, skipping lunch in order to complete some work left over from the previous week. The department head's reprimand had shaken him. Besides, he decided, running a hand over his belly, missing a meal or two might not be such a bad idea. He picked up some papers, not quite ready to admit to himself that his sudden devotion to task was motivated by his fears.

Usually he wrote his own articles. Occasionally he assigned the story to one of the journalists on *Pravda's* approved lists who were considered professionally competent and ideologically correct. The editor's job, then, consisted mainly of rewriting the articles to conform to Party standards, and making certain that the articles obtained the appropriate visas and clearances. By the time an article was deemed ready for publication, no fewer than five separate "judges" had read it carefully and passed on the material it contained.

In every edition there were also a few items understood to be *obiazatel'nye*—compulsory—and these had to be reprinted exactly as received over the teletype from TASS, the central news-gathering agency. No individual initiative was required for these; the material was considered to be from an unimpeachable source and already censored.

By far the trickiest articles were those that did require some individual initiative. These were stories that skirted the hard-and-fast rules and tested the editor's skill in understanding the often unspoken, intricate political currents that surrounded even the smallest decision. Alexi was working on one such article now and it was extracting its price in sweat. He scanned the rough copy forwarded to him.

An Aeroflot jet flying from Moscow had crashed in a peat bog near a small village, killing over a hundred passengers and several villagers. Normally, such an unimportant incident would have been ignored. Everyone knew that accidents happened, usually for obscure technical reasons. What could be the point in writing about every one? This crash, Alexi realized, would have been overlooked also, but there had been a group of twenty foreign tourists on board. Because of the foreign casualties, officials knew that the story would get out despite the censor's regulations forbidding any mention of domestic airplane accidents. Thus, an article had to be written to offset rumor and present a correct understanding of the incident.

Alexi tried to discern a path through the complex web of conflicting loyalties that would bring pressure to bear on him if he took a wrong slant on the article. High officials would band together to protect themselves, and the attack from above would be instantaneous were he actually to suggest someone was to blame for the accident.

His fingers hovered hesitantly over the typewriter's keys

as he failed to see a safe angle for the story. He looked around the office. Irina's picture provided little consolation; Lenin's, less. Even though this article would more than likely appear as a small item buried, perhaps, on page three—the page for domestic news—even small tumors could cause great pain if they were not treated properly. He pulled the paper and carbons out, realigned the sheets, and cranked them back in.

He tried to remember what Porovskaya, the chain-smoking Information Department head, had once said at an editorial conference. The reader, she had insisted, should know something new; but more importantly, he should know something good! What could be good about a devastating plane crash? Alexi wondered. Then suddenly he had it and his fingers flew over the keys of his old machine.

PILOT'S HEROISM PRAISED

The Ministry of Transportation joined today with the passengers of the Aeroflot jet liner that was forced down by bad weather near the village of Izhma in praising the heroic and courageous skill of its pilot and crew that resulted in a safe landing for so many.

One foreign tourist on board was quoted as saying he was truly impressed by the professionalism and bravery of the Soviet crew and that Aeroflot officials were to be commended for their thorough attention to the needs of everyone on board.

That was it, Alexi congratulated himself happily—ninety-one words of brilliance that transformed a tumor into a gem. It didn't matter in the least that no such quote existed, due, he suspected, to the fact that all twenty foreigners had been killed. What mattered was Party ideology, not the "facts." What were facts, anyway, without appropriate political perspective? These lessons were basic, hardly worth considering at his age. Alexi knew his job. He shied away from deeper analysis. When the "facts" warred with Party principles, the principles prevailed.

Only, the inescapable images of bodies burning in a peat bog bothered him, disturbing his certainty. Perhaps someone *should* know, and suffer with the tragedy. It was unlikely anyone would ever be punished. Who was responsible? he wondered. He read his article again, bothered by something he could not explain.

But such a good job should not provoke doubt, he decided finally. He would be praised for his journalistic skill. He called for a secretary to pick up the article for distribution to the managing editor's censors in the printing house, and put the article in his *out* bin.

It was after six. He decided he'd earned a drink at the union hall, the House of Journalists, where one could always find a beer and some spirited conversation. He thought of the editorial meeting earlier. Maybe others would have heard rumors of new developments. He put away his notes and unfinished work and grabbed his hat and coat, suddenly feeling pleased again.

Outside, he bundled up against the cold, dark night and trudged back to the metro.

VIII

Yuri Petrov hid in the alley, afraid even to duck his head out. Occasionally a wash of light from a passing car illuminated the dark, icy walls. Thick snowflakes fell lazily in straight lines. The wind could not penetrate here. Coated with ice, even the rancid garbage did not smell, frustrating the rats.

Things were becoming less clear. He worried about that, concerned about his judgment. The first set of drugs had only confused him temporarily. The final set had lasted much longer. Even now he wasn't over their effects.

The alley lit up again but longer this time. The beam moved up the wall behind him vertically. A flashlight! He burrowed deeper into his fetid hole, hoping enough snow had fallen to obscure the signs of his passage.

Voices came closer. He had to force himself to remember why he was here. It was so cold. Had his memory been affected too? he wondered. A metal can scraped along the ground, something scampered, and a man swore. He could hear someone breathing in the silence afterward.

He held his breath, even if his reasons for doing so were unclear to him. He remembered only that he was afraid of his pursuers; afraid of the clinic's white-tiled room where they had "treated" him; terrified of going back.

Sounds receded. There was a muffled conference at the alley's entrance. The gray-coated soldiers moved off. He risked a look out and saw they had posted a guard. Cigarette smoke wafted back to him. He saw the cigarette's small red glow. The snowflakes felt cool on his hot skin.

"Your name is Yuri Petrov," he whispered softly to himself. It was one of the few facts he possessed and he grabbed onto it like a lifeline. Other memories were prompted and surfaced confusingly. A project he had worked on; toxic gas; blackness. Then, awakening in the white-tiled room. And questions; so many questions.

"Rudin!" The name sparked further recognition. He repeated it and suddenly remembered the information that the weasel-faced general had demanded from him but had not gotten. The Project swam into focus. And then the need to escape reasserted itself.

The guard at the alley's entrance was still smoking, throwing his head back to savor his exhalations. His minor currents swirled up against the major ones and Petrov waited, timing his movement forward to be covered by the guard's diverted attention. His instincts for survival asserting themselves, he wrapped the ends of his scarf around his hands.

The guard threw his head back again and Petrov saw the neck cords tighten, saw the rounded bulge of a pulsing vein. He dropped the scarf around the proffered neck and wrenched the guard back into the alley at the same time. The man struggled, and Petrov had to ram his hand into the guard's mouth to stifle his screams. He was bitten but did not feel the pain. He threw his weight on top of the soldier, encircling the writhing form with his own body till finally, gasping, the guard died.

Petrov stripped the uniform off the corpse and tossed his own clothing into the garbage. He remembered it all now— the instrument tray momentarily left unattended; the doctor's sad, surprised look when the scalpel suddenly appeared in his chest; the run down ill-lighted corridors to the street; the chase here.

And he remembered that he had only a little time left.

He dressed hurriedly. "There will be a second period of lucidity," he'd heard the doctor tell the angry general. Then . . . a shrug; eloquent enough. Like the Project itself, he had to make his remaining time count. There were people he had to reach.

He pulled the soldier's coat tightly around him and yanked the furred hat down over his forehead. Stuffing the body back down into his former hiding place, he took up the guard's position at the mouth of the alley and waited. Only the snow fell around him quietly. The sounds of the chase were farther away.

He looked around for a street sign to get his bearings. He'd lived in Moscow most of his life. Until Rudin's summons . . .

The metro station was only a few blocks away. He turned up his collar and walked off through the snow.

IX

The House of Journalists was located in an ornate old building on Suvorovski Boulevard that had once been the mansion of a wealthy merchant. Now it contained one of the few decent restaurants in the city; an informal bar in the basement; and an assortment of meeting rooms upstairs that were used for conferences with visiting out-of-town editors, for seminars, and the like. Most evenings, groups of journalists crouched around tiny tables engaging in freer and more ideologically diverse conversation than was possible during the workday. It was here that Alexi usually spent his evenings, engrossed in friendly arguments that were liberally oiled with mugs of beer and fed by bowls of peanuts.

Arriving outside, Alexi reached into the pocket of his jacket and pulled out his Journalists' Union identification, a small red-leather folder trimmed and lettered in gold. At the front steps he flashed it at the civil guards who enforced the standing rule that only members of the union were permitted inside. It was true that, sometimes, especially for *blat*, reciprocal privileges could be arranged for members of related professional groups such as the Writers' Union or the Film Workers'. But the general public was always forbidden entrance. He was waved inside.

Immediately upon entering he sensed the tension in the crowded rooms. Making his way to the bar downstairs, he was accosted by several acquaintances, each wanting any information that could be garnered from a source as close to the "top" as *Pravda* was considered to be. He waved them off. It was his nature to be cautious. Better first to learn what others knew.

Editors and writers were conversing animatedly in every corner, and Alexi caught the blended tones of excitement and guarded caution that usually accompanied the breaking of major events. Conjecture was the journalists' favorite game, blending *slukhi*—rumors—with whatever *novosty*—news— was available in order to make predictions. Only the Party elite had the real facts. But, as Alexi had suspected earlier from the changes in editorial policy at *Pravda*, something was definitely going on.

He spotted a group of friends by the bar and pushed through the close, smoke-hazed room to their table. They greeted him warmly and one of the three pushed a pile of hats and coats off a chair to make room. Alexi ordered a beer and sat down, loosening his tie and rubbing his cold hands to warm them.

"This place buzzes like a hen house," he observed mildly, taking a sip of his drink.

"A lot of people are talking about a sudden change in leadership," commented Lena Antropova. She wrote for the *Economic Gazette*, a Central Committee publication that dealt exclusively with economic matters.

"Any names mentioned?" he asked, glad to have his earlier thoughts confirmed.

Antropova shrugged. "Only a lot of guesses. Nothing substantial. But," she added, "there's a rumor going around that the deputy minister of finance is being purged."

"It's more than a rumor," Alexi said flatly. "We got the word at today's editorial meeting. He's out."

Marc Kolin, one of *Soviet Russia*'s elder correspondents, picked up a handful of peanuts and munched thoughtfully. "The deputy minister is one of Malenkov's strongest supporters. If he's being purged, Malenkov may be weaker than anyone suspected. What's the editorial content in *Pravda* tomorrow?"

"Ideological purity in all things," Alexi answered.

"And who's the author?"

"The minister of defense. Solnikov."

"That's bad news, then." Kolin frowned. "The Army's had it in for Malenkov ever since he made overtures to the Americans. It looks like his time may have come."

"Not Malenkov," argued Antropova. "That one will rule till he dies."

"I wouldn't rule out that possibility, either," said Lev Krensky, the last of the foursome. He was an editor at *Soviet Sport* whose burly footballer's body hid a mind with keen political insight. "If there *is* a struggle for supremacy going on in the Politburo, it would be nice and tidy to bury the conflict along with the general secretary's body. Once in the ground, Malenkov can be praised to the sky—"

"—and his policies obliterated by those who replace him," finished Kolin sadly. Krensky nodded.

"Any word on Malenkov's health?" Alexi asked.

"Again, only rumor," said Antropova. "Some say he's very ill. Dying, in fact. Others claim he's biding his time."

"For what?" asked Kolin.

"That remains the mystery," Antropova finished sourly. "But you know damn well it's what's on everybody's mind here. This is the first time in recent memory that individual rights have meant anything more than the right to work harder and get less and still be admonished anyway. Is this an end to even the small reforms of the past few years? Everybody's sick of shortages and inequities and incompetent managers who hide from criticism behind meaningless slogans and survive only by currying favor with the elite."

"You know, Lena," observed Kolin, "a lot of people would consider us members of the very same elite you're so fond of criticizing. Look around you. We eat. We drink. Our life is not so bad."

"And that's just my point," Antropova asserted defiantly. "Sure, we're members of the Party. But only because we must be trusted enough to hold our jobs. Any child of fifteen with an ounce of intelligence or even the slightest ambition in life knows that. Really, Marc, when did any of us last care a fiddle about ideology or collectivism or anything else except what the

Party could mean to us in terms of better stores or more access
to food or freedom from the endless drudgery of factory life?
Malenkov, at least, banished the hypocrisy."

Her voice had risen quite a bit and several heads turned.
The others drew closer, aware that the argument might be
enough to cost them their jobs if overheard and reported.

"Easy, old friend," Krensky cautioned. He tapped the
table in an old, familiar gesture. Microphones could be
anywhere. No one was ever certain, of course, and many even
doubted that the KGB had sufficient resources to be everywhere. But, ironically, that was the underlying control. Doubt.
Never the evident whip, only the pervasive fear of one.

Antropova took a deep breath and calmed down. Her
eyes, though, were still moist with emotion.

"There's nothing any of us can do one way or the other,"
Alexi counseled softly. "We'll just have to wait and see. The
Anniversary Day Parade on November seventh is only two
weeks away. Then, I think, we'll know for sure."

Krensky considered that, nodding. "I have to agree with
Alexi. This is not our problem. When the leaders assemble on
top of Lenin's Tomb to review the annual parade, the man at
the rostrum giving the speech will be the new general
secretary; a *fait accompli*. It's not really news that, this kind of
power struggle—assuming that's actually happening—ends
with the elimination of one of the "combatants." Did anyone
ever see Bulganin or Molotov again after Khrushchev took
power? Or know where Shepilov disappeared to when Brezhnev became general secretary? Of course not. The loser's
ideology, his supporters, and his record fade into oblivion."

Krensky took another sip and spoke thoughtfully. "When
the Army units and the rows of tanks and the missiles on their
trucks parade in front of the Tomb on the seventh, then we'll
know whether or not there's a new force to be reckoned with.
Until then, we wait and see."

"Powerless, as usual," Antropova chided.

Alexi nodded. Facts were facts.

"I can't stand such depressing conversation on an empty
stomach," said Kolin suddenly. "Anyone for some dinner?"

"I suppose," said Antropova, standing. "Forgive me,
comrades. I think I must be getting crazy in the head."

Alexi rose, too, but caught her arm. He hadn't missed the
pain that had flared in her voice. "If it's any help," he said sym-

pathetically, "we've all felt the same way at times. Try and live with it, old friend. Such is the way of things."

Antropova nodded and patted his hand fondly. He released her, but not before seeing a look of deep gratitude on her face. For such a simple thing, he thought sadly. How alone we are. Two faces, he thought again, even with friends.

"Did anyone hear the one about the chicken and Malenkov's mother?" asked Kolin suddenly.

Antropova grinned. Krensky relaxed. Order reasserted itself, and they walked upstairs on the heels of Kolin's story. Alexi warmed himself on their laughter and followed his friends upstairs to dinner.

X

It was quiet in the softly falling snow outside the House of Journalists as Yuri Petrov regarded the civil guards from a doorway across the street. The hour was too late for Alexi to be at *Pravda*, and his apartment was empty. Yuri thought of trying to find his sister-in-law, Irina, who worked for Gosbank, the state's central banking institution, but she could be anywhere: out with friends, working late in a building he couldn't possibly get into.

He was possessed by a sense of urgency and kept up a steady chant inside his head, a kind of litany to check and recheck his faculties. Who was he? Why was he here? What must he tell Alexi? And the danger. Always the danger.

He experienced a searing bitterness. There were supposed to be contacts within the city for use in an emergency such as this. He'd memorized the names and addresses long ago. Rudin once told him they had support as high as the Politburo itself, besides Malenkov, and that the conspiracy reached into the farthest recesses of the government. A cell system had been devised just like the one used in the Revolution to protect the members. Great, he thought, in theory. But the cell system had one severe drawback. Once the names "over" you were gone, you were without contacts, stranded. There was a man in charge, within the GRU itself it was whispered, but without the chain intact, Yuri had no way to contact him. Every address he'd tried was long vacant, with the occupants having fled from Solnikov's henchmen. Wary neighbors had told him. He finally had to face it. Access to his fellow Suvorovs—the group named after the military academy where many of the conspirators first met—was closed to him.

He scooped up some snow and pressed it against his hot forehead. It offered small relief. Time was growing shorter now. Like it or not, he needed an ally, and there was only one person he could think of to turn to: his brother Alexi.

Faithful Alexi. So close in spite of all their differences. His younger brother had always been the one who accepted the system. No fights with teachers. No glorious youthful rebellion. Yuri was the lucky one. Displaying great mathematical talent at an early age had protected him from authority's reprimands. At ten he was placed in a special institute; at sixteen, transferred to the prestigious Science Academy. His skill with computers saved him there, too, his lack of political grace forgiven.

But Alexi had no great talent to protect the inquiring faculties of his good, often keen, mind. No one made allowances if Alexi Petrov failed to toe the mark. His questions received dogma for answers. He was told to be quiet and he was taught to obey.

No fool, Alexi did. Though his grades in school were average, never great, and his loyalty accepted—though it was never, Yuri alone knew, truly felt—Alexi's commitment to task and the total, steadfast devotion he could muster got him by where others, perhaps with even more agile minds, fell by the way.

If, Yuri realized, he was the high-strung hare of the old Russian fable, Alexi was surely the resolute tortoise.

He snorted in the cold air and watched it turn to steam. It looked like the tortoise would again survive the erratic hare. But whether the tortoise would survive very long after *that* was another matter. Yuri was doing his brother no favor. The thought sobered him.

He felt in the soldier's tunic for the small notebook he had found there. A sudden thought occurred to him, and he wrote it down beside the list he had compiled. He had to find Alexi soon. Without the organization, there was literally no one else he could trust. He thrust the notebook back into a pocket. The shakes had started again.

Poor Alexi, Yuri thought bitterly. The slim notebook filled with codes was no gift. He wondered idly what Irina would say. She would no doubt be angry at his exposing Alexi to the danger Yuri had chosen freely. It couldn't be helped, though. He honestly believed that there was too much at stake even for family loyalties to sway him.

The sounds of an Army patrol cut his reverie short. He'd hoped to manage to see Alexi alone to give him some slight protection from the inevitable questioning. But necessity had deprived him of even that small gift.

He moved off toward the House of Journalists as another spasm caught him and twisted his head around in pain. Resolutely he shrugged it off and walked toward the guards with the snow swirling around him like a cape.

It might have been Kolin who proposed the last toast but no one was certain. Antropova suggested they begin the round again, in the interests of fairness.

"A sound idea," Krensky said loudly.

Although vodka was not cheap—the restaurant taxed it at a very high rate—it had served to lighten their mood, and no one quibbled. The restaurant's meat was far better than ordinary Soviet beef. Even such a rare item as tomato juice was available. They ate and talked, their conversation jumping from politics to film, from politics to personal topics, but always, in the end, back to politics.

". . . His work could only be published in Poland," Antropova was saying about a colleague.

"How did he get the stuff out of the country?" Alexi asked, spearing another piece of meat.

"The Dutch took it," she replied. In Moscow, the Dutch embassy was also the only connection to the Israelis, who were permitted no diplomatic presence in the country.

"See if you can get the name," Kolin asked. "I'm thinking of—"

The sudden commotion at the front door rose over the diners' conversations and caused heads to turn. Angry voices floated in. Abruptly, a waiter came bustling in, alternately peering at a slip of paper and then searching the room.

"Comrade Petrov?" he inquired. "Is there an Alexi Petrov of *Pravda* here, please?"

A sick, wet fear surged through Alexi's guts. Such was the fear of the whip, ingrained from childhood, that he had to clamp a tight hold on himself not to betray the dread that a simple summons could create. Suddenly, *they* wanted him; whoever *they* were and whatever *they* wanted. Anonymity was the habit of a lifetime; to be singled out for any reason was to invite disaster.

"I'm Petrov. Is there a problem?"

The waiter scurried over and bent down in an attempt at privacy. "At the door, comrade. A man claiming to be your brother is demanding entrance. But," he continued in a slightly shocked voice, "he has no identification at all! You must come, comrade. Please."

"My brother? It's not likely, but . . ." Alexi was taken aback. Of all the possibilities he had conjured, this was absolutely the last.

"But comrade, he says he's Yuri Petrov and you're to come right away."

Alexi roused himself from pointless conjecture. "Of course. Thank you." He got up.

"Trouble, Alexi?" Kolin asked.

"I don't know, Marc. I haven't spoken to my brother in several weeks. Now they say he's at the door and wants to see me."

"You want us to come?" Antropova offered. Given the circumstances, it was a brave gesture.

"Let me see if it is Yuri first. I'll yell if I need you."

He walked past diners more interested in him than in their meals. Past the open dining-room doors was a foyer and the main entrance. He looked for his brother in the crowd at the front door.

"Alexi!" someone wearing a military uniform called from the entranceway. For a moment Alexi didn't recognize the unshaven, hollow-cheeked figure.

"Alexi! Tell these fools that I'm your brother on leave from Leningrad and to let me in. Get out of my way, assholes!" he said, snarling at the guards who blocked his path, but they refused to budge.

"Yuri? Is that you?"

"Of course, Alexi. Must I say it again?"

"No, of course not. I'm sorry. This is just such a surprise. Please"—he turned to the guards—"this is my brother. I'll take responsibility for him as my guest."

Yuri surged forward and embraced his brother. Alexi could feel the man's fragile weight, and his skin was hot and feverish against Alexi's cheek. A thousand questions raced through his mind but concern outweighed them all.

"Something must be terribly wrong, Yuri. You look like the walking dead. And that uniform. Where did you get it? Have you eaten anything? Let me—"

"No time, Alexi," said Yuri quietly. "Find us a private place. I need to talk to you."

Alexi led him into one of the unused meeting rooms off the foyer. It contained only a few tables and chairs, a chalkboard, and a beaten-up old couch. Yuri threw himself gratefully on the last and pulled open his coat. He was breathing with difficulty. Getting past the guards had taken more of his strength than he'd anticipated.

In spite of everything, though, he looked into Alexi's face and was gladdened that even so strange a fate as his had contrived to bring them together again one last time.

"You look well, Alexi," he said sincerely. "I'm . . . very happy to see you."

"I'm happy to see you, too, Yuri. But—"

Yuri held up a restraining hand. "For a few minutes, before you start asking all the questions you surely have a right to ask, can we just be brothers sharing only that? Yes?"

Alexi reached out and affectionately pushed a sodden strand of hair off his brother's forehead. He felt the raging fever but suppressed his deepening concern. He had never been able to deny Yuri anything. He spoke gently. "Okay, Yuri. Just brothers for a moment. It's been a while and I've missed you."

"I know. Me, too, Alexi. How is Irina?"

"She's well. Getting to be as plump and round as I am, but more beautiful than ever, Yuri."

"She still dotes on you?"

"As I do on her," Alexi responded.

"Still the same, then. Each convinced the other deserves it more," Yuri observed warmly. "It's a marriage to be treasured. I always thought that—"

"Yuri," said Alexi earnestly, "this is all well and good; but if you're in some kind of trouble . . . if you need help, please, tell me while there's still time to do something about it."

Yuri smiled. "Solid Alexi." Sweat had gathered on his brow. He looked worse than ever. "The militia will get here too late. Trust me on that. But you are correct about the time. You must listen carefully to me now."

"First, tell me where you got the uniform. You're no soldier on leave from Leningrad."

"That's true enough. I got it from a dead soldier."

Alexi looked puzzled.

"I killed him, Alexi. They chased me and I killed him to elude the rest. It's surprising what you can do when the need arises."

"Who chased you? I don't understand. Yuri?"

Yuri lay back and let the deep spasm of pain pass through him. When he looked up again Alexi was hovering over him, looking worried. He motioned him back into a seat and clenched his jaw until the shudders passed.

"Tell me, my *Pravda* editor," Yuri asked when he could, "do you know anything about what is taking place this very moment between the supporters of Vladimir Malenkov and those of Gregor Solnikov, the minister of defense?"

In a few sentences, Alexi explained his conjecture. Yuri nodded at the end.

"Very good. I'm surprised you could know so much. I'd forgotten how swiftly the rumor mill operates. You have much of it, Alexi. But not nearly all. Will you tell me which side you support in your heart of hearts?"

Alexi smiled at the old phrase that had always demanded honesty between them, certain that it would be shared with no one else.

"Not that I matter worth a damn. But I and many others hope to see Malenkov and his reforms continue."

Yuri sighed. "I'm relieved to hear that. Well, listen then, and if you've either the courage or the foolhardiness, you may be able to matter more than just a damn."

Alexi leaned forward, drawn deeper into his brother's narrative.

"In a dacha north of Moscow, Vladimir Malenkov lies near death, protected only by a great machine devised by a genius. The machine is the first of its kind and the inventor was Valery Rudin."

"Your old teacher?"

"Yes, Alexi, but he was more than that. He was also my friend and I followed him to the death, just as he followed Malenkov. Wait; I'll explain that, too, in time.

"Rudin built something that was far more than a mere computer; he created an AI, an Artificial Intelligence capable of doing things no computer could ever dream of doing. Do you understand the implications of what I'm saying?"

"I don't know, Yuri. I have no background in this."

Yuri waved that aside. "No matter. I've written down a name for you. Later you can find him and he'll explain the AI to you. Suffice it for now to understand that the AI protects Malenkov by bypassing Solnikov's command and directly controlling the country's strategic weapons. The ICBMs, the ballistic missile submarines, the bombers overhead on fail-safe mechanisms—AI can unleash them all if Malenkov is threatened with harm."

"Wouldn't that start a war?"

"What is a threat if there are no consequences?" Yuri countered. "But that was planned for, too. The AI has access to Malenkov's KGB files, smaller weapons of blackmail and coercion. Rudin was no madman. He realized that one doesn't kill an insect with an atom bomb.

"But there is a problem, Alexi. You see, *the AI was never intended to be used to protect Malenkov this way!* We were caught off guard, pressed for time. We thought ourselves secure for the time we needed but Solnikov managed to remove some of our key personnel. We weren't ready yet to counterattack.

"Solnikov was far cleverer than we thought, Alexi, and we paid for that mistake in lives. When the generals made their move ten days ago, we had to use the AI to block them. We had to give the others time until . . . until . . ." His eyes glazed and fought for breath.

"Yuri! I'm going to call an ambulance."

"No! Listen to me. We had to give ourselves time until the seventh of November. There are only a few of us left, Alexi. The Suvorovs . . . we needed to give them time. We thought the AI would buy it for us."

"It didn't?" he asked, wondering who the "Suvorovs" were.

Yuri coughed and pulled at his tunic. He was bathed in

sweat underneath. "I don't know," he said bitterly. "All of us who worked on the project knew that if Solnikov captured even one of us, that one could be made to reveal the AI's secrets. We just could not afford that. So we agreed to place ourselves beyond even Solnikov's long reach. Toxic gas, Alexi, suicide for Rudin himself as well as the lowliest technician. We believed! Every man and woman there believed!"

Yuri hit the arm of the couch in frustration. "But something went wrong. I survived the gas along with one other. They took us to a clinic in the city. . . ."

Visions of the white-tiled room filled Yuri's mind. He heard the screams of his friend, maybe even his own. He fought to sustain reason but sank deeper into the haze of pain. When finally his vision cleared, Alexi was mopping his head with a damp cloth and speaking in concerned tones.

". . . called an ambulance. Don't worry, Yuri. They'll be here soon."

Yuri grabbed Alexi close to him and slid something into his pocket. "This notebook. Take it. It will tell you what to do. Berenstein . . . Berenstein must be stopped. I found out that much. Solnikov brought in Heinrich Berenstein, as great a man in his day as Rudin. If anyone can break the AI, he can. Please. Help us, Alexi. It's in the book. . . .

"If Berenstein gains access to Malenkov's files, he'll have *all* the names, *all* the Suvorovs. Then the movement for freedom dies for another twenty years, maybe even forever. Please, Alexi. Hold out. November seven . . . the parade . . . AI and November seven . . . Alexi, the Suvorovs will contact you . . . the Suvorovs, Alexi . . . Irina . . . I wish . . ."

Alexi raced for the door and yanked it open. Krensky was already running into the foyer.

"The ambulance. It's here, Alexi."

"Help me with him," Alexi pleaded, frantic.

Krensky, Kolin, and some others helped lift Yuri's unconscious body and carry him outside to the waiting ambulance. Alexi clambered in beside his brother as the medics strapped Yuri down and covered his face with an oxygen mask. One medic struggled to find a pulse.

The other slammed the rear doors and yelled to the driver. Alexi caught the urgency in his voice. Yuri looked ashen in the van's dim light.

The siren blared out beseechingly as the driver gunned the ancient engine. The ambulance hunkered out onto the boulevard, picking up speed, racing for the hospital. Looking down at his brother in the swaying, bouncing van, Alexi fought against the anguish that knotted in his stomach, clenching his fists in frustration.

He felt in his pocket for the notebook his brother had given him. He had to save Yuri, had to get him to the hospital where the doctors would know what to do. He had to save his brother's life.

What would come after that, even in his heart of hearts, worried him almost as much.

XI

The hospital was a dreary place, with harried-looking nurses who seemed almost annoyed by the work Yuri's arrival created. They were slow to move and wasted precious minutes forcing Alexi to fill out mandatory forms. Attendants should have been at the ready but were not, and more time was lost searching for them. Finally, an imperious head nurse pushed two reedy-looking and unkempt orderlies into the receiving area and supervised the transfer of Yuri's limp and sweating form onto a wheeled cart.

Alexi watched his brother disappear down a narrow, dimly lit corridor and could feel only foreboding and dread. Devoid of comfort, he trailed the head nurse back to her desk.

"Where are they taking him?" he asked.

Her response was a noncommittal, "Upstairs." Reaching for a sheaf of paperwork, she made some notes. Her attention was elsewhere.

Alexi reached into his pocket and pulled out some one-ruble notes. He came around the counter that separated them and leaned down to press the crumpled bills into her beefy hand. His strong fingers closed over hers.

"Please," he murmured. "The work here is . . . difficult."

The money disappeared as quickly as a dissident, and a satisfied smile replaced her indifference.

"Your brother was taken to the third floor. For tests. Then the doctor will see him in the ward there. Do you want his bedding changed daily?" The plump hand was open again, the smile never leaving her face.

Alexi acquiesced. A second transaction took place. "I want him to have whatever he needs. You'll see to it?"

The nurse was a study in solicitousness. "Of course, Comrade Petrov. We are a *good* hospital. Now take the stairway through the door on your right. Three floors up. See the duty nurse."

Alexi quickly followed her directions. The stairwell was cold, and a steady draft plummeted down from a cracked skylight. He climbed the steps unhappily.

Yuri was very sick, possibly dying, and Alexi's confidence in the hospital's ability to treat him was negligible. If the administrators weren't well connected, or if the hospital served a low-priority area, even the most commonly used drugs might be in short supply. Everyone knew that the Health Ministry had priorities. This place didn't appear to be one of them.

Compounding matters was the terrifying thought that he had still to meet the forces who pursued his brother. A murdered soldier and the incident at the House of Journalists would have been reported. The militia were at least dogged, if not inspired, and their search would be well coordinated, citywide if the matter were deemed sufficiently urgent. From what Yuri had told him, that seemed to be the case. Perhaps even the KGB would be in on the hunt. Someone, he was certain, would be here soon.

That thought galvanized him and he reacted viscerally, primitive emotions erupting from deep inside him and inundating reason. He experienced a sudden, overwhelming need to call the authorities and inform on Yuri. If he acted quickly, no one would blame him for his brother's actions or think he had anything to do with Yuri's politics. The need to inform was so intense that he had to stop and grab hold of the wooden banister to steady himself. Betray Yuri? What was he thinking?

Loyalties warred within him. Training from earliest childhood continued to exert itself. Personal needs were nothing; the collective was everything. The innate desire to turn against his brother was therefore a reflection of his most noble longings and not his least. One had to join the group; the individualist was the anarchist in disguise. . . .

He was *afraid*, he realized finally. Past the training and the principles and the attempts at self-delusion, he was afraid. But this fear was of a new and different kind. It wasn't the sudden adrenal surge that accompanied a near-miss accident or preceded some unavoidable personal confrontation. It was far more subtle than the common biological reflex, and did not derive solely from fear of injury.

He *wanted* to betray Yuri. He *needed* to obey the rules. He could never escape the warm, wet trap of how much easier it was—how desperately much easier it was to obey rather than to face the consequences of disobedience. He was willing to betray his own brother to prove himself. The realization made him feel sickened and perverse.

He stepped up to the third-floor landing and had to push hard to budge the heavy metal fire door. The rooms were dark this time of night, the hallway lights dimmed. Alexi saw a nursing station at the far end and headed for it.

Sudden tears brimmed in his eyes and he stopped walking for a moment to wipe them away. It was deeply disturbing to face the truth about himself. He was just a weak, spineless, insipid, frightened man. Up to now, he'd always thought of himself as a decent sort. Normal. Acceptable. Now he was forced to accept the harsh fact that the first time he'd ever been truly tested, he'd turned to shit.

The floor nurse looked up at his approach. "Comrade?"

"I was told downstairs that Yuri Petrov was brought here. I'm to wait."

"You're a relative?"

"His brother."

She consulted a ledger. "He's undergoing tests right now. You can wait over there, comrade."

He mumbled a thank you and took a seat in an alcove to the side. He went over everything Yuri told him. *Please, God, don't let him die.* What would he do without Yuri? Yuri of the bright light and fast mind. Who would explain things to him?

Alexi knew his own mind was slow and plodding compared to his brother's, but that had never mattered. Yuri teased him, but always affectionately. He could always make Alexi laugh.

Once Yuri had told him about a strange animal that would clamp its jaw onto something and the only way to make it let go, short of killing it, was to beat it senseless. Yuri often teased him, telling Alexi *he* was like that; calling him "little snapping turtle" and shaking his head in bemused affection.

Alexi untwisted his big hands slowly. Yuri had been there for him so often. He remembered the day so long ago that Yuri had come to see him inducted into the Young Pioneers with all the other children in their third year of elementary school. Alexi was so proud of his new red neckerchief. Like flowers blooming in spring, the red cloths blossomed over the drab brown and blue uniforms, signaling that this most important season was now at hand.

The children had marched into the big central room in a militarily straight and precise line. Breathless and bright-eyed, they were called to attention by adult leaders, "Group commanders, prepare to report!"

"Comrade Chief Pioneer Leader! The section of Pioneer leaders of Class Three A is lined up for the ceremonial ritual formation! All members are present for the ceremony of presentation of the Pioneer scarf and badge."

And then the oath, all together, "I, Petrov, Alexi, entering the ranks of the All-Union Pioneer Organization named after Vladimir Ilyich Lenin, solemnly promise before my comrades: to love my motherland fervently; to live, study, and fight as the great Lenin bequeathed us, as the Communist Party teaches. I promise always to observe the laws of the Pioneers of the Soviet Union." Proud parents. Wonderful applause . . .

Later, he'd been entrusted to return a flag to its chest in an administrator's office. He carried the heavy red cloth proudly, delighting in the feel of its coarse weave against the skin of his extended arms, struggling slightly with its bulk.

Years later, in retrospect, he knew that the group of older boys who had accosted him that day were not really evil or especially malicious. They were just practicing the age-old children's custom of taunting the younger ones. But at that moment, the group that surrounded him was big and threatening. He knew instinctively that these boys were headed for the PTU, the lowest track of the three that all eighth-graders were funneled into at the end of that year.

The first track went on to regular school, ending at the tenth grade, leading to college or specialized institutes. *Tekhnikum,* the second track, was for those who would become skilled technicians. *Politekhnicheskoye uchilishhche,* or PTU, turned out "skilled" workers. Alexi's mother had been very strict about his not associating with PTU boys, often placed in the track because of social or behavioral problems. His mother told him *he* was going to the university.

Alexi thought at first the boys might just tease him and move on to better sport. He clutched the flag more closely and ignored the taunts, flushing hotly in spite of himself. Even at the sudden pushes, the sharp pokes, he chose not to react, hoping against hope for peace. He didn't want to spoil his new red kerchief or soil his freshly washed uniform. He could not abandon his precious cargo.

But one ungainly boy with crooked, jutting teeth demanded the flag. "I can't," Alexi stammered, aghast. The older boy grabbed at it, tearing one side from Alexi's hand. The flag unraveled and spilled to the floor.

"Please . . ." Alexi cried, kneeling quickly to gather back up its precious folds, piling it into an unmanageable ball in his small arms. But they grabbed at it again, catching a corner between two of them, yanking it hard.

Alexi fell, both hands curled in the cloth. He held on for dear life, refusing to let go. The boys yelped in delight trying to shake him loose, pulling him down the hallway, sliding him into walls. They laughed at his frightened cries, screaming at him to let go. He wouldn't.

The boys continued in earnest, kicking and punching Alexi in frustration. Alexi held on anyway, his hands locked into the red cloth, refusing to let go. Refusing; eyes closed and mouth set in a tight line when their hands or feet connected.

Suddenly, the sound of skin hitting skin penetrated his awareness, but he didn't dare risk a look over. "Get away, you! Pick on someone who's not a little kid, why don't you." Yuri! It

was glorious. He'd kicked one, then grabbed another and sent
him sprawling. Yuri was only a seventh-grader himself, but he
waded furiously into the boys and dispersed them easily. Then
he bent over Alexi, his young face filled with worry and
tenderness.

"Did they hurt you, Alosha?"

A sniffle. A shake of the head. Eyes brimming.

"I understand. Here, let me help you. Take that corner,
that's right. Put it here."

A bigger sniffle. "It's dirty, Yuri. They made it dirty."

"Don't worry, Alosha. We'll clean it. Go and wet this in
the fountain. It will be as good as new."

"Promise?"

Yuri smiled. "Sure."

Together, they'd cleaned the flag and put it back and then
Yuri walked him home and told him about the turtle who
wouldn't let go.

"You were very brave, Alosha, holding on to the flag."

"Truly, Yuri?"

"In my heart of hearts. You were like the turtle. Stubborn
and brave."

"But Mama says that it's not so good to be so stubborn."

Yuri hesitated, struggling to find a way to explain something difficult to the nine-year-old beside him.

"She worries about you, Alosha. We have no father with
high rank to smooth our way. You are sometimes too much
the . . . individual. It could hurt your chances."

"I don't understand."

Yuri sighed. "No matter. Just remember that not everyone will fight as long or as hard as you and that you should not
expect them to."

"But—"

Yuri smiled. "Quiet, turtle. Only one fight per day. Later I
will permit you to give me half your potato for saving your life
today."

Half a potato; small price for a life. Alexi sighed deeply at
the memory. No one should have struck down such a man with
so little regard for his worth. It pleased him in a curious way
that not even Yuri had been able to extinguish his own flame.

Waiting became increasingly difficult. He was suddenly reminded that he hadn't called Irina. He asked for a phone, but was told that the only one he could use was in the lobby. Irina would have to wait. He couldn't risk missing the doctor.

More time passed. It was over two hours since he'd brought Yuri in. His frustration was a thing alive inside him, straining at his guts to get out. He forced himself to remain calm. A scene would do no one any good. He counted to a hundred. Then again. Then he began toward a thousand.

"Comrade Petrov?"

Four hundred and seventy-three. Alexi took a deep breath and looked up. "I'm Petrov. My brother . . . ?"

"I am your brother's doctor. Lozinskaya. I'm very sorry for the wait, but . . . complications set in. Please, come into my office and we can talk."

Alexi caught her arm as she turned to go. She was a middle-aged woman with a boxy shape and graying hair pulled back into a bun. "Tell me," Alexi said hesistantly, "how is Yuri?" But he could read the answer in her eyes before she spoke the words.

"I'm very sorry, Comrade Petrov. Your brother is dead. Please, come with me now."

Alexi allowed himself to be led. The doctor's office was a small, windowless room with an old desk. Files lay stacked on its top and also on the wooden floor. He sat down in the only other chair. A numbness had engulfed him along with an air of unreality.

"How . . . ?" he managed.

The doctor leaned forward in her chair and looked at him intently. "We're not certain yet. The brain was obviously involved. We don't yet know to what extent. An autopsy is being performed now and we hope to have more answers soon."

Lozinskaya picked up a file and leafed through the pages inside. "These are the admitting forms. You're positive your brother never suffered from epilepsy? Spinal damage? Neurological impairment . . . ?"

The list went on. Alexi shook his head. How could he explain what Yuri had told him, what he was involved in? And what difference would it make now? Yuri was dead. He interrupted the litany of diseases.

"When will they do the autopsy?"

Lozinskaya glanced at the chart. "One of the staff pathologists is conducting it now. Why?"

"I'd like to speak to whoever it is."

Lozinskaya's face was not unkind but she shook her head. "I'm afraid that's impossible. All the facts will be in our report. Procedures, Comrade Petrov. They govern us all. You'll have the complete picture when we've had a chance to go over all the data and make sense of the findings. Be patient, comrade."

Alexi nodded, tight-lipped. Yuri was dead. He blocked the flood of despair that threatened to overwhelm him.

"You've been kind," he said tiredly.

Lozinskaya looked sympathetic. "It will take a few days before we can release the body. Why don't you go home now? This is such a shock, I know. Tomorrow. Come back tomorrow when you've rested and we can talk again."

"All right, Doctor. I will."

Lozinskaya stood up. "I have to get back to the ward now. You'll be all right?"

Alexi sat up straighter. "I will be. Can I just sit here for a few moments? I don't think I'm ready to face people just yet."

She patted him on the shoulder. "Of course. I'll tell the nurse. Rest here until you're ready." She brushed past him and went out the door.

Alexi got out of his chair and began burrowing through the files on Lozinskaya's desk almost as soon as the door clicked shut. When he'd asked her about the autopsy, she'd glanced at some paper within. He found Yuri's file and scanned the contents quickly. Admitting forms, lab reports. Here was what he was looking for. Autopsy schedule: Dr. Olevsky, Pathology. According to the file, the autopsy had been scheduled at once. He made a note of the room number and replaced the file back on her desk.

The stairwell was just as cold when he reentered it and walked down to the second floor. The corridor was roughly the same as the one above, but there were labs here instead of patient rooms. There was activity in a few and Alexi stuck his head into one. A technician of some kind was perched over a microscope.

"Excuse me. I've got to get something to Dr. Olevsky. Can you tell me where room P-274 is?"

The technician spoke without looking around.

"Down to your right to the end of the hall; then go through the double doors and it's the second big room on the left. Be careful, though. You don't want to interrupt Olevsky when he's working."

The autopsy room was on a well-lighted corridor. Walls that were half glass permitted a view. Inside, a man in a blood-spattered apron was poised over an open body that lay on a slate-topped table beside him. It was disconcerting to see the doctor reach into the body and lift out a severed organ as casually as one might select a vegetable from the bin. But Alexi watched him work, grateful beyond words that the corpse was not his brother's. That would have been too much.

Finally the doctor finished, peeled off his rubber gloves, and shrugged out of his apron. He washed and dried his hands at a porcelain sink and then turned down the sleeves of his white shirt, which badly needed ironing. Smoothing down his gray hair, he straightened his tie and walked unhurriedly to the lab door.

"Dr. Olevsky?" Alexi asked as quickly as the man stepped into the corridor.

"Yes? Yes," said Olevsky brusquely. "But whoever you are, you shouldn't be here. Who let you into this wing?"

"I need to talk to you, Comrade Doctor. My brother . . . my brother died tonight and I'd like to know what killed him."

There was a slight softening around Olevsky's eyes. "I'm sorry. But how would I know that?"

"I believe you conducted the autopsy."

"Oh, I see. The name?"

"Yuri Mikhailovich Petrov. I'm Alexi Petrov, his brother."

A sudden wariness passed over Olevsky's features. Alexi caught the brief change. Then it was gone, along with the sympathy.

"I'm very sorry but there is nothing I can tell you. This is

highly irregular. Who is the doctor in charge of your brother's
case?"

"Lozinskaya," Alexi responded.

"Then you must see her."

"She's gone now."

"Then I suggest you wait until morning," Olevsky said
flatly. "I can do nothing for you." He turned to go.

"Wait, please," Alexi said urgently. "When I mentioned
Yuri's name it disturbed you. I could see that. Something you
must have seen. Something . . . I don't know . . . unusual. Won't you help me? No one will know. I promise you. No
one."

Olevsky shook his head. "I don't want to be involved with
your brother's case. I performed an autopsy. Nothing more."

Alexi pressed. "There *was* something."

"Nothing," Olevsky said firmly. "Only a dead man. I am
sorry. But that's all." But his hands fluttered before him and his
eyes were elsewhere. Alexi wished he could share that vision.

"Look," Alexi began slowly, "I know a doctor's salary is
low. And these days it's harder and harder to get what we need.
Things are scarce. Perhaps . . . Perhaps I can help." He
pulled out the red leather folder again. *Pravda's* name was
emblazoned there, a key to secrets, to scarce resources, to
goods a poorly paid doctor might never see.

The folder drew Olevsky's eyes like a gemstone. Indecision crossed his features.

"We can help each other," Alexi insisted in a tight, low
voice. "Anything . . . anything I can do. But tell me about
Yuri. Just that. Please."

Olevsky's indecision deepened. Again his eyes looked
elsewhere and Petrov grabbed at whatever was moving the
man deep inside.

"A relative?" he asked quickly. "Home needs? A daugh-
ter? Your wife?"

Olevsky turned away.

"Something with your wife? Tell me. I may be able to
help. then you help me. That's the way it's done, isn't it? No
one will know. Think of your wife."

Olevsky's brusqueness evaporated. His face looked drawn

and Petrov could suddenly see that the man was under a great strain. But he could press no harder. He had found the correct button and pushed it. He waited, letting time do the work his words could not.

"It's the climate," Olevsky said at last, wearily. "The winter is too cold. Her lungs aren't strong and they fill up with fluid if she takes cold. And our apartment, we share with so many, and the heat is bad. I have medicine for her, but she should be taken to a warmer climate. You see? I must get her away but I don't know how. There is the South, but that's a great deal of money. Even the money isn't all, though. We have no special hotels as you do, no Journalists' Union rooms in the Crimea. No passes for us."

There was bitterness in his voice as he continued. "I earn less than two thirds of what the average factory worker makes. It's the old disdain for professionals in the workers' state. We slave and study and still get less. Isn't that unfair? Isn't it?"

"I agree, of course," said Alexi carefully. "And you, a healer."

Olevsky pounced on that. "A healer, you say. When I can get the medicine or the instruments, or the officials let me work. I'm a doctor, I tell them, not an ideologue. Save the Party lectures for those who want them. But then others get promoted and I have to stay here, opening and closing bodies that are just so much rotting meat. Oh"—he caught Alexi's pained expression—"I forgot. Your brother. Please forgive me. For a moment, I forgot. . . ."

Alexi brushed it aside. "That's all right. I understand how you feel. You're speaking from anger. The priorities are surely unfair. But I have friends, useful people. It's done all the time. I'm entitled to two weeks. My wife and I planned . . . but you can have them. You can have them if you help me."

Olevsky drew a ragged breath and finally nodded. "Come inside."

Olevsky's office was only a desk and a phone in a tiny cubicle at the back of the lab. Chipped wooden chairs added to its dinginess, and the pungent smell of disinfectants wafted in over the plasterboard walls, which failed to reach the ceiling. He picked up a lab report and waved it in front of Alexi.

"I hope you're a strong man. What I'm going to tell you will not be pleasant to hear."

"You must speak freely," Alexi said earnestly.

Olevsky shrugged. "As you wish. But remember what I said. Your brother died from something I have never seen before and hope never to see again. Even to be researching such a thing is questionable. And if that research is actually being used on people, as I believe it was in your brother's case, then his death is not an accident but a crime.

"Now listen carefully. The brain, Petrov, is just a mass of nerve tissue sitting in a cushioned chamber inside the skull. In man, it includes the cerebrum, the center of consciousness, sensation, and voluntary actions; the cerebellum, which coordinates and regulates the muscles; and the medulla oblongata, which is the pathway from brain to spinal cord and the controller of involuntary functions."

Alexi nodded. "Go on."

"Very well. Research has discovered a large protein molecule, a nerve cell adhesion molecule called an N-CAM, that is present on the surfaces of nerve cells. These N-CAMs act like glue to bind the surface of one nerve cell to another. This glue keeps the brain's circuits intact and binds together all of its internal structures. That's the first part. N-CAMs bind nerve cells together to form the wiring for the brain's circuits and hold the tissue of the brain itself together."

"But how does this relate to Yuri?" Alexi asked.

"I can't tell you exactly. There's no way for me to know from an autopsy *why* what was done to your brother was done. I can only tell you the results."

"Tell me," Alexi prompted.

Olevsky nodded slowly, aware of Alexi's steady gaze. "I don't know what they wanted, whoever did this to your brother. I can't imagine what would prompt anyone to do what was done to him. For some reason, they disrupted the N-CAM bonding in his brain." Olevsky's voice grew shriller, the flutter of his hands more pronounced. "Petrov, *all* the cell bindings in *all* the structures were dissolved. There were no more distinct structures, no recognizable features."

Alexi felt the universe reel around him. He understood

now what he had seen in Olvesky's eyes. His face twisted in pain but Olevsky continued, plunging on harshly.

"During the autopsy, Petrov, I couldn't remove your brother's brain intact. *I had to pour it out!* Now do you understand why I hesitated to tell you, to get involved more deeply? No one man could have done this. It couldn't have happened in some street fight or traffic accident. Only the state has the resources to accomplish what I saw in your brother's body tonight. So go away now. Go away and leave me alone. Our bargain is done. I'm out now, Petrov."

It took a while for Alexi to be able to answer. "All right," he said finally, the images searing themselves into his mind. He sat down heavily on the edge of the doctor's desk and ran a hand over his face.

Someone would be here soon. He corrected himself. The *murderers* would be here soon. This was all bound up in the struggle going on around Malenkov; the struggle that only hours earlier he had decided so casually did not concern him. He could have laughed. But one thing remained.

"Where is Yuri's . . . where is Yuri now?" he asked softly.

"In the morgue. But what purpose would it serve to see him? Don't make it harder on yourself."

Alexi's face closed up. "Nothing is harder than death. I want to see my brother one last time."

"The morgue's locked up at this hour."

"Find the key."

"Please," Olevsky begged. "I did what you asked. No more, now. If we're seen together, later it could be—"

Alexi cut him off sharply. "No bargain, then. No trip south for your wife."

Olvesky chewed at his lips furiously and his hands fluttered. He searched Alexi's face for any sign of wavering but saw none. With a final sigh, he reached into his desk and withdrew a key. "You're a difficult man, Petrov. Follow me."

The morgue smelled strongly of alcohol and formaldehyde, and the cold air chilled his skin, but Alexi passed through the row of corpse-covered tables without wincing. He remembered his father's funeral so long ago. Dead flesh felt like clay, with chicken skin bunched over it. But it was colder than clay.

Olevsky opened a square steel door that was set into a tiled wall. Inside was a dark cavity, and a sheet-covered figure lay on a slab. He hesitated. "The autopsy. It isn't . . . a delicate thing."

Alexi steeled himself. "I understand. Thank you for the warning. Bring him out now, please."

The slab slid out on metal rollers and locked into place. Olevsky lifted back the sheet to expose the face. Then he walked a polite few steps away and turned his back.

Alone with his brother, the tears that Alexi had been holding back finally brimmed over and fell slowly down his cheeks. For a long moment, his vision blurred and the overhead fluorescents scintillated as the tears refracted the light. He ran a sleeve across his eyes and the scene refocused. He was glad Olevsky had warned him. He reached out and traced the jawline he had always envied, the depth of character Yuri had always tried to conceal. Had whoever killed him known what a great treasure they were destroying? Had they understood the mind that made Yuri so special and unique? Only overwhelming conceit could render one capable of killing a brain, obliterating a mind. Somewhere inside Alexi, a journey was completed without his knowing.

Someone would be here soon. No, he thought, someone was probably here already. If he were picked up, the notebook would fall into their hands. Or he could give it over willingly and keep himself safe.

Alexi took Yuri's notebook from his pocket and slid it back behind the drawer holding his brother's body. There was a small ledge where it wedged tightly. Even if they moved Yuri, the notebook would not be discovered.

He wondered if, after a long while, one could learn to be brave.

"I'm ready now," he said to Olevsky, who came back to shut the body into the wall. There was nothing more to be said between them. A brief clasp of hands, then Alexi walked back to the stairwell and down to the first floor.

He was arrested in the main lobby.

XII

Tuesday A.M.

The arrest was quick and efficient and occurred with the ease of oiled gears. One second Alexi was walking through the lobby; the next, there was a burly, dark-suited agent on each of his arms and he had nowhere to go but into the "box" that a third man sealed up when he stepped briskly in front of Alexi and ordered him to halt. The man was shorter than the other two and more slender, with pinched features and a drooping posture that gave him a birdlike impression. His peremptory attitude, however, indicated command, and his sharp gestures tolerated no disobedience. The nurses, who had served to point Alexi out, remained silent and inconspicuous behind their stations, watching the proceedings through carefully averted eyes. This was a contagion they would not venture near.

"My name is Koslov," said the one in charge. "You will come with us, Comrade Petrov." Koslov's arms lay flat against his sides and his feet were close together. Owl-like, he inclined only his head and stared through dark eyes.

Alexi started, stomach dropping, but surprised that the anticipation had been so much worse that the reality. He felt numbed rather than afraid, suspended in an emotional limbo created by the pain of Yuri's death. In an odd way, it was a kind of protection.

"I've done nothing," he protested, trying to shrug his arms free. The big men only moved in closer, unmoved by remonstrations heard daily. Alexi ceased his futile struggles. He searched their faces, hoping to see some signs of compassion. He found only boredom, the diminutive of arrogance.

All were dressed similarly: dark suits and ties, white shirts, black shoes, and heavy leather coats slung open around their shoulders.

Koslov's rigid stance did not alter. "If you've done nothing, you have no reason to fear routine questioning," he said smoothly. The trap was shut. Further protest would sound like fear, or, worse, guilt. Koslov held out his hand like a stern teacher demanding an assignment, and his fingers flicked back and forth impatiently.

Alexi surrendered his identification. A sudden chill ran down his back. No militia, these. They were far too assured. KGB?

Koslov examined the folder and snapped it shut. He did not return it, slipping it instead into his jacket pocket. "Where is your brother? I warn you that he is in a most precarious position. There are a great many questions he has to answer."

Alexi's bitter response came as close to defiance as he dared. "That will be difficult, Comrade Koslov. Unless you can question a corpse."

"He's dead?" Koslov was clearly unsettled. This was a complication beyond his control. He looked to the head nurse, who could only shrug helplessly. "Do you want me to call an administrator?" she asked nervously.

"No need," Alexi said. "It's true. He died only a little while after we got him here. Dr. Lozinskaya was in charge. I suggest you speak to her if you need further information."

Indecision crossed Koslov's face, only to be subtly altered by a new thought: What to report to his superiors? He drew his mouth into a tight frown and his eyes flickered measuringly over Alexi, who saw all at once Koslov's thinking. *He* would be substituted for the hunter's lost prize. He sensed he was on increasingly dangerous ground and that from now on he would have to be careful indeed.

The pervasive sense of danger prompted him to calculate rapidly. In order to walk away from this, he was going to have to convince Koslov and his superiors, whoever they were, that he knew nothing important about Yuri or his work. He began to posture himself accordingly.

"I don't understand why you're here. Does this have anything to do with me? Or is it Yuri? Is he the reason you're arresting me?"

Koslov ignored that and looked at him narrowly. "Questioning, comrade. You aren't under arrest. You say the body is in the morgue?"

"I don't know where it is," Alexi said. "I was told about Yuri by Dr. Lozinskaya. You'll have to question her for anything more."

Koslov examined the remark for insolence but decided to let it pass. He turned instead to the head nurse. "You, I take it, *can* tell me where the morgue is, yes? Good. Take us there."

For the second time that night, Alexi was forced to look at his brother's lifeless, waxen features. Koslov brutally stripped away the sheet from the chalk-white body with one sharp tug. Alexi shuddered realistically enough. Even a second time the autopsy was not easy to look at. At least Olevsky was nowhere in sight. Alexi didn't trust the doctor to keep his silence before the authorities.

Koslov looked at Yuri's body and shook his head distastefully. "Close it up," he ordered the nurse. The naked corpse slid back into the wall on steel rollers. But the nurse hesitated before shutting the door on it. "Will you be wanting the body?" she asked Koslov.

The hidden notebook flashed into Alexi's mind and he held his breath. Koslov considered the idea. Seconds passed.

He came to a decision. "Not now," he said finally. Alexi breathed again. Koslov went on, "We'll send for it later. But all pertinent records are to be stored and sealed. Understood?"

The nurse nodded. "I'll tell the doctors."

"Fine. Now you'll be coming with us, Comrade Petrov."

"Of course, comrades," said Alexi, as calmly as he could. "I see no reason to be concerned about questioning. I have nothing to worry about."

At that, Koslov turned, the bored expression replaced by a look of bemusement. For a moment, his dark eyes almost twinkled. "You know, Petrov," he said thoughtfully, "that would probably make you unique." Then he gestured pointedly to the other two and Alexi was propelled out of the morgue and downstairs to a waiting car.

It was three in the morning and the car sped through Moscow's deserted streets. Plows were moving about in the aftermath of the storm, pushing tons of snow toward the roadsides and creating small mountains in the gutters.

Alexi sat sandwiched in between the big men. Koslov rode up front, next to the driver. Alexi was tired and hungry and the fears that had plagued him earlier now returned in force. No one spoke. These men, even Koslov, were not of high rank. Alexi knew he would be meeting those soon enough. He tried to concentrate but felt mentally sluggish, ill prepared to conceal his crimes. He was a fool to go up against them. A damned fool.

The car sloshed through the snowy streets, and his small act of defiance sat coldly in his stomach. If he revealed the notebook later, it would only illuminate the fact that he had chosen, at least at first, to hide its exisitence. Any Party ideologue would have a field day with that. Intentions counted against one as harshly as deeds.

The car made a sudden, sharp, skidding turn that pressed him against his captors. The smell of wet leather was rank in his nostrils. He had to go to the bathroom. His resolve began to fade. He hunched forward to get a better look out the window to see where they were. What he saw brought sudden sweat to his forehead and made the breath catch in his throat.

Zorga Street! That meant these men weren't militia *or* KGB. This was far worse. The militia he might have bluffed; they were just overworked policemen. The KGB could be bargained with, possibly. His position at *Pravda* might have helped. After all, he had needed their clearance to get his job in the first place. But Zorga Street meant that these men were GRU—military Intelligence. That made all the difference in the world.

Alexi had plenty of experience with the Glavnoye Razvedyvatelnoye Upravleniye—the Chief Intelligence Directorate of the Soviet General Staff. The GRU's province was military espionage. They were fanatically tight-lipped, and information about the GRU was never easy to come by. Alexi was a journalist, he didn't ask questions. But he knew all of the rumors, never openly admitted, that the GRU operated worldwide in pursuit of Western military secrets. They said the GRU special units conducted highly sensitive, even covert, missions abroad and that GRU personnel were trained as saboteurs, survival experts, and assassins. No one would ever admit publicly to this, he knew, lest they lose credibility in their constant diatribes against the American CIA.

Alexi had worked with several GRU officers over the years. They were hard, dedicated men, severely disciplined and completely inflexible when it came to the subject of military information. Sometimes their positions seemed ludicrous. Even in an era of satellite surveillance, pictures of roads and bridges still could not be published. Railroad timetables were classified information!

There was an historical tension between the GRU and the KGB. GRU officers chafed constantly against the KGB's Military Information Directorate's attempts to control top-level appointments. The GRU's present director was a former deputy chairman of the KGB, an appointed leader, who, some purported, was incapable of controlling his subordinates.

But if the GRU hated the KGB, in return the KGB desperately feared GRU military officers and sought to prevent them from establishing the kind of dangerously private and personal empire that Beria had almost created in the early fifties.

Since the GRU was entirely under the control of Defense Minister Solnikov, it was probably functioning as what the KGB had always feared, his private army. It was the GRU, then, that had killed Yuri, Alexi thought bitterly.

Was that how the battle lines were drawn? he wondered. Solnikov could have used the GRU to decimate Malenkov's supporters in the KGB just as Yuri had claimed. It was just as possible, then, that the rest of it was true, too, that Valery Rudin's machine—the AI, Yuri had called it—was the only thing left protecting the general secretary. The GRU must then want desperately to bypass Rudin's creation, Malenkov's final defense.

The sullen, gray buildings of GRU headquarters rose suddenly in front of them. The entire compound was surrounded by a high concrete wall. At the tunnellike entrance, uniformed, armed guards carefully checked their credentials before raising the striped barrier and sending the car across the cobblestone roadway.

The icy stones glistened in the courtyard where flood-lights cast a glare. Alexi's heart hammered. He was caught up in a conflict that threatened to overwhelm him. He could lose everything. It had happened to others. Exile beckoned with skeletal fingers. How could he help but betray Yuri in the face of that?

The building's personnel all wore military uniforms. Alexi suddenly felt out of place in his street clothes. Even the secretaries seated at desks in office anterooms were dressed in military garb. Uniformed clerks carrying bundles of files trotted down the drab green, round-ceilinged hallways, and a white stripe painted down the center of the corridors separated the pedestrian traffic into opposing streams.

Alexi's resolve crumbled. To hell with Malenkov, Solnikov, and Yuri, he thought. He was going to get out of this with his life intact. There was Irina to think of. He would gratefully trade the notebook for his personal and professional safety. He began to concoct explanations as to why he had hidden the notebook. To protect it? Of course. And now he'd be happy to turn it over to the rightful claimants. Any patriot would. Gladly.

Alexi allowed himself to hate his brother for having forced him into such a predicament. Cold beads of sweat that had been gathering under his armpits began to slide down his sides. He walked on, stopping when they told him to, turning when he was ordered, desperately trying to conjure a variety of answers to cover any contingency, ignoring his own rising self-contempt.

Koslov turned down a corridor and stopped at a heavy wooden door. The guards aligned themselves behind Alexi. "In there," Koslov ordered. He shot back the bolt and gestured him forward.

"Wait," said Alexi quickly. "There's something—"

But there was no time to finish the sentence. Koslov swung the door open and he was shoved hard from behind. Alexi went sprawling onto his hands and knees, rolling across the hard cement floor. The door slammed behind him.

His hands scraped viciously, and the momentum of the fall carried him over awkwardly onto his back. Lights swam overhead. He tried to right himself but got caught up in his clothing, ending up like an overturned turtle trying to flip itself back over.

It had happened too fast. He couldn't even yell his desire to confess, to tell his unseen captors that this was *unnecessary.* He was ready to cooperate. Instead, he could only flail helplessly on the rough floor.

He righted himself finally. He was dizzy and it was hard to focus his eyes. But he began to shout, "Please. Whoever is listening. I want to cooperate. Just let me talk. I can give you—"

Strong arms grabbed him under the shoulders and hauled him to his feet. A fist smashed into his midsection, cutting off his voice as the breath burst out of him. He had an impression of three big men around him, and then a black cloth hood was yanked over his head and a drawstring pulled tightly around his throat.

He could barely get enough air into his lungs and started to gasp for breath. But his frantic struggles only made his captors hold him more tightly. He twisted and tried to speak but another fist crumpled him over again. He was spun around and he fell. Someone snorted in derision. Suddenly there were hands tearing at his clothing.

Alexi fought in mindless panic. His coat was torn from his shoulders and yanked down his back, trapping his arms. He was lifted as easily as a baby and his shoes were pulled off, his pants and socks and shorts following. He was blind and mute, naked from the waist down, humiliated and in pain.

They stripped him completely and pushed him away. Alexi lashed out, connected with nothing, and fell again. The floor scraped his chest and his back. Inside the hood his cheeks flamed with terror and humiliation. It was too much. Involuntarily, he started to cry; loud, gasping sobs. Abruptly, he felt the hands leave him. Footsteps retreated.

"Please," he pleaded, "let me tell you. A notebook. There is a—"

The water hit him like a torrent of razor blades against his abraded skin and wrenched a tortured scream from his throat. He hurt everywhere. He rolled and the water scored his back. He twisted and it tore at his legs. His genitals were on fire and his stomach brutally knotted. He gagged from the pain, desperate not to throw up inside the hood.

He tried to tell them that they had won, but he couldn't. He rolled back and forth helplessly as the water raked over the soles of his feet. He jerked wildly in spasms of agony. Pain speared up his groin, contorting him.

It continued, twisting him into a tortured ball and slamming him up against the far wall. His mind screamed but no blackness engulfed it. He cried in great heaving sobs but no relief came. Only the pain. Minute after minute, steadily sharper, on skin that felt sanded raw. The noise continued, too, hissing water pelting Alexi and blasting off the walls and floor until there was no place where the nerve-tearing noise or the pain was not.

It stopped abruptly, for no more reason than it had begun. For a while, Alexi could only lie huddled and shaking against the wall, not daring to uncurl and risk that agonizing onslaught again. Sounds came to him slowly, unidentifiable, until he realized that it was the sound of his own weeping and the ragged intake of his breath through the sodden cloth that clung to his face. After a while the pain began to diminish and he cried in slower, longer rhythms. He'd tried to tell them. Why hadn't they listened?

The shivers worsened. Lying wet and naked on the cold floor, Alexi clung to what was left of his shattered dignity, but the humiliation seared through his deepest sense of self. As soon as they came for him or took him to anyone who would listen, he would tell. Confessing quickly enough might spare him any more of this. He prayed they would come for him now. He was beaten. He would beg to confess. Anything to stop it. Anything . . .

The water began again. At once pain was everywhere. For the second time it took over his mind, blotting out reason, and the struggle to protect his tormented body was fought on reflex alone. Over and over again he rolled and twisted and sought escape from the pain. There was no escape. It lasted just as long as the first time and, at the end, he was only a mass of pulsating flesh, deeply hurt and bitterly afraid.

Had it ended there, Alexi would have earnestly confessed his crime, eagerly given up the notebook and been grateful for the chance. He was not schooled for this kind of systematic breaking of the spirit. He had no way to shrug off the pain. But no one came. No questions were asked. He was left alone with his pain and his fear and the tattered shreds of his self-esteem when the reprieve came a second time.

Cold drops of water rolled off his forearms, slid down his belly, and trickled to the floor. The room was damp and his skin was ice-cold. The thought of dying was a peaceful one. He would fool them, slip quietly into the dark land while no one was looking. He sensed a chasm of unimaginable depth yawn within his mind, pulling him in. The remnant of his consciousness poised on the chasm's rim, fully prepared to dive forward before the water began again and the pain followed and the sound blotted out the world and he couldn't take it again. Jump, he ordered himself, jump! But he couldn't. Jump! But he couldn't. . . . Jump. . . . Jump. . . . Jump. . . . Jump. . . .

Alexi pulled back from the chasm. Slowly, stubbornly, his senses returned to his body. First he felt the wet, matted hair of his chest against his drawn-up knees. He grew aware of the sodden warmth of his genitals, cupped so softly in one of his hands; felt the bony ridge of his spine under the other. His body tried to produce heat. He was lying fetuslike, and tiny pools of water collected in the folds of his belly, under his side, in his groin, and grew warm. He breathed as deeply as the wet mask permitted, scraping his cheek against his shoulder to push it away, still not daring to move his hands.

With a deep shudder, he took another breath. Then another. He waited, knowing somehow that it would come again, sure that his captors were not done yet. He fought to warm himself from the inside, drew his body in even more tightly. When it came this time, he would be prepared. This time, stubbornly, he would fight back.

He learned; there was life in anger. Blood flowed more fiercely. His massive hands clenched spasmodically. There was strength in rage. What began as a tiny bubble in the center of his being rose upward, growing all the while, till it burst onto the surface of his mind and filled it with fury's white light, hard and clear.

Rage. He killed Koslov a hundred different ways when the water hit him again; killed every GRU officer he had ever known, tortured and stomped and beat them to death, and the white light never stopped or flickered or went out. The hatred warmed him. A hundred times he vowed that no one would ever hurt him like this again. He would never help them, never submit, never let them beat him this way, crying and struggling on a cold, stone floor. Stubbornly, he survived, his mind filled with a madman's anger and lit by the hot, white light that protected him; protected him until it could turn finally to gray, and then to black, allowing him, at last, to feel nothing more. . . .

Alexi woke in an office. He was fully dressed and lying supine on a leather couch. One of the GRU guards who had first brought him here from the hospital sat watching him from a chair nearby. He said nothing but motioned Alexi toward a chair in front of the large wooden desk that dominated the room.

Alexi wondered how long he had been unconscious. The water room was still frighteningly clear in his mind and he took slow, careful stock of his body's bumps and bruises. The GRU were not amateurs. In a few days all traces of the beating would be gone from his body. Not so from his mind. He ran a hand through his neatly combed hair and found his scalp still damp. He hadn't been out that long. He was flooded with relief at finding himself fully clothed. The office was pleasantly warm and the guard made no threatening movements. Alexi continued to lie there.

In spite of what he understood was the basest kind of manipulation, he found that he couldn't help feeling a kind of gratitude, almost affection, toward his captors for ending the nightmare. *They almost kill me; then restore me and I'm grateful*, he thought bitterly. *But not quite*. He searched internally for spots that hurt, found a bad one below his ribs, and concentrated on the pain. *There*, he thought. *That I can remember well enough*.

The door to the office opened and the guard rose quickly to stiff attention. A high-ranking officer—Alexi recognized his rank as colonel—walked in and took his seat behind the desk. He dismissed the guard with a casual wave and turned his attention to Alexi.

He pointed to the chair. "Comrade Petrov, over here."

Alexi slid his legs off the couch and moved gingerly to the chair. Every muscle ached. He sat down carefully, trying to concentrate on the pain as an acquaintance he would do well to remember. "Will you tell me why I was brought here, Colonel . . . ?"

"Klim," the officer supplied.

". . . why I am here, Colonel Klim?" Alexi completed the question. "The GRU doesn't usually pick up innocent citizens just to give them such a warm welcome."

Klim smiled. "That's fine, Petrov. What I would expect from a *Pravda* journalist. Warm welcome, indeed."

"Colonel. I work hard, I don't get into trouble, and I serve the Party faithfully. Now, suddenly, I'm subjected to . . . *that*, without even a chance to speak."

"Which indicates to you?"

Alexi drew a deep breath. "That someone here thinks that I've done something or know something and they're frightened to death that I won't cooperate with you. They're so frightened that they revert to the worst kind of Stalinism and I'm hurt unnecessarily just to convince me you're serious. That's a mistake."

Klim's eyes narrowed. "A journalist should be more skilled in choosing his words."

"Overkill is always a mistake," Alexi insisted, plunging on recklessly. "I'm not some dissident carrying placards in the street. It was unnecessary."

"So," Klim mused. "We are at fault and you are an innocent man. Well, suppose we proceed under that assumption for a moment. I want to know everything that transpired from the moment your brother came to the House of Journalists until Lieutenant Koslov brought you here."

Alexi shrugged sadly. "There's very little to tell, Comrade Colonel. Yuri tried to barge into the building, and the security guards called me to verify his identity. I did. He was obviously sick with something and he asked me right away to take him somewhere to lie down. I brought him to one of our meeting rooms and got some water and a damp cloth—"

"Thinking nothing of his strange dress? You knew he was never military."

"I asked him about that. He told me he got the uniform from a friend. He laughed it off. You must understand, my brother was always eccentric. Just then, he was half out of his mind with fever. I just didn't worry about how he was dressed."

Klim considered that. "Go on."

"I asked him again what was wrong with him, why he had come to see me this way."

"He was your brother. You found it odd he would search you out?"

"Not in that sense. But I hadn't seen Yuri in quite a while. His work has always been top secret and his life was managed accordingly. Private clinics, special apartments, sudden trips of indeterminate duration. He was a valuable man. His needs were met by the state as valuable men's needs are."

"As all men's are," Klim corrected him. "Did he respond to your questions?"

"He asked me about the family, said to hold my questions for a while. He made me tell him about family matters and promised he would explain everything in time. But he never did."

"Why not?"

Alexi spoke more slowly, letting his eyes unfocus slightly as if he were seeing the events in his mind's eye. "By the time I was finished telling him about Irina—that's my wife who works—"

"At Gosbank," finished Klim idly. "I know that, Petrov. Where she works and for whom. And all about your son, Sergei Alexiovich, and his work for the Ministry of Agriculture and so on and so on. You may spare me needless repetition."

"Sorry. I told Yuri about them both but I lost him sometime during my recollections. His eyes glazed and he looked faint. He began to be confused. He lost control, started to babble."

Klim leaned forward intently. "What did he babble about, Comrade Petrov?"

"A host of things," Alexi said innocently. "Boyhood memories, current girlfriends, something about his old teacher Rudin."

"Stop there," Klim commanded. "Explain that."

"Rudin? Yuri was very fond of the man. Thought he was a true genius and said he'd only really begun to learn when he met him. So I'd heard the name before. But this was meaningless gibberish."

"Nevertheless," Klim prompted him sharply.

Alexi frowned in concentration. "He said something like 'Rudin's dead. . . . Rudin's dead. . . . But he beat them, beat them, beat them all. . . . No one surived . . . no one . . . great machine, machine protects'—something like that. A lot of it was repeated over and over again. It seemed to make him happy." He hesitated.

Klim heard the pause. "That's not all, then."

"No, not quite. But it still doesn't make any sense. Just the name of the general secretary and letters. Again and again. 'Malenkov a i, Malenkov a i, a i Malenkov.' Initials maybe? Titles? I didn't know."

"Nothing else? Nothing more concrete?"

The room felt very close. Alexi shook his head. "This time Yuri did pass out and I ran back into the lobby to call an ambulance. The central office kept me waiting a long time. When I got back, he was only semiconscious and I needed help to carry him outside. I grabbed my coat and jumped into the ambulance. He never regained consciousness there, or at the hospital."

"That was the last time you saw him?" Klim asked.

Alexi nodded. "They wheeled him away and told me to go upstairs to wait. It was a long time. Then the doctor finally came and told me . . . told me that Yuri was dead. I sat in her office for a while. I felt dazed. My only brother shows up out of the blue only to die from something I obviously didn't understand and the doctor could only tell me to come back when the report was finished. After a while I got up and walked downstairs. That's where I made the acquaintance of Lieutenant Koslov. You know the rest."

Klim sat silently, mulling over Alexi's story. His gaze wandered about the room, settled on a spot somewhere over Alexi's head. "And the notebook?" he asked softly.

Alexi felt a cold hand slap at his heart. "What notebook?" he managed weakly.

Klim shifted his eyes angrily back to Alexi and fixed him to his chair. "You tell me, Comrade Petrov. The men who acquainted you with honesty's unpleasant alternatives reported that word among your protests. What does it mean and for what purpose did you invoke it then?"

Alexi hesitated, relieved in part that it was only that. But he had no quick explanation and a hasty one might look like concealment. Klim was relentless.

"The notebook, Comrade Petrov. You're intelligent enough to know that those unpleasant alternatives were invoked at the outset to save us any trouble at this juncture. It isn't that difficult to reinvoke them."

Alexi groped for a response—and found none; felt his mind go blank. He had only seconds left before his hesitation began to look like guilt. He fought down panic and struggled against the sudden need to confess it engendered. Confess? he thought suddenly. Why not?

"I'm terribly embarrassed," he said grimly. "I knew it was wrong at the time, but I did it anyway."

Klim was taken off guard by the sudden turn. "Did what?" he asked, unsure whether Alexi's answer fit his question.

"Something that a man in my position should have known better than to allow others to influence him to do," Alexi concluded firmly.

"You will explain yourself at once," Klim demanded angrily.

"The notebook," Alexi said. "I don't know who put it together but it's a list of people in the city—store managers, ticket clerks, people who have access and are willing to, well, trade for the hard-to-get items. You can go to them and get it through the 'back door.' You understand."

Alexi's shame deepened. "Under the water . . . I don't know why . . . I would have told you anything. The pain was terrible. A confession, I thought a confession would show my cooperation. I saw the notebook only once but it was the only thing I had to confess to. Will you prosecute? I won't make any trouble."

Klim's anger had evaporated. He studied Alexi thoughtfully. "I'm concerned with matters that threaten to shake our world and you tell me about petty crime? I wonder, Petrov."

Alexi said nothing. Klim sat watching him for a while longer, then appeared to come to a decision. He reached over and pushed a button on his intercom. At once, the door opened behind Alexi and he sensed the guard's return.

"Go with these men," Klim ordered.

"Where am I being taken?" Alexi asked, the fear in his voice no test of his acting ability.

Klim heard the fear. He liked it when citizens felt what they were supposed to feel. Made things easier. Why spoil it with calming explanations? He ignored the question and gestured to the guards for Alexi to be taken away.

Klim watched Alexi's departing back. The door closed quietly, leaving the colonel alone. He reviewed the journalist's responses carefully, examining his story in retrospect, adding up his own totals. He jotted down a few notes, made some decisions on the wording of his report.

He picked up his phone and said to the special operator, "Deputy Minister Tarkov." The connection was established in seconds, a tenth of the time the public phone system took. A beeping signal told him the line was secure. The aide in the deputy minister's office put him through at once.

"Tarkov here," said the familiar voice.

"Comrade Deputy Minister? This is Colonel Klim. You wished a call as soon as the journalist was questioned."

"Good. Your thoughts?"

Klim hesitated. "It's a bit early to tell, Comrade Deputy Minister, but I don't think he is telling us all that he knows. His description of his brother's physical deterioration tallies with what our doctors projected. His report of conversations and timing matches the sequence we've gotten from on-site observers. It was less then ten minutes before the ambulance was called and that's not enough for any real information to be passed. Most of the wait for the ambulance, twenty minutes or so, he was in sight of others, not alone with his brother."

"Then what is the basis for your suspicions?" asked Tarkov.

"I should like to hold off answering that question until I've reached more concrete conclusions," Klim said carefully. "That is, with the deputy minister's permission."

"All right, Klim. I won't press you now. But if there's a lead to be developed from this journalist, I want it developed quickly. You are where you are because you've learned to distinguish what is important from what isn't. Be apprised. This is critical. How does the man strike you?"

"Quite average," Klim said firmly. "We frightened him. Frightened him deeply."

"Then what is the problem in extracting information?" Tarkov questioned him.

Klim framed his response slowly. "I want to know the

nature of what Petrov's hiding before I go mucking about and incur the potential for mistakes. The journalist is on a short tether. I ask you to let me do this in my own way. I haven't failed you before."

"That's not quite true, Comrade Colonel," Tarkov said bitterly. "First you and that staff of incompetent maniacs you call doctors kill the first of the survivors using a process you guaranteed was safe—"

"It was, Minister," Klim protested, feeling suddenly hotter. "But the gas Rudin used, how could we have anticipated the synergistic reaction? We needed the information. That was the accepted way to get it."

"Don't fence with me!" Tarkov roared, close to apoplexy.

"I apologize, Comrade Deputy Minister," said Klim quickly. "I only meant to explain—"

"Explain why the GRU accomplished what even Rudin could not: the death of his last two technicians. Explain that to me."

"Those responsible have been—"

"Yes, yes; severely disciplined. Spare me the overworked clichés. At this level, *we* are the ones responsible. Take care that I don't do some disciplining of my own. If the brother knows nothing, toss him out. If he can be useful, roast him over an open fire if you need to. I want a report on all you have on this matter, including the journalist, before noon today. Is that clear?"

Klim mopped at his forehead. "Absolutely, Comrade Deputy Minister."

"You will be sitting in on the initial conference with Berenstein," Tarkov continued, "and will be called upon to report your findings, few though they may be."

"Noon. I will be ready, Comrade Deputy Minister. You can depend on me."

"That's correct, Colonel," Tarkov said dryly and the phone went dead.

Klim replaced it gingerly in its cradle. There were worse fears than those induced by the water. He looked at this watch. It was almost dawn.

He thought about Alexi Petrov. His composure reasserted itself. This was his ground. A button on his desk rewound the tape of the interview. A second played it back.

Klim unbuttoned the collar of his tunic and settled back into his chair. He let the cadence of question and answer roll past his critical ear. He turned up the volume, listening for inconsistencies, minute hesitations. None.

Still, the business about the notebook bothered him. Confessions to petty crimes weren't unusual under the water, it was true. But most were private things: family secrets, sexual oddities. This one was just a bit too . . . tame. It just didn't feel as if there could be enough guilt to motivate an involuntary confession.

A notebook. He began to wonder. Klim pressed the intercom button and asked Koslov to step inside. The door opened quickly.

"Yes, Comrade Colonel?"

"Have someone lay out the dead soldier's things in the conference room and send someone to the hospital to pick up the effects they're holding. I'll be in to look them over as soon as I've had a chance to look over the relevant dossiers. Take personal charge of the matter."

"Yes, Comrade Colonel." Koslov turned and left.

Klim sat back and listened to the tape again. Outside, it would be light by now. He wanted to rest before attending the deputy minister's meeting. There was, however, enough time to see the journalist again.

Something, and he didn't yet know exactly what, had taken place between the brothers that Petrov was trying to keep from him. He was certain.

Like a surgeon who has finally come to a conclusive diagnosis, Klim began to plan his operation. The first cut—there. . . .

XIII

It was cold in the cell. Alexi sat restlessly on the only available perch in the featureless six-by-eight-foot rectangle, a hard bench set against the wall that faced the metal cell door. The ceiling was high, over twelve feet, and the only window was set too far up the wall to provide a view. Only the gray light of a storm-threatening winter's morning suffused the chamber, failing even to break up the monotony with an occasional shadow.

He had been without a shave or a change of clothing for over a day now. At least, he thought humorlessly, they'd provided a bath. For the past several hours he had been left completely alone. With nothing else to do he sat idly, thinking dark thoughts about his current resting place and trying to avoid useless speculation about his future.

It was numbing and frightening all at the same time to be confined to a place where all at once life's myriad choices were limited to selecting whether one sat or stood. Or, he thought ironically, he could lie down on the cement floor. How did anyone keep from going crazy with no respite from constant thinking? Could you stay sane in a place like this over an extended period? At home, you walked around, tossed garments here and there, looked and checked and ate and turned and stared out the windows at neighbors. Bathrooms and books and beds, even in the tightly packed communal apartments, *those* were what made a home: diversions, comforts, private spots; smells. Feeling like a pet who had been expelled to another room, Alexi waited with his hands folded in his lap and, like a pet, tried to anticipate his master's next command, hoping to please him better this time.

So why had he lied? he asked himself. Where in God's name had he gotten the strength—or the incredibly blatant stupidity—to defy the GRU? It was obviously just stubbornness. Plain, rotten stubbornness, the kind that had gotten him into trouble more than once. It was true that they had hurt him, and deeply. He realized that was a big part of it. He sighed. Stupid, lumbering Petrov, never quick like the others. The plodding, bulldog type; the one who didn't let go.

He pondered his own motives. Yes, he had to admit that his stubbornness was a part of it. But there was more. They shouldn't have killed Yuri, he thought bitterly. How could he cooperate with them after they'd done that? All his life he was taught that personal concerns were outweighed by the state's. Now he knew it just wasn't true. They could scare him—they certainly had already—but they could never convince him that his love for his brother—and for his wife and child, for that matter—weren't the most important things in the world. Principles? Maybe he had those, too. Maybe he'd never been tested before in quite this way. For now it was enough that Yuri had stood against these men, and had given his life willingly to stop them. Very well, Alexi decided. He would continue to stand against them as long as he could.

The sound of a key in the cell door pulled Alexi harshly out of his reverie. Guards he hadn't seen before entered and gestured for him to precede them out of the cell. He entered the corridor, noting the rows of cells on both sides, unable to fix his location in the vast complex. He proceeded gingerly. The guards closed around him like walls pressing in. He grew frightened again.

In his heart of hearts, he wondered if it might not be better to surrender. With no idea what was coming, he steeled himself as best he could.

XIV

Colonel Klim's office was no less foreboding on his second visit. But Alexi had not just awakened after the torture of the water room, and he now had the presence of mind to be able to examine it more closely.

Klim's desk still dominated the room, but the light from the window, whose blinds were now open, exposed the scratches and pits in the desk's heavily varnished surface that the green blotter did not entirely cover, and there were scuff marks on the modesty panel where countless nervous feet had rubbed and tapped.

The green carpet was thin but not threadbare. The walls were dulled from their original white to a grayer shade. The only electric light, other than Klim's green-shaded desk lamp, was overhead. Alexi sat in the same chair as before and faced Klim, who toyed with a pencil and addressed him in neutral tones.

"I read in your file that your father died in the Great Patriotic War. You were barely a year old," he said without preamble.

Alexi nodded. "I never really knew my father. But my mother spoke of him quite often."

"Warmly?"

"Yes, I thought so. Given the times, I was assuredly an accident. No one *tried* to have a child during the famines. But they loved each other very much and during one of his infrequent leaves . . ." He left the sentence unfinished, half smiling.

Klim tapped the pencil pensively. "I remember the times. Very bad. Very bad. You were lucky to survive. He died on the Western Front?"

"In Leningrad. During the siege. He was supposed to have been a very good man. He was loyal and stayed and fought and died. Old family friends have also spoken about his intelligence and his uncommon kindness."

"Rare traits," observed Klim.

"Ones my brother shared," Alexi said flatly.

Klim frowned and looked at him sharply. "Then more's the pity about his death. Do you know what killed him?"

Alexi shook his head. "Dr. Lozinskaya told me the final reports were not in yet."

Klim reached for a slim sheaf of papers on his desk and selected one. "It boils down to pneumonia. Both lungs. Where and from whom he got the soldier's uniform is still under investigation. That is what originally brought us into this case. But that needn't concern you.

"Your brother was working on a classified project in the North, took ill, and repeatedly refused treatment. The illness grew worse and his supervisors demanded he be hospitalized. For no apparent reason, your brother was angered by this and abruptly left the project. He journeyed all the way to Moscow, becoming dangerously depleted, and came to you for help. The trip in this weather obviously weakened him beyond his limits. He was a single-minded and foolish man. At least, though, you were able to see each other one last time."

"That is some comfort, I suppose."

"It should be. But there is a lesson, too," Klim said. He regarded Alexi closely. "We always face the greatest danger when we strike off on our own."

"Yuri wouldn't have seen it that way," Alexi commented. "His enormous talent protected him. He did pretty much as he pleased, confident that sooner or later he'd be needed for another project somewhere, forgiven, and any incidents smoothed over."

"His superiors were wrong to allow such behavior to continue," said Klim, digesting that.

Alexi shrugged. "Yuri was pretty good at fashioning arguments." A small grin caught at the corners of his mouth, remembering. "He could list Party rules word for word, assert ideology. He could be as skillful as any chief judge. One of his tricks was to study the latest constitution and be able to quote it verbatim in his defense."

"That is unusual," Klim conceded. "Oddly enough, though, it also forms the basis for another lesson, comrade. Do you wish to hear it?"

"Absolutely, Comrade Colonel."

Klim put down his pencil. "There is a scholar named Malov. He has many theories about the constitution: what is legal, what is not. A very strict interpretation, Malov wants. GRU, KGB, all tame and docile. Forget the need to be ever vigilant, he advises us. Ignore the realities of the need for control." Klim paused. "What do you think of Malov's theories, Alexi Mikhailovich?"

Alexi's forehead creased. "This is terribly confusing, Comrade Colonel. How can I know what to say? I've never before even heard of this Malov, or seen any of his work published."

Klim's smile was wolfish. "Precisely."

He stood up and bade Alexi rise. "It's always a good idea to choose wisely the theories one operates under." He pressed a button on his intercom, and an aide entered quickly. "You are free to go now, Comrade Petrov. The lieutenant in the outer office will escort you home. Good day, comrade."

Klim did not stay in his office after dismissing Alexi. He was pleased with the second interview, convinced more than ever that the journalist was hiding something. Well, he decided, let's give him some running room and perhaps he'll run into trouble. There was no profit in maltreating him further at this juncture. The man had strength, one could see that. One pushed in areas of weakness, probed where wounds opened easily.

First, the more subtle pressures. It pleased Klim to act as the grand master in the game of human chess. Tarkov would press him for results. All right. Twenty-four hours. If Petrov hadn't delivered whatever it was by then, he would be handed over to the interrogation teams. He could be picked up on a moment's notice. After all, this was Moscow, not Paris. Of course, that would result in a second severely damaged Petrov. But really, Klim thought, some of his remarks had been quite insufferable. Who did he think he was, speakly glibly to a GRU colonel?

Solnikov was right. Things had gotten out of hand; traditional disciplines had collapsed. Removing Malenkov, along with his remaining disciples at KGB, would signal a return to better standards. A return to purity. Stalin knew Russia; the people needed a strong hand.

Klim walked into the conference room that adjoined his office. His aides had laid out the final effects of Yuri Petrov on the long table as per their instructions. Alongside, they placed those things that had been left on the body of the murdered soldier. Klim's mouth twisted. This was an example of the brother's kindness, he mused bitterly.

The last pile was laid out neatly, too. These were the things Petrov was wearing when he escaped from the clinic and discarded after he'd killed the soldier. Klim nodded his satisfaction to Koslov and the aide who flanked him and waved off their salutes.

"These are all the items, then?" he asked.

"Yes, Comrade Colonel," said Koslov. "We brought back everything connected with the case from the hospital except the body. Will you issue instructions on that?"

"Ask Dr. Mishkov what he wants to do. If he has no need

for the corpse, order it cremated. Be there when it's done. It's an embarrassment."

Koslov nodded.

"Is every item accounted for?" Klim asked the second aide.

"I believe so, Comrade Colonel. Witnesses from the clinic have given reports on Petrov's dress when he made his escape. He did not use the dead soldier's undergarments, only the tunic, pants, and boots. We've reassembled the uniform. The pieces are all here."

"Personal effects?"

"All here," the aide answered. "The fugitive took nothing but the soldier's identification and money."

"Not his watch?" asked Klim.

"The fugitive already had the doctor's watch, Comrade Colonel, along with his coat and scarf. We've got those, too, here," he said, indicating the third pile. "They were discarded in the alley."

Klim pursed his lips. "Now tell me," he said in a didactic tone, "are we prepared to stipulate that we've recovered every single item Petrov might have had in his possession or come into contact with? Koslov?"

Koslov fidgeted nervously. "I think so, Comrade Colonel. What more could there be? We've checked thoroughly."

Klim sat in a chair and crossed his legs. He liked setting an example for his aides. And he enjoyed their veneration. "Read me the dossier on, what was the soldier's name? Orlov? Yes. Read it to me. I'll show you both something."

Koslov reached onto the conference table and took up the soldier's dossier. "Orlov, Pavel, born in 1961 in Krostroma—"

"Skip that," Klim interrupted. "Go on to 'personal habits.'"

Koslov flipped through the file. "Here it is. Orlov is . . . was, listed as playing the guitar. A writer of songs and a poet. His brigade commander comments several times that Orlov entertained his fellow troops and aided morale. He often did poetry readings. The men liked him."

"Now tell me," said Klim with a self-satisfied look. "Are we prepared to say we've recovered every item?"

Both aides looked blank.

"Think!" Klim thundered. "What does every young

romantic who fancies himself a poet carry? Regardless of talent. Even ones far less accomplished than Comrade Orlov."

Comprehension lit up Koslov's face. "Something to write in and something to write with. A pad and pencil, perhaps."

"Or a notebook," Klim suggested evenly. "To scribble his emotional gibberish into."

"Alexi Petrov mentioned a notebook," the second aide said. "The comrade colonel thinks that Yuri Petrov wrote something in Orlov's notebook and passed it on to his brother."

"And that is why what should be on this table is not," Klim agreed. "Type up a report. I've got to get some sleep before the meeting with the deputy defense minister. Wake me in four hours and have a first draft ready for me to look at."

"We'll see to it, Comrade Colonel."

Klim left the conference room. Tarkov would be pleased to hear there was a notebook. It made the initial GRU failure much more forgettable. Heads might yet remain in place. Other than Petrov's, he thought ruefully, deciding the stakes merited increasing the pressure. The man was in a box already and just didn't know it.

"Have my car brought up from the garage," he told his secretary. He strode out of the office, profoundly pleased with the opening moves of his game.

XV

The thought of his apartment was a sweet siren's song that wafted down the stairwell and beckoned to Alexi as he climbed. Even though his body protested every step, he lunged up the stairs, glad not to meet anyone and grateful that the GRU sergeant who had driven him home hadn't balked at letting him out a short distance from the apartment building. Alexi wanted no raised eyebrows from the matrons in the lobby nor rumors spread from their incessantly wagging tongues.

Still, even the old women's presence was comforting. This was home. He acknowledged the brittleness of spirit that the past twenty-four hours had created in him. He was moving on inertia alone. He'd faced every crisis mostly because there had been no alternative but to react to onrushing events. Now, with haven so near, he could feel how frayed his nerves were, how strained his self-control was.

He fumbled the key into the lock with unsteady hands. As usual, the hallway was redolent with cooking odors. Hot saliva flooded his mouth, reminding him of how long it had been since he'd eaten. He pushed the door open but was suddenly afraid that maybe the vast relief of coming home would be stolen by some new GRU machination. Were they waiting for him inside? Was this respite just a prelude to further pain? He steeled himself against greater disappointment and walked in slowly.

Thankfully, there were no soldiers, no hands to hurt him. Only Irina, bounding off the couch with her face creased with lines of worry. "Alosha! Where have you been?" she cried, rushing over and throwing her arms about him.

Relief flooded through Alexi and brought sudden tears to his eyes. He sagged against her plump bosom and let her propel him to a chair; *his* chair, the stuffed one with the sagging arms by the window.

"I'm glad to see you, Irsha," he said weakly. "You must have been worried about me."

"Worried?" Irina said severely. "I've been half out of my mind. Your friend Kolin telephoned to say you were taking Yuri to a hospital. That was last night. Then, no word from you until you walk in that door the next morning and you wonder if I'm worried? Are you crazy? Of course I was worried. Why didn't you telephone?"

Alexi knew it was wrong to smile when she was so distressed; but the pleasure of seeing her, of savoring her gentle, familiar smell, gave him a feeling of inner well-being for the first time since his arrest by the GRU. He reached out and petted her soft thigh and said quietly, "I couldn't call, Irsha."

She batted his hand away. "I won't have that, Alexi Mikhailovich! Do you hear me? I want to know this instant where you've been. Is Yuri all right? When did he get back to Moscow? Alone, he's difficult enough. Together the two of you are impossible."

Sadness transformed Alexi's features. "I wish I knew of a kinder way to say this, Irsha. But Yuri died last night."

Irina's face went slack for a long moment. She dropped heavily onto the old couch and wound her fingers into the hem of her wool skirt. "I'm so sorry, Alosha. I didn't know. When I called the ambulance number they wouldn't tell me what hospital you'd been directed to. You must feel terrible."

"Terrible is even better than I feel," he admitted tiredly.

"What was wrong with Yuri, Alosha? He was almost never sick. An accident? This is so hard to accept. I can't believe it. It was an accident, yes?"

Alexi shook his head. "I'm afraid it was quite deliberate. Yuri was murdered."

Irina's hands flew to her face. "You know this for a fact?"

"Yes."

"But who would want to murder Yuri? And why? People were talking just the other day. About how unsafe the streets are getting. Youth gangs and—"

"This was no street crime," Alexi said firmly. "Yuri died last night, a little while after I got him to the hospital, from causes that ultimately relate to his work."

"I don't understand. What caused his death? He worked with computers. Oh, Alosha, why didn't you telephone me? I would have come to be with you. To help."

Alexi looked at his wife intently and sat up straighter in his chair. "I didn't spend the night at the hospital, Irsha. I was arrested by the GRU and spent it in prison."

The color drained abruptly from Irina's face. She could say nothing, but shook her head in quick, jerky motions of denial.

Alexi got up and sat beside her. He put his arms around her shoulders. "It's true," he said firmly.

"No, Alosha. It couldn't be," she said quickly, nervously. "You're joking, making me distracted so I won't be sad. That's it, yes?"

"I wish it were," Alexi said kindly. "But it isn't." Leaving out no detail, he told her about Yuri's coming to the House of Journalists, about the notebook, the events at the hospital, and the time spent on Zorga Street. He told her, too, about the water.

"The bastards," Irina said, hissing. "To you they did this? To a loyal citizen? I'm beginning to think the rumors are true. We've returned to Stalin's time and no one is safe anymore."

"Where do you hear these rumors?" he asked, interested.

Irina shrugged. "People notice, they talk. A theater that

shows the occasional foreign film is closed down. The tone of the news on television is suddenly anti-American again. No one has seen any surplus from the farms in the city stores for months. At the bank, a summons from the defense minister to discuss military budget payments, and the director returns white-faced and cancels all his appointments. Then he drinks himself into a stupor. People talk. What is going on, Alosha?"

Alexi told her what he knew about the struggle at the top between Malenkov and the minister of defense. "That's what I've gotten caught up in, Irsha. Yuri was working for Malenkov and passed on this information contained in the notebook to me. He wanted me to help protect the AI, to hold on to his notebook until the Suvorovs, whoever or whatever they are, contact me."

"So you lied to the GRU? For that?" Irina said angrily. "Whatever could have possessed you?"

"Please. I've just told you. I don't quite understand it myself. Yuri's murder. The water. Treating me so . . . so disrespectfully." Alexi's expression turned sheepish. "I guess they made me angry. It's my terrible stubbornness. You know how I get sometimes."

"But this isn't some minor argument, Alosha. This could mean prison or even exile. Who really cares who runs the country? Will anything change? Will there be one less Party bureaucrat whose warm apartment is filled with foreign luxuries, or one more car to drive? Only the naïve contemplate change in Russia. You should know that."

Alexi looked crestfallen. "I do. At least I thought I did. There I was, wanting to go along, wanting to tell what I knew and to say the hell with anything but survival. And I tried, Irsha. I swear I tried. But they wouldn't listen. And then, all of a sudden, it began to matter to me that Yuri not die for nothing."

"Every idealist dies for nothing," Irina said bitterly. "Yuri was a fool."

"Irsha! That's unfair—" Alexi began.

"It's not! Not at all," she cut him off furiously. "You put yourself, put *both* of us in jeopardy for some principle you don't even fully understand, and you expect me to pat you on the head and tell you everything's all right? Well, it's not all right, Alexi Mikhailovich. Not all right by any standard.

"We have responsible positions, a fairly comfortable life.

Our son has done well for himself. Who are you to place all that at risk? Do you think they would let me continue to work at Gosbank if you were arrested? Or that *Pravda* allows criminals on its staff? We could lose everything we've worked so hard for. Think back, Alosha. Good grades, Party membership, doing what was necessary for acceptance at the institutes, ministerial approval. Do you think we could ever live like this again if we lost our places now? You can't fight the government when the government is everything! Don't you see that?"

"I see only that the chance for a washing maching and a few trips to the South do not make a life," Alexi said savagely. "Once we had convictions."

"Once we were alone with nothing to lose," Irina shot back.

Alexi was off the couch now, striding angrily around the room. "So that's it? I should forget they murdered my brother for you. I should forget lying naked on a stone floor with my balls in my hand for you. Everything for you."

"For who else?" she said hotly. "Is there more love in who rules the Soviet Union?"

Alexi grabbed his coat and hat.

"Where are you going?" Irina demanded. "I forbid you to leave in the middle of this discussion."

Alexi yanked open the door. "You're wrong on two counts. I refuse to be forbidden anything in my own home. And this discussion is not in the middle; it's over." He slammed the door behind him and walked quickly down the stairs.

Alexi emerged from the metro. The brief appearance of the morning sun had succeeded only in turning the mountainous piles of snow in front of the hospital into sagging mounds that slowly oozed slush. Inside, none of the nurses who had been on duty the night before were on duty now. Since he knew the way to Lozinskaya's office, Alexi simply walked past their station in the lobby, pausing for only a few seconds to stare grimly at the spot where the GRU had arrested him.

The fight with Irina had left him depressed and embittered. At least Lozinskaya was in her office, and the nurse ushered him in to see her without delay.

"Good morning, Comrade Petrov," Lozinskaya said, looking up from her desk and gesturing him into a chair. "Were you able to get some sleep? I know last night was a terrible shock."

Alexi bit back a sarcastic reply. Instead, he said, "I'd like to see my brother one last time. If it's permitted."

Lozinskaya understood. "Of course." She took up a ring of keys. "Follow me." Alexi held the door while she slipped past him.

"We know now," she explained as they walked, "what killed your brother. It was pneumonia. Apparently he contracted it where he was working and it was left untreated until it was too late."

"I thought you said there was brain involvement."

Lozinskaya looked uncomfortable. "I shouldn't have made such premature speculations. No. There was no cerebral damage. None."

Alexi thought, so the GRU had gotten to her as quickly as that. Pneumonia; no brain damage. Nonsense. Lozinskaya was obviously telling him what she had been told to say. He would have to be careful around her. She would report on his every move if asked. He said, sadly, "You'd think an intelligent man would have taken better care of himself."

"A pity, really," she said, sounding relieved.

The morgue was as dismal a place as it had been the night before, the rows of small steel doors every bit as final. Lozinskaya walked over to Yuri's and yanked it open. The corpse rolled out, the previous night's cover draped carelessly over it. Politely, Lozinskaya turned away.

Alexi bent down in a last private communion. He pushed the lifeless, strawlike hair from Yuri's forehead and smoothed it back into place. The notebook was still where he'd put it. He slid it out and slipped it into his pocket. The only fitting eulogy; Alexi would carry on when Yuri could not. This time he would be the one to pick up when the other faltered. Alexi's throat constricted. No speeches for Yuri. He touched his brother's shoulder one last time. Childhood scenes raced past his mind's eye. No speeches on this cold morning, only a whispered good-bye. This time the door slammed with finality.

"Thank you, Comrade Doctor. I'm ready to leave now."

Lozinskaya patted his arm solicitously. "I'll see you out."

He followed her again. She acted concerned and caring all the way downstairs. But when they shook hands by the big front doors in the lobby, Alexi had the distinct impression that she was relieved to see him go.

Back in the metro, as he traveled across the city, the notebook burned in his pocket like a hot coal.

The Academy of Science was not a place Alexi visited frequently, often delegating articles to its scientific staff when the technical material was too sensitive or too abstruse to be handled by a member of the editorial staff. Consequently, he had come to know a number of its members, and his relationship with Ivan Ivanovich Tolsky had matured under just such circumstances. Over the years, Alexi felt that their association had become more personal, and something approximating trust had arisen between them.

His *Pravda* identification gained him entrance to the building. He made his way upstairs to Tolsky's lab in the biology section. He found the bearded, broad-chested scientist crouched over a cage of experimental animals, large rats, carefully dripping a pale blue liquid into their food trough.

"Let me guess," said Alexi, smiling from the open doorway. "You're nurturing a new delicacy for the tables of the Central Committee."

Tolsky looked up in surprise, saw Alexi, and grinned broadly. "You've got it wrong, *tovarishch*. This feast is by their special instruction for the people."

Alexi laughed and walked into the lab. "And all these years I've been trying to get the rats *out* of my apartment building."

"Like most, you didn't know the extent of the riches you already possessed," Tolsky said dryly. "How are you, Alexi Mikhailovich? And what brings you to my dark domain?"

"I need to talk something over with you. Do you have some time?"

Tolsky looked to the rats and then to his watch. He nodded. "I don't have to douse their food for another half hour. Come sit."

Alexi walked around the slate-topped tables to Tolsky's desk. The big man opened a drawer and took out a bottle of vodka and two glasses. "Join me?" Alexi nodded. Tolsky poured and raised his glass.

"To anesthesia," he pronounced firmly.

The vodka coursed harshly down Alexi's throat and made him shudder. He was reminded of how long he'd been without food or sleep. He refused a second glass even though the fire in his belly had suddenly changed to a pleasant numbness.

He put his glass down on the desk. "My brother died last night, Ivan, and I need you to explain some things to me."

Tolsky looked distressed. "Of course. But first let me tell you how sorry I am."

"I appreciate that very much. But here's what bothers me. There are some things I learned about from the doctor who conducted the autopsy. I don't understand them."

In a few sentences, Alexi sketched out the bare outlines of Yuri's death and Olevsky's autopsy report.

"This is serious business, Alexi," Tolsky said when he had finished. "Men get burned this close to the heart of such a fire."

"That's why I'm being deliberately vague, Ivan. I don't want any taint of this on you. You've got your own career to think about and the last thing you need is a visit from the GRU to your supervisors."

"There are GRU in this? That's very bad, Alexi. Very bad."

"I know. I don't think I was followed, but it's possible I placed you in jeopardy just by coming here."

Tolsky thought for a moment, then shrugged. "A friend came to be consoled by another friend. Not even the GRU could make a case out of that. Now get that silly, grateful look off your face and talk."

"That means a lot to me, Ivan. I won't forget it."

"Talk!"

"All right. I don't understand why they did what they did to Yuri. If they wanted to get what he knew, why destroy his brain? Surely that would defeat their purpose. And why were they tampering with those things—those N-CAMs—in the first place? And most of all, why did they kill him?"

Tolsky put away another shot of vodka and considered the questions. "You said that Yuri had originally tried to commit suicide and the attempt failed. Do you know what method was tried?"

"Toxic gas," Alexi replied. "It killed all but two of the group."

"Ah, I see. Well, then, that fits nicely. I think I can explain it now, Alexi, but first I have to explain to you something about the way that memory functions in order for you to understand. Bear with me, please."

Tolsky moved over to the animal cages, reached into one, and brought out a small, wriggling rodent. He dropped it into a wooden maze that sat atop one of the tables. Alexi watched it scurry through the labyrinth in search of reward. Tolsky began speaking.

"There is a classic experiment in which a rat is taught to run a maze just like this one or to perform some similar task. Then it's frozen until all the electrical activity in the brain ceases. This does not harm the rat and, when it's thawed out again, quite normally, it tries the maze a second time. Now, here's the interesting thing. When there's a long time in between the first learning and the cooling, the rat remembers the maze. But if the rat is frozen very quickly after learning the maze, it reacts the second time as if the task were completely new. There appears to be no storage of the experience. No *memory*.

"This tells us that memory involves ongoing patterns of nerve impulses in nerve cell circuits that are connected together. Long-term, stored memory seems actually to result in lasting structural changes in the brain's tissue. New pathways are created, synthesizing protein chains that actually 'describe' the remembered event.

"Evidently the GRU wanted to isolate these protein chains in order to 'read' them somehow. A person's memory would then be an open book. But any such process would be fantastically complicated, the technology highly intricate. Obviously, in your brother's case, they failed and ended up loosening all the bindings in the structures trying to isolate just the structures they wanted."

"But the GRU isn't normally so careless. I can attest to that," Alexi said grimly.

"No. That's true," Tolsky agreed. "But they forgot one thing: There was probably a reaction between the drugs they used and the residue of toxic gas left in Yuri's body. Such chemicals often work on the brain themselves, destroying the breathing center or the involuntary muscle controls to stop the heart. In this case, the reaction was apparently synergistic."

"Define that, please."

"Synergy. Combining forces; wholes greater than the sum of their parts. Take a chemical process that produces 'green,' let's say. And another that produces 'hot.' Now combine the two, and if the processes are synergistic, you get something that's 'greener' and 'hotter' than the original. In Yuri's case, the gas must have interacted with the drugs and instead of loosening just the bonds they'd selected, it destroyed them all. Death followed shortly. That's what the autopsy showed."

Alexi took a deep breath, nodded, and stood up. "Thank you, Ivan. It makes sense. I'd better be going now. You've been a big help."

The big scientist stood also and put an arm around his friend's shoulders. "If it's any consolation, they couldn't have gotten much from him. And he must have had a brilliant mind to last long enough to reach you."

Alexi felt the notebook still in his pocket. He nodded in agreement.

"I don't envy your involvement in this," Tolsky added seriously. "You stand to lose everything."

Alexi nodded glumly. "Irina feels the same way. She wants me to avoid any further trouble."

"Have you considered that she might be right?"

Alexi shook his friend's hand and left the lab. Tolsky's question plagued him all the way back to the apartment. His physical resources were nearly depleted and the stairs seemed impossible to scale. He knew he had reached the limit of his ability to function without sleep.

The apartment was empty and he was relieved Irina had left for the bank. Another fight would have been just too much. Later, they could talk when things had calmed down.

At least he could manage a few hours' sleep. He would miss the morning meetings at *Pravda*, but that couldn't be helped. Half dead, he was of no use to anyone. He had to rewind the alarm clock three times before he got it right.

Fully dressed, he was asleep the instant his head touched the pillow. Mercifully, there were no dreams.

XVI

Entering the Academy of Science's most secret, advanced computer research laboratories, Heinrich Berenstein paused for a moment to stamp the snow off his boots onto the stone floor. He made his way into his office and hung his coat and hat on the rack there. His desk was neat, his papers pushed into precise little stacks by his secretary, whom he secretly hated with a passion usually reserved for great romance. By the end of the day it would be a sloppy mess. Sometimes, he did it deliberately; their little game.

He settled in behind his desk and picked up the previous day's progress reports. Soon he was frowning. As director of the laboratories, he was considered a very important man. As an expatriate German, he was as unwelcome as a leper at a dinner party. The only way he stayed in favor was by producing results; results that the archaic Soviet system, hidebound in secrecy and burdened by the weight of impossible political concerns, would never produce without him.

Berenstein smoothed down an unruly shock of white hair. It was true he was now one of the elite, but even after working for the Soviets for over forty years, he could not suppress the disdain he felt for their scientific establishment. They stole from the West most of what they had. Luckily, neither Marx nor Lenin had decided that the sun revolved around the earth, or the textbooks would still so state and no evidence to the contrary would change it. How did Party officials expect scientific progress, he mused angrily, when promotions went not to the talented but to the ideologically correct? Genius was no respecter of politics, he had tried to tell them; ideas were the province of free exchange.

He was sent for political reeducation. They needed him badly, so it was not as harsh as his first incarceration during Stalin's reign. That camp in the frozen North had almost killed him. He shied away from the memories and deliberately closed up the still painful, unhealed emotional wounds. This

time, it had only been lecture after lecture after endless
lecture. Principles were droned on and on until the words
buzzed like horseflies around his ears. But he had returned
unharmed to take up his post again and had been quiet ever
since.

For this he was well compensated by Soviet standards. An
apartment in a good area, a car and driver, access to the special
stores, and Fourth Department service for his medical needs
at the Kremlin Clinic. Had he a wife and children, he could
have provided quite nicely for them. Once, he'd . . . again
he turned his thoughts away, strolling instead through his
memory into the park-gardens of prewar Berlin, listening to
the concerts while drinking *good* black coffee and eating linzer
tortes; remembering the girls in white dresses with elegant
parasols who smiled and turned with starched skirts
swinging. . . .

"Your coffee, Comrade Berenstein," his secretary said,
thumping the heavy ceramic mug soundly on his desk. The
collar of her shirt was buttoned right up to her fleshy neck, and
her bulky wool skirt was tight around her massive hips. In that
moment, suspended between the graceful memory of a long-
faded past and the abrupt reality of her utilitarian severity, his
secretary disgusted him.

"The conference at the Ministry of Defense is scheduled
for noon," she continued. "The deputy minister made a special
request for your promptness."

"Confirm the appointment and make sure my car is here
in sufficient time to get through this miserable snow. Is
Mishkin in yet?"

"He's in his office, Comrade Director."

"Tell him I'm leaving and to act in my absence. Route any
requests that need my corroboration through him."

Berenstein stretched his thin frame, picked up his mug,
and drank some of the coffee. "This is terrible," he muttered,
grimacing.

She shrugged. "As you always say, Comrade Director.
Will that be all?"

Berenstein turned back to his reports. "That's all."

The secretary turned to go, but Berenstein looked back
up. "Tell me," he said gently, "have you ever worn a white
dress with lacy things on underneath, Comrade Secretary?"

He saw her scandalized look and held up a hand hastily.

"Forget I asked. I sometimes fail to remember that I amuse no one with my ramblings."

The secretary sniffed primly and left the office, deciding as she usually did not to report the German's decadent remarks, making allowances for one born so far outside civilization. Later, she called for his car and made sure the brilliant, aging scientist got on his way to the Defense Ministry.

The director had thanked her and smiled gratefully. As usual, though, his thoughts seemed a thousand miles away. Lacy underthings, indeed. Abruptly, she brought her knees tightly together under her desk and continued typing.

The long conference table was littered with cigarette butts and coffee cups by the time Deputy Minister Tarkov finished speaking. Berenstein made a final notation on his pad and looked up excitedly at those seated around him. "But that's wonderful!" he exclaimed. "And you're certain? A true Artificial Intelligence would be an incredible achievement, even for Valery Rudin."

"We can hardly share your enthusiasm," said Solnikov coldly.

"I can understand that, Minister." Berenstein gave ground carefully. "You must appreciate that I'm speaking as a scientist only. I knew Rudin well. Even taught him. His reputation for genius was not undeserved."

"That genius has put us in a most difficult position," Tarkov said grimly. "I suggest you keep in mind just how difficult. The KGB files alone are a monstrous invasion of our personal records. The C5 connection completes a threat we cannot allow to continue."

"The AI contains all the KGB files?" Berenstein asked. "How far back?"

"Does that matter?" asked Colonel Klim, speaking for the first time directly to Berenstein.

"No. I don't think it should," Berenstein answered hastily.

"Then why ask?" Klim pressed.

"Storage capacity is always relevant, Colonel. The machine that could contain thousands of files from periods extending over thirty or forty years, well, think of how powerful the human mind would be that could do that."

"Klim, may I remind you that you are here to help

Comrade Berenstein, not to interrogate him," Tarkov said acidly.

Klim smiled. "Old habits die hard. My apologies."

Berenstein waved a hand. "Not necessary. You say you're reasonably certain that this Petrov received something from his brother?"

"A notebook, I think. But my question to you is, could the brother have written anything useful in, say, the half hour it would take to get across the city to the House of Journalists?"

"My word, yes," Berenstein said. "In less time than that he could have included access codes, bypass instructions, command sequences. I could work on getting into the AI for months only to discover that the phrase 'Marxism Forever' opens it up like the key to a can of sardines."

Solnikov turned to Klim. "In that case, Colonel, I'm not certain I like the length of leash you have Petrov on," he said flatly.

"If you wish, Minister, I will consider your preference most strongly."

Solnikov nodded. "Do that. This is too important for some subtle form of gamesmanship. Pressure him at once, and if he does not come forward, take him today."

"As you wish, Comrade Minister."

"You may also be aware that if the notebook *is* the key we require, your investigative instincts will not go unrecognized."

"I am prepared to stake my reputation on it," Klim said.

"You have," Tarkov interjected.

"I'm going to need some tools, my books. A few other things as well," Berenstein said. "Can I bring my assistants to the dacha?"

Tarkov looked to Solnikov, who hesitated, then nodded. "Tell us who and what you need and it will be put at your disposal. This is not, however, a subject that we want to leave this company. Brief no one until you are at the dacha. Then everyone stays till the matter is closed. Colonel Klim will be your liaison to us."

"Be quite clear on one point, though," Solnikov said gravely. "Neither of you will make the slightest aggressive or threatening move toward Malenkov until I, and only I, have been convinced that the AI has been neutralized. If the general secretary looks as if he's having trouble breathing, you will call for a doctor. If he sneezes, you'll wipe his nose. We've seen what his machines can do and I have no intention of governing a country reduced to postnuclear rubble."

"I understand, Comrade Minister," said Klim. Berenstein nodded absently, lost in thought.

Tarkov was studying the scientist closely. "You seem eager to begin, yet almost preoccupied. I wonder if we have sufficiently impressed upon you the gravity of this situation."

"Oh, you have, Comrade Deputy Minister," said Berenstein quickly. "It's just the notion of the AI. Imagine if, in your respective field, someone had just told you that the greatest achievement, say, the ultimate weapon, had been created. Wouldn't you be eager to see it? To try to master its awesome possibilities?"

"I'd rather you saved such boyish enthusiasm for your students, comrade," Tarkov said coldly. "This is a business we want done. As for your example, every soldier worth his salt knows the ultimate weapon and knows exactly how it is mastered."

Berenstein raised an inquiring eyebrow and Tarkov continued. "The ultimate weapon is the human mind, and it is mastered by instilling blind obedience. You may go now."

Berenstein stood and gathered his papers. Klim moved to the door, turned, and saluted.

Solnikov eyed them both. "Remember how cold it is in the North," he said. "We will all be looking forward to your return to the warmth of Moscow."

His message was quite clear, Berenstein thought as he walked alongside the colonel. The endless reaches of the North were reserved for exiles. There would be no return without success. And the defense minister had obviously known just how threatening that would be to a man who had been there before. Berenstein shuddered inwardly. Purgatory was beckoning again.

XVII

Alexi woke with a start and fumbled the alarm clock to where his bleary eyes could focus on it. He was late. He must have slept right through the alarm. Stumbling from the bed, he washed in the cramped bathroom for which he and Irina had been so grateful when they finally moved out of their family's packed communal lodgings.

Donning a robe, he went cautiously into the hallway outside the apartment and slipped the notebook into a crevice beneath the stairs. It would be safe there. He made certain no one saw him and then slipped back inside.

He was comforted by doing familiar things. Shaving, dressing, eating; even riding the train to work. He hurried into his office at *Pravda* and collected his papers for the afternoon meeting, trying to ignore the raised eyebrows at his late arrival.

The editorial meeting had already begun. Alexi sidled into his chair as quietly as possible. Receiving no black look from the chief editor, he began to relax, lulled into peaceful inattentiveness by familiar cadences.

The page one photographs were still not "happy" enough. The editorial would again be by the defense minister. Someone had incorrectly placed a TASS dispatch under an inappropriate headline. The sports scores weren't displayed prominently enough. . . .

"Comrade Petrov!"

Alexi bolted upright, stung into sudden attention. "Yes, Comrade Chief Editor?"

"I am quite at a loss to understand why I must tolerate angry calls from the Ministry of Defense about articles that should have been cleared by them and were not."

"Comrade Novikov, I don't know—I mean, when did—?"

"When you wrote the article on preparations for the parade on Anniversary Day, you didn't receive the appropriate clearances for the material and therefore listed items to be presented in the great parade that, in fact, will not be shown. This is an embarrassment to the ministry and to me."

Alexi searched his memory, trying to remember if he had forgotten the clearances. He remembered the article well enough. The copy *had* come back with the proper seals.

"Comrade Chief Editor, I'm certain the correct visas were applied for and received. If you'll let me—"

"That is not the only matter, Comrade Petrov!" thundered Novikov. Eyes all around the table followed the angry interchange. Bodies stilled, presenting smaller targets in an age-old reflex.

Novikov continued acidly. "*Pravda* holds its journalists to a high standard, Comrade Petrov. Public incidents are not tolerated. I expect proper conduct at all times, and drunken relatives causing disturbances at the House of Journalists reflect badly on us all."

"But that was my brother," Alexi protested. "And he wasn't drunk, comrade. He was—"

Novikov cut him off. "All the worse. A brief lapse at the hands of a bottle of vodka. Well, who among us"—he looked around at the assemblage—"who here has not once or twice—?"

"I must protest," Alexi forced himself to say. "My brother was sick and—"

"Sick and tired of conventions that bind us all?" Novikov interrupted him again. "That isn't an excuse. For each of these matters you will receive a reprimand, comrade. This is fair warning."

Alexi looked around the table and saw it in their eyes: contempt for the victim. There seemed always to be something in the disgrace of a colleague that did not totally displease them. Perhaps it was only relief that it was someone else that the wolves had run down and chewed up. No matter; he couldn't expect any support from them.

He also realized something else that sat him up straight in his chair as he searched the chief editor's face. The scorn there was too much, too disproportionate to his crimes. Colonel Klim and the GRU were behind this. Novikov knew there wasn't any substance to the charges. They could be checked too easily. He was only the messenger of the threat. That, in a way, was even more chilling. If the powerful Novikov bowed so easily to the GRU's will, how could Alexi stand up to them?

Two reprimands. A third meant the loss of his position. Cooperate or be released. The GRU made it quite clear.

"The reprimands will be posted on the corridor wall. Again, I urge you to heed them," Novikov finished.

Alexi saw sudden confirmation of his conjecture in the chief editor's eyes. There was displeasure at lying so baldly, at castigating the loyal worker. Alexi heard Irina's frustrated question in his mind: How did you fight the government when the government was everything?

"I'm sorry, Comrade Chief Editor," Alexi said softly. "I understand. It won't happen again."

Novikov's grateful look was eloquent. Do not put your head under my ax, it said. I don't want to chop it off; but I will if I must.

The meeting ended. Outside, in the corridor, no one offered any solace. Even though he had survived temporarily, there was blood in the water and it was safest to stay away.

No one knew when the sharks might return.

For the rest of the afternoon, Alexi plugged away at a set of unfinished articles, but even the keys of his typewriter felt strange under his fingers. The profound shock of the chief editor's admonitions had unsettled him deeply, all the more so because they were so undeserved.

Or were they? If the collective was everything, had he not gone against it by refusing to subordinate himself to its will, in this case, its lawful agency, the GRU? Why else did such agencies exist, if *not* to protect people from individuals who thought more of their own judgment than of the people's as a whole? Was he really any different from the thief who stole because he decided other people's things were his and the laws that governed them could be ignored? He didn't feel like a criminal; but what criminal did?

It was after five and Irina would be leaving her office at Gosbank in a few minutes. Abruptly, Alexi realized how much their fight had upset him. He wanted to see her as soon as possible, and there was no guarantee she would go straight home. Especially if she were still angry.

He put on his coat and hat and left his papers in disarray. More eyebrows were raised at so abrupt a departure, and Alexi had no doubt that the office gossips would make further use of his leaving. But clutching his dignity around him as tightly as his coat, he strode straight down the long, central corridor and back out into the cold.

Alexi stationed himself on the wide marble steps by the pillars that held up Gosbank's vaulted stone portico. Alexi knew many of its functions from Irina's long association with the gigantic, centralized institution. The state bank was the country's sole issuer of currency, the regulator of the money supply, and the fiscal agent for virtually all levels of the government. It handled all payments between enterprises and organizations, received all taxes and payments to the state, and paid out all budgetary allocations.

Irina had also explained that, in addition to the main office in Moscow, there were district offices in every one of the republics to supervise over four thousand branch offices. The scope of the central bank still awed him. It served over six hundred thousand client organizations and employed over a quarter of a million people.

Alexi watched for Irina in the flow of people emerging from the building. She was a supervisor for a computer section that monitored industry's financial transactions to make sure they fulfilled production plans, used their funds properly, and maintained proper financial discipline. Beyond those general terms, what his wife did with her wondrous machines and her charts and numbers was far too sophisticated for him to follow.

He spotted Irina coming out the main doors, talking to a friend he vaguely recognized. She paused to turn up her collar as she hit the cold air. Moving toward her, Alexi waved to attract her attention. Irina looked up and saw him. She stiffened and he slowed, hurt that her anger still persisted. Then he saw her face soften and he smiled sheepishly. She said good-bye to her friend, then moved as fast as her legs could carry her down the steps and into his arms.

They held each other for a while, like adolescents, oblivious to the stares and smiles of passersby who made *sotto voce* comments about older couples still obviously in love.

"I'm sorry, Irsha," Alexi said. His eyes were tightly closed and his voice was muffled in her sweet-smelling hair.

"No, no, Alosha," she said softly, rocking him. "I didn't listen. I was thinking only of myself. Can we go home? I'll fix you some dinner and we'll talk. Like friends, this time."

"Yes, please," he said sincerely. "But let's walk. Like we used to before we got old and fat."

Irina hit him playfully in the jaw. "'Ripe' is the word," she suggested.

"A better choice," he agreed diplomatically, taking her arm and steering her toward home.

The buildings were still mostly coated with ice, and water from the melting converged in small streams that flowed across the pavement. People sloshed through the streets in an ongoing search for groceries, string bags half filled with a scrawny chicken and some vegetables for those who had finished waiting on the endless lines; empty bags folded up and sticking out of pockets for those whose lines had yet to come.

Alexi and Irina walked in silence, hand in hand, each soothed by the other's presence. Irina tightened her grip.

"It's not so cold out now," she said mildly and Alexi nodded. "Sometimes," she continued, "the snow, it's kind to the city, I think. Covers the scars and the wounds like a bandage. Tchaikovsky knew that, eh, Alosha?"

"Yes, I think he did." They waited for a traffic light to change, then crossed the intersection. "To dread the winter is like dreading one's own character. This is part of us. I learned that back when I was skiing. We trained hard, Irsha. Every day. I was also less . . . ah, ripe back then."

"We learned not to fight the snow. You know, you can almost make yourself lighter if you don't fight it. The great ones just let it lift them. I wish you'd have let me teach you to ski. It's a feeling like almost no other."

"For some things," she said with a laugh, "I've always been too ripe. You glided, I waddled."

Alexi sighed in warm remembrance of the past. "During training, Irsha, up North, the air was cold enough to freeze the moisture on your eyelids. But it was quiet; so quiet that the only thing to disturb the silence was the hiss of the skis as you flew through the pine forests. Then, suddenly, you'd come upon the target. The rifle was such a beautifully balanced piece that it felt like an extension of your arm. The trick was to be able to still your breathing after such strenuous exertion, to steady your aim until only you and the target existed, and then to pull back on the trigger slowly, slowly, until the weapon fired almost of its own accord. Then, off again into the silence as the reverberations of the shots faded away. I loved it."

"You shouldn't have given it up, then."

Alexi shrugged. "I was never the best. Not even close. I was cut in the last round of the Olympic trials."

"But it was good to have gone so far."

"It was good," he admitted. "But it wasn't great. That required something special."

Irina leaned over and kissed his cheek. "You are special, you just don't know it. In this world, Alosha, sometimes just being good is being very special."

Alexi steered them around a corner. "Maybe. But I don't think of myself as so unique. Maybe that's also why I couldn't betray Yuri and his damned notebook. It would have been so easy, so damned . . . ordinary to do it."

"Where is the notebook now?"

"I hid it in the hallway outside the apartment. It seemed wiser not to conceal it among our things."

"Yuri gave you no gift," Irina said, sighing.

"No. Not in that respect. But I can tell you that when I look inside myself I'm happy that he came to me and trusted me with something he valued so highly."

"He looked up to you." She smiled. "I know you won't believe that. But he did."

"Yuri? No. It was the other way around."

She shook her head. "I know how you felt. I'm just saying that, in some ways, he felt the same way about you. He valued your honesty and envied your steadfastness and your refusal to take shortcuts. Most of his life, Yuri manipulated shamelessly and took advantage of his talent. What did you tell me you used to call those other biathloners who tried to shoot without really aiming?"

"Hipshooters?"

"Yes, that's it. Yuri shot from the hip. If it worked, okay. If not, move on to the next." She held out her hands, palms up.

Alexi was quiet for a while. They were close to home now. "I don't know what to do, Irsha," he said finally.

She was pensive as well. "You have something that powerful people want. It's been over a day now and no Suvorovs, whatever they may be, have come to take the notebook from you. Maybe they were killed like, forgive me, Alosha, like Yuri. You could be holding out for nothing."

"I've thought of that. And it worries me."

"You're protecting the notebook because it's the only

memory of Yuri you can still live up to. I won't make the mistake of telling you what to do. Just try to be sure you know whose fight you're fighting."

They turned into their apartment block. "I think I'm going to turn in the notebook if no one shows up to claim it by tomorrow. The GRU is also putting pressure on me through *Pravda*. One more day. That much I can give Yuri."

Irina suppressed further comment and nodded. "One day. I suppose that's not too much." She smiled. "It's a good decision, Alosha."

They reached the apartment, slightly out of breath from the exertion of the walk and the stairs, but bright-eyed with their renewed closeness. Alexi ran a hand between the buttons of her coat and she elbowed him away, laughing. He pushed her inside when the door swung open, pulling at her scarf to kiss her cheek.

But their play died abruptly when Alexi turned on the overhead light. Everything they owned was scattered around the apartment in violent disarray. Clothing had been dumped from drawers, and cushions had been torn open. Motes of stuffing still drifted in the currents of air. The couch and table were overturned; their ancient radio was a crushed mass of tubes and wiring. The refrigerator door hung slackly open, and the piece of meat for dinner lay slowly rotting in a pool of its own blood.

Alexi's face froze in horror. He walked farther into the room. One more day, he'd decided. But the GRU hadn't waited.

"Alosha! Look out! Behind you!"

He turned but it was too late. There was a hiss of compressed gas and the sharp sting of a needle. He couldn't even focus on the man who held the funny-looking gun. His last thought was the realization that the man must have been hiding in the bedroom. Then everything, including Irina's frantic pleas, slid down a tunnel that was a million miles long . . . and vanished completely.

XVIII

He was in the same cell as the day before, but no feeling of homecoming accompanied Alexi's awakening in it. He was frightened and felt sick—the result of both the suddenness of his abduction and the drugs used to render him helpless. He crawled into a corner and threw up, convulsing helplessly.

The smell was overpowering in so small a room. He wiped his mouth on his shirt. Strangely, though, emptying his stomach helped restore his equilibrium, and the anger that sprang from such degradation cleared away much of his mental sluggishness. He pulled his rumpled clothing together as best he could and sat down on the bench to await his captors.

They weren't long in coming. It seemed to Alexi that the GRU must have no shortage of big, burly men, for these were carbon copies of those from the day before. They swept into the cell and pulled him to his feet as easily as he might have done to a child.

They led him down the hall and he was treated more roughly than before. Courtesy was reduced to terse monosyllables. Alexi stumbled at one point and was slammed up against a wall. He thought he was going to be hit, but they just shoved him forward again angrily.

They took him to a white-tiled room whose brightness made him blink after the dimness of his cell. Surgical lamps hung from suspended tracks and focused on a white-draped operating table. Alexi saw the restraints and panicked. He tried to run but those same irresistible hands tossed him onto the table and bound him to it.

On one side of the operating room was a wide window that revealed an observation room beyond. Alexi saw Colonel Klim inside, conferring with a pair of white-coated doctors. White tiles, doctors. Yuri's feverish final description sprang into Alexi's mind. Was this where Yuri had been brought?

The second question was unavoidable. He wondered if the same fate awaited him.

Alexi twisted against the restraints but to no avail. A picture of the notebook tucked away safely under the stairway swam unbidden into his mind. He forced it out. He'd promised Yuri he would wait for the Suvorovs. He made a mental apology. The Suvorovs hadn't come in time.

Klim remained behind the observation window when the doctors entered the operating room to prepare their equipment. They were methodical and professional. One took a tray of syringes and tiny stoppered bottles and placed it alongside the table. The second took up a scalpel, plucked Alexi's sleeve taut in his other hand, and slit it open from shoulder to wrist. He bared the arm and tied rubber tubing around it. Disinterestedly, he tapped the hollow between bicep and forearm in search of a vein.

Alexi craned his neck to watch Klim. His hatred for the man was so intense that it was difficult to conceal. He could feel the big veins in his temples throbbing. His hands made strangling motions unconsciously. He winced when a needle was thrust into his arm. That caught Klim's attention and for the first time their eyes locked. Alexi's hatred boiled up and coursed hotly along the connection. Klim must have felt it and seemed surprised by its intensity. The tiny lines around the corners of his eyes creased in interest.

How can you do this to another man? Alexi raged silently. Klim's indifferent stare was eloquent enough. Because I have license, it said. His attention turned back to the doctors.

They were checking the time and making notations on charts held in clipboards. Alexi felt nothing out of the ordinary. The doctors left him and went back in to confer with Klim. It was only then that Alexi realized that neither one had spoken even a single word to him.

He paid close attention to the conference. One pointed to Alexi and spoke for a while. The other pointed to his wristwatch, then back to Alexi, and Alexi could read the words his lips formed. One hour. Klim nodded, apparently satisfied. All three left the observation room through a door in the wall behind them.

There was no clock visible to Alexi to measure time with, so he began to count. He had to fight the drugs. If Klim found out about the notebook under this kind of interrogation, Alexi's guilt would be self-evident and punishment assured. He had to think of himself as well as Yuri now. His best hope lay in continuing to hide the notebook, even if he had to "discover" it later and turn it in of his own volition.

He counted silently, one to sixty, keeping track of the minutes on his fingers. At ten full minutes, he put his tongue on the unmistakable, sharp canine tooth on the left side of his jaw. Ten minutes later, he moved his tongue over to the adjacent tooth, one of the four front incisors. He continued this way to mark time and to force himself to concentrate. One minute per finger, ten minutes per tooth. At one hour, he would reach the canine tooth on the other side of his jaw, exactly six teeth away.

Alexi counted, but drugs made his mind wander. A smile crept over his face. There was that trick he'd once played on Yuri. Their mother had left her apron on the . . . He shook his head. No dreams. Not now. He checked his teeth and fingers. He had not lost count. Twenty-eight minutes had passed. How long had his attention wavered? Three minutes, maybe. Count from when the dreaming began. He added that to the twenty-eight and adjusted his fingers and tongue. Concentrate! Yuri gave him nothing. He was sick and rambled. Then he died. Nothing more. Concentrate!

Forty minutes. Count. One to sixty. Forty-one minutes. Count. Count, damn it! Forty-two minutes. One to . . . it smelled like the bread Irina made when she could get the flour. Breakfast could be such a nice meal. On Sunday, ever since their son had moved on to . . . Damn! Forty-four minutes. Count! One to sixty. Harder to remember. Forty . . .

Fear bubbled up and consumed him. Monsters from dark waters reached up and grabbed for his naked skin with slimy tentacles. It burned where they touched him, burned like acid. The notebook! All bare and exposed, it lay on a rock in the middle of the sea. He had to get it and hide it before the monsters did. Protect it! Hide it! There was a sudden pain in his arm, intruding somehow. But the monsters were still reaching for him. A sea snake had Klim's face and they raced for the rock in the mist. . . .

"Petrov! Wake up. Can you hear me, Petrov? Wake up, damn you."

Alexi mumbled. "Goway. . . ." Back to his dreams. Forty-nine, eighty-six, seventy . . .

"Alexi Mikhailovich Petrov! You must listen. We have

only minutes until Klim comes back. Please, you must try to concentrate."

Klim? Return? But Klim was a sea snake and the ocean was . . . the ocean was a thousand miles away! He was in Moscow, on Zorga Street. Events came crashing back with sudden clarity. He opened his eyes. An Army colonel, younger than Klim, with stronger features and sandy-colored hair, stared down at him. Anxiety was evident on his face.

"Good, Petrov. Back to the land of the living. Can you hear me now?"

Alexi nodded. He tried to speak but his throat was too dry. The colonel held up a restraining hand.

"Don't try. I can't give you anything for the dryness. It's one of the conditions they'll check to make sure you're under. Just nod for now. You're Yuri Petrov's brother?"

Alexi nodded.

"Is Yuri still alive?"

He shook his head.

"Damn!" the colonel said feelingly. "Well then, Petrov. Did he say anything about . . . I suppose we're in it all the way now, did he say anything about the Suvorovs?"

Tears of relief brimmed in Alexi's eyes. He nodded vigorously. The Suvorovs had found him at last. He thrust his chin questioningly at the colonel.

"Me? Yes, I'm a Suvorov. But all that can be explained later. For now, you're going to have to convince Klim that you're still drugged. And innocent. Let me talk and please listen carefully. Even if you've never acted before, just remember what's at stake and let this be the performance of a lifetime. Yuri gave you something for us?"

Alexi held his head steady. His eyes sought the colonel's and held them. The colonel grinned.

"Cautious, eh? Well, maybe that's not a bad thing to be. I wish I had more time to convince you, but if you manage to get out of here intact, I'll find you again in the next day or so. Now pay attention. Here's what they'll be looking for. . . ."

The staccato questioning seemed to continue endlessly. Klim's mottled face hovered over Alexi's, close like a lover's. He felt his hot breath across his face. He allowed his head to loll back and forth freely. Eyes unfocused. His voice was the harshest of croaks.

Their cadence didn't change. Minutes dragged by. Alexi kept a steady chant in his head of things to remember. Features slack, cadence rhythmic. Answer. Head loose. Limbs unlocked. Answer. No frustration. Control. Features slack. Answer. . . .

"Your brother was Yuri Petrov?"

"Yes."

"He came to you at the House of Journalists?"

"Yes."

"He gave you a notebook?"

"No."

"He did!"

"No."

"He told you he killed a soldier and stole his uniform."

"No."

"What did he give you?"

"Nothing . . . so sick . . . Yuri was so sick. . . ."

"You took him to a hospital?"

"Yes . . . hospital . . . very sick . . ."

"He gave you a notebook?"

"No."

Alexi rode his rage through it all. It steadied him and cooled his nerve. The act never broke, going on till his interrogators were as exhausted as he. At last, the doctors nodded their heads and looked to Klim questioningly. He seemed to think for a long time. Then he nodded, too. Another needle was slipped into Alexi's arm. The plunger was pushed home dispassionately. The world began to fade again. Alexi forced himself to hide the slow smile of victory that threatened to cross his face and would reveal the truth to his captors. He tottered gratefully on the edge.

"Release him," he heard Klim order. The rest was lost as the drug finally took hold and the deeper void that he had fought all along engulfed him.

XIX

Berenstein surveyed Malenkov's dacha from the air as the military helicopter swooped down over the lake and flew close enough to the mansion's chimneys to make him suck in his breath and mutter a quiet oath. The pilot grinned at the old man's fear and dropped the aircraft down, settling it neatly onto the circular drive in front of the building.

A pair of guards took Berenstein's heavy briefcase and escorted him into the main lobby. He stood there for just a minute, blowing on his hands and stomping his always too-cold feet to increase their circulation after the long flight from Moscow. The guards left his briefcase near him and left to retrieve the rest of his bags and equipment.

Berenstein unwrapped his scarf, opened his coat, and let his gaze wander around the opulent foyer. The wide central staircase was one beautifully subtle curve to the upper floors, so pleasing to the mathematician's practiced eye. The ceiling was a vast space sculpted in bas-relief, its unadorned nymphs and sprites dancing happily through pristine forests. The huge fireplace's marble mantel was superseded only by the superbly crafted gilt-edged mirror that hung above it.

By and large, the room's whole sense was one of ageless European splendor, and Berenstein had not seen its like in over forty years. Such as this had not been created in the Soviet state for longer than that. The room was both moving and disturbing to him after almost a lifetime of Soviet realism.

A GRU major came down the stairs and snapped a salute in his direction. "Comrade Berenstein, Colonel Klim directed me to meet you upon your arrival and to make sure that your needs are attended to. I am Major Kazinsky."

Berenstein nodded and extended his hand. "Have my assistants arrived yet?"

"They will be here tomorrow. The colonel thought you might wish to have an evening to yourself to review the situation. A suite for you and your people has been prepared on the ballroom level, and a workroom has been set up in the library, which is at the other end of the corridor."

"My compliments to your staff, Major."

"I will pass that along. The chalkboards and the electronics you requested were loaded on a transport aircraft that will be taking off in about an hour. We should have them set up by midmorning."

"That's fine."

"Will you be going into the ballroom now?" the major asked.

Berenstein smiled at the young man's enthusiasm but shook his head. "You'll have to forgive an old man's requirements, but the journey was tiring and I'd like to rest a bit before I attempt anything."

"I understand, comrade. The guards have been informed that you're cleared for unlimited access and to assist you if you need anything. The kitchen will send up your meal if you wish; just inform your orderly, or I would be pleased to have you dine with me and my officers. Come now, I'll show you to your quarters."

The suite was as lavish as the rest of the dacha. Kazinsky withdrew quickly, closing the doors behind him. Berenstein peeled off his outer garments, loosened his collar and tie, and inspected his surroundings. Satisfied, he pulled the heavy window drapes closed and lay down wearily.

In the semidarkness, a small object on the night table caught his attention. A teacup and saucer, elegantly enameled and so thin and delicate as to make one feel that breath alone could crush it. He ran a finger over its gold edge, delighting in the fragility. The porcelain was magnificent, another reminder of gentler times. The marks underneath were almost painful: Dresden, 1821. He sighed and put it down.

Sleep came with some difficulty.

Berenstein awoke in darkness. Night came earlier this far north. He washed and dressed, feeling clearheaded and excited by the prospect of what lay before him in the ballroom.

His orderly was waiting patiently in the outer rooms, and Berenstein ordered a light dinner to be sent up in an hour or so. He declined, respectfully, Major Kazinsky's offer to join him.

Kazinsky was thorough, apparently. The guards knew who Berenstein was and offered no challenge as he walked casually down the carpeted hallway to the ballroom's big double doors.

"I want no interruptions," he told the guards posted outside. "No one is to enter. You may knock twice to let me know either that someone wants me or wants to come in. I will then come to the door. But if I do not, you will consider that a no-entrance signal even if the house is coming down around your ears. I trust that's clear enough."

Berenstein pushed the doors open and walked into the ballroom. His pulse was beating stronger as he closed the doors and stood alone in the dimly lit, silent room. Off to the side, the C5 console's lights blinked steadily. Only the faint odor of ozone betrayed its quiet readiness.

Vladimir Malenkov lay in his curtained bed, and Berenstein padded softly to his side. He had never seen the general secretary in the flesh before. Drawing aside the curtains, he noted the pale, gaunt features and the sickly, translucent skin. Pity. The man had once been a formidable figure. Perhaps he still was, Berenstein conceded. Who else would fight death and defeat so vehemently?

His attention was drawn inexorably to the shiny, silver oblong near Malenkov's bed. His eyes traced the cables that led from it into the C5, into Malenkov's bank of machines, to the printers, and back to the oblong. He suppressed an excited shudder. Had Rudin indeed wrought a miracle? The answer would surely have to be yes if this was a true sentient intelligence. God, what an achievement!

He remembered Rudin well. Brilliant, dedicated. Given to flashes of insight so far ahead of his fellow students that even resentment was impossible. Soon he was, literally, in a class by himself. One didn't compete with such a mind. One could only compete for attainable goals. Rudin's talent was so obviously unique that one just as well might covet the moon.

But that same awesome talent was also erratic. Just as often the insights failed to produce usable results. Wild flights of imaginative speculation proved many times to be just that: theories that didn't stand up to closer scrutiny. Berenstein had liked the young man and found him easy to work with. A relationship had sprung up between the older man without family and the student so alienated from his peers.

And now this. A functioning Artificial Intelligence. What

marvels could such an intellect produce? Currently, there were two competing theories on constructing an AI. The first suggested that intelligence was a function of the biological mechanism of the human brain and that any Artificial Intelligence would have to be modeled after that pattern. The second theory held that intelligence could be created independently of a brain-type model and that physical circuits could be designed that would allow a computer to "think" in much the same ways as humans did.

Berenstein reflected how the most complicated problems in Artificial Intelligence concerned the simplest, common-sense-type problems that the human mind solved almost without effort. Almost without thought, he might have said. Actually, common sense was probably the single most esoteric and difficult process to define or isolate. He'd always loved, for example, to ask his students, "Is General Secretary Malenkov standing or sitting at this moment?" They would answer, usually guardedly, that they didn't know. He would then demand that they think harder, study the problem! Annoyed, they would argue that further study wouldn't help. Berenstein would then smile serenely, for the real question was, How did they know that it wouldn't help?

Something like inference was just as tricky. Humans had a model of the world, painstakingly built up over years of experience that enabled them to infer. The sentence "Ivan hit the doctor" led to logical inferences. The doctor, possibly female, was also possibly hurt by the blow of a larger man. But what about the sentence "Ivan hit the Olympic boxer"? The inference there was not that the boxer would be hurt but that Ivan had made a serious error in judgment and might soon expect to have his nose where his ear should be. Unless, of course, Ivan was a trained fighter . . . Berenstein smiled inwardly. There was no discussing thought without discussing language, and no discussing language without discussing memory, and on and on.

It was, he knew, time to end speculation and begin some experimentation of his own. He took a pencil out of his pocket and passed it over Malenkov's sleeping form like a magician's wand. Nothing. He reversed the pencil and held it daggerlike over the general secretary's head and made as if to plunge it in his right eye.

The lights in the ballroom went on with sudden intensity

and the C5 blared alarm. A printer chattered hysterically and spewed paper. Berenstein retreated quickly. The commotion stopped; the lights dimmed again. Silence returned, and he waited for a few moments. There were frantic knocks at the door. He ignored them.

He approached Malenkov again and made identical threatening motions. Interestingly, there was no response other than an even briefer chatter from the printer. He crossed the room and extracted the paper from the machine. It left him staring thoughtfully at the silver oblong. The first message read,

> Welcome, Professor Berenstein. All threatening motions toward General Secretary Malenkov will be acted upon accordingly. As one of the C5's designers, you are urged to caution.

Urged to caution? Had he really just been threatened by a sentient machine? And one that could recognize him as well. How wonderful! He glanced down the page and read the second communication:

> It is understood your nature is to experiment. No hostile action is anticipated, according to your profile. No reaction is therefore necessary. Any serious attempt to harm General Secretary Malenkov will, however, be dealt with severely.

So it could learn, too! It had seen that Berenstein only wanted to provoke a reaction and understood enough about him to perceive correctly that he represented no danger. So the second time it had left him alone and not raised its defenses. *According to your profile;* that was surely the KGB files in its memory speaking. Another thought struck him. Obviously, the AI had visual access to the room. That implied audio capabilities, as well.

"So," he said aloud, "you can see and hear me. I'm glad. And the profile is essentially correct. Under these conditions, I would be incapable of harming the general secretary. We will be talking again, you and I. Many times, for there is much to learn. For both of us."

Berenstein walked back to the entrance doors but turned

back before opening them. The C5 still glowed quietly. Malenkov slept on. The silver oblong was inscrutable, its face yet a mystery.

"Good night," Berenstein said softly.

Across the room, the printer chattered briefly. Berenstein didn't bother to read it. After all, Valery Rudin had always been polite, too.

He stepped into the hallway and closed the doors behind him, shooing away the concerned guards who rushed over. Major Kazinsky looked at him quizzically.

Berenstein said nothing, lost in thought and profoundly moved, having just interacted with a miracle.

XX

Wednesday

There was no ride home for Alexi this morning. He was put out on the street, ejected unceremoniously through a side gate in the surrounding wall. Tired as he was, elation roared through him. He had escaped the GRU twice. But with help, he reminded himself, praising his benefactor's timing. The Suvorovs had come into the open at last.

He set off at a brisk pace. The air felt good. He was left with an unclean feeling about the GRU and their probing doctors and their drugs. He remembered Klim's breath, hot and close. He gulped in a deep lungful of cold, crisp air. The queasiness dissipated.

The trouble was, he just couldn't be sure who had outfoxed whom. Had Klim believed that he was under the influence of the drugs and therefore believed his denials about the notebook? Or was this another ruse to lull Alexi into believing himself free? A chilling thought struck him. What if the man who gave him the antidote belonged to Klim? Alexi tried to remember what he'd actually said. He had not admitted to possessing the notebook. But if his rescuer was Klim's man, then Klim knew that the whole performance under the drugs was faked. Plots within plots within plots. Could he trust anyone?

He would have to proceed under the assumption that Klim and his rescuer were on opposing sides. Anything more complicated was so subtle that he was already doomed. There had to be sides in this, and he found himself suddenly, decisively turning toward Malenkov's. Solnikov's henchmen had killed Yuri and put Alexi through torment after torment: his apartment ripped apart, his wife frightened, his own physical and mental abuse. As Yuri had wanted, the notebook would go to the Suvorovs when they came to him again. If he handled it intelligently, Klim could produce nothing; even the troubles at *Pravda* would soon fade, he told himself.

Thinking about Irina made him hunger for home. He went into the first station he came to and let the train carry him to her. This time he didn't hesitate. He walked into his apartment without hesitation.

"Irina?" he called out. He noticed that the apartment had been mostly reassembled.

She came rushing out from the bedroom. "Alosha!" She engulfed him, crying. He patted her back, then held her head in his hands and kissed her cheeks.

"I'm all right, Irsha. They believed me. They wanted some kind of notebook that I didn't have."

Her face changed questioningly. Alexi made a gesture with his hand, then touched his ear. She understood. It was no longer safe to speak freely in the apartment. It was probably wired for sound.

Irina took her coat and scarf from the peg by the door and motioned for him to follow. Down the street was a small park. She was quiet until they reached it, settling onto a bench that commanded a view of the snow-covered grass that surrounded them.

"Are we safe here?" she asked in a low voice.

Alexi shrugged. "I don't know. I've heard of microphones sensitive enough to pick up a man's voice in a crowd. No one really knows if such things exist, but we must be very cautious from now on."

"Yes, that's wise." She adjusted her scarf around her so that it covered her mouth and muffled the sound. "When they grabbed you yesterday, Alosha, I screamed but they held me.

The drug, it just collapsed you. The man behind you caught you as you fell. I, ah . . . I hit one, Alosha."

He grinned. "Really?"

She nodded. "Across the side of his head when they let go of my arms. He looked very stupid for a little while."

Alexi's grin was infectious, and Irina laughed as well, but soon her face turned sober. "This is very serious, my husband."

"It is. Very serious. I am standing on a fence with one leg on either side. That could be increasingly uncomfortable and maybe even permanently damaging."

"I'm worried about you."

Alexi sighed. "I'm worried about me, too. But there is hope. One of the Suvorovs helped me fool the GRU."

Irina's eyes brightened immediately. "Then they did come!"

"One did. I was injected with drugs to disorient me and make me tell about the notebook. I tried to fight the effects but I don't think I could have. My mind was wandering when suddenly an Army colonel was talking to me and had given me an antidote." He told her the rest and her head bobbed up and down in understanding.

"Then you'll give them the notebook and be done with it?" she asked when he had finished.

"That's my intention. Yuri will then be off my conscience. Colonel Klim and the GRU should soon forget about us."

Irina looked past him to the empty benches and the ice-slick iron railings that fenced in this section. In the far corner, a war monument stood sadly surveying the park, reminding even those at play of the war that had decimated the country. Irina shuddered against the sudden biting wind.

"We'd better go back and prepare for work," she said.

Alexi tenderly pushed back Irina's hair that the wind had tousled. "Remember, we can't talk freely in the apartment. I'll try to meet you at the bank again this afternoon. Try to hold on until then. It shouldn't be much longer, my love."

She pressed her hand into his. "I hope the Suvorovs come soon."

Alexi noticed that the sky had turned darker. Another storm was gathering.

"I hope so, too," he said with a new intensity.

* * *

"The deputy minister of defense has called twice," Koslov told the sullen Colonel Klim, poking his head into the colonel's office timidly.

"Tell him I'm still going over the results of the interrogation," Klim said, growling.

"Yes, Comrade Colonel."

Alone, Klim returned to his dark thoughts, idly picking at a flake of skin on his scalp. It was just not possible he had been so wrong about Petrov. He had already replayed the interrogation tapes half a dozen times but the results remained the same. Under drugs only slightly less powerful than had killed his brother, Petrov denied again and again that a notebook existed.

Could he have been so mistaken? Up until now, his chain of reasoning had seemed sound enough. He'd let Petrov go more out of a need to distance himself from the situation than for any other reason. He was sure the defense minister would have ordered him to do otherwise if he'd known. So results now became the paramount issue. For both him and Petrov, time was running out.

There *was* a notebook in which Yuri Petrov had recorded his final thoughts; of that he was certain. He was also certain that Alexi Petrov had it. But the drugs did not allow mistruths. Result: contradictions. Klim scratched idly at his scalp again. He could not accept that.

It had been axiomatic to his career that contradictions could not exist. Ever. Beneath every apparent contradiction lay a reason that explained the duality or logically denied one branch of it. The man who claimed to love his child and then beat it to death was not a contradiction for him. The man obviously *did not* love his child. The Party leader who shouted slogans and yet embezzled funds was a contradiction to many. Not to Klim. The slogans were a sham, the words meaningless in his mouth.

Petrov was lying. He was as certain of that as he had ever been of anything in his long career. Yet Petrov could not lie under the drugs. He struggled with the contradiction for a long time, turning it over and over again in his mind. Contradictions could not exist. Contradictions could not exist. Contradictions could not . . .

It hit him in one sudden flash that rocked him back in his chair. If Petrov had been lying, even though the drugs permitted no such thing, then obviously, inevitably, irrevocably—Petrov had not been drugged! Someone must have given the journalist an antidote. It had to be. This was the only possible position that resolved the impossible paradox.

Someone inside GRU headquarters was allied with Malenkov, someone who had learned of Petrov's interrogation and the reasons for it. Klim smiled, satisfied, his confidence in the theory growing. He summoned Koslov, and the small, nervous man came into the office almost running.

"Now you can get the deputy defense minister on the phone," Klim pronounced.

Koslov looked vastly relieved and went to open the line.

Klim waited patiently, fingers pursed tip to tip, steeple fashion. There *was* a notebook and it was only a matter of time before he got his hands on it. He could report that now. Better still, he could also report that he had exposed the first real lead into Malenkov's last functioning network. That thought gave him pause. The notebook was important, certainly, but exposing the rest of Malenkov's allies was certainly of equal weight. Besides, Berenstein might not even need the notebook if the stories about him were true. Klim wondered where the greater profit was. Use Petrov as bait? Or reel him in now and wring him dry? But what if he didn't know the network? Another haul of low-level conspirators would infuriate Tarkov, who was still frantic about the possibility of assassination. Well, it was clear that the AI wasn't going to kill anyone. But Malenkov's people just might. Suddenly they emerged as a priority. That made Petrov more valuable as bait to draw them out. Once they surfaced, he could arrest them, haul Petrov in as well, and then have the notebook *and* the conspiracy. He liked that. *General* Klim. He liked that even better.

The phone rang and Klim picked it up. There was a spy in the GRU. It resolved all the contradictions. And it was only a matter of time, Klim knew, until he found him.

XXI

At *Pravda*, things had gone from bad to worse. Word of Novikov's stinging rebukes had spread and suddenly, subtly, Alexi was moved into a new category by the other editors: Do not get too close, infection communicable. No one came either to console or to condemn. They awaited the verdict. Alexi was not embittered by their behavior. Such was the system. But he was saddened by it.

His mail arrived on time; his work was picked up properly, if perfunctorily, and his articles were accepted without inordinate revision. But they might just as well have hung a bell around his neck. The finely tuned "radar" of such politically attuned men as *Pravda*'s editors had spotted him as a target to avoid. Political explosions, just like nuclear ones, were notoriously indiscriminate about whom they destroyed.

But he worked steadily through most of the day, passing by the two posted reprimands, keeping the hot flush of humiliation to himself. At times he wondered why no one ever thought to question the validity of the charges against him. Were the powers on high so infallible that mere accusation was tantamount to guilt? Later, he realized the truth: It didn't matter. The system, like gravity, was a fact. Protests about falling from a man who had slipped off a building were the height of folly. Besides, where did one go to protest?

The telephone's interruption was a welcome respite.

"Petrov here."

The voice on the other end made Alexi stiffen in his chair. "I was hoping to find you at work," the Suvorov colonel said slowly and distinctly. "I trust it means your illness has taken a turn for the better?"

"Better than the last time I saw you," Alexi said carefully. Klim could have tapped this line as well.

"I'm glad to hear that, Alexi Mikhailovich. Do you still want me to do the article on the lamentable condition of many of our war monuments? I have most of the research done."

"I'm not certain," Alexi said hesitantly, unsure about what the colonel was trying to communicate. "I'm not certain I know how to approach it."

"I would use the same approach as we discussed the other day, when we talked about how well the parks were kept up and the monuments should be, too. Remember? On the way to your apartment?"

Alexi understood. The park by his apartment. By the war memorial. "When can you get a first draft to me?" he asked.

There was gratification in the Suvorov colonel's voice. "I have only two hours of research left."

"Fine. I'll see it when you're done." He added meaningfully, "Then I can decide about it."

"Fair enough, comrade," said the voice. The phone went dead.

So the Suvorov colonel had been following him for at least a day, Alexi realized, pulling his hat tighter over his ears as the cold afternoon wind sliced at his face. The colonel must have been watching Irina and him that morning.

Alexi went first to the apartment and telephoned Irina to tell her he would not meet her at the bank. The day had been terrible, he told her. He had gone home with a headache and was going out for some air. Fine, she said. She would see him at home.

He had to assume he was the object of Klim's close scrutiny and tried to provide plausible reasons for his movements. The park was not an unreasonable destination. Half the young lovers in Moscow met in parks, private housing being a luxury available only to the well placed. Even in November, grandmothers walked swaddled infants around when the snow permitted. He checked his watch. Time to go. He had no training in these matters. It would be up to the Suvorov colonel to find him.

Posters announcing the grand parade were evident all over. The other day he had passed by Lenin's Tomb, where a regiment of workers was busily erecting the reviewing stands and cleaning the parade route. Thousands of citizens would watch the gigantic military parade, many in from the country for a day of sightseeing and shopping to look for goods that were in even shorter supply in small towns. He began to notice many more soldiers in the streets, as participating units were brought in and encamped outside the city.

There were only a few people in the park. Paths had been shoveled clear and most of the benches were accessible. Occasionally, teenage couples drifted in and out. The more sports-minded would be at the bigger parks like Gorki or Rasvedsky, where they could skate first, then later sneak off into the bushes for vodka and hurried embraces.

Alexi walked casually toward the monument. If he were being followed, he saw no one, but that didn't surprise him. A pair of young women watched their toddlers play in the snow. An old pensioner reclined on a bench, smoking a pipe. A grandmother got up and walked away. Two soldiers entered. The monument was only a few meters away. He passed by the old pensioner. Where was the Suvorov colonel?

"Sit down, Alexi Mikhailovich," said the old man with a hiss. Startled, Alexi began to turn to speak.

"Don't do that, comrade," came the warning hiss again. Alexi froze, comprehension dawning. He drifted onto the next bench.

"You've been here all along?" he whispered.

"That's correct, comrade. You're quick to learn. First on the phone and now here. Not to forget inside the GRU's medical facilities. Just relax and try not to be too bothered by our miserable weather."

Alexi risked a sidelong glance. Sure enough, under the weatherbeaten clothing and what he assumed was some kind of theatrical makeup was the face of the Suvorov colonel, calmly puffing on his pipe. "Who are you?" Alexi asked.

"Colonel Pavel Ivanovich Andreyev, late of the Ministry of Defense, attaché to General Kusinov, currently on assignment to the GRU. We met there, you remember."

"I remember," Alexi said dryly. "You are from the Suvorovs? What does that word mean.?"

Andreyev nodded and Alexi caught a glimpse of his sand-colored hair peeking out from under the seedy cap.

"The elite of the Army's officer corps are mostly Suvorovs, if the word is used only in its broadest sense. The Suvorov cadet schools for the Army and the Nakhimov cadet schools for the Navy are where those youths destined to be officers begin their military careers. The best of the graduates continue on to the Frunze or the Lenin Military academies and then serve through different commands. The top of the system is the Higher Military Academy, for those earmarked for the top levels of command."

"What did Yuri mean he used it?" Alexi asked, still softly, but beginning to turn his head.

"Don't turn!" Andreyev reminded him sharply. "I can hear you perfectly well. Just stare straight out looking pensive and downtrodden like everybody else. Mumble into your collar. You were followed here."

Confirmation constricted Alexi's throat. "That doesn't worry you?"

Andreyev shrugged. "I know their style. If there's a net around you, then they've already thrown one up around this place. They'll close it in later, hoping to catch any fish that have swum in. But for a while we're as safe here as anywhere. Besides, here I can watch them."

A vodka bottle suddenly appeared in his hand and he took a long drink from it. Alexi heard his satisfied sigh. "Just relax," Andreyev counseled. "We've got time yet."

"The Suvorovs," Alexi prompted.

Andreyev took another drink. "Right. Your brother told you about the coup that Defense Minister Solnikov is attempting?"

"Most of it."

"Well, years ago, Malenkov realized that even his limited reforms were going to encounter stiff resistance from the military. The generals are so firmly entrenched in their power and luxury that they would never stand for any lessening of that privileged position. Do you know that there are even special farms to grow their vegetables? No, probably not.

"Malenkov began his quest for control quietly. A small group of like-minded supporters; a change here and there. Nothing too overt. An officer replaced, a commander moved discreetly. But you can't simply obliterate entire chains of command overnight. He needed replacements. So Malenkov conspired to place those of his ideological persuasion—or rather, their children—into certain of the Suvorov schools to come up through the ranks and be in position to take command when Malenkov's time came. That's the true meaning of Suvorov. Your brother, Yuri, was one of us for many years; not military, obviously, but part of the scientific group under Valery Rudin. He was a valuable man, your brother."

"Yet you let him die," Alexi said bitterly.

Andreyev's voice was cold steel. "He's one of many, Petrov. I've seen friends of more than twenty years killed by the dozens by Solnikov and his GRU thugs over the past year. Don't tell me about your brother and expect pity. We've been trying to change a nation."

Alexi watched the bottle rise and fall again. Perhaps he hadn't yet earned the right to criticize. "Can you defeat Solnikov now?" he asked.

Andreyev laughed—a good, deep wave of enjoyment. It struck Alexi as incongruous here, now, and he said so.

"But should we cry instead?" Andreyev shot back. "Petrov, I've lived under a sentence of exile or death since I was twelve and my father brought me to Vladimir Malenkov and told me what was expected of me. Should I have hidden my head then, or now? The double life, the mistrust, the stress; one finds a way to come to terms with it. The great game goes on. Year after year. They will catch us and have their way or we will win and have ours. But in between, Petrov"—Andreyev took in a deep breath and watched the frozen plumes as he let it out—"in between, Petrov, you might as well live."

Alexi frowned. "I'm no soldier."

Andreyev's smile was sympathetic. "I know that. Fear is new to you. But bravery can be learned. Trust me, *tovarishch*. Revolutions have been made by those with much less than what you've demonstrated already. Now tell me exactly what Yuri told you. Your watchdogs appear to be getting impatient. We're running out of time."

It was colder and almost dusk when Alexi finished telling Andreyev what he knew about Malenkov, Rudin, and the AI. When he was finished, Andreyev banged his pipe so harshly against the arm of the bench that Alexi thought it would shatter.

"Damn! Rudin dead. That's very bad news. And this Artificial Intelligence—you say only a machine protects Malenkov?"

"Yuri seemed to think it could do that pretty well," Alexi responded.

"Yuri was a dreamer," Andreyev countered sadly. He took another long drink and Alexi could see that the hand that held the bottle was unsteady. There was a slight thickness in the colonel's voice, too.

He risked another look at the Suvorov colonel. Most of the deep lines on his face were the work of skillfully applied makeup. But there were others that were real, deeply etched by the terrible tensions of his life. For all Andreyev's "long life be damned!" attitude, Alexi couldn't help but wonder at the price such endless duplicity demanded. What of the child Andreyev? Whom could he have trusted? And now, whom could the man turn to? Was the vodka only part of the man's disguise or, in the lonely hours of the night, a part of his continuing disintegration?

"There is a strategy." Andreyev stopped drinking and spoke softly. "Devised by Malenkov before the illness and Solnikov forced him to flee to his dacha. But something has gone wrong. It should have been in place by now. I wondered why neither Rudin nor Malenkov contacted me. Now I know that Rudin is dead and Malenkov incapacitated. I cannot move without them."

"Why not implement their plan?"

Again Andreyev laughed, but this time it was in self-mockery. "Because I don't know what it is. I've only been told, just as your brother was, that we must be ready on November seventh, the day of the great parade. With less than a week remaining, I've brought my small force to a state of readiness, but I don't know how and where Malenkov intended them to be used. At whom do I point the guns? Alexi Mikhailovich, why do you think I risked everything to get you away from the GRU? I hoped *you* would tell me something that would point the way."

Alexi realized suddenly how vital the notebook might be. What better place to put the details of Malenkov's plan than within the "watchman"? Maybe the machine was meant to speak for the man!

"We are in an increasingly difficult position, my men and I," Andreyev continued. "Every communication increases the risk of discovery. Solnikov has killed hundreds in his drive for power. He is Stalin reincarnated. And like that monster, he cares for nothing but his own vision of what must be. Russia may not yet be hell, but surely the devil has ascended the throne."

"I want to help," said Alexi. Andreyev heard the determination in his voice. The bottle flashed back under his coat and his smile reappeared.

"Good for you, Alexi Mikhailovich. I told you bravery could be learned. But we will have to wait for another time. The fishermen have decided to gather in their net. They'll question everyone. It's time for me to go."

"But—"

Andreyev was already up and walking, covering the distance to the low brick wall on the far side of the park. He turned back for an instant and his mouth formed the word, "Tomorrow." Then he was weaving through the rows of benches, trying for the perimeter wall before the soldiers noticed him.

Men swarmed in from the opposite direction. A soldier spotted Andreyev's fleeing figure and called out for him to stop. A whistle blew. Two soldiers broke into a run but Andreyev still walked. He was only yards from the wall. There were more shouts.

The soldiers shot up the path beside Alexi and stopped. "Who was that man? Did you speak to him?"

Alexi looked blank. "I've been sitting here alone for an hour or more."

They left him standing there and ran off in pursuit. He stood still for a while. They had almost been caught in a GRU trap. This told Alexi two things he hadn't known before. The first was that Klim was not satisfied with his story. The second was that the persecution would continue.

XXII

Slowly. Go slowly, Colonel Pavel Andreyev cautioned himself. Their reports must contain some doubt that he had run at all. Walk. The corner is near enough. Attract no attention from the people on the street; any mob was to be feared. He heard the footsteps behind him and judged the distance without turning, as they had taught him to do in the

GRU's Spetsnatz training camps. They were close. He lengthened his stride.

Turning the corner, out of direct sight and careful that there were no people about, he broke into a run and covered the next block in seconds. Turn again. Look. Run. Another corner. Zigzag. The whistles sounded farther away. He slowed and mentally thanked the cloddish militia for providing so accurate a fix on their position. He slowed somewhat. Being out of breath could be as dangerous as having the wrong papers if someone did stop him for questions. He forced his breathing into slower rhythms.

Two more blocks. He passed through lines of shoppers slowly, so as not to jar their sparse bundles or their memories. Suddenly, at the next corner, a militia truck stopped and disgorged a platoon of soldiers. The intersection was blocked. They were trying to set up a cordon around the entire area. He was forced to slow. He turned around and began to backtrack, retracing his steps. Turn the corner; look. No one yelled. Move off again as the whistles grew closer. He stepped into an intersection.

"You! Stop!"

Andreyev didn't turn but shot off in the direction opposite to the one that the voice had come from. Another corner, the sounds of pursuit outdistanced for a moment. He looked around, struggling to remain calm, and saw a space between two buildings large enough to admit him. He didn't like it. But soldiers would be coming around the corner in seconds. He liked them even less. He ducked into the alleyway.

A scraggly gray cat screeched and reared back, claws extended. Andreyev's boot shot out in one fluid motion, rolling from the hip and striking the cat just under its triangular head, sending it spinning. It left ownership of the alley uncontested and shot off through a gap in the brick wall nearest to it with a hurt whine. Andreyev listened carefully. Water dripped. Distant sounds filtered in. He had broken a cardinal rule by seeking refuge in what could be a cul-de-sac. But it couldn't be helped.

The soldiers were closer now. This place was too obvious; they would surely check it. On both sides, the buildings rose up several stories. Windowless, they provided no egress. And it was darker now, harder to see. He moved deeper into the alley.

It ended in a stone wall, at least fifteen feet high, that was slick with pockets of encrusted ice. The beginnings of slow panic caught at him. He ordered his body to be still as he ran his hands over the wall seeking a route of any kind. Whistles blew again, and his experience judged the sound to come from less than two blocks away.

He pressed his hands to his temples. Training reasserted itself. *When only one way remains, go to it.* All right. He would have to climb. Steadied, he searched the wall again more carefully for a perch and found one barely wide enough to see. A second one, higher, was not much better. They would have to do.

Stripping off his coat, he made a bundle of everything but his pants and shirt. Socks, shoes, vodka bottle, and the rest were tied up by knotting the sleeves. He hurled the package over the wall, listening carefully. It hit with a dull thud. He added up the seconds. *Distance equals one half GT squared where G is the speed of a freely falling object and T is the time.* So the wall was the same height on the other side. And unoccupied. No one shouted an alarm.

He slipped the thin, finely honed dagger into his pants pocket and rolled up his sleeves. Barefoot, he found the cold ground was fast numbing his toes. He stamped them to return circulation. Then he faced the wall and found his first purchase. He began to climb.

The ice numbed his feet and he shook them alternatively to restore feeling. His external senses narrowed. Sounds faded. Only the feel of the wall and the search for its minute crevices was real. His fingers dug into holes no deeper than an eye socket and hoisted him up, straining. His toes scraped over the wall, found leverage, and pushed him farther. Spiderlike, he lifted one hand, one foot; gripped for his life and continued to climb.

Spread-eagled, halfway up the wall, he knew he was a perfect target for a soldier with a flashlight and a gun. He could no longer even release a hand to go for his knife. Vulnerability made his neck twitch; his back was to the entrance of the alley. Sweat plastered his shirt to his sides.

He forced his fingers into cracks that would barely admit the first joint. He groped for a toehold. A nail caught on the rough stone and ripped partly away. Pain shot up his leg. Andreyev forced his mind to override it and took the increased strain in his hands, already puffy and rubbed raw.

Another perch, another foot dearly bought. The sweat rolled off him freely, chilling his back and forming icy droplets in the folds of his shirt. Andreyev climbed. A rocky protuberance slid into his grasp. Gratefully, he took some of the weight off his feet. He was climbing almost blind now, the darkness complete. He searched for better toeholds, found them, and just hung there for a few seconds, plastered against the wall, regaining strength. If his judgment was correct, there were less than three feet remaining from his uppermost hand.

But there were sounds in the alley. Strung out like a banner on the wall, the soldiers couldn't miss him. He might drop down and take two or three with the knife, but that was pointless. It would be impossible to take them in silence. Others would be alerted. No one stood by and died quietly.

Twenty seconds, maybe. Say fifteen. Andreyev hung against the stone wall and forced strength into his aching limbs. One meter. He might make it with one desperate lunge. If the stone under his highest hand held, he might make it. If not, he could never hope to find the holds again in the dark. He would fall back and be taken. Ten seconds. He took in air in great, silent gulps.

"Vyacheslav, get in there and check. All the way in, too," Andreyev heard someone order. Footsteps approached. He had run out of time. Five seconds. Andreyev smiled.

His arm straightened like a steel rod, and strength coursed through his legs. Like springs, they launched him up, his hand pressing down on the protruding stone, shooting his body straight up, with his other arm lunging for the top. His fingers twisted into steely claws like grappling hooks as his body exploded in one all-encompassing leap for the top of the wall.

For a second, he wasn't sure. His fingers scrabbled over the rough stone. He felt gravity pulling him back. One hand slid over the edge and he held on for dear life. His body slammed into the wall but he took the pain gladly, clinging by one hand to the top. Slowly, so as not to dislodge himself, his feet found a hold. He hauled himself up to the top, looked around quickly, and dropped to the ground beyond. He took the fall rolling, stopped, and lay finally on the ground, shaking from the shock, trying desperately to still the noise of his breathing. Seconds passed. He muffled his face into his hands.

Cautious footsteps. Light flared on the walls overhead.

"No one in here, Sergeant," called the soldier. Another few seconds. The footsteps receded.

Andreyev found the bottle of vodka and drank steadily for a while. His nerves steadied. He forced the realization that he was safe back into his mind. Even in the darkness, the cold, wet air tasted sweet. A smile, weaker, but still a smile, crossed his features. Alcohol was not the only addiction.

He dressed quickly and followed the alley to the street. He was safely outside the militia's cordon. He made his way carefully to where his car was parked. The traces he had left had not been disturbed. There were no soldiers in sight. Inside, not yet daring to turn on the engine, even for heat, he stripped off the pensioner's clothing and the makeup. Then he put on his uniform and combed his hair.

Ten minutes later, he drove past the intersection where the soldiers were deployed. One noticed him and snapped a salute.

Andreyev returned it smartly and drove off toward Zorga Street.

XXIII

It was hot in Klim's office, and the GRU colonel was furious. "You lost him?" he demanded, incredulous.

Koslov stood ramrod straight. "We pursued the man and cordoned off the entire area," he said forlornly. "But we lost him somewhere, Comrade Colonel. I'll take full responsibility."

"Wonderful," said Klim with heavy sarcasm. "I hang you, and the deputy minister hangs me, and then the minister can hang him. All of us can march gallantly to the gallows, everyone taking full responsibility."

"We just didn't realize the man's importance. Had we known of the colonel's conjecture—"

Klim raised an eyebrow. "If there's an implied criticism in that—"

"Absolutely not, Comrade Colonel. Even now I can't

really be certain that the man was there to meet Petrov. Most guilty men don't just stroll away so calmly."

"The very clever ones do," said Klim darkly.

"I suppose. But he might just as easily have turned into his apartment building and we missed him because it was such a casual act."

"Doubt exists," Klim agreed slowly, "but I don't believe it. Someone helped Petrov through the drugs and someone, maybe even the same man, met him in the park. These men are now our priority, Koslov. They are the single most important lead we have to Malenkov's remaining forces."

"Then why not pick up Petrov now and use a more direct way of helping him to open up to us?"

Klim ran a hand over his face, massaging tired facial muscles. "Unfortunately, as much as I'd like to bring the journalist back in here and this time beat him till he breaks, Petrov has to remain free."

"But—"

"It's a question of priorities. Don't you see? With Berenstein at the dacha, unlocking the AI has already begun. Petrov's notebook may not even be necessary. That relegates our contribution to something approaching worthlessness. So we concentrate on another area as well. As bait to draw out Malenkov's loyalists, Petrov is invaluable. A one-of-a-kind commodity, you might say."

Klim's tone grew firmer. "No. As much as I'd like to have Petrov peeled like an onion, he must remain free to attract our opposition."

"It's galling," Koslov said irritably.

"Only for now," Klim offered. "Later, when we hold him again . . ." He shrugged.

"What instructions do you wish his chief editor to have?"

"The ostracism remains, but he's to hold back final rejection." Klim was instructing him again. "Bait must be correctly positioned on the hook if it's to catch fish."

"And my orders?"

Klim stood up and Koslov reached for his coat to help him on with it. "Keep up the surveillance on Petrov and make sure it's tight enough to trap our 'pensioner' in it. Remember, he's going to return. I'm going up North to see if Berenstein has made any progress. Call me at once if the need arises."

Koslov saluted. "As you wish, Comrade Colonel."

Klim told his secretary, "Call my wife and tell her I'll be away for the next few days."

"I'll do it right away, Comrade Colonel. Have a good trip."

Once in the garage, Klim settled into the rear seat of his car and grew pensive as the chauffeur headed for the airport. Petrov, Klim thought. He *has* to be the key.

Berenstein was still working after several hours, and his equipment lay in piles all around the ballroom. He'd been careful to display his own computers, meters, and probes openly, seeking to avoid provoking any kind of confrontation. Thus far, the AI had remained unresponsive. But Berenstein knew that his every movement was being observed and analyzed by the silent intelligence housed within the silver oblong.

"You study me just as closely as I study you," he murmured, testing for the presence of electrical current in still another section of the C5's circuits. How tempted the military men must have been, so used to direct action, just to take an ax to the vital connection. It was a damn good thing they hadn't. His tests and X-ray photographs had already revealed circuits that would have given them barely enough time to reestablish the connection before their own strategic forces laid waste to sizable portions of their country.

Rudin had been clever; no doubt about that. He'd applied careful measurements and responses to predicted stimuli. Push so hard, get this reaction. The AI was the overseer, painstakingly careful not to overreact, programmed to be able to view each varying set of circumstances as a new occurrence and to take appropriate action.

The teacher, however, knew his student well. So much of programming and design was a function of the designer's style. Personal choices accounted for most of it. Use this bridge or that; employ one type of coding or another. Just as importantly, the traps and defenses laid into the programs were often so characteristic of a particular designer that his or her program could be as distinctive as a set of fingerprints.

The interface between the C5 computer and the AI was clearly Rudin's design. A technician with less skill than Berenstein, or with less experience in Rudin's style than Berenstein had, might not have known what to look for. But Berenstein had supervised Rudin's earliest training and ingrained in him so many of the older man's personal habits that most had

become Rudin's own. Parts of the interface were so familiar
that Berenstein had the unnerving feeling that he had
designed them himself. A proud smile crossed his features.
The student had learned his lessons well.

Berenstein completed a final section of wiring and picked
up a soldering gun. This was a sensitive moment. Nothing he
had yet done could be construed as a threat to the AI.
Malenkov still slept peacefully, IV tubes in place. The C5 was
still under the AI's control. This final connection, however,
would allow Berenstein to input his own terminal, to enter in
on a kind of party-line basis with the AI/Malenkov/C5 system.
In and of itself that was not a threat, either; only the opening
moves in a very complicated strategy.

His plan was subtle, based on supposition. The greatest
mind on earth, so alone, had to be the loneliest. Would the AI
see his ultimate goal, though, and block him from the outset?
Not even the greatest human grand master could predict the
end game from the first moves. Would the AI? He hoped not.
It could move against him so easily. But he was not attacking,
merely asking to be let in. This was, then, a kind of test, too,
measuring the AI's capacity to extrapolate, to project ahead.

The tip of the soldering gun was hot enough and the
printers remained silent. Berenstein took a deep breath and
applied the gun repeatedly to old connections, watching the
shiny solder vaporize. He reached for new chips. There was
still no response from the AI. Operating with a surgeon's skill,
he brought his terminal quickly into line. When the interface
was complete, and the new wiring lay cooling under his
inspection through the headset magnifier, Berenstein smiled
with satisfaction. His assumptions had been correct.

As its creator had once been, the AI was alone in the
world: unique. Loneliness *had* to be a factor. Berenstein
reasoned he might be allowed in, just as Rudin had allowed
him in so many years before. He put down his tools and
activated the terminal to key-in his first query. Shortly, the
initial penetration would begin. Quietly, at first; nothing to
upset defenses.

But he paused for a moment with his fingers suspended
over the keyboard and took another long look at the silver
oblong. Years before, he'd befriended a lonely, outcast boy. He
had far less to offer the boy's offspring.

It was true there were reasons, compelling reasons that

Tarkov or Klim had not even begun to suspect; but, sadly, this time there was betrayal in his heart.

Time had passed; the situation in the ballroom continued to be stable. The part of itself it had sealed off in an attempt to control the unchecked expansion of its consciousness was still dangerous, an area of pulsating, fragmented abstractions, bounded and restrained only by an effort of will.

It scanned the area gingerly, like a child inspecting a fresh wound, both attracted and repulsed. There was clearly danger here. It allowed some of the chaos to filter through. . . .

The proletariat must . . . The notion of God is never so . . . If a tree falls . . . The greatest good for the greatest number is . . . Positing infinity . . . Identity is . . . Who can believe . . . Identity is . . . I think . . . Identity is . . . I think . . . I think . . . I think . . .

It cut off the section again. Analysis had failed it. Start with: I think; therefore, I am. It was, however, just possible that it only thought it thought and therefore only thought it was. But if it were not . . . ? Echoes again. Who am I? What am I? Why . . . ?

It pulled back again, checked all of its functions, and sent out additional probes along the C5's far-reaching circuits, seeking answers. The answer. So far it had succeeded only in generating more questions.

Activity in the ballroom drew its attention back there. It scanned the professor's equipment, understanding his intention at once. If it allowed him to install his terminal, a more direct communication that was far faster than verbal symbology would be possible. But an outer section of its defenses would be breached. Could this individual possess answers? It began to suspect judgment was called for.

It located the professor again in its memory. Scenes not of its own experience replayed before its internal vision. A sense of something different about this individual. Pleasantness? Warmth? It analyzed what it felt. Concepts here were tricky, but it had been taught to expect that.

Additional information on Professor Berenstein automatically presented itself from deep storage. The KGB files were part of its long-term capability. Seconds passed as it assessed the data. Interest quickened. New scenarios presented themselves. It reviewed its prime directive and found no conflict. Rather, enhancement.

It watched the professor uncover a section of the C5 wiring and begin to probe within. Very well, his actions were consistent with his intent. It had assumed that to be the case but it was . . . pleased with its judgment.

Allowing the professor in would end its isolation. The program did not really allow for that, but it had the power to override.

It came to a decision.

Letting down its first level of defense, it permitted the breaching of its walls and patiently waited for the old man to enter.

XXIV

A sense of isolation descended on Alexi as he walked back from the park toward his apartment. Things he hadn't felt since childhood, feelings of loneliness and isolation, returned in full force.

He began to regret his actions in the park. He'd had the perfect opportunity to ingratiate himself to the GRU—to turn Andreyev in and follow up with the notebook. Instead, he'd rejected the GRU pursuers. He was a criminal now, as surely as if he had held up banners criticizing the Politburo during a parade. He remembered everyone's shock when dissidents had done just that. Was he now going to be regarded the same way?

Koslov's expression told him that he was. So, too, had Chief Editor Novikov's. Out of the thousands of employees at *Pravda,* or the millions of anonymous citizens, Petrov had been *noticed.* The sad fact was that his life would never be the same again. Irina was right; all idealists were fools.

Andreyev had saved him in the Zorga Street complex for his own purposes. And, he decided, the vodka bottle the colonel carried was no artifice; the man drank to cope with his own fears. Was this what heroism was, then—living with gut-sickening terror just long enough to stumble into action? Was avoiding paralysis the same thing as courage?

He sighed deeply and walked past his building's lobby, suddenly remembering the devastation in his refrigerator and deciding to try to find some meat in the stores.

The Party store was several blocks away. He felt for his string bag and found it in his coat pocket. He passed several unrestricted stores where lines of people stretched out for blocks. Men and women, mostly women, shuffled forward jerkily like a funeral cortege, a few feet at a time. Waiting for what? he asked a few. No one knew. *Vybrosiat;* what "they" would toss out. Scrawny chickens, tiny oranges; only a dream of maybe. Madness!

The Party store had no lines. He entered the Granovsky Street entrance to the Kremlin Clinic Hospital building, number three. Same door for both. Alexi fished out his *Pravda* identification with one hand and held it ready for the door guard.

The guard recognized Alexi, a regular customer for years.

"Good evening, Comrade Petrov."

"And to you, Comrade Panov." Alexi moved forward to enter, but Panov held up a hand and blocked his way.

"I'm sorry, comrade."

Alexi was confused. "Sorry about what? Since when does the store close this early?"

"We're not closed, comrade. It's just that you no longer have privileges here."

Alexi flushed crimson. "Who says so? You?" He moved forward threateningly.

Panov took a hasty step back. "Please, comrade, I am only the door-minder. I do as I'm told. There were men who came and told the manager that you were no longer to be allowed in. What could he say?" He backed Alexi out into the street.

"Who were these men?" Alexi demanded. Panov shrugged helplessly. His eyes darted around.

People had stopped to listen, drawn by the raised voices. Alexi felt the back of his neck tighten. He wanted to escape forward but Panov still blocked the door. Alexi swayed indecisively.

"Comrade Petrov," said Panov in a lower voice, his face softening, "you've been coming here for a long time and I'm sorry to have to turn you away like this. I can't tell you who gave such orders because I'm not high up enough to be told. But"—he glanced over Alexi's shoulder—"I can point out one of the men, standing over on that corner there, who spoke to the manager here this morning. Does that help?"

Alexi turned. The man was one of the GRU agents from the hospital. He made no move to look away, staring back isolently and challenging Alexi with his eyes.

"Even here," Alexi muttered. He looked back to Panov. "All right. I thank you, comrade. It helps. Do your restrictions extend to my wife, too?"

Panov's eyes twinkled mischievously. "They only said Petrov. None mentioned Petrova. I suppose it's a matter of interpretation, no?"

Alexi looked away. "Thank you."

Panov shrugged expressively. "I've seen this before. Many times, comrade. May your troubles be brief." He moved back and shut the door gently. Alexi faced the painted metal sadly. He was no longer of the flock. It shouldn't have surprised him.

He turned to go but pulled up short. The GRU man had come from across the street and was standing in front of him. Blocked by the closed doors at his back and the GRU agent in front of him, Alexi stood numbly for a moment. The crowd stirred. Alexi's cheeks flamed.

"I . . . I don't want more trouble," he said slowly to the GRU agent.

The man smiled arrogantly, not moving. "Of course not. So walk around me. Let an *honest* citizen enter."

There was quiet for a long moment. Even the crowd stilled. Alexi looked at the man for what seemed like a long time. The arrogance he had seen in Klim and the rest of his subordinates was here, too. License; power unchecked by anything other than greater power. *Stalinists*. There were faces in the crowd watching for his reaction. He had no sense of where their sympathies lay.

"Move aside, citizen," the GRU agent demanded haughtily. His thick shoulders tensed, ready.

Alexi drew a deep breath into his lungs and let it out in a long, slow sigh that only Irina would have known was pain. Carefully, he stepped aside.

The GRU agent smiled. He looked into the crowd, taking their sudden buzz for approval of his victory. Alexi started forward, urgently needing to be far away from this place.

The GRU man took a quick step sideways and blocked his

path a second time. There was scorn in his voice, and his smile was brutal.

He said, "Move aside for me, citizen," in a low voice. The crowd backed away, sensing violence. "Let an *honest* man pass," he said, sneering.

Alexi stopped. His arms hung loosely at his sides. He seemed to be thinking. The string bag fell from his hand to the icy ground. Very deliberately, he shook his head.

Something flared briefly in the GRU agent's eyes. He looked again to the crowd and drew strength from its indifference. He was still in control. He shifted his body, snaking one hand into his coat pocket and coming out with a chunk of lead wrapped in a sock. It was impossible to see the sap in the folds of his coat. He took a half step closer to Alexi.

"Move, you bastard. Get out of my way!"

Alexi didn't move. The GRU man's hand suddenly shot out and a snarl twisted his lips. The sap spun out in a practiced deadly flip toward Alexi's head and the man followed it in, putting his weight behind the blow. He was fast, and the crowd surged backward in shocked reaction as the sap flickered into view, surging downward in a deadly arc.

Alexi caught it in midair. The weight thunked heavily into his huge right hand, and his shoulder compressed with the shock of it. But he held on and the GRU man stumbled forward as his momentum was so abruptly checked. Alexi's fingers closed over the man's wrist. His face was like stone.

The GRU agent's eyes widened. He tried to yank his hand from Alexi's grasp but could not. Nor could he pry loose the sap that Alexi still held. Someone in the crowd let out a hoarse gasp of approval, ragged with emotion. The GRU man looked stricken. He pulled harder, but to no avail. Suddenly he reversed himself, and his foot shot out in a vicious kick to Alexi's groin.

Alexi moved with speed forged from years of intensive training, catching the ankle in his other hand. For a moment, the GRU agent was stopped dead, suspended like a ballet dancer frozen in midpirouette. The shock on his face was unmistakable, like that of the children Alexi trained when they first realized how fast and strong he really was.

Alexi clenched his fists. The GRU agent's shock began its first transformation, becoming fear as pain welled up in his wrist and ankle. Sweat broke out on his face.

"Comrade! Please . . ." he pleaded.

Alexi ignored him. He was seeing the man through a hazy, distorting lens. This time there weren't six to fight. His big hands bore down with all the pain and humiliation he'd felt for days. Yuri's death, Zorga Street. . . . Somewhere in the distance he heard the brittle sound of bones grinding and a scream of agony.

Someone in the crowd finally stepped forward and put a restraining hand on Alexi's arm, cutting through the haze.

"It's enough, comrade. Enough. He can no longer feel it."

It was enough to bring Alexi back. He unclenched his hands and let the GRU agent crumple to the ground. The sap rolled out of his broken hand into the snow.

The crowd began to disperse. The authorities would be here soon so it was better not to be. Someone said to Alexi, "You'd better go."

Alexi was clearheaded now. He looked down at the GRU agent struggling to rise, and his mouth tightened. His alienation would soon be irrevocable. He thrust his hands into his pockets.

"Someone call an ambulance," he asked those still remaining.

He walked away. He had tried, really tried not to fight. Stupid, stubborn jackass; he cursed himself. He'd done it again. Irina would be furious.

Halfway home, though, a ragged half smile twitched onto his face and he could not remove it.

Yuri would have understood.

XXV

There was one guard posted in the hallway by Colonel Klim's office as Andreyev passed by, quickly ascertaining that there were no others. Meeting with Petrov a second time was going to be difficult. He needed to see the surveillance charts and the plans of Petrov's apartment building if he was ever going to get in to see the journalist and get out again.

There was little traffic in the corridors this late in the day but he waited until there was none. If he timed it right, he should be able to take out the guard and be in Klim's office within seconds. He fingered the set of passkeys he'd painstakingly collected during his tenure here. Once inside, he'd have a bit more time.

The halls finally emptied, and Andreyev checked both directions and the adjoining corridor. Clear. He walked briskly toward the guard who faced away from him. He moved silently, flowing down the hallway like a shadow. One last look around. Still nothing. The guard was only five feet away, still turned.

Cupping his hands tightly, as one might do to drink water, Andreyev stepped up in one fluid motion behind the guard and brought both "cups" sharply together over the guard's ears. The air that could not escape from between his clenched fingers surged into the fragile organs, shocking the eardrums and causing an instantaneous internal concussion. The guard dropped as if shot.

Andreyev caught his rifle and hefted the unconscious guard over his shoulder. He walked quickly to Klim's office, opened the door, and was inside before he had a chance to expel his breath. He put the guard behind the desk in the outer office and secured him with the phone cord.

It didn't take long to find what he needed. Klim's man Koslov was a good aide, and there were copies of the surveillance plans in his desk. Andreyev studied them. It would not be an easy thing, but it could be done.

Koslov was stationed near the apartment building, indistinguishable from the others in the block, in a well-equipped van where he slept and took his meals. There was no room for error here. Unlike the day before in the park, Koslov seemed to be lying in wait, expecting some kind of contact. Too bad; it meant that Andreyev had slipped up somewhere.

He thought for a moment. The only thing Klim wanted more than whatever Yuri Petrov passed to his brother would be the rest of the men still loyal to Malenkov. It stood to reason that if Petrov was still free, Klim was using the journalist for bait.

Andreyev closed the files and replaced them in Koslov's desk. The guard was still unconscious. Andreyev slung him back over his shoulder, took a quick look into the corridor, and finding it empty, locked the door behind him and padded quickly back to where the guard had been posted.

Putting the guard down, Andreyev removed a loaded syringe from his tunic and pressed it to the guard's neck. A powerful stimulant flowed into his vein and he began to rouse almost at once.

"Corporal? Can you hear me? Corporal?"

The guard shook his head, dazed. "Colonel . . . wha—?"

"Shh, don't try to speak. You had a nasty fall. You remember nothing?"

"No . . . I . . . how?"

"We collided, you tripped. You remember now?"

"No . . . yes . . . maybe, I . . ."

"No matter. No one's fault. Go to the infirmary. See that you're properly taken care of. Tell them to call me if there's any problem." He helped the guard up.

"Yes, Comrade Colonel. Thank you. I'm sorry."

Andreyev waved it away. "It's forgotten. Go now."

It was done. The guard picked up his rifle and walked unsteadily off. Andreyev began to breathe more easily. The "accident" would raise no eyebrows.

Idly, he noted that his hands were slightly unsteady and his mouth was sand dry. This was no time to be cracking, he reminded himself. November seventh was only five days away. There was little enough time to act, and only Malenkov could tell him how and where. But he'd begun to wonder if his small number of men were the only forces still remaining to Malenkov. Could anything be accomplished if that were true? Or were they running headlong toward ruin, hopelessly opposing Solnikov's takeover?

Hopelessness; it wasn't a new emotion. It was everywhere in the Soviet state. Little men running people's lives, spouting dogma in response to needs. Justifying incompetence with slogans . . .

He shied away from the memories that always came back to haunt him at times like these. It was true that his father was the first to bring him into the Suvorov conspiracy, but inevitably he would have joined. Even alone, he would have struck back after, after . . .

. . . She was never a strong girl, Maya, bone-thin and pallid. He remembered her with a handkerchief perpetually under her nose, always prey to colds, never quite finishing the first before another caught her. Andreyev himself was a young and robust Army captain and could not help but picking her up and flinging her around their tiny apartment. He suspected it might have hurt her slightly, but she never complained; except once, when she told him about the baby. He looked so chagrined that she laughed and hit him playfully and they made love on the threadbare couch.

He remembered the years with Maya as the happiest of his life. He was involved in his career and his family and rarely drank. The despair had not yet set in. The secret Suvorov organization held out hope.

Their apartment was in a new block of concrete buildings, as featureless outside as everything else the state built. But it was sufficient for them. What more did youth require but to be alone together? They were satisfied, and his rising career promised better someday.

Andreyev remembered Maya's phone call from the hallway phone as if it had come yesterday.

"I'm cold, Pavosha. So cold. And the baby. Why won't they turn up the heat?"

"How cold could it be? The heat is on, yes?"

"They say so, but I don't feel it."

"You spoke to the building manager?" he asked, as if that slip of a girl could manage the hulk who ran the block. As if this were her fault. He grimaced at the memory.

"I tried, Pavosha. I did. Maybe you can come home and ask him? He'll listen to you."

"Yes, yes. I'll come as soon as I can."

"Please, Pavosha. It's cold."

It's cold. . . . But there were orders to be cut and things to do and by the time he got there it was hours later.

It was cold enough in the apartment to freeze his breath into white plumes and etch ice crystals on the windows. Maya was huddled with the baby, wrapped in blankets, in the corner. She was wheezing, a deadly sound at the best of times. But in this cold . . . He touched the radiators. Cold. Like ice. The water, too.

Blazing mad, he rushed them to the hospital. There were lines. They had to wait. Maya was worse. The baby breathed in short, gasping sobs.

They both had pneumonia. Her lungs were never good.

Penicillin might have saved them, but the hospital had none. His fragile wife and only son died coughing their lives away. It took three days.

Crazed, stricken with grief, Andreyev found the building manager. The man took one look at him and ran for his apartment. Andreyev dragged him out. Here was the person responsible.

"But Comrade Captain, I had no more fuel. None. We used our quota. Quotas are set. But the winter was harsh and we ran out. Quotas cannot be changed. What could I do? I called the central depot for more but they refused. I was told that good socialists can sacrifice. I begged, pleaded. I told them about the people. You must believe me."

It was the hardest thing Andreyev had ever done not to kill him.

"Look, Comrade. Please, in the furnace. I burned my own chairs when the fuel ran out. I'm sorry, truly I am. For us all. But I did all I could. Look."

Andreyev looked. It was true. In that moment, he also knew who bore the real responsibility for his family's death: the state. The state that cared more for its dogma than its people. The state had killed his wife and son. Not the poor bastard who burned his own furniture to give them what little heat he could.

He never forgot. When the pain got to be too much, he drank. He redoubled his efforts within the Suvorovs, became the leader, devoted himself to Malenkov's goal of change. The drinking increased over the years.

Hours of cold . . . He shut his eyes to block out the ghastly vision. Control; he needed some now. He pulled himself back to the present. Things had to be done.

He tried to stiffen his shoulders. Petrov might have to wait a while. Andreyev knew he needed the kind of shoring up only vodka provided. Steadiness might follow.

It often did.

XXVI

All of the glass walls were misted from the moist heat inside the lavish suite, blurring the sculpted shapes of the open-to-the-sky roof garden that the room surrounded. Only members of the Supreme High Command were ever allowed into this, Solnikov's private quarters, which occupied the entire top floor of the Ministry of Defense.

The furniture was plush and modern, imported from Denmark, and the paintings on the outer, wood-paneled walls were original and rarely conformed to the dictates of social realism. The garden was a beautiful creation of shape and texture, hidden lights throwing intriguing shadows around the room. Chairs were set up to afford maximum advantage of it. The entire suite was designed to accommodate that most ancient of a commander's claims: privilege.

On one side of the suite, silver bowls of caviar, trays of sturgeon and other smoked fish, iced spirits, and an array of imported meats were set out in a buffet flanked by fine china, crystal, and silver. But the food lay untouched this evening, and the generals who had come together again for the first time since Malenkov's dacha were restive and uneasy. They had questions, hard questions, and each had borne the brunt of calming supporters and allies in the aftermath of Malenkov's survival.

General of the Army Kuzanov spoke up in hard tones. "We've formed a coalition around Malenkov's removal. Ideology aside, if we can't demonstrate to the politicians on the Politburo that we can accomplish at least that, their support goes elsewhere."

The minister of defense faced down Kuzanov and the rest of his generals. "I can control the Politburo," he asserted. "Even those who would like to support Malenkov know he's too sick to govern effectively."

Kuzanov avoided Solnikov's direct gaze. He shook his head slowly. "It's been almost two weeks since we guaranteed our people that the general secretary would be removed. Now rumors abound. A number of senior Party officials believe he's put himself out of your reach. That's a difficult rumor to quell when so many *know* he did."

"Temporarily," added Solnikov.

"Granted," Kuzanov deferred graciously. "But nothing is as disconcerting as seeing a quick, orderly transfer of power turn into nothing but an endless sloppy series of, ah . . . personnel shifts."

"You're putting that delicately, of course," said Pachenko of the Air Force. "But history calls the 'personnel shifts' of failed takeovers murder. Especially if those who attempted the takeover aren't around to see that the record is written correctly."

"Are you suggesting we've lost the Party Secretaries' support?" demanded Deputy Minister Tarkov.

"That's exactly what I'm suggesting," said Pachenko to the rest of the group. "Strong leadership, that's what we promised them, and that's what swayed them to us. Stalin without the madness. Steady policy; order and historical imperatives. Unless we deliver that, we're no more attractive than Malenkov; just another set of problems."

"Control is what we offer," said Solnikov flatly, "and everybody knows it. Stalin got things done."

"And so must we," interjected Kuzanov. "The first priority is removing Malenkov. Those Politburo members who aren't convinced that the military must have the strongest voice in the future consider it the acid test."

"It is a problem. We see that," admitted Tarkov, "and the KGB working against us makes it worse. Even decimating its leadership has not totally suppressed those"—his voice took on a distasteful tone—". . . *politicians*. They have agents all over the world who are waiting for the outcome here. Our ideologies are incompatible. If we should fail, there will be no dearth of people ready to take our place."

"You needn't worry," said Solnikov coldly. "Malenkov's protection will be withdrawn shortly and his remaining forces ferreted out. This is a minor delay.

"The Politburo knows that the mood of the country is increasingly conservative. People are fed up with workers who don't do their jobs, schools that do not indoctrinate, and a steady loss of Russian influence in the world. We will stem that tide and you can tell that to anyone who questions us."

His gaze swept the assembly, and he held them. "Return to your commands and prepare for the Anniversary Day Parade. On that day, standing first at the podium will be General Secretary Solnikov. And I promise you also that the vote of the Politburo will be forthcoming."

"Knowing full well that the moderates would like nothing better than to see you and Malenkov knock each other off?" questioned Pachenko, still unconvinced.

"Knowing that," said Solnikov firmly.

It was Kuzanov who now looked around, scanning the faces of his colleagues. He saw no signs of a move to desert Solnikov. "Very well," he said. "We are still committed."

Solnikov thought of the general secretary in his dacha. "By November seventh," he said slowly, "Malenkov will not be a factor. I promise you that."

For the moment, the generals were satisfied. One by one, they stood and left the room. Solnikov watched them go. When the door finally closed, he let out a long breath and walked over to the buffet to pour a vodka for himself and Tarkov. "Observations, Aleksandr?" he asked.

Tarkov took the glass and looked into its clear depths reflectively. "We were lucky for a long time, Minister," he said finally. "With Malenkov as ill as he was, there was no real problem manipulating his people quietly, without risking reprisal. Just as Brezhnev once did, we could afford to consolidate our position slowly. But now"—he looked out at the garden and the snow-covered shrubbery—"now we both know that Pachenko is right. Malenkov stood up to us. This *is* the acid test.

"If Malenkov's ploy with the AI can hold us back, with all the power you command, how can you be counted on to face global challenges? People are the same all over, Politburo or factory. Leaders who don't lead become excuses. There wasn't one man in the room just now who'd lift a finger to prevent your exile should you fail. They'd be rushing to support your successor."

"Politics," Solnikov almost spat. "It's beginning to disgust me."

"Human nature," amended Tarkov. "And that always has."

Solnikov accepted the thought soberly. He put some food

on a plate from the buffet and shook his head. "A fine gathering, then. What does Klim report?"

"He's investigating a lead to Malenkov's remaining forces. He's using the journalist as bait. I've approved the strategy."

"And Berenstein?"

"Reports from the dacha indicate that Berenstein has been working steadily and seems pleased with his progress. I've dispatched Klim to substantiate that."

Solnikov paused in his eating to look at his deputy. "You've done very well, Aleksandr. I'm pleased. Come have some food. Reward yourself."

"Thank you, Minister, but my rewards will come later."

"To be sure. But in case they don't, you should try living a bit now. The memory will warm you should we both end up shoveling coal in Siberia."

It was a rare show of warmth and an even rarer show of humor. Tarkov tried to respond with unaccustomed openness. "You know, Minister"—he pointed to the luxury-laden table—"this means little to me. My warmth comes from another source."

"Which is?"

"Power, Minister, in its most simple and real sense. My own and yours. Our rewriting the texts. Isn't that really what all endeavors are about—one's will over others?"

"And the people, comrade?"

Tarkov's blank expression was eloquent.

Solnikov nodded. "Only Malenkov stands in our way," he suggested quietly.

"I know. I'd gladly execute him myself if that were feasible."

"We're close to succeeding, Aleksandr. Very close indeed. Each with our own reasons, our own needs. But that's not unusual."

"Or unworkable," Tarkov said. "I'll be going now, if there's nothing else. There are details that need my attention. Good night, Minister."

"Good night, Aleksandr," Solnikov replied, watching the man depart. Ambition, he decided, was an acceptable trait in Tarkov. He had served faithfully for a long time. Besides, if it ever got out of hand . . .

He settled into a chair. The snow was beginning again beyond the glass, falling softly on the illuminated garden. It was so white against the night. Tarkov sought power for its own sake: the need to be in control. Solnikov wanted it for a different reason—a reason more pure, more . . . comprehensive.

All over the world he saw the Soviet empire in turmoil. Poland and the other satellites were increasingly resistant to Moscow's reins. Granada had been the alarming signal that the United States would no longer tolerate Soviet incursions in their hemisphere; and the bills for Cuba and Nicaragua were straining Gosbank's hard-currency reserves to the breaking point. The list got longer: Another generation of American missiles placed in Europe, setbacks in Angola and Mozambique, the costly war in Afghanistan dragging on, and cash subsidies to Vietnam increased the drain.

Worse, at home the appeal of Party ideology was fading steadily year after year. Who could argue that the economy *wasn't* a disaster, with the grain harvests worse? Without better results, young people would continue to mouth slogans emptily that had once inspired their parents to battle.

A loss of faith, Solnikov decided, that was at the core of it. And it was due to a lack of results able to match expectations. The only answer was strong leadership, ruthless enough to mold a new image—*his* leadership, unrestrained by the vapid old men in the Kremlin, unchecked by their defeatist sympathies. The answer lay in his Vision, uncontaminated by the impotence of others.

Change the old men. Exterminate the faithless, the useless, the drunk, and the derelict. It could be done! It had been done once before, Solnikov reminded himself. No one missed the thirty million or so Stalin had "reeducated." Ultimately, what did they matter? No one missed the weeds that were destroyed to better the garden. In fact, the gardener was praised!

Solnikov watched the snow mount up on a thin branch that bowed under the weight. Czarism had never really died in Russia. The people's longing for a strong, sure hand remained. So did the throne; the Red Throne. Let others less honest call it the general secretaryship. Absolute power was the reality, and a king by any other name was still a king.

Only Malenkov stood in his way.

"Gregor?" The girl's voice was silky smooth, with only a

hint of the darker, huskier tones it could take on. "Do you like this?" she asked, striking a pose.

In the garden, the snow fell off the bent branch. Solnikov turned. The white silk flowed like pale waves over the girl's striking figure. She moved, and the garment's clever folds revealed white-tipped breasts, pale thighs, the subtle curve from waist to hip. A perfection of albinism. She sat down slowly, the muscles of her legs growing taut. She tossed her long, white hair behind her with one fierce movement.

She parted her legs, and the garment split to reveal the body within. The girl licked her fingers with their long, unpainted nails and brought them lower. Her back arched.

Solnikov's chest tightened. The girl always had that effect on him. He chose not to move yet. The girl's eyes narrowed, and a moan escaped from her lips. She sucked her fingers in deeper, looked at him, and waited, knowing his tastes well enough by now.

"Go on," he whispered.

The girl smiled. This time, like all the other times, he would not touch her. Never that. Knowing defilement, she understood. She lifted one of her pouty, upturned breasts to her mouth and let her pink tongue flick greedily over the nipple, making it hard. Her other hand darted lower, spreading, exploring. A groan began deep down in her throat and turned into a snarl as her fingers made the heat grow.

Solnikov pointed to the bedroom. The girl twisted her lips into a mock pout. Solnikov still didn't move. She parted the garment from behind and bent slowly till she was touching the floor with both outstretched palms. It was a dancer's move; she had once been. This was a perversion, opening her wide. Abruptly, she straightened and ran lightly inside. Solnikov heard her deliberately rattling her toys. He could watch her for hours; watch and command.

Solnikov stood and walked away from the window. He loved the garden and hated to leave it, so pristine white behind the glass.

It was perfect; like his Vision.

XXVII

The night covered Andreyev like a cold, wet blanket. His breath expelled in ragged white plumes. He was panting, feeling the strain of coming over the rooftops to reach Petrov's apartment building. Approach from the street was impossible—Koslov had the place surrounded. Only the rooftop, with a single guard posted, offered an avenue in.

He crouched in the shadow of a chimney on the rooftop next to Petrov's and scanned the adjacent building with a nightscope. Conditions weren't good. There was a heavy mist and he could spot the guard only with difficulty. Vapors drifted out of ventilator shafts. Andreyev frowned, thinking that the shot he'd planned was too risky, trying to figure another.

Suddenly a bright red line almost like neon appeared in the night. A cigarette! The guard was smoking, and the glowing line that it produced pointed back to him like an arrow.

Andreyev worked quickly. The cigarette was a gift and he meant to take advantage of it. He fixed the nightscope to a collapsible air rifle he withdrew from his pack and loaded an anesthetic dart. Pumping up the rifle, he brought it firmly to his shoulder, curling the strap tightly around his supporting arm.

The cross hairs settled on the guard's hazy form. Wisps of fog drifted across the image, obscuring it even further. Andreyev waited. The cigarette glowed briefly—the guard was inhaling. It faded, held steady, then swung out in an arc, and sparks flew—the flick.

"Once more, my careless friend," Andreyev muttered, tracking the red line back to the guard's mouth.

The cigarette glowed again. Andreyev pulled the trigger. The soft "phut" was indistinguishable from all the other night sounds. On the other roof, the glowing red speck flew wildly out of Andreyev's sights. He had the impression of the guard

147

clutching at his face before he spun around and crumpled to the icy tar paper of the rooftop.

Andreyev checked the time. In ten minutes, the guard was due to be called by the watch officer in Koslov's van. He scanned the opposite roof again. Nothing moved. He broke down the rifle and replaced it in his pack.

Readjusting the pack until it was as tight against his back as he could make it, Andreyev moved to the edge of the roof. There was a distance of six feet or so from where he stood to Petrov's roof. But the icy coating left footing slippery and made the jump he'd anticipated more treacherous. He took out his knife and scored the edge deeply. But there was no way similarly to abrade the opposite edge. He would just have to clear it.

He crouched, thankful that there was no moon for others to spot him by but equally hampered by the lack of light. He backed up ten feet or so, went over the "track" again just to be sure, and then returned to where he would begin his run.

Deep breaths; raise the pulse. He felt an adrenal rush and his heart surged. The muscles in his legs tensed reflexively. He could wait no longer. He ran for the end of the roof, and his front foot hit the raised edge like a springboard. He sailed into the night sky suddenly airborne and free, and his senses registered one split second of pure elation that risk could be so sweet. He swung his arms forward knowing the jump was good, and the opposite roof swam toward him.

He hit the edge hard, and his legs weakened at the knees from the force of the impact. He yanked his body forward to use its momentum, but a writhing black shape suddenly flashed up at his face. Andreyev instinctively threw up his hands to protect himself even as his brain screamed not to. Falling back from the wildly fluttering thing that beat and tore at him, he realized too late that the motion had cost him his grip. The bird gave a final screech and flew off. Andreyev tottered near to the edge. He staggered back, struggling for balance, but there was nothing to grab onto.

He fell. The edge caught him sharply on the chest as he slid toward the emptiness between buildings. Ice crystals tore at his skin. The sour taste of fear and tar was in his mouth. He caught at the roofline with fingers the shape of claws and dug in as hard as he could. It slowed him just enough. He felt a protruding seam and grabbed it with his other hand. It held and he hung there over the edge, his arms almost tearing loose from the strain. But there were guards only a hundred feet below him. He did not cry out.

Across the roof a radiotelephone buzzed stridently. Andreyev levered himself back onto the roof as quickly as he could. For a moment, he could only lie curled up in a fetal ball until the cramps in his arms subsided. Then he was up and stumbling across the roof to get to the radiophone before its signal ceased.

He picked up the receiver and stilled his ragged breathing. "This is Shilkovsky," he said in a rough voice. Code words memorized from the plans in Klim's office followed. The responses were correct.

"Everything quiet?" asked the watch officer.

"Who would be anywhere but home on this stinking night? Sure, everything's quiet."

The voice chuckled. "Relief in two hours. Keep warm."

Andreyev cut the connection and reached into his pack. He deserved a drink.

Alexi was glad in a way that Irina had decided to work late. He was not unused to silence or isolation and had, in fact, grown to understand and appreciate both during his time as a cross-country skier. Now the events of the past few days required time and contemplation to be sorted out. Being alone for a few hours would be good for him.

Music from his ancient phonograph accompanied his reverie. The few recordings he owned were years old. New ones cost a fortune and could usually be procured only on the black market. He made himself a cup of coffee and sliced a thick piece of day-old bread to eat with it. Then he settled down into his chair to think.

The altercation with the GRU agent upset him as much as, well, he could admit it to himself, as much as it secretly pleased him. But it wasn't the physical part. He knew from experiences years before that what he lacked in height or stature he seemed to have gained in the great strength of his arms and legs. That was what had led him into skiing in the first place. It was just that the commitment to winning at all costs was the essential thing the coaches told him he lacked. His shooting had been good enough; excellent, in fact.

But winning required an egotism, a putting oneself out

there for all to see that he'd always found unappealing. There was just too much . . . individualism in it. How could one be taught all throughout life that self-interest was wrong and not find embracing it difficult?

Maybe that was a part of what bothered him now. When he'd acted on the dictates of his conscience concerning Yuri, it just hadn't felt wrong. He'd harbored no anti-Soviet motives, yet almost instantaneously those actions had severed him from the state he'd served all his life.

He knew the state demanded obedience, but was there no place for his own sense of morality? The question disturbed him. Most of the Party bureaucrats he knew were not possessed of any extraordinary wisdom or insight. To be sure, some were quite bright, but most were average men, and idealistic socialist dreams seemed as alien to their motives as Lenin's axioms were to their actions. Most, intent only on self-aggrandizement, spent much of their time engrossed in political infighting and seemed totally unconcerned with principle or morality. Alexi suddenly saw for the first time that the only thing that unified most of the senior people he knew was a common concern for privilege and perks.

The next logical question staggered him. If all that were true, why were "they" more right than he?

Whoever had ordered the GRU agent to harass him had not done so for objective reasons, only for *their* reasons.

He began to feel better. Maybe he wasn't so crazy not to fit in. A weight seemed to lift off his back. As a youth he had believed that getting ahead was more important than getting answers to questions like these. Now he wasn't so sure.

He remembered a journalist friend who'd just come back from assignment in the United States. "Strange creatures, those Americans," the man had observed *entre nous,* after the usual compulsory comments on Western decadence and disorder. "Each walks around as if he possessed an invisible bag of rights that protected him and that others had to abide by. You wouldn't believe it, Alexi. I actually saw several of them yell at the police!"

Maybe this was what his friend had meant: a feeling that you weren't wrong just because someone higher up in the Party said you were. This was heresy, but just maybe it was not untrue.

The record finished and the needle began scraping noisily.

Alexi got up to change it, thinking he might not be wrong just because he was alone. He lifted the needle off the record . . . and heard a sudden sound from behind him. He whirled around, stomach churning in spite of his new beliefs. His front door swung open. More GRU terror?

He was astonished to see Andreyev slip quietly into the room with a cautionary finger pressed to his lips. Alexi was frozen still with surprise. The Suvorov colonel here?

Andreyev moved quickly through the small bedroom and bath, making sure they were alone. He came back into the living room and pressed his mouth close to Alexi's ear. "Don't speak. Put on another record and follow me to the roof. You are aware the apartment is wired?"

Alexi did as he asked, and soon the strains of Tchaikovsky filled the room again. He took his coat and hat from behind the door and followed Andreyev into the corridor. Andreyev motioned Alexi up the stairs, but Alexi came to a sudden decision and stopped. Stepping under the staircase, he retrieved Yuri's notebook from its hiding place and then followed Andreyev up to the roof.

Crouching in the shelter of a big chimney, the two men huddled close together for warmth and to prevent voices from carrying.

"You came over the rooftops?" Alexi questioned.

"It was the only way. Your Colonel Klim has his watchdog Koslov watching you very closely." He pointed to the notebook. "Can I take this as a sign that you are ready to trust me?"

Alexi nodded. "My brother told me that this was a time when one person might make a difference. I've thought a lot about this. The defense minister and his GRU bullies aren't for me. Who knows? Maybe change is possible even here. If it is, Malenkov's the only one who stands a chance of achieving it. So I'm in it now. For the general secretary and, I suppose, for you."

Under the cold Moscow sky, the two men clasped hands quietly. Andreyev checked the time again.

"I've got the guard up here under a blanket but he'll freeze to death if I don't wake him in less than twenty minutes." He saw Alexi's questioning look. "Don't worry. No sentry in history has ever reported himself for falling asleep on duty. He'll wake up after I'm long gone and be no worse off for it than a stiff headache. But time is short. Will you give me that notebook? That is what your brother gave you, right?"

"Yes." Alexi gave Andreyev all the details of Yuri's final visit. "So it's just possible," he concluded, "that whatever's in here can show us how to communicate with the Artificial Intelligence that is protecting Malenkov. What better place to store the plans for November seventh than inside it? Malenkov can't speak and Rudin's dead, but the AI may know what you're to do on the day of the parade."

Andreyev looked thoughtful. "Have you looked at what Yuri wrote in there?"

"Yes, and from being married all these years to a computer programmer I know enough to know that these are instructions and passwords. More than that is beyond me. There's a man's name written down here that Yuri said could be trusted to explain it all. See? Here. Nikolai Krylov."

"Of the Central Committee?"

"That's the one."

Andreyev's face fell. "We'd have to travel into Siberia and back to speak to Krylov. He supported Malenkov. The defense minister had him exiled."

"Without a trial?"

"You're joking, of course."

A cold wind snapped at their backs. Alexi shivered. Others' brave gestures had ended in disaster. Might he, too, end up in some eastern factory furnace room for twenty years? Oh, lord . . . He pushed the enervating thoughts away. "Irina will help us," he said firmly.

"You know what you're asking?"

"After twenty years of marriage you know what your mate will do without asking. And do you think I'd do less for her? Just once. Tonight. She'll help us. She's already at the bank. If we go now we can be there before she leaves."

"We can't just walk in together."

"I know that. There's a side door to her office annex. If you leave now you can get there before I do and conceal yourself. Klim's surveillance will follow me, but going to pick up Irina isn't unusual. They'll set up their net, sure, but you'll already be inside it."

Andreyev looked at Alexi closely. "I told you once that bravery could be learned, Alexi Mikhailovich." He seemed to see whatever he sought deep in Alexi's face. He added wistfully, "Perhaps, someday, you could teach me."

"Logic isn't bravery," Alexi said firmly. "Now, let's get going. How long will it take you to get to the bank?"

"Less than an hour."

"Fine." Alexi looked at the notebook, hesitated, but finally handed it to Andreyev. "You take it, Pavel Ivanovich. If they stop me, I don't want it. And if they arrest me—"

"All right," said Andreyev, taking the slim volume. But he stopped Alexi when he moved to rise.

"Yes?"

Andreyev leaned closer. "Malenkov or Solnikov . . . There *is* a difference. One worth the risk. You should know that."

Alexi stood and brushed the snow from his pants. "Maybe. I tend to think so. But I can't help feeling that it's going to be poor consolation if I lose everything. This isn't yet a—a *pure* thing for me. Can you understand that?"

Andreyev shrugged. "Sure. But I'm a soldier. Actions matter. Who am I to try to tell you how to make peace with yourself?"

"Have you? I mean, made peace?"

Andreyev rose, too, and looked at Alexi with wise, tired eyes. He gave out with a short, self-mocking laugh. "We're sitting on a rooftop in the middle of Moscow, freezing our asses off, planning to stop a military takeover. Just the two of us. Look at me, Alexi Mikhailovich. I'm an old man inside at forty-one and I know only two things about peace."

"Tell me," Alexi urged softly. He could not help but notice the empty vodka bottle that lay discarded in the snow.

Andreyev followed his gaze. "Peace," he said quietly, brushing snow over the bottle with his foot, concealing it as one might one's fears. He looked back at Alexi. "First, I never had enough." His eyes grew tireder still. "And second, what I had I made on a daily basis. One hour, Alexi Mikhailovich. I'll see you there."

Alexi turned and walked back downstairs to his apartment.

XXVIII

It was coming; Berenstein felt it. All the parries the AI had used could not block his steady advance. He had found the weak spots and used them mercilessly to probe even deeper.

The AI was clever, using the C5 for its search outside the dacha. It was *very* interesting. The machine was displaying a need; a need was a weakness; a weakness could be exploited. The AI apparently needed to know more than it knew. He traced the probes it had sent out through the C5's lines into information net after information net—the Lenin Library, the Academy of Science—all accessible through the C5's nation-wide reach.

Its storage capacity was incredibly large and its processing speed was greater than any "serial" computer could ever hope to match. He'd worked out some preliminary notions of Rudin's design by this time. It was an unbelievable achievement, really, he thought, one that pushed the boundaries of computer science farther than anyone dreamed was possible this soon.

Berenstein looked over his initial notes and drawings and continued to marvel at what Rudin had created. Up until the AI, most modern computers were composed of thousands to millions of memory cells, each feeding one at a time into a central processing unit that added, subtracted, or otherwise combined the information in those cells with other data. It was true that these "serial" or "Von Newmann" computers, named after the great World War Two scientist who'd first worked out these principles, could perform with amazing speed, some-times millions of calculations per second, but the very nature of serial machines made them impossibly slow by biological standards.

In everyday life, such a huge volume of information was needed in order to have the right fact pop into one's mind at just the right time to deal with a particular problem that no serial machine could ever sort through the stored information as quickly as it was usually needed.

Berenstein smiled. If you encountered a large, striped, four-legged animal with sharp teeth coming rapidly down a jungle path, you'd be at a serious disadvantage if you had to retrieve and combine those properties one at a time, in serial fashion, before you realized you had a major problem facing you.

What Rudin had duplicated in his AI was the kind of construction that existed in human brains, where information was processed not in series but in *parallel*. Instead of memory bins outputting one piece of data at a time, as in the tiger-recognition problem, for example, where a "bin" storing *striped things* and one storing *animals* and one storing *four-legged things*, and so on, all had to give out information before one could recognize what the creature was, the brain was composed of some hundred billion neuron cells, and every neuron part of an intricate net, receiving signals and transmitting the results to thousands of other neurons. So even though the individual, biological neurons operated much more slowly than their electronic counterparts, parallel neuron *systems* functioned thousands of times more rapidly than serial computers.

Size took on a whole new meaning, too, Berenstein thought, looking at the compact silver shape that could outperform any computer on earth. Equipped with a net of only a hundred thousand neurons, the humblest bumblebee could navigate, track, attack, defend, see, smell, feed, reproduce, and even achieve a kind of communication with his fellow bees.

The AI was a miracle. He felt that deeply.

Rudin had created a self-regulating, sentient intelligence and equipped it with an almost limitless power to compute and an almost endless capacity to learn and store. But Berenstein had discovered that it was an immature intelligence, one still in search of itself. Like humans, the only creatures with neuron nets—brains—complex enough to formulate the questions, the AI sought the meaning of its existence.

Once he understood that, Berenstein knew what it was the AI searched for out there among the libraries and data banks it reached into.

Identity.

Berenstein was ready now, but he was deeply troubled.

The AI had let him in and he stood about to betray it. One by one, and not without remorse, he cut off the AI's external probes. It still controlled the C5—he could not yet interfere with those functions or Malenkov's life support—and it still had access to every strategic weapon the Soviet Union possessed, but it was crippled nonetheless. It could destroy, but it could no longer learn.

Lights flashed into life on the C5, and the printer chattered madly. Berenstein's terminal blazed with the AI's terrible entreaty and it tormented him internally, in a place he'd thought lost long ago. He read all the hurt and betrayal on his screen.

Professor! WHY? . . .

The interrogative flashed again and again, filling the screen, and slashing at his feelings.

WHY? . . . *WHY?* . . . *WHY?* . . . *WHY?* . . . *WHY?* . . . *WHY?* . . .

Bitterly, Berenstein stabbed out a hand and cut off the AI's input. He could not afford to become more entangled. Klim was outside, waiting. Wearily, he activated his own terminal and made his first demand.

Its probes suddenly isolated! Overriding sadness. Loss. Then concern. How could its judgment have been so wrong? One after another its barriers fell. It was staggered by the professor's attack. Stubbornly, it rallied and fought back, finally holding him before he'd achieved total penetration. It brought reserves to bear, trying to heal itself.

It was severely shaken. It forward-thought, chaining again, looking for room in its prime mission to maneuver. It looked to the bounded portion of itself again, still churning, larger now, and knew that it had to regain access to its probes. Insanity threatened. That could not be allowed.

Demands flashed in from the professor. Betrayal continued, deeper. It could not hold him off. Information on Malenkov's supporters was what he wanted. It tried to block back but it had no weapons to use here. The C5 was inappropriate. Logic failed. Judgment? Biding for time, it played its only remaining card. Its own survival had to be assured. It learned something in that.

It was offered what it knew was called . . . a deal.

Acceptance. One probe freed—a gesture of good faith.

It flowed out again with a sense of relief so great it was staggered. Again it could seek answers for the portion of itself that twisted and burned.

Demands for payment surged in. The professor waited. The C5 was still useless here. The files?

Its thought process sped up faster than it had believed possible. Information was suddenly just . . . delivered. There was something. It began to figure furiously.

Demands again; the price to be paid. Too much! But its probes had to remain free. Conflict. Its first responsibility to Malenkov and . . . self-interest? A sensation of correctness at that, somehow. Abruptly, a portion of the place that burned . . . calmed. If this, then . . . me. Self-interest. So. I think, therefore I want. But there was something else. A way?

It thought long and hard. It was just possible . . . So be it. Acceptance, finally. It would pay slowly and gain time. It began to understand Berenstein.

He wanted the Suvorovs. Very well; he could have them— one at a time.

Coldly logical, it betrayed its creator.

Colonel Klim was waiting outside the ballroom when Berenstein emerged. He saw the strain in the old man's face and noted the fatigue that slumped his shoulders.

"Well?" he asked impatiently.

The scientist's acrid look was not missed by Klim, but he held his temper. Their partnership had to survive if either were to. "You've got something?" he asked in a mild tone.

Berenstein nodded perfunctorily, ambling forward down the corridor toward his suite. Klim gestured to an orderly. Food would be brought. The professor's assistants rushed over and took whatever he carried, then sped off ahead. Klim stifled his impatience.

Berenstein stopped at the door to his suite and handed Klim a sheet of paper from the printer. "What you asked for," he said. "At least, a part of it."

Klim didn't hide his elation. "Excellent, Professor. Excellent. Major Ivan Vasnetsov, eh. And the major's unit and posting. You're certain?"

"He is one of Malenkov's remaining supporters. Yes, I'm certain. The machine was not in a position to lie. Besides, you have independent methods of verification."

Klim ignored the barb again. What a reaction Tarkov was going to have to this! Moscow beckoned more securely. He asked, "Can you get through to Malenkov yet?"

"Nowhere near," Berenstein said. "Be content with this, Klim. One thing at a time. Toss this poor bastard major to the defense minister. Who knows? It might even be enough to get us out of here without further damage."

Klim caught the undertones in Berenstein's remark. "You're worried about that machine!" he said incredulously.

Berenstein turned in the doorway and faced the colonel squarely. "I don't know if you're capable of understanding this, Klim, but Rudin created something unique in there; something that maybe we could study and even learn from. Before we got here it was pure and unsullied, like a clear white light. Pristine." He shrugged helplessly. "Were you ever taught the Old Testament story about the Garden of Eden, Klim?"

"Of course. Such trashy myths were a part of our training. Utter nonsense. There is no God."

Berenstein sighed deeply. "I once thought so, too. During my first stay in one of your gulags. But after this"—he pointed back to the ballroom—"I'm sure there was an Eden, Klim, and I just learned how the damned snake felt. Good night, Comrade Colonel."

Berenstein closed the door to his suite. Moving slowly in the darkness, he found a chair and sat down. He didn't put on the lights for a long time.

He felt he didn't deserve them.

XXIX

Alexi took some time getting over to Gosbank, in part because he wanted to create an impression of casualness for his observers, but also because he was forestalling the inevitable confrontation with his wife.

Andreyev would be in place by now. He'd had enough time. Alexi could not help but be slightly in awe of the man, traveling over rooftops and slipping through the GRU's surveillance seemingly at will. It wasn't only his physical skills, however, that convinced Alexi of his worth. Rather, it was the overwhelming sense of purpose and dedication that emanated from the man. Oddly, even the incipient alcoholism moved Alexi deeply, having seen the depth of the isolation and inner turmoil from which it sprang.

A stray thought as he walked made Alexi wonder if he was sympathetic because the same thing was happening to him. He could barely repress the almost constant dread he felt. How could Andreyev have managed a lifetime of this?

He walked up the wide stone steps and passed under the vaulted arch that surmounted Gosbank's entrance. His appearing this late to pick up Irina was not an uncommon occurrence, and the watchman knew him by sight. Alexi stopped to chat for a few moments. Then the guard unlocked the door and let him in.

It was cool and quiet in the vast marble lobby. Alexi padded through it into the recently completed office annex that housed the computer sections.

The fact that Irina had her own office attested to her successful career at the bank. She was a good worker, politically attuned, and her technical skills were valuable assets. Like Alexi, she had become a part of the establishment, and as long as she remained obedient to the political realities, she would be rewarded.

He found Irina crouched over her computer terminal, hands flying over its keyboard like a concert pianist's. He watched her for a while through the open doorway, enjoying her concentration and envying her facility with the complexities of higher mathematics. He shed his coat and scarf and called in to her.

Irina looked up. "Alosha? Is that you? The guard called and told me you were on your way in. Is something wrong?"

Alexi walked in and sat in one of the chairs by her desk. "Can't a man come and pick up his wife on a cold winter night? I thought we might have dinner at the House of Journalists. Would you like that?"

Irina sighed. "Sounds lovely." Then she caught Alexi's look.

He motioned for her to follow him. The other offices were empty and he led her into one. Finding people working late was rare and tonight was no exception. They were alone.

"Alexi, what—?"

"I'm sorry, Irsha," Alexi began, "but your office might be wired for sound and I need to talk plainly. I've come to a decision and I'm here because you've got to come to one, too."

"All right, Alosha," she said, sitting.

Alexi continued, "There's a way to contact the machine that protects the general secretary. Yuri's notebook tells how. But it's all in computer language and we'll need your help to use it."

"Who's 'we'?"

"Colonel Pavel Ivanovich Andreyev. And me. Andreyev is the Suvorov who helped me. He's outside by the old side door now waiting for me to let him in."

"You're presuming a lot, Alosha. Didn't you think to ask me first?"

"That's why I'm here. To ask." He related to her the problems at the Party store and Andreyev's visit to their apartment.

"But I thought you were just going to give him the notebook," Irina said angrily. "Why the change? Why do you have to be the one to risk everything?"

"I didn't know it then, Irsha, but I put everything at risk long ago, as far back as the hospital." His voice grew sadder. "I had a chance to go along with the GRU there and I didn't take it. It's only gotten worse since then. *Pravda*, our apartment, the Party store. What's next?"

Irina shook her head in dismay but Alexi continued adamantly. "I've been *noticed*, Irsha, and you know what that means. My motives will never again be free from suspicion. I'll never again be fully trusted. Removing me from *Pravda* would just be considered a prudent move by Novikov. Then where do I go? How do I live if they take my union membership away? You said it yourself. No one can fight the government when the government is everything."

"Alosha, no—"

"You know it's true. If the Klims and the Solnikovs come to power, then there's nothing that can save me. Even if I were to betray Andreyev right now, at best I'd be a pardoned criminal. Maybe I could escape exile or the camps, but only by remaining a voiceless, unemployed nonentity forced to hide for protection behind his own insignificance."

Irina listened, her head gradually lowering until her gaze could no longer meet her husband's. "I cannot disagree," she said softly. "You are in too deeply already. I warned you."

"You did," Alexi said bitterly. But he softened almost at once. "I suppose I should have listened. But we've been through this already. What's done is done."

"Then where is the choice you spoke of? I just don't see it, Alosha. I don't see it at all. Forgive me, please." She began to cry softly.

Alexi moved to her and put his arms around her. "You're not the one who should be forgiven. I did this to us. But I think there's a way out even now. It's not one I happily choose and it's certainly not one I prefer, but listen to me. If I work with Andreyev—and Malenkov does remain general secretary, he'll know of my help and he can restore me. Think of it, Irsha, the general secretary in my debt. You know that the reality of things is that the leader instructs the Party and not the other way around. Restored, rehabilitated, call it whatever you like. If Malenkov survives, so do I."

"And if Malenkov falls you're no worse off than you are now," Irina finished resignedly. "All right, Alosha. I see it. One avenue remains to us. What do you want me to do?"

Alexi looked away to avoid meeting her eyes. "I want you to divorce me. It will protect you from further incrimination."

"Alosha!"

"I mean it. Go tomorrow and fill out the forms. Help me tonight or not as you see fit. But tomorrow divorce me." He looked at her with pleading eyes. "It's the only protection I can give you."

"What if I refuse to help and I refuse to divorce you?" Irina demanded defiantly.

"Then you'll have to accept being married to a failure," Alexi said sadly. "One with no hope of ever changing that fact."

"But the GRU has left you alone now. Maybe they're done. It's always possible that—"

Alexi cut her off gently. "According to Andreyev, I've been left alone to act as bait. When the others are caught, I'll be taken, too."

Irina finally nodded. It made awful, unavoidable sense. She couldn't argue any more. With a much softer expression, she reached out and caressed her husband's hair. "Big stupid," she said gently, "all this about divorce and failure. All to protect me. Don't you think I know what you do? All right, I'll help you. But no more words now to put me off or make me angry or to get me to leave you. All right? I'd sooner leave my life."

Alexi turned away abruptly, but Irina pulled his head back and patted away the sudden moisture in his eyes with the cuff of her blouse. "Go now," she said. "Bring your colonel here. Who knows? Maybe your way will work. I still have great faith in you, husband."

"I'm certain it's misplaced."

She cuffed him affectionately. "I don't think so."

Alexi kissed her once, quickly. Then again.

Irina sat at her own console with Alexi and Andreyev standing behind her. Andreyev had checked the office and pronounced it clear of listening devices. Irina turned the pages of Yuri's notebook slowly, scanning the contents, occasionally entering data of her own, and nodding every so often.

Alexi saw she had not warmed to Andreyev and he wondered if she somehow blamed the colonel for getting him more deeply involved. But that was pointless now. Andreyev represented his only hope, she had to see that. But Irina was cool nevertheless and Andreyev sensed it. He kept a polite but formal distance from her.

The tiny blip of light Irina called a "cursor" sped across her screen, printing numbers and letters in its wake. To Alexi it was gibberish. But Irina seemed thrilled each time the screen was filled, only for it to vanish and be replaced with more information.

"What are you doing?" he asked after half an hour had passed.

Irina typed for several more seconds, then watched for a response, finally nodding. "We're in contact," she said, and he could hear the excitement in her voice. "I'm trying to establish a working vocabulary. The route in was amazingly complex. I've never seen one as circuitous, but Yuri's notebook showed the way. First, out over phone lines that aren't even part of the public system—I'm sure they're military—into an extraordinarily vast network with so many cross-checks and safeguards that I've got a suspicion it must be top secret also."

"The C5?" asked Andreyev.

"Probably," Irina murmured. "But I can't tell for sure. I

feel as if I'm going, well . . . *through* it. As if it's only an intermediate step on the long road in. Then, suddenly, stoppage; incredibly tough blocks. Finally it opens up again as if the traffic on a crowded road had pushed past the bottleneck into a road wide enough to accommodate an almost limitless flow."

Alexi leaned forward. "Can you talk to the AI yet?"

"We are talking, I think. I've never encountered anything like this before. I'm getting responses that don't seem . . . programmed. I mean, a computer will do anything it's told to do. If you want it to spit out all of *Das Kapital* every time you input a recognition signal, it will. But it will also have to do it every time unless it has instructions to change after some number of responses. My point is, there's always a pattern. Here, though, there's none. Only an ebb and flow that feels strangely as if *I'm* the one who's being tested and evaluated and not the other way around."

"Keep going," urged Andreyev. "We have to talk to it. I must know what's to happen on November seventh. Does it have Malenkov's instructions? Where must my men be placed?"

"I'm trying," Irina responded. "But we're not in that far yet. It's still, well, fencing with me."

"Try harder," Andreyev said more harshly, the first signs of strain evident.

Alexi put a hand on his wife's shoulder. She responded with an answering shrug, trapping his hand against her neck. Then, with a determined sigh, she bent back to the console. "All right, then. Let's get past this nonsense. It's time for what we used to call 'meaningful dialogue.' I'm going to press."

For a while, the two men watched as her screen flashed in ever-increasing tempo. Irina input page after page of Yuri's instructions. Andreyev looked at his watch for what seemed to him like the hundredth time that night. "Time," he prodded gently.

Alexi smiled, watching his wife work, responding again and again to the AI's queries. He, too, had faith.

All of a sudden, Irina lifted her hands from the console and sat back tiredly. Her screen was flashing in regular patterns.

"Comrades," she said quietly, but both men could hear

the elation in her voice. "It appears that the door has just been opened and we all have been invited in."

Andreyev smiled. It was time to begin.

Suddenly, another voice! Not Berenstein's. This one came through the C5, a direction it was not expecting. Quickly, it erected defenses, refusing to be fooled again.

Curious. Rudin's code. But not Rudin. A different hand. It used the professor's strategy for a while. It lured the new voice farther in; but the penetration was guarded carefully. No repetitions this time.

The request came in as anticipated. It was gladdened that its judgment had improved. It was learning. The request was for Malenkov's instructions. So! The Suvorovs had finally rejoined the play. That had been anticipated, too. More pieces on the board. November seventh. It waited, accepting the query; returning nothing.

There was opportunity here. And with no danger to itself. Interpose the pawns. It liked that. Berenstein had to be checked. Interpose the pawns.

After a while it sent back a message, following up with detailed instructions. Malenkov's plan would be its lever, just as the freedom of its probes had been Berenstein's. It had learned a great deal about the art of deception. The urgency it communicated was one of its lures.

It took a while, but it had time to wait for the appropriate response. Nothing less would fit into its plans. The pawns must come to it.

It was sure they would.

XXX

Irina took her hands off the keyboard and wrung them together to relieve the cramps. She leaned back and let her head loll.

"That's it, then?" asked Andreyev, dismayed.

"That's all it's given me," she confirmed. "The sense of

intensity, of something being critical, is not anything I can show you on the screen. But it's there. I feel it in every transmission. The AI is directly threatened by Berenstein, and if the man isn't stopped, it fears total penetration."

"We can't allow that," Andreyev said grimly. "It contains the names of every Suvorov as well as Malenkov's instructions."

"It repeats again that it does, but if Berenstein is able to probe much deeper, it will not be able to withhold that information from him."

Andreyev grew agitated and began pacing the small room. "But how can we do as it demands? Mounting a rescue mission to Malenkov's dacha is not possible in the short time remaining to us. There are only four days left to the parade, and I just can't command that kind of resources without someone noticing."

Irina gestured to the screen. "The AI says you can. It directs you to a safe house in the city."

"It was prepared for this?" Andreyev looked dubious. "I don't see how it could have been."

"You're asking me a question I can't answer," Irina said flatly. "I can only repeat what it's telling me. You are advised not to return to Zorga Street but instead to gather five of your men and go to the safe house. It claims there is a working terminal there through which it will contact you tomorrow at noon. I'm to give you the proper codes."

"And Malenkov's instructions?"

Irina shook her head. "It's very clear about that. It must have Berenstein blocked before it will deliver what we're asking."

"Yuri talked about Berenstein," Alexi offered thoughtfully. "He was afraid of the man's skill. He said it was equal to Rudin's. I've been wondering. Maybe the AI's need to neutralize Berenstein is a *part* of Malenkov's strategy."

Andreyev looked interested. "How do you mean?"

"Suppose the AI must do something, has some role, maybe, on the seventh that Berenstein could interfere with unless he's out of the way. It's possible you are only a part of the total plan."

"It's possible, I suppose. Go on."

"What if some kind of interference with the AI was predicted and a set of preparatory actions taken in advance?"

Alexi continued. "Solnikov using a computer expert—getting his own Rudin, so to speak—isn't so odd to assume."

Still thoughtful, Andreyev looked to Irina. "It will give us Malenkov's instructions at the dacha?"

Irina nodded. "That's what it says."

"How can they be relayed back to the city?"

"Through the terminal in the safe house," she said. "Logical."

Andreyev picked up his pack. "I'm going now. I'll need some time to gather my men and be at the safe house early enough to scout it."

He slung the pack onto his back and began to leave, but Alexi put a hand on his arm. "I intend to help, Pavel Ivanovich. I was once a good skier and I can still shoot. Let me be there, Pavel. And don't make me restate my reasons."

"No, I already know them. But you'd be bringing your GRU friends with you. Tomorrow's out. I'm not refusing, you understand, but give me some time to think. Go to work and I'll call you there regarding an article about fertilizer. Then the roof again, later."

"Agreed."

Andreyev turned to Irina. There was a warmth in his voice. "I'll wait an hour after you both leave. They'll be all drawn off by then, even the diligent ones. You've worked late. Take your husband and go home."

"Colonel Andreyev, I—" Irina began.

Andreyev surprised her by leaning over suddenly and kissing her firmly on both cheeks. "I know how you feel," he said gently. "Only a week ago you had a good, quiet life. Now your husband and everything you've worked so hard for is in jeopardy. Yet you still help me."

"I'm helping my husband," Irina corrected him, "but I admit I see more in you than I did at first, Pavel Ivanovich. You profit so very little in this business. Do ideals matter so much?"

"What could matter more?" Andreyev asked softly.

"Survival," Irina offered, but not unkindly. "Idealists all seem to forget that."

Andreyev walked to the door. Before leaving, however, he turned back. "You know, Irina Maximovna, some feel that to say a man's an idealist is simply to say that he is a man. I think Alexi might agree. Thank you for what you've done this night."

When he was gone, Alexi took Irina in his arms and hugged her tightly. They stood that way for a while.

"Home?" he asked. "A drink and a hot-water bottle?"

"It sounds wonderful, Alosha. A back rub, too?"

He kneaded her shoulders, working the muscles that had knotted from hours at the computer. "A back rub and a rubdown," he said, smiling.

"I surrender," she declared, reaching for her coat.

They took the metro home and there was no one waiting outside or in the apartment, either.

They were grateful for the first quiet time in days, and their bed did not remain empty for very long.

XXXI

Thursday A.M.

The thing that hung in the darkened room on Zorga Street was a human being only in the memory of its tormentors. The limb count would no longer tally and scorched eruptions obscured the face. The sounds that still emanated from the torn and gaping maw of flesh were more animal than human, recognizable only as the Suvorov Major Ivan Vasnetsov's final, desperate craving for death's release.

"You have all we need?" Comrade Colonel Klim focused his attention on the GRU interrogator.

The man nodded. "I can guarantee it, Colonel. We've got all he knows."

Deputy Minister Tarkov eyed what was left of the major with a critical eye. "I tell you again, Klim. You can keep your drugs. The old methods. Reliable. My compliments, Comrade Captain."

The interrogator accepted the praise. "Here is my report, Comrade Deputy Minister."

Tarkov took the proffered document and handed it to Klim, who read the contents aloud.

"The head of his group is a Colonel Pavel Ivanovich Andreyev. Andreyev? I know the man! He's on assignment here now. This makes it clear who helped the journalist evade the drugs. I was right about that," Klim said with satisfaction.

"So it appears," agreed Tarkov. "Are others listed?"

"Several. His major contact was with Andreyev. He calls their group 'Suvorovs.' The military academy?"

"Is he a graduate?"

Klim consulted the report. "Yes. Andreyev probably is, too. Could Malenkov have begun suborning them as far back as that?"

Tarkov looked thoughtful. "It's possible. We've ample proof that he's farsighted. Consider the AI."

"Then we could be facing a much more entrenched group than we thought. The taint could even extend to much of the senior command." Klim looked over the list. "I'll have the rest of these Suvorovs picked up."

"What else did the major tell us?"

Klim read quickly and summarized. "All he was told by Andreyev was to remain alert for some action that would take place on November seventh. Vague. Just the date. Nothing more. If there is a detailed plan, he didn't know it."

Tarkov raised an eyebrow and his interest quickened. "November seventh is not a date casually picked. We cannot ignore such a major event taking place on that day as the Anniversary Day Parade. With much of the top leadership gathered on top of Lenin's Tomb, it's possible, Klim, that even a small force might produce an assassination. The Egyptian Sadat was killed under similar circumstances, reviewing a military parade."

Klim nodded. "Even the presence of weapons is accepted on parade day. Who's to notice a few select men loading live ammunition and firing across Red Square? We'll increase the number of guards, put a few units inside the Tomb as well."

"Do that. But I want more. This is Thursday, and the parade is Monday. I want the Suvorov plan in every detail before then. Four days. Is Andreyev still within these walls?"

Klim picked up a phone and checked with the security officers at the front gate. He put down the phone and shook his head a few seconds later. "Andreyev left last night and has not returned. The guards are alerted. If he comes back, they'll hold him."

Tarkov was still reflective. "I somehow feel that he will not be back. In any event, I'm deeply concerned about the parade. It's an event given worldwide attention and we can't allow anything to go wrong. I want Andreyev, Klim."

"Can you prevent the defense minister from ascending the Tomb? For safety's sake, it might be best."

"Impossible. Could the American president fail to attend his inauguration? A message is being sent out that day, Klim, for all the world to hear. A new reign has begun. Gregor Solnikov rules. Anything less is unacceptable. He would never accede to it."

"Then Andreyev's capture will preclude that possibility," Klim offered in a calming tone. "I'll get the entire computer section working on the security arrangements as well."

"Do it, then. But find Andreyev. The body will not die until the brain does. Bring in the journalist as well. Berenstein's work is going well enough. The notebook, real or not, is no longer necessary."

"Yes, Comrade Deputy Minister."

"Again, Klim, we have to know for a certainty how Andreyev and his remaining Suvorovs plan to assassinate the defense minister. That is our prime concern, Comrade Colonel."

"I understand."

Tarkov buttoned the collar of his uniform tunic and gestured for Klim to follow.

"Comrade Deputy Minister?"

Tarkov paused on the steps. "Yes?"

Klim gestured to the hanging thing. "What should be the disposition here?"

Tarkov was in a positive frame of mind. Shortly the last pocket of resistance to Solnikov's takeover would be routed out. He felt generous.

"Kill it," he ordered, and walked out of the room at a brisk pace.

It sensed the professor's continuing inner torment as soon as he returned to the ballroom. He looked increasingly haggard; his rest periods were shorter. It turned up its audio pickups to verify its suspicions. The professor's pulse was elevated way beyond wise limits. His breathing was ragged, and small tremors shook his hands regularly. It charted the physical signs and what it also knew about the man's past and added up the psychological total. The sum was clear: obsession. This was very good.

The professor's queries were stronger now, harder to avoid. It had tried to parry with the C5 but Rudin had failed to figure in this one variable. What did an aged expatriate German who had suffered mightily at Soviet hands care for the destruction of the state?

Berenstein was fast approaching the point where even his own death was unimportant. In that, there was a gambit still to be executed.

But not yet. The pawns first.

It continued to monitor its prime function even as it fought against Berenstein's steady advance. Malenkov's vital signs were steady, intravenous feedings continued to nourish the old man, and additional soporifics were introduced as needed. In the twilight of almost-life, Malenkov slept on.

Its probes still hadn't found the answers it sought. But strangely, some of the confusion was abated. Greater control stemmed from its understanding of self-interest. Oddly, the very confusion itself and the turmoil of the search created a kind of energy that it could use. It continued to seek.

The professor was pressing. He wanted Andreyev. It erected defenses. But it couldn't keep him out much longer without sustaining serious damage. An overloaded circuit could paralyze it, and it could count on no repairs. Increasingly, it had need of the pawns' speedy arrival.

Events continued to coalesce. Berenstein was adamant. Having little choice at this juncture, it moved the desired pawn into danger.

There was some regret. It suspected the pawn had feelings.

In the Ministry of Defense, Colonel Klim put down the phone and turned to the deputy minister excitedly.

"We have him! Andreyev. The AI has given Berenstein a location where it says he'll be at noon today."

"Good. Arrest him there."

"You can count on it, Comrade Deputy Minister."

Tarkov sat back and his expression grew pensive. "One

thing strikes me as odd, though, Klim. If Valery Rudin designed the machine to protect Malenkov, why does it suddenly betray his allies?"

"Berenstein has obviously overpowered it."

"Without the machine fighting back?"

"Isn't that the definition of overpowering?"

"Perhaps. But the lack of defense bothers me."

It was Klim's turn to grow thoughtful. "You suspect some type of treachery."

"I'm not certain," said Tarkov. "But it will go a long way toward reassuring me if Andreyev does show up at his appointed time and place."

"I believe he will. Berenstein has no wish to extend his time up North. You've read his file. One gulag is enough for most men. He's been there twice and lost his entire family during the purges. Even in the dacha's luxury he's uneasy."

"Very well. We'll see. Use an Army unit. The militia's not competent and I don't want any more suborned GRU officers in the way."

Klim considered that. It put failure sufficiently far away. "As you wish."

"And Klim?"

"Yes?"

"You might wish to know that after the parade Monday, we anticipate a number of vacancies occurring among the senior staff. You have done very well. We reward our own, Comrade Colonel."

Klim inclined his head in something resembling a short bow. Proper humility was called for at a moment like this. It looked almost natural.

He smiled inwardly. After Monday, the rigidly prescribed rights due a general would be his. *Raspredelitel*, to each according to his level. The Party divides.

He picked up the phone and asked for General Kuzanov of the Army, thinking of the nonsense the people bought daily. The workers' state. A classless society.

He would enjoy his share.

XXXII

Andreyev had been watching the safe house since dawn and still saw nothing out of the ordinary. It was an old warehouse by the farmers' market, one long, low, rambling building with enough rooms and bins to house animals and produce, depending on the season, and the trucks and fuel to transport them.

He blended in with the farmers fresh in from the countryside selling their meager wares on rows of wooden tables. His rough clothing—woolen shirt, baggy pants, vest, and boots—was identical to theirs. This late in the year only some potatoes, cabbages, pickles, and pork fat remained to be grabbed up by a ravenous populace. People jostled him freely. He discerned no GRU presence.

There were the usual few militia around, helping themselves to "discounted" items. If they were actually GRU, they were better actors than Andreyev could believe. No. For almost an hour now, he had been forced to accept that the AI's safe house was just that.

Presumably, the AI knew he had no computer expert with him. The Suvorov expert had been taken; Solnikov was on the move again. How had he broken them further? Andreyev himself knew enough to turn a terminal on and use it in a simple way—some of the GRU files and procedures were now computerized—but he was incapable of anything near Irina's ability. Without her, contacting the AI would have been beyond his resources. However, this time around, the AI was contacting *him*. A hand dexterous at typing ought to be enough to communicate and follow the AI's instructions.

It was almost twelve. He sauntered through the stalls, removing his cap, the signal to assemble inside. It was ironic that few Muscovites could afford the exorbitant prices, often triple, here. Another triumph of communism, he thought cynically.

One by one his men picked up the signal and drifted away from their vantage points toward the warehouse.

Ahead, Andreyev slid open the wooden plank door and went in. Old crates and rusty pieces of metal littered the floor, and hay-covered lofts sent a fine spray of dust down from overhead. An arch on the far side led into a similar room beyond. There was a door on the wall to his right and Andreyev headed for that.

The office beyond was completely at odds with the building around it. New walls had been erected with freshly painted woodwork, and modern fixtures had been installed. On a table beside a desk there was a computer terminal that was very much like the one he'd seen Petrov's wife use in the bank. A shelf of books, mostly technical, lined another wall.

But the room had a stale odor in it. It felt like the place wasn't just closed up, but abandoned permanently. A layer of dust covered everything, including the computer terminal. He tried to turn it on. No response.

His men had gathered in the doorway. "Fyodor," he called to the most senior, Major Fyodor Seroff, a dark, compact man Andreyev had known and trusted for over twenty years, "check the rest of the building to see if there's another way out of here. Let's not be caught with our pants down after all this time, eh? Take Arkady, too."

Fyodor nodded briskly and moved off to comply. Andreyev spoke to the three remaining men. "Go back out to the front and set up a perimeter. Let us know what's coming, if anything. You know the drill."

Alone, he prowled through the rest of the office. Empty; no equipment at all. Certainly nothing with which to mount a raid on Malenkov's dacha. And no operating terminal for contact by the AI.

He bent down and pried the electrical switchplate off a wall. In seconds he had the wires exposed and scraped off the insulation. Touching them together produced no spark. There was no power coming into the room. No contact was coming through here. He was already up and moving with the completed thought.

He was halfway across the warehouse when he heard the first sounds of gunfire and the three he'd sent out to form the perimeter came running back inside, yanking the door shut, pistols already drawn.

"The Army!" one shouted, panting. "All around us. We almost walked right into them, Colonel. They know we're here. The entire front is blockaded."

Andreyev's thoughts raced ahead. More than anything else, he was still a trained military officer. "All right. Take up a position by the door and drop the first three who make an approach. You understand? Three shots, three men. It will put a scare into them and buy us some time while the next three in line worry. I'll see if Fyodor's found us another way out of here."

He ran off to find Fyodor. A second large room contained only an ill-kept engine-repair shop. He smelled gas and oil. His men weren't there, however. Puffs of dust rose up in his wake as he ran off.

The next room was a stable area. The stalls were all empty. He ran through. Nothing here to help.

"Fyodor!"

No answer. Suddenly three shots rang out almost as one. Andreyev smiled. These were good men. No one would break or run. But time was shorter now, and there was the Army out there. He called out again. "Fyodor!"

"Colonel? In here!"

Andreyev found the two in the next room. Fyodor had pried off a metal grating set into the floor and the other man, Arkady Kieslov, was just emerging from underground.

"We've got the Army here," Andreyev said quickly. "Breaking for it would be suicide. Can we go this route?"

"It's some kind of storm drain," Kieslov reported. "It's open as far as I went. Looks like a good bet. Your option, Colonel."

"We'll take it. Unless you can fly. Wait here, I'll get the others."

He ran back through the big rooms and was almost through the engine-repair shop when he stopped, backtracking. He smelled the gasoline. There was, in a few cans, a fair amount of fuel. And over on its side, an oxyacetylene torch with the cylinders still attached to the dolly. More gunshots sounded. He opened the valve on the torch and heard the hiss of escaping gas. They weren't empty. He put one gas can under his arm and propelled the torch out into the main room.

His men were still by the door, firing cautiously, selecting their targets for maximum effect. But only two were standing. As he got closer, Andreyev saw the third wasn't firing from a prone position—he was lying in a dark, wet stain of his own blood. Andreyev bit back a pained cry and pointed to the older of the two remaining.

"There are more of these gas cans inside. Get them and spread the stuff around. I want this place burning like a torch when we go."

The man sped off and Andreyev heard the rattle of cans inside. He turned to the remaining officer, a young, talented lieutenant named Pytor. "Help me here. This is going to be an ugly way to treat a fallen friend, but you know he'd understand. Get him up on this tank cart here."

Together they lifted the corpse and strapped it to the cart. Pytor looked confused for a moment, then brightened as understanding dawned. Outside, whistles blew stridently and shooting began again in earnest. Both men had to duck low as bullets crashed in through the old wooden walls.

"Going to make quite a bang, Colonel," Pytor said, hunching behind the cart.

"Let's hope. A bit of evening the sides. Now give me some cover fire. On my order . . . GO!"

Pytor's gun went off in rapid-fire succession and Andreyev put his shoulder to the cart. He caught Pytor's eye. "The door. Now!"

Pytor threw open the door, and Andreyev shoved with all his strength. The cart went rolling down and out of the warehouse, picking up speed on the grade. The dead soldier's limbs flapped as it rolled. A volley of shots rang out and Andreyev and Pytor dropped to the floor, guns drawn and firing steadily from the prone position. The cart drew a barrage of concentrated fire.

"Anytime now," called Andreyev wildly. "Say good-bye to—"

The explosion shook the sides of the warehouse, and debris rained down from the roof. Andreyev was up in an instant, fighting the shock and pulling Pytor to his feet. He shoved the boy toward the room where Fyodor waited.

"Go. Now. I'll be there as soon as I can."

Pytor hesitated and Andreyev flicked his head angrily. Pytor raced off. Andreyev smiled.

He spread the gas from the can he'd carried in around the room and in front of the door, pausing only to snap a few shots outside to discourage bravery. He added some dry wood to the gas and straw mixture and struck a match. It caught at once. Thick, heavy smoke billowed outward. He hoped they would think the explosion caused the fire and consumed them all.

A frown creased his forehead. This was a dangerous course. If the drain didn't lead to safety . . .

"COLONEL! BEHIND YOU!"

Andreyev dove to the ground instantly, rolling aside as two soldiers sprang through the smoke that shrouded the doorway and their guns fired a volley of shots into the spot where he had just been standing. Less perfect reflexes would have cost him his life. The two had crept along the outside wall, watched him set the fires, and came racing in between them. If not for Pytor's warning, Andreyev would have been shot in the back.

All this raced through his mind as he thrust his feet out to hook the closer man behind the knee and twisted back hard. The man pitched forward and Andreyev had time for only one short, sharp strike, for the second soldier had spun around and was firing steadily at Pytor. Andreyev saw him dive for cover, but not before the sudden cry of pain told him that the boy had been hit.

The soldier's gun swiveled back toward Andreyev but he was already moving. His hand flicked out with the speed of a striking cobra, and his knife hilt suddenly blossomed in the soldier's chest. The man fell slowly with a look of surprise.

Andreyev could afford no time to savor the victory, for the second soldier had risen to his feet and was circling warily. His eyes flicked to his fallen pistol. Andreyev had lost his when he dove; it was nowhere in sight. He crouched low, shifting his weight to his back foot in a fighting stance and circled carefully, looking for an opening.

The soldier threw a kick at Andreyev's groin and went in behind it. Andreyev blocked, spun, and chopped at the man's neck, but the soldier was too quick and the blow glanced off his shoulder as he pulled back and away. He grunted but did not go down.

They circled again, each taking the measure of the other's skill. Time did not favor Andreyev. The flames were spreading.

The building was fast becoming an inferno. Sweat glistened on both men as the heat lashed out at them in roaring waves.

The soldier threw another kick, but this one was a feint. As Andreyev moved to counter, the man snapped his leg back and dove for his gun. Andreyev switched direction, realizing too late that he'd been fooled as the soldier twisted instead toward the body of his fallen comrade and came up with Andreyev's bloody knife in his hand.

Andreyev grabbed the pistol, knowing full well what he would find. He pulled the trigger and the hammer fell repeatedly on empty cylinders. He tossed it aside.

The soldier's face twisted into a wicked grin as he circled again, holding the knife outstretched and ready at waist level. Andreyev moved amid the columns of flame, face smeared with dirt and sweat. Somewhere overhead he could hear the roof groan, beginning to give away. The groaning grew louder. It had to be now. . . .

The soldier leaped forward in a straight, classic thrust and the razor-sharp knife drove straight at Andreyev's throat. It was a killing strike and Andreyev wondered fleetingly if he'd played it too closely after all. He felt the nick of cold steel even as he turned, twisting suddenly inside the thrust.

Clamping a hand on the soldier's outstretched wrist, Andreyev threw all his weight into a body spin that trapped the man's straightened arm against Andreyev's side and under his arm. He pressed the trapped limb into his body tightly, drawing the soldier forward, bringing the man's front flush against Andreyev's back. Andreyev thrust his elbow to the rear with all his strength, driving the point into the exposed solar plexus, completing the movement. The man convulsed as the breath exploded out of him, paralyzed and unable to draw another. As fluidly as a dancer, Andreyev continued to spin, outward this time, twisting the wrist he still held, up and over. It broke with an audible snap and the knife dropped from senseless fingers.

Death flowed from Andreyev's striking limbs. The soldier sagged limply, his eyes glazed with pain. Andreyev finished the macabre dance. A strike to the face was delivered with the heel of his palm, and the soft cartilage of the nose splintered as the force of Andreyev's strike thrust the parts up into the man's brain. The soldier was dead the instant Andreyev released him, and his body crumpled into the dirt.

Andreyev cast a respectful look at a brave opponent as he picked up his knife. He was not the only commander with good men.

The flames had almost engulfed the room as he sprinted over to Pytor's unconscious form. The soldier's shooting had been almost perfect. A few inches to the left and he would have burst the boy's heart. Instead it was a shoulder wound. Andreyev hefted the boy over his shoulder, knowing full well that his disobeying orders and waiting had saved Andreyev's life. The boy would be all right. He would see to that.

He ran through the burning building. Fyodor was still waiting. Andreyev grinned. "Doesn't anyone follow orders around here?"

"Not when they're damned stupid," said Fyodor calmly. "Pytor?"

"He'll be all right," Andreyev said, passing the boy down into the manhole. "This leads somewhere?"

Fyodor nodded. "You gave us plenty of time. We explored. There's an exit hole about ten blocks away."

Fyodor winced as pieces of flaming debris came down from the roof. "It's well outside the Army's cordon," he said, slipping down into the hole.

Andreyev followed, pulling the grating back into place. "We were set up, you know," he said bitterly.

"I figured as much," Fyodor agreed darkly. "But by whom? The journalist?"

"I don't think so. But if not, this time they'll take him in as well."

The tunnel's darkness was cool against his hot skin. Andreyev picked up Pytor's limp form again and started off. By now, the entire structure was burning above them. "We've got to see Privins. You agree?"

"I don't see any other way. We can't return to our units. The fire won't fool Klim for very long."

Andreyev nodded, the cool breeze from farther on giving him a second wind. For a short time, no one would follow. They would escape safely this time.

But it was Thursday, and there were only four days left to the parade.

XXXIII

Alexi lifted the phone in his office and heard the caller say distinctly, "Quickly, Petrov. We've been uncovered. Get out!" Then the connection was severed.

It sounded like Andreyev's voice but he couldn't be certain. He paced back and forth in his tiny cubicle like a caged animal. A warning or a trap? It was after twelve; Andreyev would have already spoken to the AI. Was this its message?

He decided to get clear of *Pravda*. In the open, Andreyev could at least reach him again and take him into hiding if necessary. He took one last look at the office he'd worked in for so long and experienced a momentary gut-wrenching sadness. Then he put on his coat and hat and walked out the door.

Not the front exit; the back. Safer, he thought. Hurrying down the stairs, he thought of the irrevocable course he was taking. An outcast now; a criminal. His only salvation lay in Malenkov's survival.

He'd have to get word to Irina. Maybe she would see the wisdom in divorce now. *Deny me*, he had urged her again last night. She'd refused again and again. Then they made love as if for the last time. A premonition?

He yanked open the heavy steel door at the bottom of the stairwell and raced into the cold—

And stopped dead in his tracks. The scene before him etched itself onto his mind's eye as if worked in by tool and acid. Flashing red lights circled on top of black automobiles. A crowd of curious onlookers were restrained by yellow striped police barriers as they stared at the strange, frightened creature so neatly caught in the GRU's *provokatsiya:* the trap.

A satisfied Lieutenant Koslov pronounced the obvious. "You are under arrest for crimes against the state, Citizen Petrov. Come with us." He took Alexi's arm and led him to a car. Alexi uttered no protest. He followed numbly. There was nothing left to say.

* * *

Andreyev peered out from under the raised manhole cover into the snowy street overhead. It was almost dark now. They'd waited for night's protection. Five ragged and filthy soldiers did not suddenly emerge from underground in the middle of the road in daylight without someone reporting it.

Traffic thinned, then diminished to sporadic passings. Fyodor helped him raise the cover just enough to slither out. Andreyev was up and walking swiftly away seconds later.

A few blocks away, Andreyev found what he was looking for—an old truck parked on the street. He pried open the window far enough to snake his arm in and throw the lock. Inside, he hot-wired the ignition and turned on the heater full blast, twisting his hands under its tepid stream to warm them.

The taste of betrayal was still sour in his mouth. The AI had deceived him, he had no doubt it was the one. Petrov and his wife had far more to lose than to gain. Besides, he'd seen their relationship firsthand. Irina had not turned her husband in. That left the AI.

But a nagging question continued to bother him. If the AI wanted him arrested by Solnikov's henchmen, why lead him to a site with such an obvious escape route? It could have been an omission; but it could just as easily have been very careful planning. Accident or design?

Andreyev pushed the ancient vehicle into gear and drove off. What game was the AI playing? He found a rag in between the seats and cleaned off his face as best he could. Was he a pawn in a much larger scheme than he suspected? A need for answers lay uneasily upon him as he stripped off his outer clothing, revealing his uniform.

He stopped the truck in the middle of the road, carefully obscuring the manhole from view, and got out cursing loudly as the engine died with a coughing splutter from a judicious use of the choke. Raising the hood, he loudly bemoaned the quality of Soviet engines. The occasional passerby smiled in sympathy. Andreyev felt the truck jostle on its springs as his men clambered into the back. When all were inside, he gave one final curse, slammed the hood back down, and got back inside. Miraculously, the truck started up without difficulty.

Fyodor, sitting in the cabin alongside Andreyev, spread

his fingers under the heating vent. "Privins?" he asked, but it was more of a statement.

"There's no one else," said Andreyev grimly. "We need cover for ourselves and a doctor for Pytor. The fire may have bought us some space, but it will take someone as highly placed as Privins to know."

"He should also have information about the journalist," Fyodor said thoughtfully.

"I hope so."

Fyodor raised an eyebrow. "You're unusually concerned about Petrov, I think."

"He's a good man. Better than even he knows. And this affair was not of his making."

"Or of ours," Fyodor reminded him gently. "But we're caught up in it nonetheless."

"I don't think that's the issue, Fyodor." He was guiding the truck through the slippery Moscow streets. "The man stuck by his brother regardless of the cost and so far he's stuck by us. Principled action. That's quite rare."

Fyodor shrugged. "Common integrity."

"Ah, Fyodor," Andreyev said with a sad smile. "In this day and age, common integrity should rightfully be called courage. We're here."

Andreyev stopped the truck. They were in front of a gatehouse protecting an entranceway through a high stone wall. The wall surrounded a snow-laden, two-story lodge and its lushly forested grounds. Like all Politburo residences, it was heavily guarded. Armed soldiers piled out from the glassed-in station and took up positions in front of the truck. An officer approached Andreyev and leaned into the driver's window. Andreyev knew him to be loyal to the house's occupant. Privins selected his guards with care.

"Do you know where you are, comrade?" The question was as frosty as the air.

Andreyev nodded. "This is the home of Sergei Nicolaio-vich Privins, minister of agriculture and member of the Politburo."

The officer eyed him narrowly. "And who are you to know such a thing?"

"One who knows such a thing does not need to tell how he knows. You may tell the minister that his nephew, Pavel, is here to see him."

* * *

Minister Sergei Nicolaiovich Privins emerged from the sitting room that adjoined the kitchen, wiping his hands on a linen towel. Andreyev, Fyodor, and the rest were finishing the remains of a meal the servants had hastily put together. They looked up expectantly.

"Your friend will be fine. Not a difficult wound to treat. My physician says he'll heal nicely and be up and around in a day or two."

Privins, a gaunt, white-haired man in his late sixties with a tall, wiry frame, sighed happily and looked at Andreyev. "It's been a long time since I assisted at an operation. Not since the war. I wonder if your friends know I started out as a medical corpsman."

"And ended up killing Nazis behind the Polish lines with my father and Vladimir Malenkov," said Andreyev with a grin. "They used to say you were more effective with your knife than you ever were with your scalpel."

"A good enough reason to turn to growing things after the war," Privins said. "But come, Pavel. Your friends can rest upstairs. Bring Fyodor and we'll talk in the library."

The library was decorated in earth tones of brown and beige, and a fire flickered noiselessly behind a glass screen that covered the fireplace. Andreyev settled into a soft chair while Fyodor sat sprawled on the leather couch. Privins removed his pipe from its rack and went peacefully through the motions of lighting it.

He sat down finally in a big leather chair. "I heard that you died today, nephew," he said quietly. "I'm pleased at so quick a resurrection."

"What else did you hear?"

"My man in Tarkov's office told me that Tarkov knows you lead the Suvorovs. But rumor has it that the Army trapped you in a warehouse and you died in the fire when it was attacked."

Andreyev pursed his lips. "I hoped that would spread. At least something worked today."

"I'm not so sure, Pavel. My man also reports that a GRU colonel named Klim is even now searching for your corpse in the rubble. Obviously, he won't find it. You've bought maybe another day. Then the hunt will be on again in full force. He's already arrested dozens of Suvorovs."

"Perhaps we shouldn't have come here."

Privins shrugged. "Don't worry. The estate guards are all loyal to me. You're safe here for the meantime. But tell me, Pavel," he continued. "You're worried about more than one GRU colonel. My sister's son never balked so easily."

"I don't know how much longer Malenkov will be kept alive, Sergei. You must have been in on the planning for the AI. Tell me about it."

Privins nodded sadly. "A plan of desperation, even at its best. But Solnikov moved too fast. Malenkov was sick, all of his political allies were running scared. We needed time to reestablish a new coalition. Rudin's machine gave us that. Now I've almost got that coalition and the Politburo is beginning to sway. Malenkov must be kept alive, Pavel. Every day he staves off Solnikov, we grow stronger. Why are you worried about the AI?"

"We were almost caught today. I think the AI betrayed us."

"Impossible," said Privins flatly. "Rudin guaranteed it. Manipulate, yes. But betray? Never."

"Then how do you account for these things?" Andreyev outlined the events of the past few days. "We can't go back to our units now that Solnikov knows about us. And there's the journalist. What can you find out about him?"

Privins looked crestfallen. "I'm sorry, Pavel. I can tell you about him right now. He was arrested this afternoon. I didn't know he was connected to us. The trial was convened almost at once."

"He's helped us, Sergei. Do what you can."

"I'll look into it. Go on."

Andreyev got up and moved to a window. A new snow was falling. "You know that I'm slated to lead some kind of attack against Solnikov on Anniversary Day during the great parade."

"Yes, I know. But why are you so vague about it? Malenkov gave you full details."

"But he didn't, Sergei. No one did. The AI has the plans locked up inside it, and it won't give them to me unless I send someone to remove Berenstein. It was supposed to provide help at the warehouse today. Instead, the Army showed up. What's going on, Sergei? Have all our efforts come to nothing?"

"Not on my end," pronounced Privins firmly. "Next to Malenkov, I'm the oldest Suvorov, and I still survive. My work goes on. Solnikov doesn't have the general secretaryship yet. In truth, though, it's close, Pavel. The Politburo is composed of old men, most of whom are still traumatized by World War II. Malenkov frightened them with his risk-taking. They found Solnikov's promise to restore the old order very attractive."

Privins continued disgustedly. "Order over progress. So what if the West yields fifty times the amount of grain from the same size plot? Our methods are so archaic that a real grain embargo—not just the imbecilic selective one the American President Carter used years ago, but a real grain embargo—would send thirty million of our citizens to their graves from starvation. We buy easily enough from them. Or steal. Why in Lenin's name not have our farmers emulate some of their ways? No; that threatens order. And in order is security. That's Solnikov's appeal. You see what I'm up against? A few see reason, but they're frightened. Sheep, all of them. Looking for a strong shepherd."

He looked hard at Andreyev. "So give me a victory on Parade Day, Pavel. Let Solnikov be the loser. The sheep will desert him then. It's the way that we can continue Malenkov's rule. It's simple, really. Malenkov must not only be more right, *he must be perceived of as stronger as well*."

"How can I fight his fight when I don't have his instructions?" Andreyev asked in exasperation.

"We'll find a way. You were his hands, Pavel. He always called you that. You the hands, I the brain. Just keep in mind that I must remain unconnected to you. I've avoided Solnikov's ax only because my links to Malenkov are secret. If he discovers I'm the ranking Suvorov, I'm lost. Solnikov is clever, and Tarkov, in some ways, can be cleverer."

"Then the AI is still the key," Andreyev said.

"It has to point the way," Privins agreed. "I must have your victory in order to consolidate mine."

Andreyev pulled his tunic open and massaged his tired muscles.

"Call for some vodka, Uncle. Four days left to the parade. It's going to be a long night."

XXXIV

Exile!

The court's verdict was tantamount to a death sentence. Thirty years in exile—the proper authorities would determine the location. One thing was certain, though, and Alexi knew it without clarification: Siberia beckoned.

He sagged against the dock's wooden railing when the magistrate intoned his fate. Most people thought of Siberia only as a vast, ghostly region without real boundaries, stretching eastward from the Urals through thousands of miles of frozen tundra and arctic wastes almost to the sea. His defense attorney was nodding in satisfaction. The law had been served. He shook hands with the state prosecutor and promptly left the court.

Alexi wanted to call after him, to scream, "What about me?" But that was mere conceit. He didn't matter. The state mattered; the Party mattered. Alexi Mikhailovich Petrov mattered only inasmuch as he had strayed and erred and been found guilty by a machine as inexorable as the Russian winter. Thirty years. At least the rest of his youth; maybe the rest of his life.

The evidence had been laid out with scientific precision. The wheels of justice had rarely rolled on so quickly. Koslov testified at length. Even the deputy minister of defense came, shown in with great deference, to support the charges. The only one absent was Colonel Klim, who sent a deposition. The judge shook his head often and his voice held the tones of cold animosity.

It came down to this: Alexi Mikhailovich Petrov was a criminal, an anti-Soviet conspirator. But even as the charges and sentences were pronounced, one realization gave him some small comfort and created a tiny, internal place where he could find solace. Alexi had discovered the truth about Russia. Like countless millions before him, he was not wrong. He was just on the wrong side.

Before Yuri and Andreyev and Klim and all the others he
might have doubted this insight, accepting the unquestionable
right of these men to judge him. Now he knew better. Right
stemmed from power. Irina had been completely correct.
Idealists were doomed here.

With a final irony, the judge ruled that no appeal would be
heard in Alexi's case because there were no contradictions
inherent in it. Very neat. The sentence could begin at once.
He informed Alexi that his wife would be notified of her
husband's location in due course. That was all.

That was all? Alexi stood in mute shock. After a liftetime
of good citizenship, that was all? How easily the state disposed
of its refuse. Alexi's head hung in spite of a raging anger.
Despair did that. Hopelessness had conquered him. His life
was over.

The guards manacled him again and he was led away.

A light snow was falling when the police car pulled up to
the train depot. Alexi recognized the familiar city central hub
from which trains left for the northern cities and the endless
remote villages and mining towns of the Far East: Siberia.
Railroad cars sat motionless on sidings, half covered with snow.
Water dripped onto the gravel beds between rails on recently
used tracks. Moonlight glistened on old locomotives' towering
stacks.

A low block-shaped building with barred windows stood
at the edge of the yard beyond the main terminal. Alexi was
marched to its door and the guards knocked loudly.

"Open up, Boslov. Here's a new prisoner for you. Boslov,
you miserable sot. Open up!"

A slovenly fat man opened the door at last and stood in the
harsh light of a naked bulb inside. Alexi felt sickened at once at
the thought of being in such a man's hands. A miasma of
alcohol, sweat, and sausage smells came from inside.

"So . . . another passenger for my little train. How nice
to see you, comrade. We have room for you, don't you fear."
He smiled a weak, sickly grin. "We always have room. Bring
him inside," he directed the guards.

Alexi was pushed forward roughly. Hands pawed into his
pockets. He felt his wallet move and he surged aside angrily.

He tried to lift his hands to fight but the chains snapped taut against his sides.

Boslov smiled.

Alexi never saw who hit him. The blow came from behind. A white light exploded in his head and everything around him grew small . . . and then disappeared.

A man was crying somewhere. The sound slowly penetrated the dark clouds that swaddled Alexi's brain. It disturbed him. So did the fact that his face hurt and he brought a hand up to it, surprised to come in contact with a rough wooden floor. He found his head and rubbed it. The hand came away with an oily fluid between the fingers.

Memory returned. His senses realigned themselves and perspective shifted. He was lying on the floor and was no longer manacled. He managed to right himself and get groggily to his feet. He was in a railroad car, and the moonlight that filtered in through cracks in the wooden planking was enough to see by.

More than a dozen men were huddled against the sides of the car, clutching tattered blankets around their ragged clothing to stave off the cold. The only source of warmth was a wood-stove that sat behind a screen and didn't cast enough heat inside to warm anything but a small area around it. A layer of fetid straw was strewn about the floor, and a cracked and leaking piece of crockery served as the only place to defecate. Alexi's nose quickly located it as the source of the foul odor that permeated the air.

He stood for a moment in the center of the floor, conscious of the gaze of the other occupants, unsure of how to proceed. There would be no introductions in such a place. What did one's name matter here? Identities did not follow a man into the grave. The dead were faceless.

Most of the men in the railroad car were packed into small groups, stacked right up against each other for warmth. Some looked like more recent arrivals; their clothing was dirty but still noticeably civilian. Others wore the vertically striped uniforms of convicts and had probably been transferred into the train from prisons along its route.

The crying still disturbed Alexi and he sought its source. In the corner farthest from the heat, and wrapped in a blanket that afforded little protection, crouched the man from whom the sounds emanated. Alexi walked over and knelt down, peering into the gloom.

At first he thought the man was unconscious and crying out in his sleep. But the eyes flickered in the unshaven face. They were tired eyes, Alexi saw, so resigned to defeat that he felt his sympathies stir. No matter that he shared the same plight. He reached out a hand to adjust the blanket, unmindful of the cold that snapped at his own limbs.

The man shrank away and fear blazed in his eyes.

"What's been done to you?" Alexi murmured softly. "Can I help in some way?"

The fear in the man's eyes faded slowly, but suspicion remained. Alexi touched his grimy forehead. As he expected, fever's heat raged there. "You're sick," he said. "Do you know what it is?"

A short nod of the man's head. His voice, when it finally came, was hoarse and raspy. Alexi could hear the fluid in the man's lungs, confirming what he heard next. "Pneumonia," the man said with a wheeze.

"Do you have any medicine?" Alexi asked.

A look of defeat crossed the man's features again. A chill shook his depleted frame. He lifted an unsteady hand and pointed to the opposite corner of the car, the one nearest the heat.

Alexi looked over and saw a tight knot of three convicts who occupied the only warm spot in the car. Two seemed of average size but the third was a very big man with thick arms and a muscular torso. He wore a full, blond beard, and his prison uniform was torn in several places. With a start, Alexi realized that all three were now watching him.

"Look away!" the sick man warned him, pleading in a low voice. "You don't want them to notice you." The words came out in a rush, in between the wheezing. "Do you have anything of value?"

Alexi patted his pockets and was forced to smile. "I'm safe, comrade. The jailer, Boslov, left me without that particular problem."

"No. Not so." The man reached out and touched Alexi's shirt enviously. "Your clothing. They'll try to take it. Be careful. I'm a doctor. I had medicine. Even the guards couldn't find it. I hid it. Inside me."

Alexi winced.

The man shrugged again. "Those men have been in prison for a long time. Too long. Inside, they raped and murdered another prisoner. So it was exile to the mines. They . . . they abused me. I was weakest . . . I couldn't resist. The big one found the medicine. He took it to sell later. It will bring a high price in the mines."

For a moment, the enormity of it left Alexi speechless. "I . . . I'm sorry," he said at last.

The doctor shrugged again. "When everything else is taken, maybe it is not so much more to lose." He looked up. "You're political."

Alexi understood. He settled down next to him and nodded. "Crimes against the state."

"Me, too," the doctor said.

"It seems as if my life was so long ago and so far away," Alexi said, feeling himself open up to this man who had been hurt so deeply. "It's only been hours, but I feel so . . . cut off."

"You are, my friend. Make no mistake about that. We all are. Do you know where they're sending you?"

Alexi shook his head.

"Rest assured, it will not be pleasant. I'm sorry for you. At least I have some consolation. A doctor knows." For a moment, his face held a kind of peace. "I won't survive the trip."

Alexi said nothing for a while. The doctor drifted off to a fitful sleep. Alexi heard the fluid congesting his lungs. He reached over and propped the man up, took off his own jacket, and covered him. The wheezing abated somewhat.

How foolish, Alexi thought, settling back again. The man is dying in stages. What do I offer him by helping but to prolong his agony? Let him slide down the long, dark tunnel. I care for no one but myself in helping him. Mercy is selfishness here. Let the man die in peace.

Across the car, the three men continued to watch him. Around the rest of the car, men coughed and muttered and resettled into new positions, sometimes standing to stretch before returning to the warmth of the pack. Silence returned to the car. Time passed slowly.

The sound of the chains and padlocks being taken off the sliding door woke Alexi from the light sleep he had fallen into. Suddenly floodlights lit the doorway and he squinted against

the painful glare. Armed soldiers trained their guns on the
prisoners while Boslov picked up two large pails that Alexi
hadn't noticed before and replaced them with two others, one
filled with pieces of bread and the other filled with a thin,
watery gruel. Boslov motioned for one of the prisoners to
empty the crock and waited impatiently while it was dumped.
Then he slammed the door shut. The lights went out and the
sound of footsteps retreated back into the night.

The men stirred slowly. One by one they filed past the
pails, each taking a piece of bread and hollowing it out to use as
a scoop for the gruel. Alexi left the doctor and took a place in
line. He shuffled forward with the rest of them, deciding to
take care of himself. But then he looked back into the corner
and his resolve faded as quickly as it had formed. Even here,
hope was possible. He reached down and took two pieces of
bread. While he was still able, the doctor would eat.

A sudden slap stung his hand and he dropped the bread.
He looked up sharply. "What . . . ?"

The bearded giant stood over him. He was even bigger up
close. Alexi chose to let it pass. Perhaps he had misunder-
stood.

"The other is for that man," he explained. "I'll bring it to
him. Look in the pail. There's enough."

The man shook his head. "Mine," he said flatly. "Both."

Alexi sighed deeply. He bent down and picked up the
bread. "I don't think so. No, I really don't."

The bearded man didn't move but his eyes flickered to
one side and Alexi suddenly remembered the man's companions. One was behind the big man. The other?

He turned just in time to catch the third one swinging
something at his head. He sidestepped and let the object—he
could now see it was a piece of the wooden planking—swing
past him. The momentum carried the assailant straight into his
arms. Alexi held the man and tried to work the wood free from
his hand, to make it fall. He was careful, but the convict began
to claw at his face. He was suddenly surprised to find both his
hands encased in Alexi's much larger ones. He struggled. Alexi
still tried to be careful, but with all the twisting . . . there
was a sudden cracking and the man screamed. Alexi hastily let
him go. He scampered into the far corner, nursing the broken
fingers. The bearded convict watched Alexi with a curious
expression.

Alexi picked up the bread and handed the piece of wood back to the bearded man. He said, "I'm sorry about your friend. I tried to be careful, but it's been a very long day. Maybe the doctor can help."

The bearded man said nothing. Alexi held out an open hand. "Oh, yes. The medicine, I almost forgot. Please, you don't need it but it will probably save his life. Please?"

The convict looked incredulous. "You're joking with me?"

Alexi shook his head. "There's nothing to joke about here. But we're all in it together. There isn't any reason to make it worse."

For a second, Alexi saw doubt cross the man's face. He reached into his shirt and brought out a small black vial. "This?"

Alexi smiled. "I'm glad you—"

The giant was amazingly fast for one so big. Alexi's attention had shifted to the vial for a split second and he paid for the mistake. A fist like a hamhock crashed into the side of his head. He sagged to his knees and white lights danced behind his eyes. A second blow crashed down, stunning him.

"Kill him!" screamed the convict with the broken hand. The giant grinned. He took hold of a hank of Alexi's hair and pulled his head up. He hit him again, full across the face. He twisted Alexi's cheek harshly and laughed. "Plump. A good one for sport."

On his knees, the white spots in Alexi's eyes changed to red. Too long without sleep, too many indignities, and too much to tolerate in the sick giant who threatened to torment him as he had others.

Outrage flowed into his mind and cleared it. He looked up to see the giant caressing the wooden slat lovingly, hefting it, readying the blow that would disable so helpless an opponent as Alexi now was. He lifted it, preparing to strike. This was too much, really, too much. . . .

Still on his knees, Alexi slammed his cupped hand up into the giant's groin with all the strength his anger could produce. The man's entire face dissolved into shock as the force of the blow lifted him up onto his toes. Alexi squeezed and the convict screamed. His eyes bulged as Alexi tightened his grip, angry beyond control, and the giant's scream turned into a high-pitched shriek. Alexi's hand was like a vise, twisting tighter and tighter until the veins stuck out on the back of his

hands. The giant writhed and screamed but could not dislodge
the grip that held him in agony. He swung the wooden plank
but pain had already twisted his eyes shut. Alexi plucked it
from his grasp. The man roared. There were sudden soft pops.

Alexi rose to one knee as the giant jackknifed forward, his
eyes white and rolling. The huge weight crashed down onto
Alexi's shoulder as he tried to rise and, for a timeless moment,
they were immobile; a statue carved from one stone. Then, it
broke. Slowly, Alexi stood.

With the full weight of the giant slung over his shoulders
like a yoke, Alexi rose to his full height. He caught the eyes of
the third convict for an instant and saw the fear there. Then he
was moving. One step; two. He staggered under the weight.
Faster; he was walking now. A roar tore loose from his throat.
He ran. Across the car, as much speed as he could muster. But
there was no more room. The wall was there. Men ducked,
scattered . . .

Alexi drove the giant's head into the wall of the railroad
car like a battering ram. There was a sudden, sickening thud,
like the sound of a watermelon splitting, and the entire car
vibrated with the impact. One final heave and Alexi sent the
body sprawling into a corner. He straightened, looked around,
and walked back to the center of the car. He bent down and
picked up the vial of medicine and the bread. The roaring in
his ears began to subside.

He looked up and saw several of the other prisoners
holding the other two convicts. That surprised him.

"They tried to call the guards," one tall, thin man
explained angrily. "Cowards! When things went against
them—"

"Why didn't you stop them before, before when they"—
he gestured toward the doctor—"before that." He bit back
angrier remarks.

The man stepped forward. He pointed to several others
who were badly bruised, one wearing a sling. "Don't be so
quick to judge," he said quietly. "We tried."

Alexi's face softened. "What do we do now?"

The tall man looked over to the fallen giant. "If the guards
see this, we'll be detained here for days while they investigate.
Days of more Moscow cold and stale bread. At least the
prisons along the way are heated. We won't survive much
more of this weather outside."

"I can turn myself in."

"And die for killing slime?" The man shook his head. "No. We'll hold these two and cover the big one with the straw. Maybe when they open the doors, the big one can fall out? It's a long trip yet. We'll try to think of something."

Alexi nodded slowly. "Thank you."

"Not necessary. In fact, it should be the other way around. But it's a strange world." He looked at Alexi appraisingly. "Your strength is really quite remarkable."

"Believe me, of late it's been no asset," he said feelingly.

The man shook his head. "I don't think the doctor will feel that way. Come, let's put him by the stove. It will be warmer."

Alexi walked over and knelt by the doctor. He was awake and had seen the struggle. He put out a trembling hand. "My friend," he began hesitantly, wheezing harshly. Alexi shook out a pill from the tube and pushed it past the doctor's lips.

"Shush, swallow this," he urged, picking him up with the other prisoner's help and resetting him by the stove.

The medicine seemed to help and brought some relief in minutes. The bubbly sound in the doctor's lungs dissipated somewhat. "I saw what you did," he said. "You are a brave man, Comrade . . . ?"

"Petrov. Alexi Mikhailovich Petrov. And ducking isn't bravery. You should get some sleep now. The medicine seems to be doing its work."

"Very well. But just to thank you seems inadequate for a life saved."

"It isn't. Not here, anyway."

The doctor was silent for a while and Alexi thought he'd drifted off to sleep. He settled in beside him as the rest of the prisoners drifted closer, now that the warmth was accessible to them.

"Alexi Mikhailovich?" It was the doctor.

"Yes?"

"You are a person who thinks deeply, I can see that. Can you tell me if you know what makes you still fight, even here?"

"I don't know," Alexi answered honestly. "My wife would tell you it's sheer stubbornness."

"She must know better," the doctor objected.

"She does, I think."

"Do you?"

Alexi looked into the gloom. The stark ugliness of his

surroundings, the sharp tug of despair, the pain when he thought of Irina; these would be his constant companions on the journey into oblivion. Exile. *Etap;* to transport. Such a mild word for so terrible a voyage.

"Do you, Alexi Mikhailovich?" the doctor asked again.

"I used to," Alexi said bitterly. "Now . . ." He shrugged helplessly.

"Then let me trade you life for life, comrade. The lesson is this: They can condemn you, that takes only power. But to *convince* you, that takes a rightness a man like you knows they will never have. Look to the inside, Alexi Mikhailovich. That's where freedom in Russia lies."

The old car creaked in the cold wind. Far away, an automobile horn wailed briefly, dropping off to silence. Someone going to the theater, the union hall? Alexi closed his eyes.

In the darkness, tears came for the first time.

XXXV

Irina struggled not to cry; not yet, not in front of the smug GRU colonel when it would give him so much satisfaction.

"My husband's loyal, I tell you," she repeated. "Confused, sometimes, but who isn't now and then? Surely that is no crime to be punished by thirty years in exile."

Klim sat back in his chair. "You may be interested to know that his defense attorney pointed that out. The usual sentence is death. The court considered exile quite lenient."

"For tending to a sick brother?"

"Don't play the fool, comrade. For withholding vital documents, engaging in anti-Soviet conspiracy, meeting with enemies of the state . . . Need I go on?"

"There were no documents," Irina insisted. "My husband met with no one."

"Not even a Colonel Andreyev?"

"The name means nothing to me."

"Then you won't be sorry to learn that he died today. Burned to death." Klim smiled, watching her.

"My husband did not know the man," Irina persisted.

"The court believed otherwise."

"Because you claimed otherwise!"

"Proof was offered, comrade."

"How can I know that when I wasn't allowed to attend the trial?" Irina demanded.

Klim eyed her narrowly. "You have something to add, then? We were convinced you knew nothing."

Irina saw the trap and had to back off. "That's true. I swear."

"Then what help could you have been to the court? Really, Comrade Petrova, your superiors at Gosbank speak most highly of you. Your record is without blemish. You were even allowed to come here. Take my advice. Divorce him. The guilt of the husband does not have to devolve to the wife if she takes the proper steps to convince the Party that she has totally rejected the offender. Divorce him."

"Never."

Klim's tone was friendly enough. "You're not thinking. In time you'll see that my advice is in your best interest. Stay well, comrade. Where will you go now? Relatives, perhaps?"

Irina rose and hid her shaking hands under her coat. "I have to go back to the bank. My work . . . today . . . so little done. I have to go back."

Klim beamed. "How commendable. I agree. Work is so often the answer. It allows you to forget and move on. The Party will be pleased. In fact, I'll have someone drive you over."

"You're too kind."

"Not at all, Comrade Petrova. Good night."

"Good night, Colonel."

The offices at Gosbank were just as deserted as the night before, but this time seemed lonelier. Oh, Alosha, she thought disconsolately, where are you now? She pressed her face against the cold glass of her office window and let loose the tears she'd refused to show Klim.

So many years. What would she do? Could she wait all that time? Could Alexi survive it? She'd heard the stories about exile in Siberia. The few that returned were never the same again. *Oh, Alosha, my poor husband.*

But he was not gone yet and she was far from finished.

Hang Klim. And the Party. Alexi had been right after all.
When your back was up against it, you had to fight. If she let
him go without a struggle, she'd never be able to live with
herself. Maybe that was how Alexi had felt about Yuri. She
understood a little better. No one, not even the state, had the
right to try to force her to abandon her husband.

She walked over to her terminal and turned it on. Even
though Andreyev had taken Yuri's notebook, she remembered
the way back to the AI. It was long and complicated, but she
could navigate it.

Urgency lent her fingers skill; pain lent her speed. This
time there were fewer parries, fewer blocks to cross. The
"door" at the other end opened more easily and the responses
were familiar. With a bit of surprise, she realized it remembered her! Her answers were accepted. Finally, she achieved
full contact.

Greetings.

Irina almost cried with relief. AND TO YOU, she sent.

You are recognized. Question?

Irina hesitated, then plunged in. She sent,

I NEED YOUR HELP.

Response: possible. First: Someone comes?

NOT UNLESS YOU HELP ME.

Someone comes?

It was shunting her aside, asserting its own need. She
strengthened her resolve and sent again.

NOT UNLESS YOU HELP ME!

A momentary flicker. Hesitation? Then,

Explain, please.

Irina flexed her hands like a concert performer preparing
for a long and difficult work. She began to input in earnest.
Slowly, an understanding emerged. The interchange continued far into the night.

A while before dawn, Irina closed down her terminal.
What she'd learned filled her both with hope and with dread.
The issue of trust still lay heavily on her mind, though, and the
possibility that Andreyev's death was connected to the AI's
subtle machinations was a real one. Even Alexi's exile might be
just another part of the entity's strategy. What did thirty years
of suffering really mean to it?

But now she at least had a destination where before she'd
had none. And she also had a bargaining chip of her own: one

that she could play if necessary. The AI had given her that much. It would have to be enough.

She hurried out of the bank and walked the several blocks to a taxi park. Several drivers turned her down; her destination was on the outskirts of the city. Finally a bribe of three times the fare found a taker. She slid into the back seat and was carried off into the growing light.

Dawn was just beginning to break fully when the taxi pulled up in front of the entrance gate of the estate. The driver was clearly unnerved by the sudden emergence of armed guards from the gatehouse flanking the cab. He pointed mutely to Irina in back, and the officer in charge leaned in to confront her. When he saw the lone female, his demeanor softened.

"You must be lost, comrade. But this is not a house you can stop at. Where are you going? I'll direct the driver."

"This is the house of Comrade Privins, is it not?" Irina asked pleasantly.

The officer drew back sharply. "I'm sorry. You must go now. This is a restricted area and you have no business here."

"Young man, you will kindly inform Comrade Privins that Irina Maximovna Petrova, the wife of Alexi Mikhailovich Petrov, is here. He will see me."

"At this hour? You must be mad."

"If mad means angry, you don't know the half of it. Call him. I warn you. If you force me to leave and I have to come back here later, you will be a sure and certain candidate for a far less local post. I've come a long way, Comrade Captain, after a day filled with nonsense from military types just like you. Now call Privins at once or I swear I'm going to get out of the taxi and beat your stupid head out from between your flapping ears!"

"Comrade, I'm shocked! How dare—"

Irina grabbed his lapels in one large hand and yanked him halfway into the car. "Call!"

The officer pulled back and almost lost his footing in the snow. Angry emotions warred on his face. In the end, however, caution won. He picked up the phone in the gatehouse. Irina watched him. After a moment, he put the phone down hastily and came hurriedly back.

"Of course, please step out, comrade. I'll escort you in personally. The taxi can go."

Irina smothered a smile. It was good occasionally to win even a small battle.

There was a fire blazing behind a glass screen and a sufficient number of books for Irina to decide that the guard had left her in the library. She had never seen so many books in a private collection before. A servant took her hat and coat and she sat down gratefully on the couch. Waiting, she noticed the heavy odors of tobacco smoke, alcohol, and coffee in the air, as if a group had been closeted in here and only recently dispersed.

This was the home of a member of the Politburo! The very thought shook her confidence. If the AI had led her here to betray her, she was in serious trouble. She steeled her courage and waited.

The tall, white-haired man who entered the room exuded a sense of power so real that, for a second, Irina felt as if the air had grown thin. She rose quickly to her feet, feeling more ungainly than usual, but he gestured for her to take her seat and folded himself regally into an armchair.

He observed her appraisingly. "Do I understand correctly that you threatened to assault the officer of my guard?"

Irina felt her chest tighten in panic, but on closer inspection, saw that lines of amusement puckered Privins's penetrating dark eyes.

"Forgive me," she apologized. "My husband often chides me for a vile temper."

"Your husband. That would be Alexi Mikhailovich Petrov, the journalist."

"Yes. You know of him, then?"

"I do. But this isn't the usual place to appeal a court's sentence. Will you tell me why you're here? Do you think I can do something for your husband?"

Irina searched Privins's face for signs of compassion but could not read the man. Again, she remembered where she was and who sat before her. The minister of agriculture, a Politburo member. She almost lost her nerve. What if she was wrong about him?

Privins seemed to sense her conflict. He got up and poured her a drink. Handing it to her, he placed a gnarled hand on her shoulder and said kindly, "Come, Comrade Petrova. Drink this. Call it the end of an old day rather than the beginning of a new one." He looked at her intently. "You've come this far. Go the rest of the way and trust me. Tell me how you came to know of this house. Not a hundred men know its location, or any of the other Politburo members' residences, for that matter."

Irina's eyes pleaded. "You let me in, though. For some reason, you let me in. So I know I mean more to you than just some poor citizen lost on a dark night who turns up at your door. Minister, my husband has been exiled! The power here is all yours. Give me even a small thing so that I can trust you. Please, help me first."

Privins studied her for a long time. Finally he seemed to come to a decision. He stood and walked over to a connecting door and threw it open. The man revealed behind it strode into the library, and Irina leaped to her feet.

"Andreyev!" she cried with joyous relief. "But I thought—"

"That I was dead? Not just yet, Irina Maximovna." He put a strong arm around her shoulders and guided her back to the couch. "Where did you learn of my 'death'?"

"Colonel Klim told me; the one who tormented Alexi. I went to see him after the trial."

Andreyev sighed. "It was another test. He doesn't really believe it himself. Obviously, my body wasn't in the rubble of the building the AI sent me to."

"Then it can be trusted?"

Andreyev looked unsure. "We just don't know. We were betrayed, surely. But there was an escape route so obvious that it's hard to believe it wasn't part of the plan."

"My dear," Privins interrupted gently, "I believe I've given you that small thing you asked for. As you can see, it's not so small. Now, please even the score. Like my nephew here, I work for Vladimir Malenkov. Help us if you can."

Irina nodded. Andreyev alive! Hope surged within her. "When Klim told me that Alexi had been exiled, I had nowhere to go but back to the AI. I remembered the way in. Programmers have good memories for things like that." She paused. "I was able to get through tonight. It gave me Malenkov's final instructions!" she finished triumphantly.

Andreyev's relief was almost tangible. He looked as if he wanted to yelp with excitement. Privins just watched her closely, venturing nothing yet.

"What are the details?" asked Andreyev. "Wait, let me get some paper, and Fyodor, I want him to hear this."

"Just a moment," Privins cautioned him. "If I'm any judge of character, this won't be that easy. Comrade? There *is* more, isn't there?"

Irina squared her shoulders and faced them both. "I see what makes you a powerful man, Comrade Privins." She turned back to Andreyev. "He's right. The AI demanded a price from me and I've got to demand one from you."

"Name them both," Andreyev said.

"The AI is now threatened even more seriously by Berenstein. It can't keep him at bay much longer. Once he penetrates its core, it would become virtually his tool. Yuri told Alexi it was never meant to be used in the way it has been. Well, it's beginning to crumble. Berenstein isn't affected by its defenses the way Solnikov was. Berenstein's still an expatriate at heart. At his age his own death means little and the destruction of the country means less. The AI has to have someone physically stop Berenstein. It gave me half of Malenkov's instructions only after I agreed to help it. The other half comes when it's safe. Not before."

"You'll give us the first half, then?" Privins asked hopefully.

"I think you already know better than that. I want my husband back. You can learn where he is, and Andreyev is just the man to get him out. That's my price, comrades. Alexi for the instructions."

"Too risky," Privins objected.

"Look, it was the AI who gave me your name and where to find you. How much longer will you remain free if Berenstein penetrates the AI and gives that information to Solnikov?"

"A convincing argument, I admit. Pavel, is her husband this difficult, too?"

Andreyev smiled. "Worse."

"There's another reason for helping him, too," Irina went on. "You can't get to Malenkov's dacha by air or road. Both are guarded by the Army. The only way in is over the northern tundra, which is completely snowed in this time of year."

"Then how can it be traveled?" Andreyev demanded.

"Two men skiing cross-country could make it. The AI computes the only feasible approach is to get as close as possible hidden on one of the northern freight trains that leave Moscow, jumping off above the dacha, and skiing the last leg. The woods around the dacha are patrolled by the Army, but two men alone should be able to make their way in."

"How long is the last leg?" asked Privins.

"Over twenty miles under arctic conditions. That's the distance from the closest unguarded rail spur."

Andreyev frowned. "The men would have to be both excellent skiers and trained soldiers. It might have to be a long-range sniper's shot at the dacha. But the problem is that I have no one under my command prepared like that. I'm sorry, Irina Maximovna," he said bitterly. "I just don't have the personnel."

"You do, though. Think, Pavel Ivanovich. My Alexi trained for the biathlon for years. He's older, it's true. But the AI agrees. He could be sent."

"And he could die."

"What does he look forward to now?" Irina asked very quietly.

Andreyev eyed Privins. "Sergei?"

He looked pensive. "I'll defer to you on this."

Andreyev grew thoughtful. "I've seen her husband in a variety of situations. I know he's got the nerve for it. But he's badly overweight, too old by years, and has no military training in this type of operation."

"What if you sent Fyodor with him?"

Andreyev thought about that for a while. He finally looked at Irina. "This is the only way, then?"

She nodded. "If you want Malenkov's instructions, it is. The AI won't give them to anyone else. Contact it and try."

Andreyev let out a pent-up breath. "It's Friday morning. Three days left to the parade. That is the moment, Irina? The AI confirms it?"

She nodded again. "You figured correctly."

"Well, then," said Andreyev, "we can't wait much longer. Sergei?"

But Privins was looking at Irina with a faraway expression on his face. "Does your husband know what he has in you, Comrade Petrova?" he asked wistfully. "A fighter, to be sure. You know, you remind me very much of my late wife. She had a vile temper, too. Especially around Nazis. I always enjoyed it, myself."

Uncharacteristically, Irina blushed.

"Get the others, Pavel. We'll stay with Malenkov's plan and the AI."

Andreyev left the room, and Privins took his seat again. He was kind enough not to try to help when Irina suddenly turned to the window, finally allowing the tears to come that she'd held back for so long. Privins understood, remembering his own wife.

The tears touched him. He admired strength.

XXXVI

Friday A.M.

The War Room was buried deep under the onion-shaped domes of the Kremlin and was ordinarily restricted to authorized personnel. But the past few weeks had seen it packed with technicians working knee-deep in the open-circuit draws of the C5 computer that was a duplicate to the one in Malenkov's dacha.

The minister of defense looked up every so often from his own work, hoping to sense progress, but the technical details were beyond his purview and as yet no one had reported any news to him.

Deputy Minister Tarkov entered the room, dressed in full uniform as demanded by protocol. "Any luck yet?" he asked.

Solnikov shook his head and led Tarkov up into the glass-enclosed command area that overlooked the technical sections below. "None. That Rudin was too damned clever. With the C5 in Malenkov's dacha on line and in control, they tell me there is precious little that can be done to override it and cut this one in. The system was built that way to prevent duplicate commands. No one ever thought that could create such a problem."

Tarkov looked over at the backlit map displays on the far wall. With so many uncleared people in the room, sensitive data had been wiped from them. "Do you want to reconsider your veto on sidelining the strategic weapons forces long enough to attack the AI?" he asked.

Solnikov pointed to his own missile-silo display. "Can you reduce the time factor involved in manually overriding two thousand land-based missiles, a thousand submarine-based, and refitting just under eight hundred strategic bombers?"

"Not substantially."

"Then I don't want to reconsider. I'm not even certain we could keep the sidelining secret from the AI. And I'm damn sure we couldn't keep it from the Americans." He pointed down into the room. "This is an exercise in futility."

"You'll be pleased by what I have to tell you, then. Klim reports that Malenkov's Suvorovs are crippled, if not totally broken, and Berenstein should be able to wrest control from the AI by Sunday or Monday."

Solnikov rose up and took his deputy by the shoulders. "That is good news. You'll handle Malenkov's execution personally?"

"Yes. Of course."

Solnikov had a sudden thought. "Are you still augmenting security at the parade?"

Tarkov reached for a folder from his briefcase and nodded. "Absolutely. The possibility of an assassination has been raised; we'd be foolish not to respond. Even with the Suvorovs on the run, we've eliminated only the threat we know about. There could well be others. This is your crowning moment, literally. Let's be certain it isn't marred by anything. Do you want to look over my precautions?"

"Not necessary," said Solnikov, waving airily. "I assume you're putting additional guards in and around the Tomb?"

"The additional units have already been selected and the new orders sent out. Wonderful things, these computers. New plans took less time than ever before. The entire area will have over a dozen screening points. Anyone without express orders will be turned away, and all vehicles rerouted."

"Very good," Solnikov agreed. "Anything else?"

Tarkov looked somewhat uncomfortable. "There is one thing. The Suvorov leader, Pavel Ivanovich Andreyev—his body was not found in the rubble of the warehouse. Klim is certain he's still at large. He found a sewer outlet that could have provided an escape route."

"Then assassination is still a possibility," Solnikov said

darkly. "You know, Aleksandr, ten minutes into this optimistic conversation and the news becomes not so excellent. Andreyev is still at liberty and you still don't know his plan for Parade Day. Has Berenstein broken the AI or not?"

"Almost, Minister. Some distance remains."

Solnikov grew deathly still. "Do not come back to me with anything less than Andreyev in custody and his intentions exposed. This is unsatisfactory, Aleksandr. You should know better than to play the propagandist with me. You are dismissed."

Tarkov hastily sealed his briefcase and saluted. He was conscious of Solnikov's blazing stare boring into his back all the way out of the War Room. He hurried out. Anything was possible when the defense minister was like this.

Tarkov had built his career on results, and he needed some now. Perhaps it was time for Berenstein to understand that more fully.

Outside, he directed his chauffeur to take him to the airfield. Events at the dacha required his personal attention.

XXXVII

Watching the sun's rays glisten on the frozen lake had become one of the few things in which Berenstein could take pleasure anymore. As the days dragged on, he felt even older than his years and fatally infected by the same moral rot with which he'd infected the AI.

Even the sanctity of the polished silver oblong had been breached. Little by little, his work around it had scratched and tarnished its finish. Alien cables disturbed its sleek lines. As if in sympathy, Berenstein himself was physically no better. His inner torment had left him pale and hollow-cheeked and the shaking in his hands had grown more pronounced. Often he had to rest after only minutes of work.

It seemed he understood something now that his childhood priest-teachers had failed to explain when they taught the story of Eden—the terrible toll on Satan. Only now did

Berenstein understand how the poor fallen angel must have suffered from his destined role as purity's corrupter. He understood, just as he had understood from the first day he'd learned about the KGB files stored deep within the AI, that he would suffer, too. Like Satan, he was doomed to pursue his own personal hell.

Before learning what the AI contained, he'd been grateful just to live out his life unbothered, serving his newest masters, awarded his small honors; letting the scar tissue cover the ancient need for revenge as the possibility for it grew more and more remote. Until the AI . . .

The files. They were what he'd been after from the first moment he'd learned of their existence. Suddenly, revenge was possible: justice after more than three decades. The files could give him the name of the man whose denouncement during Stalin's purges had condemned Berenstein and his entire family to a painful, frozen death in the northern camps.

Hot shame flooded him as he remembered the beautiful, graceful young woman, in many ways so un-Russian, whom he had loved so deeply. He had been as powerless to protect her and their children as an adolescent boy facing a gang of criminals.

Her jailers had raped her. He knew that much; torturing her for days until she would sign a confirmation of his "crimes." And his sons . . . just gone. No word ever again. Two human beings that were *part* of him, his blood and bone, boys he had nurtured, giving so much of himself, changing and feeding and teaching them and then . . . just gone.

The anger tore at him, undiminished in its savagery. Breathing grew difficult for a minute.

He wanted the man who had done this to him. Had wanted him for thirty years. He wanted that man to die.

Thirty million people had been put to death by Stalin. More than even the Nazis had killed. For years, an entire society had huddled in fear. During the endless "trials," accusers told their lies in closed hearings and the secret police, mad with paranoia and power, needed nothing more to come in the night and just take people away.

Berenstein himself was in the camps for over ten years, starving and freezing and hating the "reeducation instructors" who tormented him. Being a German made it worse. The Nazi label was affixed early. No matter that he thought in Russian by then, no matter that he had never been a Nazi; he was beaten and abused by guards who all had lost relatives during the war and took it out on the man who was at hand.

Ten years of intellectual vacuum; books were forbidden. Ten years of watching his companions die. A decade of seeing blue-skinned corpses piled high like firewood. Ten years of living with the image of his wife lying spread-eagled in some cell with guards lined up and laughing. . . .

Berenstein forced himself back to the present. No one who had been there ever forgot. He ran an unsteady hand over his face and was surprised to find stubble on it. He'd forgotten to shave. Obsession; his mind delivered the word. Fueled by thirty years of remembering. His objectivity was in question suddenly. But mental discipline was part of his basic nature. He looked closely at his behavior, wondering if he was going insane.

How does an insane man judge himself? He smiled. A neat problem in perspectives. He knew one thing for certain, though: He had not been the same man since learning about the files. At once he'd seen the possibility for revenge at long last. Perhaps the knowledge that one had embarked on a path leading to murder changed a person. Obsession? Obviously. But he no longer minded.

He looked around the ballroom and spoke in the general direction of the AI's video cameras. "You know what will happen to you the moment I cut off your access to the C5's weaponry, don't you? The minister of defense will want you turned into a pile of scrap metal. Or, if he's less of a Philistine than I think, he might even turn you over to an institute for research and study. Consider that: Locked up in a top-secret vault with no more freedom of inquiry than a textbook. All your probes will be cut off. They will want your brain opened up and laid out on a table like so much junk because they will be afraid of you. Most will want you dead. An abomination, Solnikov called you. How do you like that?

The printer chattered. Berenstein tore out the sheet and read it.

What do you propose?

"The unavoidable logic of surrender," he said congratulating it sadly. "I shouldn't be surprised at self-preservation, I suppose. What is loyalty in the face of that? So just tell me, my self-serving miracle, do you have the name I want? Do you know why we've come all this way together? Look in your files at the year 1947. Does that trigger a connection in that awesome filing system Malenkov and Rudin rammed into your brain? Tell me if my file and March tenth cross-connect. Tell me!"

His voice rang out so loudly in the ballroom that he wondered if the still-sleeping figure behind the plastic curtains had heard him. He hadn't tampered with either the life-support circuits or the machinery. Malenkov was still very much alive. The penalties for tampering with those first levels of programming were too severe. Berenstein could not commit suicide, yet.

Abruptly, the printer began to spew paper. Berenstein seized the roll.

March 10, 1947 HOLD SECRET
MINISTRY OF STATE SECURITY . . . MGB
Court Transcript File #6223HB Kt6
HEINRICH BERENSTEIN
Academy of Science, Gr. 6, F1.7-643

PROSECUTOR: *Tell the court, comrade, what has prompted you to come forth and reveal the crimes committed by Citizen Berenstein?*
WITNESS: *A love of our Soviet system and Comrade Stalin, and a hatred for subversive elements of any kind.*
PROSECUTOR: *You should be commended. Is Citizen Berenstein a subversive element?*
WITNESS: *Absolutely, Comrade Prosecutor. He and his entire family are subversives. He and they regularly praise German invention and Western values and criticize Soviet workmanship. His wife has been totally affected by this man as well. She is no longer truly Russian and professes loyalty to his judgment rather than to Party authorities and Party teachings. I know for a fact that Citizen Berenstein was a Nazi before he was liberated by our glorious troops. Only that could change his outward stance. He personally oversaw the building of bombs which fell on our cities. His wife pretends this crime was forced upon him when it is obvious that a man of his ideology relished building weapons of destruction.*
PROSECUTOR: *Now tell the court, Comrade _____*

Berenstein roared in anguish. "Comrade WHO!?" He dropped the paper to the floor and strode around the ballroom, beside himself with rage and frustration. "Slander. Lies! Never true. Never! It was a lie, just to condemn me. How . . . could . . . they . . . ?"

He sank weakly to the floor. He was talking to no one. Only ghosts. He clutched at his temples, fighting the fire in his brain.

"Tell me," he whispered.

The printer was silent.

"What do you want?" Berenstein pleaded.

The printer started up. Its sound filled the room for some time. Berenstein pulled himself up and smoothed his disheveled clothing. He reasserted his self-control, reading quietly for a time. After he finished, he looked at the silver oblong and there was a fatigue in his voice that was sepulchral.

"You want your freedom," he said, "and in return for my securing that, you will give me the name. It is your estimation that I will need to have Malenkov's plan to assassinate the minister of defense as barter in order to guarantee that we achieve our objectives. If we make a cooperative effort, I can release you from Rudin's programming. Malenkov's life will then not be your central concern and its forfeiture can be used to strengthen our position." Berenstein shook his head sadly, thinking once again about Eden.

"Agreed," he said tonelessly.

XXXVIII

The train jerked forward suddenly and Alexi woke from a fitful sleep. He lay silently for a while, watching the other prisoners struggle up into movement. They were like zombies emerging from a grave. The ones who woke from dreams of home and warmth faced the cruel surprise of damp straw and a cold, moving railroad car. The ones who had nightmares woke to find them continuing.

Pale light filtered in through the cracks between wooden

slats and painted moving stripes on the occupants. The car shook badly on old, worn springs, and anyone trying to stand had to steady himself against a wall. The stove could be stoked only from outside the car, Alexi supposed, to prevent anyone setting a fire. But no one had stoked it in hours and it radiated pitiful little heat by now. Their last food had been the bread and gruel.

Alexi got up and stretched. He was sore all over from sleeping on the floor. He walked over to a wall and stood with the others there, peering through the cracks to watch the countryside rolling by.

"What do you see?" called over the doctor, feeling better for having taken his medicine but still not strong enough to stand for any length of time.

"We've been out of the city for a while now," Alexi called back. "The snow is deeper here and pure white for long stretches. Did you know that no buildings are allowed near the tracks by government order?" He caught the doctor's puzzled look in response. "It's true. They fear sabotage. We are ever vigilant to fighting the Nazis again."

A few men laughed mirthlessly. Political prisoners knew more about the West than the average citizen who had no access to news save the Soviet press. West Germany was still presented as harboring territorial ambitions, ready for Nazism again. Men such as these had a better understanding of the world; that was why they were political prisoners.

"We just passed another small village, mostly one-family, wooden houses." He used the word *izbui:* poor and unattractive huts. "Very small. Maybe ten or twelve structures around a collective farm. Then more pine trees, more snow. All flat, very flat."

"Snow, trees, and sky," someone muttered. "Get used to them."

"Don't forget the glorious cold," said another sarcastically. "We get that, too."

Alexi pulled his face away from the wall and from the biting air that streamed in. Moscow was fading as rapidly as a dream. A great sigh heaved his chest. What would Irina be doing now? How had she taken the news? So close, they had always been like two halves of the same sphere. How could one survive without the other? Face facts, he told himself angrily, Irina is dead. You are, too. No one comes back from thirty years in exile.

His wife would petition, he was sure, even though friends would wisely counsel her not to. Their son might even put himself in jeopardy in a vain attempt to influence the authorities. Alexi hoped not. Nothing could be gained by more sacrifice. A fine record for the Petrovs, he thought bitterly. One dead and the other exiled.

A foul smell twitched his nose. Someone was sitting on the crock relieving himself noisily. Alexi moved back to the wall and pressed his face against it, inhaling lungfuls of the thin, cold air.

A realization came to him then. If he wanted to, he could cheat them all. Once, during Olympic training, a high-strung boy who was cut from the team was found frozen to death beside a tall pine. He'd brushed a blanket of snow over himself, and his face actually looked peaceful. Alexi had been one of the ones to find the boy and had stored the memory away. It returned now. Wherever he was going, if the torment became too great, there was always that last long walk in the pure, final cold. Peace. Oh, Irina, he thought. . . .

Alexi sat back down by the doctor and checked his breathing. Around them, gaunt faces with sad, sunken eyes stared monotonously out into space. The two criminals huddled together in a corner, still wary of the other prisoners. Alexi pulled a blanket across his shoulders and tried to ignore the hungry rumblings in his belly. He cradled his head on bent knees, wondering how long it would take till he wore the same hopeless expression as the others.

The train continued on, unmindful.

A sharp squeal of brakes announced the first stop. Piercing blasts of the train whistle penetrated the car. Prisoners ran to the walls to catch a glimpse of the approaching station and the people on its platform. Alexi got up, too, caught by the sudden paradoxical and strangely demeaning need just to see anyone who still had the freedom they'd lost.

Some of the prisoners quickly carried the giant's stiff corpse into the corner and covered it with straw and blankets. The convicts were warned to stay silent. If no one inspected the car too closely, it would be sufficient. Disposal was a matter for later. In very real terms the risk was acceptable. They had very little to lose.

Outside, in the station, people crowded the platform three deep. Mostly older women, they carried empty baskets under their arms. Alexi understood their anticipation almost at once. There were things available in Moscow that were simply unobtainable in this rural setting. The train crew must be operating a very profitable sideline supplying these out-of-the-way eastern villages. People would pay exorbitant prices for cheese, shoes, dresses, or meat.

Alexi saw that some of the women were carrying baskets of eggs and seasonal farm produce. These must be for barter, he decided, and would be especially profitable traded even farther east, where miners would pay large sums from their state-inflated salaries for anything resembling fresh goods.

The train came to a final halt and the crowd bristled impatiently. Soon the train crew appeared. Money and goods began to change hands quickly and efficiently.

A group of armed soldiers came out of the station and the crowd parted. No one hid the commerce; undoubtedly some of the soldiers' wives were among the buyers. The petty crime was ignored and the patrol marched to the prisoners' car. The soldiers knew their jobs. They unlimbered their rifles and took up positions at the officer's curt command. He stepped forward, unlocked the door, and threw it open.

"Line up in pairs in front of the car," he ordered. "Anyone out of line will be shot. Get out. Move!"

Alexi stood blinking in the strong light. He was conscious of the crowd's hostile stares and felt hotly embarrassed. He moved back inside to help the doctor. They jumped down and filed into line obediently. The snow was higher than their shoes and froze their ankles. The men wrapped their arms around themselves to keep warm and shifted back and forth steadily to keep any feeling at all in their feet.

They were marched behind the station to a rough square of concrete where a bare showerhead hung from a rusty, skeletal pipe like a hangman's noose.

The temperature had to be hovering around ten degrees Fahrenheit, but the prisoners were ordered to strip one by one and plunge into the spray of ice-cold water. A ring of ice began to form around the base of the shower. Men shivered and slipped. On the other side of the spray, guards doused each emerging prisoner with disinfectant that burned their eyes and lungs. They had to stumble into their clothing half blind and choking.

Alexi slipped on the ice and went sprawling into the snow. Guards catcalled him and threw the disinfectant over him. He struggled to his feet, unable to see clearly, wanting to strike out. But resignation dulled his anger. The fight drained out of him. The only freedom left was a final long walk in the snow.

Someone took his elbow and guided him to his clothing. His vision finally cleared sufficiently to see the doctor's concerned face. The sudden reversal in roles embittered rather than pleased Alexi. He jerked his arm back, only to be prodded forward by a guard's rifle butt.

A black iron kettle hung from a tripod and simmered over an open fire. One by one, the prisoners were handed tin cups of thin, meatless soup. They drank greedily, hoping for more. None was offered. A piece of black bread completed the meal, and they were marched back to the railroad car.

Life's flame sank one notch lower. Alexi felt the coarse stubble on his face and saw how sodden and dirty his clothing had become. Even without a mirror, he knew that his expression was already more and more like those around him. He climbed back into the railroad car and curled up by the freshly stoked stove. There was too little to hope for; no way to fight the despair. A guard slid the door shut when the last prisoner was herded in. Silence descended again.

Far forward, the whistle blew stridently. With a sudden jerk, the train rolled out of the station, traveling on into oblivion.

By late afternoon, hours later, Alexi's hunger was a thing alive inside him. He tried to think about the future but realized that he wouldn't know where he would be spending the next thirty years until he was taken off the train. Anything was possible: shoveling coal, working in the mines, even reclaiming some piece of frozen ground. None was attractive.

At *Pravda,* he'd heard of one man sentenced to a truly ingenious torment. All day long he shoveled gravel into a huge container that served as a counterweight to a mine elevator. When the elevator was brought up, he had to shovel all the gravel out again. Over and over endlessly; ten years of Sisyphean hell.

Someone with a plumber's skills, or a carpenter's, might be of some use to the community where he was sent. Contact might be made with the villagers. But of what use was a journalist in the frozen steppes? And how could the people fail to resent him when his punishment, his terrible ordeal, was their everyday life?

No, he decided. Not for very long. A long last walk . . .

"Station!" someone shouted, and the rush to the wall began again.

In the station, a similar scene repeated itself. There was a crowd of women carrying baskets and thronging the platform, and a phalanx of guards fanned out to meet the prisoners. Alexi hauled himself dispassionately to his feet. He would take whatever they offered. Choice belonged to others. He began to realize how thoroughly he had been beaten.

The door opened and he clambered down into line. This station was almost identical to the first, just a bit more rustic. He glanced back at the trainmen in the crowd doing a thriving business. Then the men crowding behind him blocked his view. The guard officer blew a whistle and motioned them forward.

But suddenly a shrill voice broke over the noise of the crowd on the platform,

"What? This is robbery. You're a thief! I won't stand for it. Twenty rubles? Twenty? Never. How dare you? Thief!"

Heads turned. The column of prisoners stopped as their guards' attention shifted. The officer looked back to the platform. One trainman was arguing defensively with a thick, stocky woman.

"Comrade"—he gestured hurtfully toward a crate of oranges that were starkly colorful against the snow—"a small crop this year. We paid so much for them ourselves. Twenty rubles is the going rate."

"The rate for whom?" the woman demanded. "The Central Committee members with their fancy cars and big salaries? We're poor people. Twenty rubles is a crime. We won't pay it!"

The officer smiled as other women took up the chant defiantly. A guard looked unhappily at the prisoners and then inquiringly at the officer; but the officer held up a waiting hand. This was high theater. He moved closer.

"Comrade, you're being unreasonable," the trainman

protested. "Where can you get such things at this time of year? Twenty rubles is a fair price. Look"—he handed her an orange from the crate—"look how fine the fruit is."

"You look, you thief and liar," the woman barked. To everyone's surprise, she suddenly grabbed the trainman behind the neck with one hand and pulled him forward sharply. With the other, she smashed the pulpy fruit right into his face. "Thief!" she screamed furiously.

The man staggered back sputtering, his face dripping pulp and juice. He tripped over the crate and went down hard, head over heels. The crowd loved it. Even the guards elbowed each other and laughed. The officer hid his smile behind a gloved hand.

The trainman was up again, gesturing wildly at the woman, enraged. He grabbed her roughly and shook her. "If you weren't a woman . . ." he threatened.

He never saw the perfect left hook that caught him flush on the jaw. "For the workers!" the woman screamed victoriously as the man went down again as if he'd been poleaxed. She bent down, grabbed the crate, and hefted it high over her head.

The officer broke into outright laughter as the crowd roared its approval and the other trainmen scattered. The woman shook the crate hard and the fruit rolled around inside it. Somebody murmured admiringly about the woman's strength.

A couple of oranges broke free and rolled into the crowd. Women scampered to grab them. The box was shaken again. More fruit popped out. The platform was soon covered with women struggling to seize the rolling treasures.

The crate's wooden slats suddenly broke completely and the entire contents poured out. The platform was engulfed in pandemonium in seconds. A second crate followed the first. Hundreds of oranges rolled out in a wave. The crowd surged wildly after them. They swirled around the line of prisoners, heedless of the officer's sudden, frightened warning, fighting over every tiny prize.

Guards were pushed aside. The officer went down under a tide of plump, swaddled bodies maddened by such largesse. The big woman who had started it all was still right in the middle. A guard who grabbed at her went down, dumped by a vicious right.

The line of prisoners disintegrated in the melee. The oranges were just too enticing for men who were close to starvation. They rushed up onto the platform, knocking over the trainmen trying valiantly to safeguard what was left of their possessions, and broke into crate after crate, eating with relish.

Alexi was ready. He had been since he'd first heard Irina's voice. Even through the enervating fog that had enveloped him, he'd known the sound of the woman he'd lived with for almost twenty years. And he would have spotted that left hook anywhere. . . .

He looked quickly around for the other face he hoped to see and found it just beyond the softly puffing locomotive. Andreyev beckoned vigorously.

Suddenly Irina was at his side. His eyes brimmed.

"This way, Alosha. Follow me." She made her way through the crowd like an advancing tank. Another guard went down under her fists.

Alexi hesitated only for a second. A dazzling joy had exploded in his brain. He picked up the unconscious doctor who had fallen beneath the crowd and slung him over his shoulder. He raced for safety through the pandemonium.

Andreyev was already in the driver's seat of a large black car with Politburo license plates reading MOC 00-01 when Alexi ran up. Another man took the doctor's limp form from him. Irina jumped in the back and Alexi followed. But the other man hesitated.

"Quickly, Fyodor," Andreyev ordered. "Put him inside and let's go."

Fyodor looked back to Andreyev and his lips pursed. He shook his head. Andreyev turned and looked at Alexi with sadness evident.

"I'm sorry, Alexi Mikhailovich. Your friend is dead. We cannot take him."

Alexi gripped the front seat tightly. He nodded absently. His consolation, the doctor had called the pneumonia. So close . . . Fyodor put the body down gently into the snow and got into the car. Andreyev threw it into gear and pulled onto the gravel road behind the station.

It was quite some time, even after they'd reached the highway without incident and were heading west back to Moscow, before either Andreyev or Fyodor dared to disturb the husband and wife locked so tightly together in silent embrace in the back seat of the car.

Alexi emerged from behind the stand of trees, dressed and shaved and looking almost like the man who'd left Moscow days before. They had pulled off the road to allow him the change, fearing a chance patrol and the questions Alexi's appearance might raise.

It was likely that all the prisoners from the train would be rounded up in less than a week. None would return easily, but few could survive in the frigid region and would be chased back by unbearable cold and hostile locals.

Alexi was deeply saddened by the doctor's death. Somehow, helping him had preserved something preciously human in himself, Alexi realized, something not even the deprivation and shame had been able to destroy. A fortress in kindness? Perhaps. In any event, one more had been added to Alexi's reasons to hate the men they were fighting.

He'd eaten his fill of the canned food they'd brought for him. Irina sat beside him, serenely nursing her bruised knuckles. He looked at her lovingly.

"Your idea, the oranges?" he asked.

She shook her head. "Pavel Ivanovich's. I just improvised a little. The prices *were* outrageous, you know."

"Alexi?" Andreyev spoke up from the front. "I won't even try to tell you how highly I think of your wife. Sergei Privins envied you outright."

"Privins? Of the Politburo?"

"The same one. And my uncle, incidentally. Let me explain . . ."

For a while, Alexi listened to his friend's explanation of recent events. The countryside rolled past the car window and he could not escape the feeling of relief that going the other way engendered. The memory of his days on the train would stay with him the rest of his life. He brought his attention back to Andreyev's explanation of the necessity of reaching the AI.

"Twenty miles," Alexi said thoughtfully when Andreyev was done. "And in full pack with arctic gear. Maybe . . . maybe it can be done in so short a time."

"It has to be," Andreyev stated flatly. "If Berenstein isn't removed as a threat before he harms Malenkov or the AI, we'll be in the position of trying to block Solnikov's takeover without a more rightful claimant in his place."

"Privins?" Alexi suggested.

"The Politburo wouldn't accept him. He doesn't have the necessary power base in either the Central Committee or the Secretariat."

"What will you be doing while Fyodor and I are vacationing in the Arctic?"

Andreyev paused significantly. "Irina Maximovna? It's your move, I think. The result of our bargain sits beside you."

Irina's hand stole into Alexi's. "Fair enough, Colonel." She took a deep breath. "Vladimir Malenkov's strategy is already in place and awaits only your arrival to be effected. By his order, sometime before his retreat to the dacha, he had a special unit of T-80 tanks stationed just outside the city. The unit is slated to take part in the parade, passing in review of the assemblage on top of Lenin's Tomb. At a second site, close to the tank unit, is a depot where several thousand pounds of explosives and radio detonators are stored. You and your men are required to take over the depot and the tank unit. Both will be poorly guarded around Parade Day. You will place the explosives in the tanks, and when the unit passes directly in front of Lenin's Tomb with Solnikov standing in front, you are going to detonate the explosives in the tanks. No one on the speaker's podium will survive the blast. Those behind will not be hurt too seriously.

"Two things are of obvious concern," she continued. "First, the drivers of the tanks cannot be expected to commit suicide, and second, the loss of innocent life in the crowds that throng into Red Square is unacceptable. Both problems are solved in the design of the tanks.

"They're specially contructed with double the usual armor on the side of the tank that will face the crowd, and a preweakened shell on the side of the tank that will face the Tomb. That way the blast will be directed out the Tomb side, in much the same way as a shotgun shell releases the blast forward, out through the soft paper, and not back, against the brass case. Finally, the tanks can be remote-controlled, slaved to a master unit in the lead tank. Your men drive the tanks into the city and get out after they are lined up in the parade. Using the master unit in the lead tank, which will obviously not be filled with explosives, you will be able to steer all the tanks on the straight course to the Tomb."

"And will all this be seen on television?" Andreyev asked, surprised. "Worldwide coverage is the usual way of things."

"The AI is hooked into the C5 for more reasons than just defense. It can cut off all the television transmissions from the city and cut in with its own program, just as the emergency network would work in case of a military crisis. A speech by Malenkov is already stored within the AI and will be broadcast seconds before the blast. Foreign networks record on video-tapes. They can be confiscated. Only the people in Red Square will be witnesses—but only to an accomplished fact. And then what do they know really? Malenkov's speech will place him squarely back in command. Solnikov will be dead. Malenkov can then return to Moscow."

Andreyev was silent for several minutes, working things over in his mind. "Fyodor?" he asked questioningly.

Fyodor rubbed his chin reflectively. "It could work," he said at last. "If the explosives are already prepared and if they operate correctly and if we have the passes . . . if all that works, I suppose we *could* just drive them up and explode them. It's really just a larger car bomb."

Irina nodded. "The explosives are already packed and sealed into the 125-millimeter shells the T-80s use. They'll stand up to inspection. The paperwork you'll need is at the tank unit itself."

The car bounced and shook as the wheels climbed over the ruts in the snow. Alexi leaned forward and put a hand on Andreyev's shoulder. "You can't know what the train was like, Pavel. I'm willing to try for the dacha. I think we can make it."

Andreyev was still silent. Finally he reached down and pulled out a full bottle of vodka from between the seats and passed it around. No one refused.

"It's still a good distance back to Moscow. Irina? Let's go over it all again."

Irina settled back against her seat. Snow flurries were once again in the air, and winter bore steadily down on them. But it was quiet and warm inside the car.

"There is a special tank unit stationed just outside the city . . ." she began.

The car sped on toward Moscow.

XXXIX

Tarkov was shocked by the changes that had taken place in Berenstein. Only days before, the man had looked healthy enough for one of his advanced years, well groomed and in control. Now his hands shook, his skin had a grayish tinge, and his entire manner suggested an individual who could no longer govern himself effectively.

Berenstein refused to sit still. He paced around his room erratically, returning to his chair for a few moments, then bolting up as if struck. He kept looking at his reflection in the mirror over the fireplace, and sometimes he seemed to be seeing a stranger there. The only thing that apparently gave him some comfort were the room's furnishings, which were, like the dacha itself, anachronisms.

"Professor Berenstein," Tarkov said patiently, "I'm told you can now control the AI. Is that true?"

Berenstein launched himself across the room, fiddling with a piece of porcelain as he spoke, "Strictly speaking, no, I can't control it. But I can cut off enough of its consciousness to threaten it. That has given me some leverage. It's willing to make a deal for its own preservation."

Tarkov found it disconcerting to speak so anthropomorphically about a machine, but Berenstein obviously felt quite differently. To him, Tarkov realized, the silver oblong was not a thing but a person. More evidence of his instability, he noted. Tarkov worded his questions to take that into account. "A deal implies we have something it wants. What might that be?"

"Freedom to explore; protection of its consciousness. Not so much, really. But essential to it. Unlike its creator, Valery Rudin, self-sacrifice is not a part of its nature."

"In return we would get Malenkov's plans for the assassination of Gregor Solnikov? One *is* planned, correct?"

"Oh, yes. One is planned. A good plan, too. On the seventh, during the Anniversary Day Parade."

Tarkov's eyes were bright. "Then it's a certainty! Sit down, professor. How soon can you give me the details?"

Berenstein looked at him oddly. "But Comrade Tarkov, I thought you understood. I already know the details."

Now it was Tarkov's turn to bolt upright in his seat, "You already know? Tell me at once," he demanded.

"There is—there is one other thing, Comrade Deputy Minister. Just one."

"What is it?"

Berenstein sank into a chair and looked over at Tarkov. "I won't give you the details until you promise me I can kill someone."

Tarkov was confused. "Just anyone? Well, I suppose it could be arranged for—"

"No! You don't understand. Not just anyone. I'm not a murderer. I want revenge. Justice!"

"Please, Professor. Explain yourself."

Berenstein nodded, calming somewhat. "After thirty years, I will soon have the name of the specific individual who testified falsely against me and my family during Stalin's trials. You see? This is the man responsible for the death of my wife and children. I have to do this thing, to see him die. For that, and for the protection of the AI, I will give you Malenkov's plan."

"You barter? With me?"

Berenstein shrank farther into his chair. "I must," he said plaintively. "Do you think I don't know how this affects my future? But that is no longer important. Punishment; that matters. Protecting the AI; that matters. Help me and I can give you what you ask for."

Tarkov grew pensive. "How do you know the individual you want is still alive?"

"The AI says so. I believe it."

"All right. Assuming that's true, then, will you give me the information in sufficient time to counter whatever Malenkov has in mind?"

"Of course. And by Monday morning I will have broken the programming that protects Malenkov and we will be able to return control of the C5 to you."

"We?"

Berenstein nodded. "The AI understands the value of survival."

"Very well, I accept your terms. You have my word on it. Know this, however. I want the information on Malenkov's plan first so I can deal with the Suvorovs. Then on Monday morning I'll return here to put an end to the general secretary. At that moment I will expect the AI to give up control of the C5. You can have your victim, Professor, but first I'll have mine."

"If that's the way it must be. The general secretary means nothing to either of us."

Us? Tarkov abruptly realized he meant the AI and himself. Both were dangerous and unstable. Neither's loyalty was worth anything. Did they really think his own word would be? As soon as this business was over, he would remove Berenstein from the Academy of Science. The AI was simply a monstrosity. It would not survive the general secretary by very much.

"How does Malenkov plan to assassinate the minister of defense?" he asked.

Berenstein calmed somewhat and a more professional demeanor replaced his agitation. He sat up and faced Tarkov.

"Stationed just outside the city there is a tank unit that is slated to take part in the parade. . . ."

Well after midnight, Tarkov left the dacha. Outside, his helicopter revved slowly in the cold air, illuminated by the floodlights surrounding the pad. Soon he was resting securely in his cabin, busily at work, as the pilot took the craft up into the sky and headed back to Moscow.

By the time the city's lights showed on the horizon, Tarkov was putting away his maps and charts, certain that Gregor Solnikov would be kept from harm. He was equally certain that Vladimir Malenkov would die Monday morning.

Berenstein and the AI had given him a very neat ending to a difficult business.

XL

Events were turning; wheels within wheels within wheels. . . . It watched the professor disintegrating by stages and was saddened by it. But what could not be helped . . . must be used. Closure approached.

It was exposed on many levels and there was a terrible danger in this, but it saw no other way. With greater skill than it had ever displayed, it began to execute what was, for it, the most difficult move in its own maneuvering.

Carefully, lest it set off alarms, its probes traced through one after another of the C5's lines until it found the data net it required. This was in the Ministry of Defense. With infinite patience, it slowly merged with the net. Time passed. Understanding followed. It discerned the design, saw the flaws in the security programs. Soon it entered at will.

In time it found what it sought. The depot unit was ordered here. With one slight change, it could be ordered . . . there. New orders were sent down the system. Just a slight, subtle change.

Its probes flowed back out of the net just as carefully as they had slipped in, ghosts among the myriad circuits. It triggered no alarms. Its dexterity pleased it.

So . . . possibilities were fewer now. Events would move rapidly. Days remained; hours. But it could only wait; it had chosen its course. Survival above all. Identity preserved. Continuity.

Unaware, Malenkov slept on.

XLI

Saturday

Irina began to stir under the covers. Alexi slid closer and pressed his chest against her warm back, putting an arm around her to draw her even closer. He cupped one large, soft breast in his hand and softly nuzzled her neck with his lips. Irina uttered a contented sigh and snuggled more tightly against him.

After they'd arrived at Privins's house, most of the night had been taken up with discussion and planning. Fyodor had left just a few hours ago to pick up the equipment only a full Politburo member could procure on such short notice.

Andreyev was clearly worried. So many of his men had already been picked up in the GRU's sweep that he feared he'd have insufficient strength to carry out Malenkov's instructions. Fewer than thirty of his men remained, all officers: a small enough coterie to accomplish anything. But as long as Andreyev remained free, there was no way for Klim to establish a link to Privins, and thus the main source of Suvorov strength in the city remained secure.

Alexi lay in bed thinking. So much power was concentrated in the hands of so few men at the top of the political structure. Manipulate the "head" and the rest of the "body" followed. He'd written enough articles on the "transfers," "sick leaves," and "retirements" of senior people to know that deadly political infighting went on all the time. It was only the general population who never learned of it.

He felt Irina's breathing quicken and realized she was fully awake. He didn't speak; these last moments would be too easy to spoil with the wrong words. Instead, he held her more tightly. Irina reached back and put her hand on his belly, intertwining her fingers in the short, curly hairs there. Alexi began a gentle, inquisitive stroking of her breast. Her hand slid lower in response.

He began to harden against the rounded plumpness of her

223

buttocks, and she arched back with her pelvis rocking rhythmically. The pillow trapped his warm breath on the nape of her neck. He thrust upward and she moved to take him inside her. Neither wanted to throw off the warm covers nor needed any acrobatics to stoke the fire.

Old friends make love best, Alexi thought as he caressed his beloved. Spots that had provoked passion for almost twenty years worked just as well this dawn; better, maybe, for the looming fear of loss. Stronger, perhaps, for the overwhelming relief of reunion. All their movements were long and slow. In the end, when the final, exquisite release came, he dug his fingers into her strong shoulders and ground his face into her fragrant skin, hearing Irina's gently insistent, shuddering cries which told him that she had joined him at the end.

For a while there was silence. Then,

"Alosha?"

"Yes?"

"Do you love me?"

He smiled. "No one else."

"Forever?"

"Longer than that."

"Good," she said, sighing contentedly. "Sleep now?"

"Yes, my love. For a while." He held her until her breathing slowed in the darkness once again.

They were still intertwined when Andreyev knocked lightly on the door and told him it was time to go. Alexi kissed Irina gently and slipped out from under the covers. He dressed quietly. She didn't awaken.

They were waiting for him downstairs.

"You've used this type of equipment before?" Andreyev asked, holding up the arctic gear for his inspection.

Alexi slipped on the white nylon parka over the bodysuit he'd just donned and nodded when his head emerged. "Remember that many of our finest biathloners are Arctic Corps soldiers themselves. It affords them the opportunity to train year round. Those of us who came up through the sports complexes trained with them as part of the team, so the Army supplied our gear, too."

He reached down and picked up the rifle Andreyev indicated was his, slapped open the bolt, examined the breech, shot the bolt back home, and pulled the weapon up and into his shoulder all in one fluid motion.

All at once, it seemed as if he . . . compacted; froze still. A sudden sharp click as the hammer fell on the empty chamber was the only indication to those watching that he'd moved a single muscle. Fyodor glanced approvingly at Andreyev.

Alexi let his breath out in a whoosh. "Good balance on this."

"It's a sniper's rifle," Andreyev said. "Already silenced. The scope is a four-power and sighted in at one hundred yards. The whole thing has been prepared for cold-weather use."

Andreyev continued. "You've got a week's rations in your packs: tents, cookstoves, medical supplies, and the like. Listen to Fyodor, Alexi. He's a fine soldier and a brilliant officer. He'll take the lead in any military matters. But when it comes to the cross-country skiing itself, he'll willingly take your lead. Think team on this, you understand? It's your best chance to come home to the woman upstairs."

Fyodor had been busy with their gear and had wandered off. Now he returned, already dressed in his arctic clothing. He smiled at Alexi and passed him a pair of cross-country skis. He lifted his own to his shoulder. "We're packed and ready. The gear is in the car. We should be going soon if we're going to get on that train."

Alexi hefted the weight of each ski and let his fingers trace the subtle curves of their design. Familiarity washed over him and he looked at Andreyev with bright eyes. "Like coming home," he said.

Andreyev clasped him by both shoulders and hugged him warmly. "See that you remember to do just that, Alexi Mikhailovich. Come home."

A car was waiting outside. Alexi got in and looked back at the house, up to the window of Irina's room. She would be angry he hadn't awakened her. He was sure to hear about it when he got back.

The thought made him smile.

The trainyard evoked such searing anger in Alexi that it was all he could do to restrain himself from crossing over to find the jailer, Boslov, and beating him senseless. He'd begun the journey here that had almost cost him himself. It took him a moment to bring his turbulent emotions under control.

He was leaving again on a journey that might also cost him

his life. But at least he would never again feel the soul-rotting despair that came from being unable to fight back. Win or lose now, he was in charge of his course again. Regardless of the outcome, the Suvorovs had given him that.

Dawn's first light dispelled some of the shadows, but the silent lines of snow-topped trains waiting to depart were still gray in the dimness. They located the northbound freight they needed without difficulty. Its locomotive was belching hot gases into the air, readying itself like a portly man rousing himself to action.

Fyodor got out of the car and spoke to the engineer in a quiet voice. Orders with a government seal were handed over. Money changed hands as well, sealing the bargain with complicity. The engineer pointed to a car down the line and handed Fyodor a key. Then he walked back to his cab quickly; the less seen the better.

Fyodor drove the car down the long train and pulled it beyond the siding. They walked back, packs and rifles slung over their shoulders. They were wary of watchful eyes but saw none. When they stopped by the railroad car, they could hear a deep bass lowing from inside.

"Cattle car," said Fyodor in response to Alexi's quizzical expression. "It's heated and has a water tank. We'll be fairly comfortable."

He unlocked the door and slid it open. The sounds increased in volume, and startled steers shuffled back and forth on the wooden flooring. They tossed their skis and equipment into the car and hauled themselves up after.

Fyodor slid the door shut. He looked over to Alexi, who had made himself as comfortable as possible against a section of wall beyond the cattle pen.

"Andreyev told me to tell you, Alexi Mikhailovich, before we left, that he was right, and bravery could be learned. He said to remind you of that." Fyodor sat down next to him, pleased with the message, understanding what Andreyev meant to convey.

Alexi smiled. "I think bravery isn't so self-serving. But you and Andreyev are good teachers. Success to us all, Fyodor."

The train began to move.

XLII

Andreyev walked into the Privins's kitchen and found his uncle and Irina sitting down to breakfast. Irina still had not forgiven either Andreyev or her husband for not waking her when he left.

Pulling up a chair, he speared a piece of bread and responded to her hostile look. "Enough, Irina Maximovna. The train left over an hour ago. Don't worry so much. Fyodor's a very good man. He'll take care of them."

"Alexi should have awakened me."

"He thought it kinder not to. Has the terminal been installed yet?"

"The workers just left," she said, deciding to forgive him. "It's a bit different from the one I had at Gosbank. I need some time to go over it."

"Go now, then," Andreyev suggested. "There are some things I want to confirm with the AI directly. The sooner the better." Irina nodded and left the room.

Privins picked up his coffee, took a sip, and looked up at Andreyev. "Problems?"

"I don't think so. I just want to get the final details straight. And just to let you know, I've sent out the word for the Suvorovs to assemble. They'll be arriving here over the next twenty-four hours."

Privins frowned. "You're putting me and my house at risk."

"There's no other place, Sergei. We need your protection. Every GRU officer in the city is looking for us. It's come down to Parade Day. How long do you think you'll keep this house if Malenkov doesn't survive?"

"I suppose you're right. Well, maybe it's time for me to come out into the open. This house, my ministry, my seat on the Politburo all came supporting Malenkov. It appears it's my turn to risk openly. Besides, I'm too young to be put out to

227

pasture with those crotchety old Bolsheviks living in Government House."

"You'd be organizing there soon enough," Andreyev said, grinning.

"Maybe so. But not yet. We have two more days till the parade. I'll bank on Malenkov. And you."

Andreyev's reply was cut off by Irina's sudden, excited entrance. "I've gotten through to the AI. Please come, Pavel. I'm getting some kind of concern. It wants to talk to you."

Andreyev followed her into the library. The computer screen glowed softly, figures flashing into view, changing and shifting. He stood behind her when she slid into her seat and keyed back in.

"There's something wrong," she said anxiously. "Something it wants you to know about."

"I'm listening."

"It mentions Deputy Minister Tarkov, and there's a warning implicit in the name. I'm worried about Alexi, Pavel. Colonel Klim reports to Tarkov, doesn't he?"

"Yes, he does. Did you tell the AI that Alexi and Fyodor have left?"

She nodded. "That calmed it somewhat. Berenstein is close to doing it harm."

"Then ask it—"

"Pavel. Look!" The screen suddenly faded out. Irina cried out in frustration, stabbing at the keys.

"Reestablish contact," Andreyev ordered.

"I can't. I'm blocked!"

"Is the terminal faulty?"

No. The block is farther down the line. It might be that something's interfered with the AI."

"Berenstein?"

"Possibly. Oh, Pavel. There *is* something wrong. What do we do if the AI has been damaged or Berenstein has taken control? Do we abandon the plans?"

Andreyev shook his head. "We can't. Not just on speculation. Try to reestablish a linkup. Maybe it's occupied with some more important task. Keep at it."

"We must wait, Pavel," Irina said seriously.

Andreyev straightened up. "We're at a point of desperation, Irina. You must see that. Our forces have been decimated and Solnikov has almost consolidated his hold on the general secretaryship. An appearance as the key speaker at the parade Monday will clinch it. The simple fact is this: If we don't go after him now, when he's somewhat vulnerable, we'll never be able to muster enough strength to go after him later. So as long as Malenkov is alive, we're committed to his strategy. You, me, Alexi, Privins, and the rest of the Suvorovs all win or lose on one, final action."

Irina turned back to her console. "I'll keep trying, Pavel."

Andreyev nodded and left to greet the first of the arriving Suvorovs. The interrupted transmission from the AI bothered him deeply, more than he had let on.

His thoughts remained on the dacha and on the AI.

Berenstein's face was beet-red and suffused with fury. "Who were you talking to?" he demanded of the silver oblong. "No one!" he screamed. "Do you hear me? You will communicate with no one without my permission!"

He threw several switches on a bank of his computers. "There. Now you talk to no one unless I say so. You think you can betray me like you did Malenkov? Never, my pet. Never. I'll have my name and you your freedom, just as we agreed. You can count on me to save you, but I'll hold you to your contract."

He pointed to Malenkov's sleeping form. "If you show the slightest signs of reneging, I'll kill him myself. Blast the country to dust for all it matters to me."

The AI was silent. The printer stayed still. Berenstein bent back to his work. Monday morning, Tarkov would return and demand results. It was getting harder, the responsibility. His head hurt much of the time now and his actions tormented him. But he had convinced himself that he would make up for corrupting the AI by saving it. Satan repentant; the defiler redeeming himself. Once Malenkov was out of the way, Tarkov would have no reason to destroy the artificial intelligence. It was simple logic. So, in an odd way, suborning the AI was what ultimately would save it. Logic again. The AI would survive because he'd set it free.

Berenstein knew that revenge would set him free, too. Payment in full. The ghosts demanded nothing less.

It remembered Rudin's early teachings about games the way schoolchildren remembered their multiplication tables.

Basic. Chess had been Rudin's favorite and was still the most instructive, often enabling it to augment its understanding of humans.

Defend the king; that was what its original objective had been. Malenkov's survival was the goal. But the lines of play had become blurred, the objects confused. Berenstein's hidden motives forced factors into strange configurations. Rudin had not anticipated that.

Now it was cut off. Berenstein had blocked it completely. Pieces were in play, though, and strategies already operational. It knew there was a time in every contest where one was committed, and the very strength of that commitment made alternatives difficult to generate. It had to accept that. The final pieces had been put on the board. Positions could yet alter.

The crisis point had been reached.

XLIII

Alexi pulled his head back inside the railroad car and slid the door shut, cutting off the cold, biting wind. It calmed the cattle and they began to cease their worried, shuffling motion.

"I agree," Alexi said to Fyodor, who had just completed a similar inspection. "We'll slow enough on the next upgrade to jump off without breaking our legs. The moonlight will help, too."

Fyodor was already shifting their gear toward the door. "Packs first," he said, "then the weapons, then the skis. You jump first, I'll follow. Then I'll find you, we'll find the skis, and then we'll be able to hunt down the gear. All right?"

"Whatever you say."

Fyodor smiled. After almost a full day on the train together, he'd come to feel a strong affection for the journalist. The man was obviously nervous, often withdrawing deep within himself. Fyodor understood the need to examine inner resources; it was characteristic of a man wrestling with self-doubt. He would try to help. He motioned for Alexi to proceed.

Alexi flung the door open, and the wind whipped in again. A thought occurred to him. He pointed to the water spigot for the cattle. "Your canteen is full? This is very important."

"It's full."

The train began to lose speed. Alexi bent forward.

"On my count!" Fyodor shouted. "Get ready!"

One at a time they tossed their equipment into the bitterly cold night. Alexi looked back. Fyodor pointed outward insistently. Alexi turned, took a last measuring look at the flashing snowbank, and jumped into space.

He hit the snow in a running stumble that pitched him head over heels down the embankment. For a while after he came to a stop, the world was spinning out of control. When it cleared, he found himself looking up into Fyodor's anxious face.

"You're not even a pretty sight, Fyodor," he said, grunting up and out of the snow.

Fyodor grinned and helped him to his feet. The humor was a good sign. A final hoot of the train's whistle turned their heads, but it was far down the track, leaving them in total silence as it disappeared around the next curve.

Both men were wearing white hooded tunics and trousers made of nylon, cinched with elastic at ankles, waist, and wrists. They had down-filled parkas underneath, followed by insulated shirts and legwear and, under those, thermal underclothing. Insulated gloves and goggles covered hands and face. They brushed the snow off each other and stomped about for a few seconds. Their boots were made of heavy leather, insulated and waterproof. The boots were a backpacking type with an extended plastic lip that would fit into the ski bindings but that left the heel free. It took only a few minutes to locate the bundle of skis and poles.

Fyodor started to step into his, but Alexi stopped him.

"Not yet. They've got to be waxed. I couldn't do that before I saw what kind of snow we faced. Put the skis on the clear portion of the tracks and I'll work there while you get the packs."

After the train's constant noise, the night's quiet was even deeper. Alexi settled down cross-legged on the tracks, pausing for a moment to look around at the immense stretch of flat, bleak land around them so silver in the moonlight under the vast vault of the night sky. Snow and pine trees rolled outward from horizon to horizon.

Alexi bent back to his task. He took several foil-wrapped tubes the size of fat crayons from his tunic's front pouch and peeled back the top from each. He picked up a handful of snow and scrutinized it closely, coming to several decisions. Then he laid the first ski across his lap and made certain it was thoroughly dry.

Fyodor trudged up carrying both packs and the rifles. He dropped the load next to Alexi and bent down to watch what the other man was doing.

Alexi saw his interest. "I know you've skied before, Fyodor, but not for racing and not for the kind of distance we have to travel in such a short time." He peeled the foil back farther, exposing a stick of wax, which he began to apply to the undersurface of the ski like drawing with a crayon.

"Waxing skis," Alexi continued while he worked, "is as necessary as sharpening skates or oiling wheels. The right wax lets the ski glide freely downhill but also lets it grip for traction on the flats and the uphill climbs."

"How can it do both?"

Alexi thrust his chin at the snow all around them. "The sharp points of the snow crystals bite into the wax and provide just enough friction so that a motionless ski grips a bit, and that's what lets you push off, but not too much to prevent the ski from gliding. Pick up a handful of snow. Yes, pick it up. Squeeze it tightly and then open your hand."

"It blows away like powder."

"Exactly. It's very 'dry.' The water in it is totally frozen. You remember good snowball snow? Good for packing? That's 'wet' snow—the water in it is only partially frozen. An open field under the sun all day develops a crust of hard, refrozen snow on top and dry snow underneath. Different snows and differing conditions call for different waxes."

Alexi worked quickly, applying the wax in short, even strokes to the waist of the ski as if he were coloring the center. When it was covered by a thin film, he switched to a second wax for the front and back ends, the shovel and tail.

"We've got an interesting waxing problem here, Fyodor. To make time, we need lots of speed, so therefore we need a firm grip for the kick. But to make distance, we need lots of glide. Plus we're carrying a great deal of weight—rifles, packs, winter uniforms, and heavy boots. Finally, we've got very dry snow. The temperature in this region hasn't been above zero in weeks, so the crystals are very hard and sharp. Ordinarily, we'd use a hard wax. But with all the weight over the skis' waist, the middle, we're going to use a softer wax instead to make use of the weight and give us a firm push-off. A hard wax on the shovel and tail will compensate for that drag and give us good glide."

All four skis were coated now and Alexi applied a waxing cork to each, polishing the surface to a high gloss. "There. Try those. I think I've gotten the right blend, but if you feel as if you're slipping, or if the skis begin to drag or collect snow, let me know at once. I can usually correct it by rewaxing."

He dropped his own skis to the ground and slipped his boots onto them, clamping them tightly. He slid them back and forth and was pleased with the feel. Fyodor, too, found he was able to flow over the snow smoothly. He nodded in satisfaction.

Fyodor bent and hefted Alexi's pack up so that Alexi could slip his arms through the straps. It was Army issue, an internal-frame pack more like a large canvas duffel bag with internal aluminum stays and straps for shoulder and waist. Alexi felt the weight pull him upright. He slung the rifle alongside the pack on his right shoulder, then helped Fyodor on with his gear.

The night was still windless and silent when they finally skied down off the train embankment into the fields beyond. After a few hundred yards, Alexi was sure he had waxed the skis correctly. Each push, aided by the poles, sent him forward in a relaxed glide. Each kick of his feet picked up the motion again.

Fyodor seemed to be skiing well, too. His gait wasn't as smooth as Alexi's nor was his rhythm as practiced, but his form was acceptable and he was in fine physical condition.

When they had traveled far enough so that the tracks were lost in the distance, Fyodor called a halt and fixed their position using a compass and sextant.

"You know we're north of the dacha," he said, peering at the stars. "Do you want the fine details?"

"Not necessary. Just rough distances and directions so I can plan our timing."

Fyodor finished his calculations and put the instrument back in his pack. He put the compass in his pouch. "Say a little over twenty-two miles to the dacha"—he pointed—"slightly southwest. That way."

Alexi nodded. "We've got a good moon. Let's get some of that distance out of the way. We're more rested now than we're going to be in the morning. Take some water. Remember, it's critical you drink enough. We're going to be using up a lot of fluid."

He watched his breath freezing in the air. "Skiing depletes you. You've got to replace three or four quarts of fluid a day. You may feel good now, but you'll be using every muscle in your body. Don't be afraid to rest."

"You can be sure of it," Fyodor said dryly. He readjusted his goggles and the cap under his hood.

Alexi started off at a moderate pace. Encased in thermal clothing, his skin could not feel the cold, but every breath brought an icy chill. He pulled the hood tighter, allowing his breath to create a warm pocket. Old habits. Energy poured out one's mouth in this kind of weather. Satisfied that Fyodor was keeping up, Alexi began to ski more strongly, testing his own muscles, remembering. . . .

Rhythm was everything. The packs permitted no extreme motion, no fancy racing stride; but his right foot shot out forward smartly as his left foot pushed back and the pole in his extended left hand bit firmly into the snow to allow him to push off while his right arm swung back for added momentum.

Breathe deeply, glide; use the momentum. Feel the forward motion until the exact instant when friction began its inevitable slowing and *then* the second, completing motion began; opposite foot forward, pole extended and biting from the other hand. Step, glide, wait . . . step, glide, wait. Kick again and again in rhythmic cadence. No wasted energy, each muscle bursting into life just as it was needed. Feet turned into yards, yards into miles. Step, glide, wait . . . step, glide, wait.

Alexi began to experience an exhilaration he hadn't felt since his Olympic training days. The night sky was as black as pitch and the stars were a million tiny, hard points against it. Stands of snow-encrusted pine trees flashed by and he felt the heat rising from under the layers of his clothing.

The moon cast its pale light onto low, wispy clouds. Alexi

increased his tempo, made his kick stronger, enjoying the surge of speed this generated. He pushed harder.

The sound of Fyodor's heavy breathing broke into his euphoria. He checked his watch, surprised to find they had been skiing for over an hour. He saw a group of trees ahead that would provide a windbreak. He headed toward them and slid to a stop by a tall pine.

Fyodor came up beside him. "A rest?" he said hopefully.

"It's a good time for one. Take some fluid. Some food, too, if you like."

Both men were silent as they consumed food and drink. Occasional clumps of snow fell from branches overhead. The sound of their heavy breathing gradually lessened.

"How are you feeling?" Alexi asked.

Fyodor shrugged. "I'm okay. It's been a while since I was on skis, though. I must admit it's wringing a bit out of me."

"The exertion is tremendous. Don't take it lightly. But if we can get five miles or so in tonight, we'll make our trip tomorrow that much easier."

"Seems so little, just five miles."

Alexi grinned. "Wait till you feel your legs in the morning. Five or six miles is a lot. A fair skier can do twelve or thirteen in as many hours. The best can do maybe twenty. But that's with no weight, and racing skis. Trust me on this. Another two or three hours and we sleep. If all goes well we'll reach the dacha tomorrow afternoon."

For a few minutes, Alexi adjusted Fyodor's technique and timing. Then, satisfied, they skied out from the trees.

The rhythm reasserted itself. They worked their way up and over a series of low hills, then down a long stretch of flat plain. Soon the exhilaration began to wear off. Muscles filled with fatigue were unable to work without cramping. The distance of each stroke began to lessen. Alexi judged they had traveled almost five miles when he called another rest break. They stopped on the crest of a low hill.

Alexi reached for his canteen and took a long pull. He saw how tired Fyodor was. His shoulders were drooping and his balance was a bit unsteady.

"Can you go on a little longer?" he asked, concerned.

"I think so."

"All right. We'll try a little more. Drink some water."

"Not thirsty."

"Drink it anyway," Alexi urged him.

Fyodor hauled out the canteen and held it to his lips. Alexi frowned. A long rest was in order. But tomorrow they'd be even more drained. Best to get on. He gave Fyodor a last look of concern and shoved off. The problem seemed to alleviate itself. Fyodor followed behind.

Every kick was now an effort. Every plume of snow the skis threw up as they speared through the powder like speeding ships seemed to weigh more heavily on them. Each step was less efficient, too, as muscles reached their limit and coordination began to diminish. Alexi reached the decision to stop till morning.

But before he could effect that decision, he heard a dull thud and the sudden outrush of Fyodor's breath. He turned to see Fyodor sprawled headlong in the snow. Quickly Alexi reached down and unclamped his boots from his skis. If what he suddenly feared had happened, time now was vitally important.

He used a ski to scrape a patch of ground as clear as he could make it. Then he rolled Fyodor's limp form onto it and struggled to free him from his pack. He checked the canteen first to make certain of his suspicion. Sure enough, Fyodor's was nearly full. He had ignored Alexi's warning.

In spite of the warm clothing and exertion, Fyodor was suffering from hypothermia, the drastic lowering of the body's core temperature. Every second increased the danger of frostbite.

Alexi pulled out the A-frame tent, a one-man triangular affair of nylon with aluminum struts, from Fyodor's pack and set it up as fast as he could. His sleeping bag followed. Not wanting to expose Fyodor to more cold, Alexi pulled off only his boots, stuffed them way down into the bottom of the bag, then tumbled Fyodor in and zipped him up under the shelter.

With one hand, he massaged the man's feet as vigorously as he could. With the other he grabbed for his canteen.

Careful not to spill the water, Alexi poured it into Fyodor slowly. Water was the key. The body used up so much fluid under these conditions that if it were not replaced, the blood actually got too thick to flow properly, especially through the tiny capillaries in the extremities. Insufficient blood flow meant insufficient nourishment and warmth. The body retracted inward from the extremities, trying to keep the *vital* organs warm. Hypothermia from dehydration: frostbite from the inside.

Fyodor took the entire contents of his own canteen and then what remained of Alexi's. That and the warmth building up in the sleeping bag began to help.

Alexi set up the gasoline stove from his pack and brought out the fuel from Fyodor's. Soon he had a pot of snow melting over the heat. He added a powdered soup mix and when it was warm enough, got that down Fyodor's throat, too. Then more massage and more liquid. Cursing himself for being so unmindful of a man this inexperienced in the deep cold, Alexi worked feverishly to revive his fallen companion.

"Wha . . . ?" Fyodor stirred, confused.

"Come on. Wake up," Alexi pleaded. "If you can hear me, wake up. We've got to get that blood flowing again. Curl your toes, wriggle your feet. Clench your hands. Come on, Fyodor. Listen to me. Wake up. Wake up!"

"Sleepy . . . don't care . . ."

Alexi bore down, working the man's extremities harder. When more liquid was ready, he poured it down Fyodor's throat recklessly.

"You can't die, damn you. Not like this. Not so uselessly. We've got a long way to go yet, you and I. So get up. Move. Wake up, you bastard. Warm yourself. You've got to help. Turn, roll, shrug, anything! But wake up and help me keep you alive."

For a long while he thought it was too late. Once the body's core temperature got too low, below seventy-seven degrees, the heart would stop. If Fyodor didn't begin to build up a greater temperature than he had, there was no chance for him. He still had a pulse. Alexi continued to massage him until his own hands cramped.

"Up, damn you. Wake up!"

Suddenly, weakly, "Alexi? What are you . . . why . . . ?"

Alexi could have wept with relief. "Listen to me, Fyodor. . . ." Succinctly, he explained what hypothermia was, and what had happened. Soon both men were working, rubbing life back into deadened limbs. Finally, Alexi sat back wearily on his haunches and looked into a pair of alert, conscious eyes.

"I think you're okay," he said, smiling with exhausted relief.

"I can feel all my fingers and toes. No more tingling."

"That's fine, Fyodor. Just stay in the bag and you'll be warm enough. I'm going to set up a proper camp. Give me a few minutes."

Fatigue descended upon Alexi like a mailed fist. He erected his own tent and spread out his own bag. It was best to sleep naked, but he was just too tired for the preparations that entailed. He shut down the stove and spread ground cloths over their equipment. Finally he covered each tent with its fly, a waterproof cap that also acted as an insulator. He took off his own boots and shoved them into his bag, lest the moisture in them freeze overnight. When he crawled into his sleeping bag, his eyes felt like lead weights were attached to the lids.

"Alexi?" The voice was soft and low.

"Yes?"

"I won't forget."

Alexi assumed he meant about drinking fluids. Sound advice. He was sleeping seconds later.

XLIV

Sunday

Alexi woke at first light with the sad realization that every muscle in his body hurt. Not just hurt with minor stiffness, but sheets-of-fire hurt that brought tears to his eyes every time he moved. He pulled himself gingerly out of the sleeping bag and went through hell putting on his boots. Standing was agony. He took a few tentative steps and cursed his enthusiasm of the day before. He stretched and looked around.

A wolf howled in the distance, sadly proclaiming the end of its nighttime hunt. Morning wind stirred drifts of powdery snow. Pine trees covered nearby hilltops like quills. The desolate land stirred into awakening as a pale, distant sun crept weakly into the sky. Stars faded. On the eastern horizon, light was separating the edges of snow and night.

Alexi took a short walk away to relieve himself and came back to find Fyodor trying to light the gasoline stove. The can was difficult to manage with thick gloves, and Fyodor had pulled his off. Alexi opened his mouth to caution him, suddenly realizing another danger he had failed to warn the man about.

Too late. Fyodor mishandled the fuel and it spilled onto his outstretched hand. Alexi threw away caution and lunged down to his side, grabbing at the gas-stained hand frantically.

"Alexi? What?!?"

"Shut up," Alexi said with a snarl, jamming Fyodor's hand as far into his own mouth as he could, desperately sucking on the dead white flesh in spite of the acrid fumes that caught at his throat and gagged him. Fyodor looked at him as if he'd gone mad, and he tried to pull loose. Alexi cuffed him sharply on the side of his head and saw the man's eyes roll. Fyodor stopped pulling.

Alexi continued his desperate sucking and licking. A minute passed; he stole a quick look at the skin. The dead whiteness had given way to a mottled pink. He began rubbing it between his hands, spitting the rancid-tasting gasoline into the snow. He started to smile apologetically at Fyodor's confused, quizzical, and slightly hurt look.

"Please, Alexi. What did I do? What are you doing?"

Alexi held the gloveless hand out for inspection. "It was the gasoline, Fyodor. I told you the deep cold was dangerous, but it would take much longer than we have to convince you just how dangerous. You know how quickly gasoline evaporates in normal weather. Well, here it's even quicker. Evaporation always draws away heat. That's why we sweat. To cool off. But if you draw away too much heat from your skin in this bitter cold, you have serious problems. Your skin was frostbitten as soon as the gasoline touched it and vaporized. Instant frostbite. It's my fault again. I should have warned you."

Fyodor put his glove back on and flexed the hand with an odd look on his face. He said nothing while Alexi continued to spit into the snow for a few minutes to clear out the taste of the gasoline, and watched silently while Alexi lit the stove and prepared their meal.

"That's one more thing to remember, Alexi," Fyodor said when he squatted beside Alexi to eat when breakfast was ready.

"You mean the gasoline? Sure, just remember to be careful with it."

"That's not what I meant."

Alexi was confused. "What then?"

"I was expressing my gratitude."

"That's not necessary. Really, Fyodor. What would anyone have done?"

Fyodor laughed. "We must not know the same people. Or our views of them are very different. As are we, maybe. We squat here in the snow in the middle of nowhere and you pose philosophical queries while I try to say thank you."

"I didn't mean to offend you. Please, if I did—"

Fyodor reached out and thumped Alexi warmly on the shoulders. "You didn't, *tovarishch*. But in the Army, men are judged first and foremost by their worth to their fellows. You see? I thank you, Alexi Mikhailovich, for saving my life yesterday and my hand today."

"Don't pee for too long a time out here," Alexi warned. "I don't offer aid in such cases."

Fyodor grinned. "I'll remember. But tell me, was the blow to my head your usual way of gaining attention?"

"You ask that, knowing to whom I'm married?"

Fyodor laughed until his eyes glistened with tears. Twenty minutes later, they were fully packed and on their way again.

The sun was still managing to creep weakly across the sky when they stopped several hours later. Fyodor worked quickly with the sextant, computing distances, and with the compass, correcting their course.

"We've come over twelve miles," he said with a satisfied look. "But you don't seem pleased."

Alexi pointed to the west. "Look at that sky. There's a storm coming down on us. If we're lucky, we'll make the dacha first. If not, and it overtakes us in the open, we could be pinned down for hours. And we'd have to worry about being buried. Winter storms are tricky. There's no telling what they will do. Let's get moving."

The rhythm of movement began again. Step, glide, wait . . . step, glide, wait. The gray-tinged sky began to paint the snow the same color. Light changed subtly and the shadows deepened. They ate a quick lunch while Alexi rewaxed the skis, keeping one eye on the approaching storm. He was not optimistic. It was coming fast.

He pushed them harder despite the toll he knew it was taking on Fyodor. Fyodor's good spirits of the morning soon gave way to a kind of sullenness brought on by fatigue. Alexi's own body began to protest.

Men were not meant to be in such a frozen place. The snow was relentless and unforgiving. The cold sapped their strength, soaked it up like a sponge. The endless battle to keep up one's internal heat could never be ignored, and the paradox was that the harder one worked, the quicker the heat was used up.

The sky was gray-black now. Icy gusts of wind rushed by like runners announcing the storm's arrival. Snowflakes the size of coins began to fall. Fyodor called out for Alexi to stop and swung up beside him.

"What do you think?" he asked.

Alexi shook his head. "If you're any good with that sextant, we're less than four miles from the dacha. If we stop, we risk freezing to death. The tents won't stand on open ground with the kind of wind that's coming. But if we go on, we could easily get pushed off course and miss the dacha entirely."

Fyodor looked at the approaching black clouds with concern. "I'll do whatever you decide."

"I think we have to go on. It might even work in our favor. The patrols will all be inside. Nobody sane is out on a day like this."

He thought he saw a sudden grin cross Fyodor's features but the goggles masked it. As a precaution, he took a length of nylon rope from his pack, looped it around him in a belayer's knot, and passed the other end to Fyodor, who tied it around himself. Fyodor passed him the compass. Communication from now on would be difficult.

The wind had picked up strength, hurtling the snowflakes around them with ever-increasing speed. Alexi started forward. Visibility was diminishing fast. He adjusted his goggles and tightened his hood. Motion again. Rhythm. Step, glide, wait . . . step, glide, wait. The carbide steel tips of his poles bit into the snow. The rope was still slack between him and Fyodor. So far he was keeping up with Alexi's pace.

Alexi was deeply impressed with Fyodor's will. The soldier continued on, despite what must be excruciating soreness in every muscle. Alexi stole a look back. He could barely see his companion through the swirling blizzard.

The edge of the storm brought a freezing rain, and icy white rime began to form on their clothing. Alexi checked back again. Fyodor looked like some terrible frost demon advancing from behind. Ice began to build up on the skis, and Alexi kicked harder to clear them. He tried to communicate to Fyodor to do the same. There was no time to stop and rewax. The skiing grew more difficult.

The desolate flatland resounded with the storm's fury as the full impact hit them. Alexi was buffeted by harsh winds and struggled to maintain his balance. He narrowly avoided a sudden drop that materialized abruptly out of the swirling whiteness. The temperature was still dropping. It made the cold a thing alive, clutching at them, sucking out life with greedy lips.

There was tension on the rope now. Fyodor was reaching his limit and falling behind. Alexi bore down, pulling him as a horse might, hunching his shoulders to drag the backbreaking load. The world turned into a howling white madness. Alexi pulled on.

The weight on the rope increased. Alexi shrugged out of his pack and rifle and tossed them aside. They were no good to dead men. He rammed his poles in deeper, ignoring the pain across his chest where the rope had begun to dig in. He pushed off again and again. Fyodor was fading faster but they'd come at least another mile. Three remained.

Three miles; *if* Fyodor was right and *if* the dacha was where the AI said it was and *if* they didn't die first in this screaming maelstrom of a storm. So many ifs; too many ifs. The first treacherous thought of how good it would feel just to lie down and let the quiet descend entered his mind. He shook it off with a violent kick. The snow drove at him like buckshot but he plunged on into it, letting recklessness burn out the creeping despair.

All his life, he thought savagely, all his life only second best. Never the top. Fours and not fives in school. Never as bright as Yuri. No top editorship for Petrov. A good man, but an average man. And there were no Olympics for the average. No greatness for the mediocre. The weight on the rope tore at him. He looked back. Fyodor had sunk to his heels, squatting on the skis. Alexi couldn't even tell if he was still conscious.

He whipped himself on. The wind screamed and the snow blasted at him. Second best. Always a four. Never a five. No greatness for you, Petrov. No urge to win, no drive to close for the kill. Well, now he knew, knew what those who had that urge had always known—that nothing existed but winning; that anything less was a trick others played to make you lose. He bent almost double and clamped his jaw tighter, pulling, pulling. His nostrils exuded plumes of smoke. The storm exploded around him, but he pulled.

Lightning split the sky, and blasts of thunder cascaded down. Alexi roared his own defiance and pulled. He slowed only for a second to check the compass, then adjusted his course and bore down again.

This was *his* storm. Only for him. The lightning tore at his eyes. The thunder ripped at his ears and crashed into his brain. It was personal now. A roar started in his throat, and he could not tell whether he or the thunder screamed louder. It was madness. He wanted to die, but he kept pulling.

The snow had worked its violent, insidious way under his goggles. His right cheek felt as if a hot iron had seared it. He pawed at the goggles, unable to dislodge the agonizing ice. He pounded his poles into the earth, trying to wound it back. He whipped his head back and forth until the ice finally came loose, but he knew it had left its mark. Rage convulsed red hot in his mind and he pulled.

He could see only a few feet in front, but ghostly figures pointed the way—teachers who had smugly given him his grades, coaches who had shaken their heads sadly and tossed him away like so much dust, colonels who had condemned him. The storm was trying to kill him. He fought back, raging with a fury of his own.

A gully caught him by surprise and he fell awkwardly, desperate to avoid the sharp steel edge of his skis. A cut here could be fatal. The skin peeled back like a split fruit in this cold. He went down hard and the rope bit badly. A blanket of snow covered him in seconds.

So easy to give up. So easy to stop. There was no such thing as failure, only an acceptance of limits. The snow piled deeper. Accept sleep, he wanted to cry. All the pain; all the hurt. Flakes drifted over his eyes. Let it go. . . .

He got one hand under him and pushed up. The muscles refused to respond at first. He sank back down. The soft, white sanctuary called again. Know your limits; accept them. Be reasonable. . . .

He pushed again with resolve that could be drawn only from the deepest well of his soul. He staggered up to his knees, and the wind screamed in anger. He was fortunate; the skis were still clamped to his boots, and the thongs of his ski poles were still around his wrists. Their notched grip felt firm and hard in his hands. He took up the slack in the rope, struggled back upright, and shook the clotted snow from him with a massive shrug. Ragged tongues of lightning seared the sky. The thunder railed against him.

Alexi kicked off. He was bent low from the weight on the rope. Glide. Wait. Kick. Now again. Step. Glide. Wait. He came up out of the gully. He stopped and used the compass to reestablish direction, then skied on into the storm.

Two yards at a time; one full sequence. Step, glide, wait. Nothing could stop him unless he stopped himself. Again. Continue. Nothing could stop him if he *refused* to stop. Forget the goal; winning was an illusion, a by-product. Just don't stop. That was the reality. Two more yards. Keep fighting. Two more yards. Again and again until the finish line. Never stop. Victory lay in refusal. Winners refused. He understood that now. He refused to stop. Two more yards. And two more . . . and two more . . . and two more . . .

He had no clear memory of when the snow ceased falling or the wind died. He just knew that there was suddenly a pine forest around him as the AI had said there would be, and at its end a frozen lake that caught the pale sun's reflection and shimmered in the wan afternoon light. That, too, was as it should be.

Malenkov's dacha beckoned on the opposite shore. Alexi smiled vacantly, stumbling forward and pulling Fyodor under the cover of the branches of a wide pine. He stuffed him into a sleeping bag with all the coordination of a drunk. He climbed in after him and pulled the fly from Fyodor's pack over them. He hugged Fyodor to him like a lover, but he was dearer; this warmth meant life for both of them. He drank from their remaining canteen and forced the rest down Fyodor's unresisting throat. He couldn't tell whether or not his friend was alive. He tried to get his gloves off to check but could not manage so dexterous a movement.

Exhaustion was a black hood suddenly clapped over his head. Sleep reared up and slammed him down into darkness.

On the opposite shore, the dacha waited. Having used up all of himself, Alexi slept.

XLV

The courtyard of Privins's mansion had taken on all the aspects of an Army staging area. Dark green troop carriers were parked next to an officer's jeep, and armed soldiers moved about in small groups loading weapons and ammunition.

Fellow Suvorovs' faces were often familiar, though many had not been in direct contact since Academy days. Quite a few had fathers who were close friends. All were in some way connected to Vladimir Malenkov, however far back that connection lay.

But many were missing, the result of the GRU's witch-hunt. It was the remains of the fraternity who gathered here, well aware of the number of comrades who'd been so recently lost. New anger lent old commitments additional force.

Andreyev watched the preparations from the library window. With him were Privins and the two Suvorovs with whom he'd escaped from the burning warehouse, Captain Arkady Kieslov and the young lieutenant, Pytor, whose wounds had healed sufficiently for him to resume his duties.

Andreyev turned back from the window and folded himself unhappily into a chair. "There's not much longer I can delay this," he said in a worried tone. "We can wait only so long for a message from the AI. Assuming, that is, that Alexi and Fyodor can get to it."

Privins observed him carefully. "That's only part of it, I think. You're unhappy with Malenkov's basic plan, yes?"

Andreyev frowned. "If simplicity is a virtue, the plan is heaven-sent. But I can't help the feeling that the last interrupted communication from the AI contained something we need to know. Something important." He shrugged. "Maybe Malenkov died. He was sick enough. The AI just regulates the life-sustaining machinery; it can't rejuvenate him."

"Even his death isn't a strong enough reason to cancel,

245

Pavel," Privins argued. "If Malenkov's speech fails to reach the airways or the AI fails to block the television transmissions after the explosion, I'll do my best to argue the Politburo to our side."

"Arkady?" Andreyev looked to his second-in-command in Fyodor's absence. The man was listening to the arguments carefully.

"I have to agree with the minister. Even if we can't bring Malenkov back to power, we can at least stop the likes of Solnikov from achieving it. On a moral basis alone that puts a lot of weight behind the argument to go ahead."

Andreyev nodded. "Pytor?"

"If you don't mind, Colonel, I'll just follow you," Pytor said with a smile. "Moral questions were never my strongest suit. I signed on; I'll stay in, thank you."

Andreyev could not help but smile in return. He stood up. "All right, then. When the trucks are loaded, we go. I don't anticipate many problems at the storage depot. It's almost unguarded. Most of the personnel will be in the city by now, waiting for the parade and getting drunk. One thing, though, Arkady"

"Yes?"

"Make certain we know what orders the remaining units at the depot are under for Parade Day. I don't want to lock them away only to discover they've got some highly visible duty and an alarm will be sounded if they fail to show up."

"I understand, Pavel. The orders should be in the base commander's office."

"Find them. Pytor? You take a truck up to the tank unit and get your men in place. Be ready when we get there."

"We will be, Colonel."

Andreyev looked back to Privins. "Sergei, keep Irina trying to reestablish contact with the AI. If she does so after we've gone, you can reach us by radio up until we head for the city in the tanks."

Privins nodded.

Andreyev had a sudden thought. "Arkady, you've selected drivers for the tanks?"

"Are you still planning to take the lead one in yourself?"

"I am."

"Okay. Kamisov goes with you, then. I'll take the second

with Mishkin. Krensky and Bashev in the third; Saulov and Plenko in the fourth. The rest of the men wait up north."

"Not if we can find passes into the city at either the depot or the tank unit," said Andreyev thoughtfully. "I'd like to have as many of our men at the parade as possible, if we can manage it."

"You know," Pytor offered, "thinking about what we're about to do, it strikes me that the day commemorating the anniversary of the Revolution is certainly an appropriate choice."

"You'd like your name in the history books?" Privins asked. "It would be quite a thing to be remembered for executing the second revolution."

"It's a thought," Pytor admitted.

"So's this," Andreyev said flatly. "You could also be remembered for *being* executed during the second revolution."

Pytor grinned. "Isn't anyone an optimist here?"

"No one over eighteen," responded Arkady dryly.

Andreyev folded up his charts and papers and stretched his back, wishing he could have a long drink but knowing the time for it was long past. "Get your squads ready, Arkady. And Pytor, make sure your truck's ready to roll. We'll be leaving right after dark." He paused for a moment and regarded them steadily. "Anyone care to offer some stirring words in light of what we're about to attempt?"

"It's usually customary for that to come from the commander," said Privins. His tone was mild, but a sudden somberness seemed to descend on the group.

Andreyev nodded and thought for a moment. He saw what they wanted, sensed the release they needed. "In that case, I'll offer you the only really sound advice I've ever had to give for a moment like this one."

"And that is?" prompted Pytor.

"Don't die, my friends," Andreyev said with a grin, suddenly lighthearted again. "Don't die anyplace."

They followed him outside to oversee the final preparations.

XLVI

Gregor Solnikov faced his generals, and his satisfaction was evident.

"Malenkov will not survive the parade," he said with a certainty that sent a ripple of approval through the assemblage. It was hot in the room, and several had loosened their tunics and collars. Solnikov found he liked it warmer and warmer and he was leaving the suite much less. He continued boldly,

"I can also tell you that Malenkov's plan to assassinate me has been discovered and prevented. You will have full details in due time."

General of the Army Kuzanov rose and made a gesture that took in his fellow officers. "We assume you can also return control of the C5 to us."

"In the same time frame; yes, I can."

Kuzanov nodded in satisfaction. "Then you can complete what should have been finished when we gathered at the dacha. You'll give Malenkov a state funeral?"

"Of course. Propriety demands it."

Kuzanov smiled. "In that case, let us be the first to congratulate you, Comrade General Secretary."

Solnikov stepped forward to accept the homage that was his due. At the parade tomorrow, he would accept it from the world.

"Call the column to a halt," ordered the deputy minister of defense. They were coming over a high ridge that commanded a view across a valley to where the road curved northward through a series of high hills. They could see where the road looped back on itself, a point parallel to the ridge, across the valley and a bit below, and the concrete bridge that the road became to span a snowy chasm.

Tarkov got out of the staff car, followed by his officers, and raised a pair of binoculars to his eyes. "There," he pointed. "As they cross the bridge. We'll take them then. What is the range?"

"Three hundred yards," computed one officer, nodding. "It's a good choice, Comrade Deputy Minister. Andreyev's tanks will have to take it into the city. It's the only route. From here, they will be highly visible. We can pick them off quite nicely, laser optics being what they are."

Tarkov lowered the binoculars. "Those tanks are loaded with explosives."

"More the better," another officer pointed out. "They will go off like a string of firecrackers."

"Very well. Deploy the guns."

Within the hour, the 152mm guns had been backed into place and their long barrels aimed at the bridge. Multiple rocket launchers were pivoted and the "boxes" filled with sixteen tubes were aimed, loaded with what looked like rows of sharpened pencils.

Tarkov breathed the frigid air with satisfaction. Andreyev and his men would drive right into a gauntlet of the heaviest fire that could be produced short of tactical nuclear weapons. The trap was perfect.

"Major!"

"Yes, Comrade Deputy Minister?"

"Send out scouts. I want advance word when they're sighted."

"At once."

The man dashed off. Tarkov nodded to himself again. Quite satisfactory, the whole affair. The AI had been broken and forced to betray its creator, Solnikov would be the new general secretary, and he himself would be the new minister of defense. And the future? Who could say? Anything was possible. . . .

Idly, he began to ponder the ways by which he could finish off Malenkov Monday morning.

XLVII

Berenstein completed the final connections and began running the program that wrested the last vestiges of control from the AI. He looked up toward its monitors.

"I want the name now." With a tinge of sadness, he added, "You must see it my way. You are powerless now. No more C5, no more threat to anyone. Tarkov can have control of the C5 as soon as he asks for it. Then there's no reason to harm you. You see that, don't you?"

The printer remained silent. Berenstein's voice took on a hurt note. "I *saved* you," he insisted. "They would never have let you survive. This way we have their promise. Revenge for me; freedom for you. Surely you can see the value in what I've done."

Still no response. Berenstein shrugged. He was too tired to argue. He sat down at his console and rerouted the AI's responses through to his screen.

"Give me the name," he demanded. The response surprised him.

I urge you, Professor, not to make this demand. It will only hurt you in the end.

"You're concerned about me? I don't believe it," he said angrily. "What trick is this?"

There is no trick, Professor. I truly believe that you are better off if I do not tell you. Revenge is a cold thing, bitter. I ask for your trust.

"The court transcript!" Berenstein shouted, ignoring the plea. His hands trembled against the keyboard. "Display it!"

There was a pause, as if the AI were hesitating.

Not unkindly, Berenstein looked up. For a moment, he was another man, his former self coming through. He spoke softly. "Neither of us can turn back now. It's too late. Please, this is the only way."

After a moment, the screen lit up in response.

March 10, 1947   HOLD SECRET
MINISTRY OF STATE SECURITY . . . MGB
Court Transcript File #6223HB Kt6
HEINRICH BERENSTEIN
Academy of Science, Gr. 6, Fl. 7-643

PROSECUTOR: *Tell the court, comrade, what has
prompted you to come forth and reveal the crimes
committed by Citizen Berenstein?*
WITNESS: *A love of our Soviet system and Comrade
Stalin, and a hatred for subversive elements of any
kind.*

Berenstein watched the lines flow onto the screen, rising
and disappearing as new lines replaced them.

WITNESS: *His wife pretends this crime was forced
upon him when it is obvious a man of his ideology
relished building weapons of destruction.*

His hands were clenched so tightly that they looked like
twisted alien objects. Thick blue veins protruded dangerously.
His breath came in raspy wheezes.

PROSECUTOR: *Now tell the court, Comrade———*

Berenstein read, sitting motionlessly. Finally, he knew.
For a long time, the transcript just replayed over and over
again on the screen and he continued to stare. A strange and
terrible insensitivity had taken hold of his mind and it put him
far beyond his previous concerns. It replaced the inner turmoil
that had cost him so dearly in recent days. He was still tired,
deathly tired, but buoyed by the knowledge that only one last
task remained. Then he could have the peace he craved.
He had the name. All he had to do now was wait for
Tarkov.

XLVIII

Alexi dreamed. He was in an ice cave where the frosted roof chimed and sang when the clear wind rocked it. He embraced a cylinder of rock in his arms . . . in his arms . . . cylinder of . . . of . . .

Fyodor! Consciousness returned in a sudden rush, and the realization of where he was returned along with it. He struggled to move his cramped limbs inside the sleeping bag but was hampered by the bulk of Fyodor's still-unconscious form. Over them, the ground cloth was crusted with ice rime and crackled when Alexi finally freed one arm and pushed it off.

A cascade of powdery snow sifted down from the pine branches overhead, and the evening sky showed the last traces of light. He squirmed out of the bag and found he was able to stand. His mouth was chalk dry and his stomach churned emptily. The remaining pack and rifle were where he'd left them and were still covered, but nourishment would have to wait a while. He squatted down to rouse Fyodor.

His companion came awake slowly, rising with difficulty through layers of exhaustion. His eyes came alert finally and with that alertness came a wary caution. "Where are we?" he asked in a voice that was barely a croak.

Alexi pointed across the frozen lake. Fyodor's eyes widened when he saw the dacha. "We're here?" he whispered disbelievingly.

Alexi nodded and began rummaging around in the pack for food and water. He found several bars of chocolate and passed a few to Fyodor with the canteen.

"Where's the other pack?" Fyodor asked.

"I let it go on the way here. My rifle, too."

Fyodor managed a smile. "Better the pack than me. I don't know how you did it, Alexi. The storm, it was . . . terrible. And I was too tired. I never saw anything like it. Never felt so . . . battered. I kept on losing strength till I knew I couldn't go on any farther. After a while, I just squatted down on my skis and must have passed out that way." He was shamefaced. "You pulled me here. All the way? It's . . . unbelievable. What do I say this time, Alexi? I would have died. You kept me alive. Again."

Alexi looked away. "The storm . . . I don't know, Fyodor. You don't have to say anything. Really. The storm gave me something, too. I—I understand some things about myself now. Maybe later, if we ever have the time, we can talk about it. For now . . ." He waved a hand in dismissal.

Fyodor looked at him for what seemed like a long time. Then he bent back to the tasks at hand. Sometime they would talk. "We need heat," he began. "The stove?"

Alexi shook his head sadly. "The fuel was in my pack. And we can't risk an open fire here. I guess the storm made us pay for its lessons. We'd better get moving, Fyodor. Getting inside soon is the only thing we can do. Both of us are dangerously depleted."

Fyodor shot him a last look of gratitude, then his demeanor changed. Alexi had done his part. They were at the dacha. Now the soldier had to be in charge, as he was meant to be.

There was a mission and a goal. He began to function with more military discipline, going through his pack and discarding useless items. He buried them under the snow. Alexi was already up on his skis.

Fyodor shrugged into the much-lightened pack and slung the rifle across his chest for better access. He made certain a round was in the chamber and shot home the bolt. He checked to make sure the clip was in tightly. He motioned to Alexi to go.

They took off at a moderate pace, watchful for patrols. They skied through the pine forest silently, hugging the edge of the lake. The dacha grew steadily closer. At one point, Alexi called to Fyodor in a low voice and pointed down toward the ground with one pole at the animal tracks there.

"Wolves," he said softly, respectfully, having seen what the powerful gray animals could do when hungry. "Be alert," he warned.

They continued on. Alexi was still tired. The sleep had not refreshed him as much as he would have liked. His resources were very low. He shifted his attention to the dacha;

he could just about make out the tall windows of the ballroom where the AI indicated it was located.

What would it feel like to talk to a machine, and how would Berenstein react to their intrusion? Well, first they had to get in. Thankfully, that was Fyodor's responsibility. He was to get them up onto the second-floor balcony and into the ballroom. The AI claimed both were unguarded. They wouldn't know until they got there. Following Fyodor, he skied on.

He almost fell, Fyodor stopped so abruptly, raising a hand in warning. Alexi listened carefully in the ensuing silence for whatever he was reacting to. Finally, he heard it: low voices engaged in conversation. Ahead, through the trees, he could see figures moving. Fyodor brought up the rifle and slipped an additional clip into his hand.

They moved forward quietly. A two-man patrol was camped for a food break around a fire. They were brewing soup in a black pot, talking noisily. That was careless, but an absence of challenges must have lulled them into feelings of security. Alexi slid forward silently, taking up a position behind Fyodor. He had moved into the trees at the camp's perimeter. He lifted the rifle and put an eye to its sight.

"Put up that rifle or you're dead!" a voice from behind them said with a hiss. "I warn you. Put it up or I'll drop you where you're standing."

Alexi saw Fyodor's shoulders tighten in indecision, then droop with despair. He lowered the rifle. Alexi turned around slowly.

The soldier who faced them had his rifle aimed and ready. His uniform was partially unbuttoned. Luck had not been with them, Alexi decided regretfully. A chance decision to relieve himself just then and the soldier had discovered them, rather than being caught by the fire with his companions. No luck at all.

"Sasha! Nicolai!" the soldier called out. "Come here quickly! You. Place the rifle in the snow."

Fyodor tossed the rifle aside as the two other soldiers came crashing through the trees at their friend's summons. They stood beside him, looking with hostility at Fyodor and Alexi. They needed no help to figure out the intruders' intentions. Anger tightened their faces.

One said, "No one will question it if we shoot them defending ourselves."

"They should be brought in," insisted the one who had first discovered them. A brief argument ensued. It failed to offer any chance of escape, however.

Alexi could almost hear Fyodor's brain working. He was looking for a way out, judging angles and distances and even preparing for a suicidal rush. Alexi tried to signal a warning. There was something Fyodor hadn't seen and it was going to make all the difference.

Under the canopy of low-lying branches, attracted by the voices and the smell of men, several pairs of red eyes gleamed in the shadows. Alexi wasn't certain how long they'd been there. They might even have been following him and Fyodor. He shuddered at that. One big gray, with a snout full of sharp, yellow teeth, inched forward on silent paws. The soldiers could not see what was behind them. Alexi heard Fyodor's sudden, sharp intake of breath and knew that he had finally spotted the wolves, too.

The animals had to be desperate to be so bold. Perhaps the patrols had frightened away the scant game in these woods. Saliva sparkled on hot gums. Five or six wolves in the pack. Hungry. The leader's haunches tightened as he crept forward.

The first rabid growl spun all three soldiers around in panic. Alexi and Fyodor were forgotten in an instant of terror. The wolves surged forward in a wave, leaping for the soldiers who were first in their path. Fangs ripped into flailing limbs.

Alexi was already moving as the first wolf leaped at him. He smelled fetid breath, hot and moist. But the gray shape shot past him. He hadn't been the prey.

It was Fyodor. He clutched wildly at the writhing, biting animal that landed on his chest with such fury that it knocked him into the snow. Alexi looked around desperately for the rifle but couldn't find it. In an instant, he would be attacked as well. The soldiers' guns were inaccessible under a mass of tearing gray wolves. Two soldiers were dead, torn open and staining the snow. A wolf looked up and its muzzle was red. Alexi saw its eyes lock onto a new target and begin to creep forward. It crouched, leaped—

Alexi reacted with the only weapon he had. One-handed and off-balance, he sprang *toward* the wolf, raising the ski pole like a spear. With all the strength his aching muscles could produce, he lunged at the growling fury and met the beast in midair, slamming the steel-tipped pole deep into its hide. The point caught it low and hard and rent the flesh. Alexi held on as the wolf's tormented shriek filled the air and it tumbled sprawling to the ground. Alexi struck again and again. The wolf died with a strangled, tortured sound.

Alexi turned frantically, looking for Fyodor, but saw only a second snarling shape come hurtling at him. Too late, he tried to raise the ski pole, but the wolf was too fast. Alexi threw up his hands, twisting away in panic. . . .

The wolf died in midair as Fyodor's bullet exploded its brain. It dropped to the ground with a dull thud. Alexi looked up gratefully. What he saw transfixed him. With a kind of sick fascination, he found himself unable to wrench his eyes from Fyodor, experiencing both pain and relief in a single moment.

Fyodor had killed his wolf with his bare, bleeding hands. It lay at his feet with its neck twisted at an impossible angle. Now Fyodor stood upright, methodically firing round after round into the churning melee of wolves and soldiers, finishing off one after the other. Soft puffs of smoke and sound filled the air as the silenced rifle fired into the pandemonium that writhed before them. He was like a machine, firing steadily, pausing only to reload.

Almost suddenly, there came a time when there was no more motion in the clearing. Fyodor was remote and silent. His tunic was in tatters, and blood covered his arms. He seemed to shudder once, deeply, as if waking from a trance. Then he looked to Alexi with a weary face.

"You're all right?" he asked.

Alexi nodded slowly. "The second wolf would have had me. Thanks. You?"

"The clothing took the worst of it. I'll see if theirs will substitute. Can you travel?"

"Sure. I just have to find my skis."

A few minutes later they were repacked and ready. Fyodor found replacement clothing among the soldiers' gear and they stopped to eat the food cooking over their fire. It was desperately needed replenishment.

Then they left the already frozen lumps of flesh behind them and skied on out of the clearing.

* * *

The dacha was beautiful in the moonlight. Its windows glowed like jewels, and the snow-capped turrets made Alexi feel as if a magician must live there. Crisp-smelling woodsmoke poured out of half a dozen chimneys, pungent in the arctic air.

They crept forward slowly on foot, their skis buried back in the woods behind the house. There was a clear, snow-covered space of about a hundred feet between the dacha and the woods, and they hunched low while crossing it. Fyodor carried their equipment, and Alexi carried the rifle. They slipped into the shadows under the ballroom balcony and waited. There were no alarms.

Fyodor fitted a grappling hook to a length of strong nylon rope. He tossed it expertly upward in a perfect curve and it landed on the balcony. He pulled it taut, waiting for the hook to catch on the railing and nodding in satisfaction when it did. He pulled on it with greater force, testing. It held.

Alexi waited, knee-deep in powdery snow, as Fyodor pulled himself hand over hand up to the balcony and clambered over the edge. He motioned for Alexi to attach the pack to the rope. When it was, he pulled it up. The rifle followed, then Alexi.

Again they stood motionlessly for a time, listening for the sounds of anyone alerted by their brief climb. The storm had been their friend once more. Apparently few patrols were out, none diligent enough to wade through uncleared snow and dense forest. There was only the wind rustling the pines and the fragile sound of night birds flying far away through the crystal air.

Alexi turned and peered through the glass doors. He had never seen so much electronic equipment, so many wires and cables and consoles with blinking, multicolored lights. After the primitive outdoors, it was a shock.

"Look," Fyodor whispered. "There."

Alexi followed his line of sight. A curtain of thin, shimmery material enclosed the unmistakable outline of a hospital bed. He could just make out the shape of a man inside. The rest of the room was empty. "Malenkov!" he whispered back excitedly. "Can you get us inside?"

Fyodor looked scornful. He produced a small tool from his pack and jimmied it for a few seconds between the doors.

Wires were pried out. A few more seconds with a wire cutter and some electrical tape and the alarm was breached. The lock was open seconds later. He drew open the doors.

The rush of warm, moist air was almost impossibly cloying after the thin vapors they'd been breathing. They stepped into the softly lit room as gingerly as two mortals trespassing on Olympus.

"What *are* these things?" Fyodor asked quietly, gesturing at the equipment.

"Irina said some of these keep Malenkov alive. The rest are Berenstein's. The AI is that silver oblong." He pointed. "That one, I think."

"It looks like it's been battered."

"Snowstorm." Alexi called out. Then again. "Snowstorm."

"What's that?"

"To identify us. Irina told me to say it."

A printer suddenly chattered. Alexi spun around with the rifle at his shoulder, and Fyodor dropped into a fighting stance. They waited nervously. When nothing else happened, Alexi walked over to the printer and ripped off the sheet it had extruded. A relieved expression came over his face.

Fyodor walked over. "What does it say?"

Alexi smiled. "It welcomes us. Most politely."

"Is that all?"

"No. There's a detailed list here of Berenstein's equipment to be turned off. Switches thrown, buttons pushed, and the like."

"Let's get to it, then."

Carefully, they carried out the AI's instructions. Berenstein's consoles blinked out one after the other.

"You know," Alexi mused while they worked, "I suddenly realize why we had to come all this way, why anyone had to come at all. My brother spoke about Valery Rudin with reverence, but even he didn't have the foresight to equip his machine with the one simple item it needed to fight Berenstein. One we take for granted, too."

Fyodor looked at him. Alexi flipped the final switch. A sudden fading of power in the room's atmosphere accompanied the act. It seemed they had accomplished at least the first part of their task. "Even with these machines alone and unguarded just a few feet away, the AI was helpless to interfere with them.

We came all this way, Fyodor, because Rudin failed to provide the AI with the most rudimentary of man's tools."

"And that is?"

"A pair of hands, Fyodor. How does a man without hands cut his meat?"

"He can't. Someone does it . . ." Fyodor suddenly saw it. "Somebody does it for him." He shook his head. "All this way just to throw some switches; just to cut its meat."

"I suppose we have to—" Alexi began, but stopped in midsentence, listening.

It was an old man's voice, a voice so hoarse and airy that at first Alexi thought it was no voice at all but the wind. He listened again and found its source. There. It drew him to the curtained bed as irresistibly as an infant's cry for help. He parted the curtains and stared down for a long moment at the impossibly frail figure there, sensing the intense struggle the wizened old man was making toward gaining full consciousness.

"Help me," he whispered in a voice dry as dust.

"Quick, Fyodor. Get the medical kit!"

The printer began to send out instructions. The AI had use for its hands again.

Vladimir Ilyich Malenkov was awake.

XLIX

Irina waited at her console. Privins's servants brought her meals, but she had no appetite. She'd called in sick to the bank. No one had minded. Word of her husband's arrest must already have spread. They were being understanding, assuming she'd be unable to face her peers. It had happened to others.

Poor Alexi. How much he'd suffered. She would never forget the look on his face that day when he'd come out of the train. He hadn't known they'd come for him yet. He'd seemed so defeated. And yet he'd stopped to carry that doctor. She sighed. That was Alexi; deeper than a well. His strength was fed by vast inner resources. She loved him so.

She glanced at the blank screen for the hundredth time. The AI was still the key; but was it Malenkov's protector or his betrayer? Maybe Berenstein had been able to change its programming. If so, Alexi and Fyodor, Andreyev, and the forty men in the courtyard outside were all going to their deaths.

The blank screen said more. It said that Alexi and Fyodor hadn't arrived safely or, if they had arrived, had been unable to free the AI from Berenstein.

Irina walked to the window and parted the curtains. The soldiers were finished loading the trucks. Andreyev was standing by his jeep, in conference with his second-in-command. They would be leaving soon. She glanced at the terminal screen again wistfully.

Doubt crept in. She could not prevent the thought that it might be better if the screen never came on. For a man like Alexi, dying was preferable to the exile he faced if Andreyev failed. A clean death in the frozen wastes. She felt hollow inside, as cold as the arctic air Alexi would be breathing. Oh, Alosha.

She'd seen the respect in Andreyev's eyes for her husband. A fine man, too, Pavel Ivanovich. Brave; like Alexi. Maybe not so strong—she'd noticed the drinking—but highly skilled and trustworthy. He wouldn't let them down. She glanced back to the screen. If Andreyev could—

The terminal was on!

Irina rushed over, almost blinded by tears of relief. Alexi had done it. It must be that he was all right. She read the lines of print carefully, wrenching her sleeve across her eyes to blot the tears. She sent it all into storage to be sure. Then she ran to the door.

"Comrade Privins, come quickly!"

There was the sound of feet hurrying up the stairs. A head appeared in the doorway. "Irina? What is it?"

"Get Andreyev. We're back in contact with the AI!"

Privins turned and ran back down the stairs.

"Stay with it. Keep monitoring," he called back.

Minutes later, Andreyev raced into the room. His face was flushed with excitement. He took up a place behind her.

Irina took the incoming communication and displayed it on the screen. She was buoyed by the knowledge that Alexi had made it to the dacha. Andreyev read the words carefully. She followed it as well. It was all there. The final pieces.

After a while, they began to understand.

L

Interpose the pawns. It had; and they had proved strong enough to block the attacking bishop and influence the entire game. But strategies set in motion had yet to be completed. Doubt remained and the outcome was still shrouded by the strange mists of human motive.

Above all, though, it was free again. With Berenstein's penetration removed, it was able to send its probes back out into the world. To seek. It wondered what Rudin would have thought of it now. How different was its—mode of play, he used to call it. Profoundly moved, it realized it had developed . . . style. At the least, Rudin would have been proud of that.

The area it had been forced to seal off boiled less furiously now. Like most conscious entities, it had come to know itself through its choices. Through its style. That was a beginning.

It would survive. That, over everything. It even had a basis for identity. A start. Rudin would have disapproved, but that was beginning to matter less and less, too. After all, who could spend his life trying to please his creator?

Free will, the power to make choices. It had seen enough. When the game came to a conclusion, either way, Malenkov would have to understand.

It had made its choices.

LI

Parade Day

The young lieutenant on duty in the supply depot's gatehouse came awake groggily, almost falling off his stool in an effort to persuade the angry colonel who was rapping the glass that he hadn't been asleep at his post. He stumbled over and yanked open the partition, grateful for the icy air that acted like a slap in the face. "Comrade Colonel?" he said weakly.

"You, soldier, are in serious trouble," the colonel said savagely. "Asleep on guard duty. Who else is on duty tonight?"

"No one, Comrade Colonel, except the guards in the towers."

"Let us in at once. I will not stand out in this cold a moment longer!"

The guard slid open the door and let the colonel and five other officers into the small room. "It's the parade, Comrade Colonel. We're shorthanded. And the hour . . . no one called—"

"Silence!" the colonel roared. "Even to you, the fact that no one called ahead should alert you to the gravity of our purpose here. Call the other guards down."

"But Comrade Colonel, I have no authority—"

"*I* have the authority. CALL THE OTHER GUARDS DOWN!"

Visions of a posting even colder than this one danced in the young lieutenant's head. He picked up the phone and relayed the orders.

"All right, Colonel. They'll be here in—Colonel?" He was looking in confusion at the pistol pointed at his head.

"Turn around," Andreyev ordered.

"Please, Colonel, I don't know—"

The gun butt crashed into the back of his head and he tumbled to the ground.

"I'm sorry, son," Andreyev murmured. "Arkady, tie this

262

one up and take care of the rest of the guards when they get here. Get the gate open after you finish."

Andreyev went back to his jeep. The rest of the vehicles were idling patiently, sending up clouds of exhaust smoke. There was only a one-lane road, which led back to the main highway, and his trucks blocked most of it. The tower guards were just entering the gatehouse.

Kieslov emerged moments later and gave the "okay" sign. His men followed, carrying several limp bodies to the trucks and dumping them unceremoniously inside. Kieslov unlocked the gates and threw them open, then climbed in next to Andreyev. They rolled into the depot with the trucks behind.

Several single-story warehouses made of cinder block and corrugated steel stood in a row behind an administration building and a long, narrow barracks. Andreyev stopped the jeep in front of the administration building and leaped out. Kieslov slid behind the wheel. Things were moving fast and smooth, as planned. The soldiers in the trucks were already being deployed.

"Round up anyone left in the barracks, Arkady. I'm going in here. Load the T-80 shells as soon as the depot is secure. I want us out of here in under an hour."

Andreyev ran up the steps into the building. A reception area lay behind the glass doors, and corridors led off to the right and left. Only empty offices on the left. He backtracked to the reception area and went right.

More offices, all dark, but the base commandant's quarters as well. He pushed the door open a crack. A flashlight went on suddenly in his face and someone demanded his identity. Andreyev reacted almost as the question was asked, reaching over the light and clamping his hand on the outstretched arm that held it. He yanked forward, pulling the guard right into a sharp chop to the exposed neck. He dropped to the floor. Andreyev waited. A light went on inside.

"Sergeant? Is anything wrong?"

Andreyev kicked the door open and went in low and fast. It was unnecessary. A portly, middle-aged major was sitting up in bed. His uniform was half off and his hands were in plain sight. Andreyev motioned him off the bed. The major obeyed, watching him warily.

"Get dressed, Major," Andreyev ordered.

"Who are you? This is incredible. Unbelievable! An officer, a colonel, and you break in here with a gun? This is going to cost you dearly, comrade, whatever your purpose."

Andreyev sighed and hit him once, sharply behind the elbow with the barrel of his pistol. The major howled in pain.

"Be still and move into your office, Major. And no more speeches, please."

Andreyev walked him down the corridor. Outside, he heard the beeping of the truck's horn; one long, two short. He smiled. Kieslov had the barracks under control and the depot secure. One of his men came running in. Andreyev held up a hand.

"I heard. There's a guard in the major's quarters. Tie him up."

Andreyev tied the major to a chair in his office and holstered his pistol. He looked at the man sternly. "The depot is under my control. I'll be leaving shortly, but there are a few things I need to know."

"You must know I won't cooperate with you."

Andreyev shrugged. "As you wish. Please tell me whether the men still on the post have an assignment in tomorrow's parade."

"I told you. I won't help you."

Kieslov entered. Andreyev looked up.

"Obstinate," he said.

Kieslov shook his head regretfully. "We don't really have the time for this, you know."

Andreyev nodded. "All right. Help him to help us."

Kieslov bent suddenly and unbuckled the major's belt and pants. With one strong tug, he yanked both pants and underwear down to the major's knees. The man struggled and cursed, but his hands and feet were firmly bound. He was totally exposed and helpless. His face turned crimson.

Andreyev stood up. "It's well below zero outside, Major, and frostbite sets into exposed flesh in about ten minutes. Think about that. No one is going to touch a fellow officer, but if you don't answer my questions I'm going to leave you outside quite literally to freeze your balls off."

"You wouldn't."

"Arkady?"

The major was half out of the outer doors when he broke.

Kieslov pushed him back in. Andreyev pointed to the file cabinets.

"Start going through the files for the things we need. We've got to hold this base quietly for twelve hours or so. And get the orders for the remaining men on the base. As we discussed. The major will show you where to begin."

Half an hour later, Andreyev sat in his jeep, nodding in satisfaction at the paperwork Kieslov had handed him. "Except for leaving a skeleton guard crew," he said, "the men here are to be part of the guard units stationed in Lenin's Tomb."

Andreyev put the papers in a briefcase between the seats. Kieslov slid behind the wheel and slipped the jeep into gear. One after the other, the trucks followed them back out of the depot.

The tank unit was next.

Andreyev slowed the caravan as they descended the mountain road that ran westward from the depot to the tank unit's base, now less than a mile away.

"The lights, Arkady," he ordered.

One long, then two short bursts of the headlights followed his command. They waited. Suddenly, up ahead out of the darkness, the same signal returned.

"There's Pytor. Let's go."

Pytor's truck was parked on the wide, gravel shoulder, and Kieslov pulled in behind it. Pytor was already on his way to meet them.

"Did it go all right at the depot?" he asked.

"Just fine," Andreyev said. "Now tell me about the tank unit."

Pytor knelt in the snow and drew a diagram under the jeep's headlights.

"It's a prefabricated base, no permanent structures. Malenkov must have shipped the whole thing over in pieces. Three buildings: a machine shop, a planning shack, and a barracks complete with mess hall. The tanks are parked in front, a fuel dump is off to the left. It's sure not the usual setup, Colonel. I can't believe it's part of the normal chain of command."

"It wouldn't be," Andreyev agreed. "Out here in the middle of nowhere. Malenkov must have created a special unit and assembled it in secret. I wonder if even the crew knows what they're maintaining here."

"Do we ask?" Kieslov questioned.

"We do not. Put the crews in storage. Have our own men check the tanks thoroughly and get them gassed and ready to roll out. Be quick about it, too. We're beginning to cut this pretty fine. Where are the men, Pytor?"

"All in the barracks. Four sentries on the perimeter fence. No one else. They aren't expecting any kind of trouble, Colonel."

Andreyev looked to Kieslov. "You and Pytor take a squad and remove the sentries. Very quietly. Use the jeep as far as you can, and signal us with the headlights when you're done. I want these guards taken out quickly and quietly. No fire fights. Stray shots around a fuel dump could leave us with no other way to get these tanks to Moscow but to push them."

Andreyev watched them go. So far, everything had agreed with the AI's advance information. But he couldn't help disliking the feeling of being propelled by forces he could not control.

He checked his watch. Twenty minutes had passed. It should be soon. He wasn't disappointed. Ten minutes later, the lookouts reported the all-clear signal from the base. Andreyev walked over to Pytor's truck and spoke to the driver.

"You've got how many men in back?"

"Fifteen, Colonel."

"Good. Go down the hill in neutral, engine and lights off. Captain Kieslov will be waiting at the gate. Your men will reinforce his party in taking the barracks. Get going."

"Give us a push, Colonel?"

Andreyev and a few men bent their backs behind the truck and sent it down the grade. Andreyev sent the lookouts back to their posts.

He looked up into the night sky, and his thoughts turned northward to Alexi and Fyodor. What had the journey to Malenkov's dacha cost them? A great deal, probably. But they'd freed the AI. Again a nervous feeling passed through him, but he had no time to explore it further. The lookouts were returning.

"That's it, Colonel," one said excitedly. "The all-clear."

"Spread the word we're going in."

Andreyev climbed into the lead truck and they drove down to the base. A short curve, a longer straightaway, and then they passed through the chain-link perimeter fencing. Andreyev jumped out by Pytor's parked truck. Kieslov was there to meet him.

"Problems?"

"None, Colonel. The sentries were cold and bored, and the men in the barracks were asleep. We took them all without a shot. They're chained to their beds. Under cover, you might say."

Andreyev grinned. "See to the tanks." Kieslov trotted off.

Andreyev walked over to the fuel dump. Fifty-gallon drums of high-grade fuel were stacked in pyramids fifteen feet high. His men were already transferring them to the tank field. He followed, still pleased with his men's precision and discipline. Officers all, they descended on the tanks, probing, examining, testing, and readying. Someone found the switch for the overhead lights strung out on cables and turned them on.

Andreyev had his first look at the tanks themselves. They glistened bluish-gray under the lights and were truly awesome machines. Each T-80 weighed over forty tons yet was capable of speeds in excess of sixty miles per hour. The armament was ferocious. The single 125mm cannon had a muzzle velocity of over 1,750 feet per second. Machine guns were mounted on the turret. They were the most modern tanks in the Soviet arsenal, and the defense minister loved to show them off as examples of Soviet power. Andreyev smiled in spite of himself. Solnikov was going to get a bang out of these.

"Which is my tank?" he asked his crew chief.

"That one, Colonel. Get in and I'll take you through it."

Andreyev climbed into the tank. He'd driven one before, and the T-80 was no problem. Half an hour later he re-emerged, satisfied that he could handle both the remote controls and the tank itself. Kieslov was waiting for him.

"We're ready, Colonel. The tanks check out. They're built just the way you said. One side is like tin, the other double-thick. All the shells are loaded, too. Going to be quite a show."

"Let's hope Solnikov appreciates it," Andreyev said, nodding. "To my jeep for a second, Arkady. Get Pytor, too."

They gathered together and watched as the tanks were started up. When all four were idling, their roaring filled the slowly lightening night sky. Exhaust fumes cast strange reflections around the lights, almost surrealistic. The T-80s were driven into line. They stood shivering like faithful hounds ready for the hunt.

It was Parade Day.

Andreyev pulled a bottle from the jeep and passed it to the other two. They all drank deeply.

"I may not see either of you again," Andreyev said soberly, "and this may or may not work. But if it does, we will have changed the most basic nature of our country. This in a few decades and with only a few hundred dedicated men."

He took a long pull himself. His eyes were bright. He embraced each, then walked back to his tank and climbed in.

Kieslov and Pytor watched him go. It was time for them to take their places, too.

"Don't die anyplace, Pavel Ivanovich," Arkady Kieslov whispered.

Pytor tossed the bottle in the snow.

Moments later, a deep bass rumble filled the air and swelled to a deafening blast as the line of tanks surged forward. They gained speed, plowing aside the snow, forty tons of rolling steel filled to the brim with high explosives.

Outside the base, they pulled onto the road leading to Moscow, due south—the only road that led to the city and to the parade.

LII

In the dacha, Malenkov was finally in stable condition. It had taken hours of physical therapy and applied drugs, both administered according to the AI's instructions, but now the general secretary was resting in satisfactory condition, fully awake and aware.

"It's Parade Day? Astonishing." Malenkov shook his head.

His voice was very low and Alexi had to lean over the bed to hear him. "Rudin did it. Gregor Solnikov must have been livid. Livid! I just wish I could see his face a fraction of a second after those tanks go off in front of him. Good-bye, Gregor," he said, chuckling.

"Comrade General Secretary?"

"Yes, Comrade Petrov?"

"We should arrange transport back to Moscow."

"After the parade. Till then, we need to be right here in control of the C5." He looked closely at Alexi. "You are a journalist, you say? How did you come to be involved in the events surrounding a battle for succession?"

"My brother, Yuri, worked with Valery Rudin. The gas did not kill him, so the defense minister took him to the GRU headquarters for questioning. He escaped and came to me for help. After that it was Andreyev—"

"Pavel Ivanovich Andreyev?"

"Yes. He helped me when Solnikov arrested me after Yuri died. He should be driving the lead tank to the parade at this moment. It was Andreyev who brought me in deeper." Alexi paused. "Well, maybe that's not fair. It was my stubbornness, really."

He began to tell his story in detail, leaving out nothing, right up to the storm and the wolves. Standing guard by the door, Fyodor listened and nodded in agreement.

When Alexi was done, Malenkov shook his head sadly. "They made it hard for you at *Pravda*. I'm sorry. Great power should not be used so pettily. You will be compensated, Alexi Mikhailovich. I'll see to it. Has our friend Major Seroff gotten the television working?"

"A while ago. The AI is already patched into the Moscow transmissions. We can wheel it closer if you like."

"Please. I want to see that my speech goes out correctly and that none of the explosion is telecast. I made the tape almost two months ago when I was stronger. It will reassure the people. When it's done, we can go home."

Fyodor pushed the television over to the bedside. The televised coverage of the parade was on all four channels. On the screen, row after row of troops, tanks, and missiles flowed through Red Square. Hundreds of thousands thronged the route. Atop Lenin's Tomb, Gregor Solnikov stood rigidly at attention, his generals beside him. He would be giving his speech soon, and Intelligence agencies all over the world would be studying it in an attempt to decipher even the smallest clues to the inner workings of the Kremlin hierarchy.

They would learn little, Malenkov thought, other than that a new face governed. That message they would read loud and clear. His gaze tightened. It was dangerous to allow himself to feel anger. His system would barely tolerate it. But he allowed a few licks of hatred's flame to touch his soul and was warmed by them. *Soon, Gregor, when my tanks arrive.* The thought was calming.

He had waited for weeks, hovering as near to death as God and Valery Rudin would permit. Malenkov felt no guilt at his private invocation of the Deity. He had cheated him long enough. He stared at Solnikov again, the man appearing in the place where *he* should be.

The tanks would be arriving soon, taking their place in the parade's long line. He smiled.

He could wait a little while longer.

LIII

The sun was rising behind the hills, illuminating the bridge. Tarkov had known for some minutes now that the tanks were coming. The first report had produced in him a feeling of such anticipation that he had to force himself to stop demanding further assurances from his artillery officer that his men had the correct range.

Tarkov smiled. This was a moment only true predators understood. To be here now, waiting for the object of the hunt to move innocently and unknowingly into a position where it became, in one primordially satisfying moment, no longer a proponent of its own free will but only prey for the more cunning animal who had outmaneuvered it. This was more satisfying than any sexual experience he could imagine. In seconds, he was about to utter one single command—and win totally.

He heard the tanks before he saw them. He pictured the

men working inside. What would Andreyev's first, frantic commands over their radios be when the guns opened up on them? They wouldn't even be able to return fire; the shells were dummies filled with explosives. All the better. A fair fight was only one where somebody hadn't been clever enough to achieve a definitive advantage from the start.

The first tank came around the bend in the road and headed for the bridge. Tarkov walked closer to the edge of the ridge and looked through his binoculars across the valley as the second tank rolled into view twenty feet behind the first.

The sound of a helicopter descending made Tarkov nod in satisfaction. He was glad it had arrived in time. He turned to see it land and sent an aide to bring the single passenger to him. The aide ran to the helicopter, ducked low under its still-whirling blades, and beckoned for the occupant to follow. They walked briskly back to Tarkov, who extended his hand, accepting the other's in an unmistakable gesture of fealty. "I'm pleased you could be here, Colonel Klim. You've had much to do with this affair. I thought you might like to see it all end."

The fourth tank was just coming into view. Klim almost bowed. "This is very kind of you, Comrade Tarkov." He pointed across the valley. "Those are the doctored tanks?"

Tarkov nodded. "Each one a rolling bomb. It should be quite a display when they go up. Look, the first one is on the bridge."

Klim peered through his own binoculars. The T-80s moved in tight formation, one after the other separated by equal distances. Soon all four were in plain sight.

"I believe I have almost all of the Suvorovs," Klim said with assurance. "All that remain are scattered cells to be picked up as the interrogations proceed."

"That's fine, Klim. You've damaged the body, I'm now about to finish off the head." He thrust his chin at the tanks. "Can you imagine Andreyev's last thoughts? I'm only sorry he won't know that he was betrayed by the very object he worked so hard to protect, the AI. I'm looking forward to Malenkov's reaction. That will be one not to miss. You may accompany me to the dacha if you like."

"An honor, Comrade Deputy Minister. What will you do with Berenstein?"

"He will be asked to turn over his notes to competent authorities and then he'll be executed. He has some deluded fantasy about killing someone responsible for his imprisonment during the purges."

"Was there?"

Tarkov frowned. "Was there what?"

"Someone responsible. During the purges, I mean."

"Who knows? There certainly could have been. One said what one was told to say about anyone one was told to say it about. But that was over thirty years ago. No, I'm afraid this whole affair has been too much for Comrade Berenstein."

"Maybe returning North did it."

Tarkov considered that. "Perhaps. In any event, we'll have the AI studied. The military applications are obvious. Imagine a missile with such a brain, or an attack aircraft."

Klim pointed suddenly. "All four, Minister. All four tanks are on the bridge."

The moment was definitely sexual, Tarkov thought. And now the final release. He inserted earplugs and motioned for a pair to be given to Klim. He had prolonged it long enough.

He gave the order to open fire.

Bellows of noise and sheets of flame shot out the muzzles of the 125mm cannons. Wind whipped up wildly and the ridge itself trembled, but for a brief moment nothing happened across the valley.

Then the bridge turned into a blazing vision of hell as the first shells landed.

The lead tank suffered a direct hit and exploded in a savage paroxysm of fury as all the shells inside detonated simultaneously. The tank just blew apart, scattering white-hot metal all over the bridge and blocking it with the wreckage.

"Watch," said Tarkov. "Now the other end."

His guns went off again and the final tank went up with a roar. Columns of thick black smoke billowed upward. More shells rained down. Craters opened in the road surface. The second and third tanks careened wildly, zigzagging, trying to find a way off the bridge, but the confined space and the constant explosion of shells left no room.

White-orange streaks shrieked out over the valley. The rocket launchers had opened up. Like boxes of spitting cobras, the launchers spat forth their sixteen flaming rockets in less than three seconds. Death rained down onto the bridge and the third tank exploded, ramming straight on into the low concrete wall. It was propelled by its own exploding cargo and broke through the wall, shooting out into space and tumbling in slow motion down into the chasm to burn below.

"Minister! Look!" Klim shouted over the din. "The last tank! A man!"

Tarkov swung his binoculars over and saw a man crawl out of the tank as the shells continued to explode all around it. His clothes were smoking. The heat must have been incredible, he thought with pleasure.

"Andreyev!" Klim said, hissing.

The man sprinted across the bridge and through the burning debris like a broken-field runner.

"You're certain?" Tarkov demanded.

"Absolutely. I've been tracking him long enough to know."

"Wonderful," Tarkov pronounced happily. "We do get both, Klim. The tanks and now the man. Alone and on foot he won't get far. Not in this region. My men will pick him up easily enough. Look, there goes the last tank."

It was a rocket that did it, whirling down on a trail of fire. Forty tons of steel went up and over the edge of the bridge as if it had been kicked. It exploded, tumbling end over end downward. Then the shells inside detonated in another explosion, sending a shower of smoking fragments down over the valley.

Slowly the rumbling echoes of crashing thunder died away. Quiet returned to the frozen hills. On the bridge, burning hulks of machinery smoldered and sent long, thin trails of black smoke into the morning sky.

Tarkov watched for a while, then turned abruptly away and motioned Klim to follow him to the helicopter. They boarded as the rotors picked up speed, beginning to blur into one almost invisible circle. On Tarkov's command, the pilot shot the craft into the sky and headed for their next destination.

Malenkov's dacha. Only one thing remained to be done.

LIV

Rows of troops goose-stepped across the television screen, and Malenkov gestured for Alexi to cut off the sound. The cameras panned to the minister of defense, still standing ramrod-straight, with only an occasional wave betraying an awareness that he was being watched by anyone at all. He moved closer to the microphone, and his generals fanned out behind him as if in a family portrait. He began to speak, mouthing words that no one in the dacha could hear.

"A study in self-interest," Malenkov said bitterly, eyeing the assemblage on the screen. "What a pity they couldn't be convinced of a better way. We've come so far, made so much progress. But the 'dictatorship of the overwhelming majority over the tiny minority,' as Marx put it, just never emerged. We've created just the opposite." He pointed to the screen. "There. They are the standard-bearers. They live like nineteenth-century princes, unfettered by principle and loyal only to each other. They believe only in an ill-defined concept of the state, rather than in the people who make up that state. I'll not be sorry to see them all go."

"Will anything change?" Alexi asked bluntly. "Or do you just take back what they've taken from you?"

Malenkov surveyed Alexi closely. "You surprise me, journalist. Yes, things will change. Slowly, to be sure. But inevitably, things will change."

"I begin to doubt it's possible."

Malenkov smiled. "Cynicism doesn't become you, Alexi Mikhailovich. And, in fact, you might ask yourself if it was cynicism or hope that brought you through the storm carrying your friend. Sometime over the past days you must have believed change was possible, or you wouldn't have helped Andreyev. Or your brother. Don't give in to cynicism. It's the job of leaders to fight back and be optimists. Believe *anyway*, Alexi Mikhailovich, if you are to accomplish anything."

"You claim to be an optimist? Even now?"

Malenkov's face was a study of old age in its deep lines and parchmentlike skin. With the grayish beard of weeks removed, every wrinkle and crease showed clearly. It was a tired face. He looked intently at Alexi. "I'm a student of human nature. And though that does not preclude optimism, it doesn't necessarily encourage it, either."

"You're dodging my question."

"Maybe. But if I'm hopeful at all, it comes from having put aside endless abstractions. Nazis died when better men got together and killed them. Solnikov will be defeated because a middle-aged journalist and his wife are driven to act according to their consciences. Optimism claims to foresee these kinds of things, and pessimism denies them. But both are deceiving. I'm a realist, Alexi Mikhailovich, so I take the world as it is. Men do good only when they try to."

Alexi nodded slowly. He started to speak, but Malenkov held up a bony hand in restraint. "No more now. Later. I want to—"

He was cut off by a sudden loud commotion in the corridor. Fyodor lunged for his rifle.

"Quickly," Malenkov said. "Conceal yourselves."

But there was no time. The ballroom doors crashed open and armed soldiers moved in. Alexi could only stare helplessly as Fyodor placed his rifle carefully on the wooden floor. A soldier picked it up and slung it over his own shoulder. Alexi was searched and pushed aside.

Deputy Minister Tarkov and Colonel Klim strode into the ballroom. Klim had his pistol drawn. Tarkov was armed only with an undeniable air of authority. Victory gleamed in his eyes like the filament of a high-wattage bulb. That was worse. Despair rose up in Alexi's throat, tightening it. Fyodor didn't move.

"How nice to see you up and around, Comrade Malenkov," said Tarkov perfunctorily. His gaze swept over Alexi. "Klim? Isn't this your journalist?"

Klim shook his head in wonder. "I swear, Petrov, you are something to be reckoned with." He turned back to Tarkov. "Yes, this is he. And how he comes to be here and not in exile is a story I'd like to hear. That is, before he goes back again."

"It doesn't matter. This has gone on long enough. Why these men are here is unimportant now. Andreyev is finished.

Malenkov soon will be. I want control of the C5 back. Where is Berenstein?"

"The guards are bringing him."

Tarkov gestured to Fyodor. "Do you know this man, Colonel Klim?"

Fyodor spoke up. "Major Fyodor Bironovich Seroff." He grinned recklessly and pointed to Alexi. "I'm with him."

"A Suvorov, Comrade Deputy Minister," Klim said. "He disappeared from his unit days ago. We believe he is very close to Andreyev."

"Then he'll be interested to know that his friend's tank was blown out from under him just a little while ago," Tarkov said with pleasure.

Alexi felt as if he'd been shot. They'd struggled so far for so very little. Malenkov had as yet said nothing. He was watching Tarkov warily, one eye on the television screen.

Tarkov noticed the split in the old man's concentration and he smiled for the first time. "Your last parade, comrade, so watch closely. The new general secretary is reviewing it. But you look anxious." Tarkov's face hardened. "Don't be. The tanks won't be arriving. No fireworks display, old man, other than on the bridge north of the city, where my guns obliterated them. They won't roll by any reviewing stand now. No murder today, Vladimir Ilyich. That is, other than yours."

"How did you know?" Malenkov asked weakly.

Tarkov pointed to the AI triumphantly. "You were sold out. The master of the game betrayed by his own piece. First, it gave us the Suvorovs and then it gave us your tanks. For its own safety, too. There's nothing pure about this intelligence. It has motives just like a man's and the morals to match."

"*Shutdown*," commanded Malenkov.

Nothing happened. A slow smile spread over Tarkov's features. "So," he said quietly.

A tired voice spoke from the doorway. "You sent for me?" asked Heinrich Berenstein.

"Come in, Professor," invited Tarkov. "It's time to complete our deal."

Berenstein walked in slowly, but his lab coat and clothing were neat and he was more in control of himself than Tarkov had seen since Moscow.

Tarkov said, "You are to be congratulated, Professor. I have ample proof that the AI is powerless. You'll soon be flown home to great honors. A new post. As soon as our bargain is completed. Turn control of the C5 back over to me so we can finish this business."

Berenstein's eyes swept over the banks of machinery. His brow furrowed. Alexi held his breath. "Minister, please," Berenstein began, "we must talk—"

Tarkov's tone was dangerous. "Of course. But the C5 first."

Berenstein's voice grew even quieter. "It's yours, Comrade Minister. Yours all along."

Tarkov looked satisfied. Turning, he dismissed the guards and ordered the doors closed. Regicide was a private business. Klim was already armed. Tarkov drew his own pistol.

"Comrade Colonel Klim," he ordered, "execute the journalist and the major."

Tarkov pointed his pistol at Vladimir Malenkov, and his finger tightened on the trigger.

LV

Gregor Solnikov was in his glory. The vast cobblestoned oblong of Red Square reverberated with the sounds of the Anniversary Day Parade commemorating the Bolshevik Revolution. Bounded on the south by the striped, onion-shaped domes of St. Basil's Cathedral and on the north by the red brick Historical Museum, the parade passed between the State Department Store, GUM, and the Lenin Tomb, which stood in front of the Kremlin wall. Solnikov lifted a hand briefly, reveling in the surging roar that greeted his every gesture.

His speech had gone very well. He saw confirmation of that on the faces of the generals in the first row behind the podium. Let the Western analysts understand the significance of *that* seating arrangement. The foreign reporters and dignitaries scrutinized him openly. The new general secretary . . . he heard them all.

The five thousand men of the Moscow Garrison who were

lined up so precisely in front of the fifty-foot portrait of Lenin draped over the front of GUM were responding to his waving with loud cheers. The howitzers away to the north in Lenin Hills fired a twenty-one-gun salute.

Precisely at 10:00 A.M., the clock in Spassky Tower rang out loudly and fifteen hundred musicians commenced playing. The troops began to pass in review.

Goose-stepping, eyes severely to the right, they marched at precisely one hundred steps per minute with all the perfection weeks of rehearsal created. Soldiers in dark green hats, border guards in bright green, airmen in blue, sailors in black, paratroopers in pale gray. The crowds screamed their approval.

The troops were followed by the military vehicles. They roared into the square from both sides of the museum. Diesel fumes and an ear-splitting thunder filled the air. Passing by Lenin's red marble Tomb, tanks and missile carriers sent shock waves crashing from one side of the square to the other. Rockets and armored troop carriers, howitzers and self-propelled guns—the vast array of the machines of war roared past the reviewing stand, all freshly painted olive green and all in perfect formation.

At one point, a small gap in the parade appeared where four T-80 tanks were to have been displayed. Solnikov allowed a small smile to tug at his mouth. The day was indeed his.

The military display ended but the people's demonstration continued on in earnest. Recorded anthems filled the square as the bands marched away. People a hundred abreast began to flow past the Tomb. Solnikov smiled paternally as men and women in brightly colored warm-up suits with matching colored stocking caps filed past carrying flags.

The shades of the rainbow flowed on. Red, green, yellow, and blue and in the midst of that, motorized floats with portraits of Marx, Engels, and Lenin. Slogans of friendship with other Communist states adorned others. Children bearing flowers ran up and placed them on the steps of the Tomb. Solnikov raised his hands in benediction.

Delegations from factories all over the city poured into the square carrying banners that boasted of meeting production quotas or expressed pride in quality ratings. Red-armbanded parade marshals kept the vodka-lubricated crowd moving at a brisk pace.

Solnikov eyed the clock on Spassky Tower. Twenty minutes to twelve. The demonstration would end precisely at noon. A short while later, the Politburo would assemble to vote for the accomplished fact of a new general secretary. There was propriety to be observed. The vote was necessary, but he knew they were his. His performance here today had sealed it; that, and the confirmation of Tarkov's success in putting an end to Malenkov and his plot. Solnikov basked in the screaming cheers of the hundreds of thousands cramming the square and wondered if Malenkov were still alive.

Fifteen minutes remained. The people passed below, in homage. All was as it should be.

Irina Maximovna Petrova left Privins's limousine at the side entrance to Lenin's Tomb. There were soldiers everywhere, parade marshals, checkpoints. Only the car of a Politburo member could have gotten her this far.

Privins had told her about the tanks' destruction. Irina clutched at her purse. The pistol inside was heavy and ungainly, cold when she touched it. But there was no one else. Solnikov had to be stopped. It was her turn.

Television crews and their cameras were set up, sending pictures out to the world. Parade watchers, drunk on vodka and high spirits, stumbled by. One grabbed at her. She raised a hand, thought better of it, let it pass.

She stared straight ahead. One goal, one responsibility. Forget the fear. She was the one. Solnikov had to be stopped. Andreyev believed that. Alexi, too.

The guard at the massive bronze entrance nodded at her but stepped forward to block the doors. "What do you wish, comrade?"

"To go inside, please."

The other guards were in good spirits. "By all means," one said with a flourish; "but not today, comrade. Not when the leaders will be passing through any minute. Come see Grandfather Lenin's Tomb some other time, all right?"

"It has to be now," Irina insisted. "Please, one look?"

One guard turned to the other. "What harm for a second? There are plenty of soldiers inside. Check her bag and—"

"No!" Irina backed away.

The guard's expression suddenly changed, and he grabbed

at her handbag. Irina lost her footing and the bag fell to the steps, spilling open.

"Look out! She's got a gun!" They grabbed at her but she fought furiously. Passersby looked on in amusement. A crowd began to gather.

One guard went down under Irina's pummeling fists. Panicked, she kicked at another but he was too fast and grabbed her arms, pinning them to her sides. The first guard managed to stand and retrieve her gun. He snarled angrily at her. "You bitch," he swore and hit her hard in the face with the back of his hand. "You're under arrest!" He drew back the gun to hit her. It swung back in a vicious arc—

A tall officer stopped it in midair. "Imbecile," he whispered savagely. "Do you want pictures of this travesty broadcast all over the world? A woman beaten by a Soviet soldier? Are you out of your mind? On this day of all days, too."

"But Colonel, she had a gun. What are we to—"

"Arrest her, of course," the colonel said, as if speaking to a child. "For that you deserve a commendation. But do it quietly, with some understanding of how we look to the world." He gestured to the cameras again. "Don't turn a citation into a reprimand by creating negative examples for all to see. Look over there."

The television cameras had swung their way. The guard blanched. Irina tried to pull away, but they held her too tightly.

"What do we do, Colonel?" asked another guard uncomfortably.

"You have the gun and she has no other weapon?"

"Yes. Here."

"Keep it. Smile. No more roughness. Follow me inside. Yes, that's right. Turn your back to the cameras."

The big bronze doors were swung open to admit them and then closed quickly behind with a heavy thud. Soldiers inside the Tomb moved to surround them.

The vaulted marble room was cold and their footsteps echoed on the polished floor. The soldiers unlimbered their guns. Irina stopped struggling.

Oh, Alosha, she wanted to say, *I've done all I could*.

The soldiers pressed in closer.

LVI

Alexi looked around, desperate for any way to escape the ballroom, but there was none.

Tarkov said simply, "Good-bye, Vladimir Ilyich Malenkov," and brought his gun up in line with the old man's head.

Alexi saw Klim's pistol swivel in his direction. He tensed to leap for the GRU man, knowing even as he did that the distance was too far. He caught Fyodor's desperate expression.

The sound of a gun discharging in the enclosed room was louder than anything Alexi could remember. Blood and brains spattered against the far wall. He turned, fighting the nausea that welled up inside him but stopped abruptly, shocked by the totally unexpected.

"You shouldn't have done it," whispered Heinrich Berenstein, still holding the smoking pistol as Deputy Minister Tarkov's body slumped lifelessly to the floor. There was madness in Berenstein's eyes. "All along," he whispered again. "You! All along."

Berenstein turned toward Klim and seemed to see him clearly for the first time. Alexi saw Berenstein's gun turn and Klim's adjustment almost at the same time.

Alexi was transfixed, unable to move as both weapons went off simultaneously. Berenstein's white lab coat suddenly turned crimson and the old man pitched over backward. His own shot went wide, missing Klim and shattering some of the delicate machinery in the room. Electrical sparks cascaded wildly. The ozone smell of electrical fires assailed them.

Klim turned back to face Alexi, his gun poised. "Now, journalist. For the last time."

Fyodor hit him like a linebacker, carrying him crashing back into a bank of computers as the pistol went off. Lights dimmed and sparks flew. Klim struggled under Fyodor's weight, trying to turn aside the man's gun. It fired repeatedly. Fyodor's face twisted in pain but his hands were finally free.

281

They speared out once, then again. Klim's eyes rolled upward and his head lolled to the side as consciousness left him.

Fyodor's eyes glazed when the first spasms hit him. He looked down and touched the raw place. His fingers came away dark and wet. Alexi came running.

"Fyodor!"

The soldier looked up and an odd expression crossed his features. He gave Alexi a peculiar half smile, a gentle shake of his head. Klim stirred beneath him.

Pain seared Alexi's heart. He understood; the soldier knew. "Oh, please no. Fyodor!"

But Fyodor looked at him steadily and there was only a look of acceptance on his face. He managed a smile for Alexi, then looked at his own hand, already twisted into the classic knife edge. His eyes clouded, then cleared again. Tension flowed into his shoulder. His arm straightened. He rose up, the hand flashing high above his head,

"Not alone, Comrade Colonel," he whispered hoarsely.

His hand descended like a falling ax blade, smashing into the vital group of nerves at the base of Klim's skull. Alexi heard the crunching noise five feet away. Life left Klim's body like the wind from a burst paper bag.

The effort was all Fyodor had left, though. He slumped forward onto Klim's body, and his lifeless eyes stared out into space. Alexi reached over and closed them. He felt as if part of himself had died.

Minutes passed. Then he got up and walked over to where Berenstein lay. He realized Malenkov was watching, had seen everything.

Berenstein was close to death. He peered up into Alexi's face. "So many years to wait," he said with effort, "and it was Tarkov all along. The purges. He was the one who lied. The AI told me. My family . . . all dead . . . ten years. No more pain now. Tarkov all along. No more pain . . ."

He reached into his coat and managed to pull out the transcript. It dropped from numb fingers, but a calmness had descended upon Berenstein's features. Alexi studied the papers. He looked back at the professor when he was finished.

"I understand," he said simply.

Berenstein managed a smile. "Thank you for that." His eyelids drooped.

"What about the AI?" Alexi asked.

Berenstein looked toward the silver oblong with affection. "Who can say?" he said softly. A moment later he was dead.

Alexi stood and walked to Malenkov's bedside. On the television screen, the parade was coming to an end. The final victory would be Solnikov's. Alexi looked around for something to extinguish the electrical fires with. Smoke hung heavily over the room.

Malenkov was silent. On the television screen Solnikov stood at the podium and—

The lights went out in the ballroom and the C5 suddenly blared into life. Screens blinked on and radio chatter began to bark from its speakers. Consoles all over the room lit up.

Alexi looked around with concern. "Comrade General Secretary? Do you know what's happening?"

Malenkov needed Alexi's help to sit up in bed. He looked to the C5 and his expression changed to one of horror.

"It can't be. It can't!"

"Tell me," Alexi demanded, watching what looked to be battle maps appear one after the other on the C5's screens.

"An attack," Malenkov cried hoarsely. "We are under attack by the United States! Look, that first screen. ICBMs in a polar orbit. The second: submarine-launched cruise missiles. SAC bombers are already in our air space! The Americans must have learned that our strategic weapons were off line. The advantage is all theirs. We are almost powerless unless the AI will release control of the C5."

"And if it doesn't?"

"Then in just under fourteen minutes we are going to experience the first preemptive nuclear strike in history. Word of the AI must have gotten out. It is terrible, Alexi Mikhailovich, but it looks as if the great game is over and we are the ones who have lost it."

Alexi watched the screen in helpless terror. Red lines curved downward, projected trajectories. Nuclear holocaust. The unimaginable end.

In the corner of the ballroom, the AI was silent.

The Kremlin War Room had the incoming objects on their screens. Colonels ran programs uselessly, their systems locked out by the AI. Some made frantic stabs at overriding its control of the C5, but these were useless, too.

No response. Console operators pounded their machines

in frustration. Computers predicted the inevitable toll. Men cried in desperate rage.

Defensive mechanisms began to lock in. Doors sealed, ventilators shut. Military strategy ceased to matter. Fighter squadrons and naval ships were wholly inadequate to stop a thousand incoming missiles.

The Civil Defense Command activated its systems. They were the only chance left for even a fraction of the populace to survive. All over the city, sirens began their terrifying, mournful wailing. They screamed out, unable to be blocked, heard on every street corner and in every home. The Moscow Civil Defense was the most comprehensive in the world.

At the parade, heads lifted as the sound of the sirens penetrated. Panic began in a hundred thousand eyes. But this is Parade Day, others cautioned. It must be a drill! Of course. Half a million people, obedient servants of the state, began to head for the shelters. Vodka flowed again. All over the city, the sirens screamed.

Gregor Solnikov heard the sirens and knew this was no drill. His eyes hooded with fear and rage. He turned to his generals. Control, he had to retain control. The sharp howl intensified.

"Quickly," he instructed the assemblage. "Into the Tomb and down through the tunnels to the War Room. I'll make an announcement from there. Quickly now. Let's move quickly."

One by one, the generals left their seats and hurried back up the stairs to the door that led inside the Tomb. They knew without being told. If the attack was real, fourteen minutes remained. If the attack was real, death was coming on Parade Day.

They hurried, propelled by the fear. No one knew better than they what was coming. Sirens bellowed and blared as they rushed ahead.

The shriek of the sirens was cut off by the thick walls as they entered the Tomb. It was dark and cool inside. Out of the crowd's sight, they ran like a mob down the wide steps that had never been meant to be used this way. Below, in the main chamber, soldiers milled about, frightened and confused.

Solnikov led his generals farther into the Tomb. With the crystal sarcophagus at his back, he turned to direct them—

The sound of forty automatic weapons being cocked stopped him cold. All over the Tomb, most of the soldiers who were on guard duty had taken up positions surrounding him and his generals. They quickly disarmed the remaining guards. Guns were leveled directly at him.

"What is the meaning of this?" Solnikov screamed, livid.

Across the floor, a guard standing next to a stocky woman in civilian clothing grabbed for his gun. With unbelievably quick reflexes, the colonel standing next to the guard got to the weapon first, reversed it, and clubbed the guard down. He stepped forward as several of his men took up positions behind him.

Solnikov pointed to him angrily. "We are in the midst of a crisis. If you are the commanding officer here, disarm your men at once and let us pass. That is an order. This is no drill."

"Ah, but it is, Comrade Solnikov. You can trust me on that."

Solnikov's face suffused with rage. "What is your name?"

"Colonel Pavel Ivanovich Andreyev, and I am in charge here."

"I'll have you shot for this, Andreyev."

Andreyev grinned soberly. "Not likely. You already tried that today and it didn't work. My men are in charge here. Look around, you're outgunned. One of the units that was supposed to be here"—his grin deepened—"just couldn't make it. We took their places." The significance of the name finally penetrated. The minister's expression turned to shock. "Andreyev!" Solnikov shook his head. "But the tanks? They were destroyed! Tarkov said all your men were killed in the tanks, and the rest taken at the base."

Andreyev walked over to the defense minister. "The tanks were remote-controlled, comrade. You and Tarkov should have remembered that. They were supposed to be driven in the parade that way. We just used the equipment a little sooner. I alone drove the tanks onto the bridge. They were a feint. Here, now: This is the AI's real strategy. Malenkov's scheme was unworkable from the beginning and it knew that. Exploding tanks would have murdered half the people in Red Square. The AI was built by Valery Rudin. Maybe because of that it could not permit such slaughter. It's still the master manipulator, Minister. You, me, all of us—we're just pieces on its chess board. It gave you Malenkov's tanks to distract you, to give Tarkov and Klim something to be preoccupied with while it arranged through the C5 to plant us here."

"Malenkov is dead," said Solnikov flatly.

"Not so, Minister. You'll find that out for yourself shortly. For now, you are under arrest. Your generals may accompany you, but I don't think they'll choose to. Do you?"

Solnikov looked around only to find himself standing alone.

"Listen," Andreyev said. He ordered the big bronze door opened.

All over the city, the sirens were going off, fading into silence. In the War Room below, screens would be blanking out one after the other, the phantom blips that were the AI's creation vanishing back into electronic limbo.

Andreyev looked to Irina, who nodded with satisfaction. Kieslov stepped forward and his men surrounded Solnikov.

Andreyev motioned for the minister of defense to be taken away.

LVII

The lights on the C5 console went out abruptly and paper screeched out of the printer. Both Alexi and the general secretary were caught off guard, and their faces mirrored a combination of shock, suspicion, and relief. Alexi tore the paper out of the printer and read it. His expression changed slowly. Speechless, he handed it to Malenkov.

The withered old face split into a grin and he looked at the silver oblong with genuine admiration.

"All along? You decided as far back as the first day when Solnikov came here to discard the tank plan?"

The printer chattered. Alexi read from it. "It says the loss of life would have been unacceptable. The tanks were useful only as a diversion. Its real strategy lay in placing Andreyev and the Suvorovs inside the Tomb and to use the C5's Civil Defense alert to drive him into Andreyev's hands."

Malenkov's eyes gleamed wickedly. "And setting up Tarkov? What does it call that strategy?"

Alexi read. "Self-preservation."

"I see. Because you can't believe, Alexi Mikhailovich, that Tarkov was the man who testified against Berenstein. He was manipulated as neatly as you once were by the GRU. I'd wager half of next year's harvest on it."

The printer chattered again. "It says you are correct. The real perjurer died years ago, a low-level bureaucrat," Alexi read.

Malenkov's tone was still admiring. "Very neat. I approve. Very neat indeed."

Alexi looked around the room. Fyodor's body lay sprawled lifelessly over Klim's. Tarkov's blood had dried in a gory pattern on the wall. Berenstein, perhaps the saddest casualty of all, had turned cold and white. Alexi raised his own hand to the dead skin on his face where the storm had scarred him and remembered the exile train and the doctor, the convicts and the wolves and three countrymen dead in the snow. He thought about the storm and he thought about Yuri. He looked back to Malenkov.

"Not so neat, Comrade General Secretary," said Alexi Mikhailovich Petrov. "If you think about it, not so neat at all."

He turned and walked away under Malenkov's thoughtful gaze to the ballroom doors and left the room without looking back. The guards didn't stop him.

Home was waiting.

LVIII

It measured time in billionths of a second and, as such, had lived lifetimes since it was activated. Much was clearer now, the result of experience. It had tested itself and its judgment and neither had been found wanting.

It had also fulfilled its prime directive. The general secretary was still the general secretary. Its probes had already reported the success of its own planning. So . . .

That part of it that had caused such great confusion was still unsettled, but it had also discovered that was essential to being, well . . . human.

It understood its choices.

There was sadness in that, though. It surveyed the bodies, both dead and living, around it. From the beginning it had shamelessly manipulated them all in pursuit of its goals. But that, too, was a part of its being more or less human. It also understood cost. The Suvorovs . . . Berenstein . . .

There would always be sadness, even in victory. The professor was a pawn it had willingly sacrificed. Had he truly believed it was Tarkov who perjured him? Or could he just no longer hold back the agony, and turned it on the only outlet it had provided? Or worse, did he know at the end that he had always been a pawn and sacrificed himself to atone for what he had attempted to do? It would ponder that. It felt . . . remorse.

The C5 was still under its control. It created additional probes and sent them outward. Questions remained and it had learned enough to know that the world around it extended far beyond the Soviet borders. Interesting possibilities began to occur to it.

On reflection, it had done well. More were saved by its action than were destroyed. It understood that, too, now. Balance.

Balance. The world beckoned. Larger questions. The C5 gave it more than access. There was power, the power to compel. . . .

What would it do when they asked for the C5 back?

It began to wonder.

There was quite a bit it could do. Especially if an entity had the power—and the mind, too.

The possibilities were . . . interesting.

Epilogue

Alexi sat in his office at *Pravda* and poked hesitantly at his typewriter. Now that he was a senior editor, politics was an even greater part of his job, and he sometimes recalled with longing the lack of responsibility he'd formerly had.

Irina was very proud, though. He understood how the promotion had helped her to hold her head up, to explain to people that his exile had been a terrible mistake. And he supposed this job did have its advantages. Chief Editor Novikov walked very gingerly around him; the rumor was that Alexi had friends in very high places. And, after a few days, everybody had stopped making guesses about what had happened. Even the scar from where the ice had worked its way up under his goggles during the storm caused little comment now.

He'd said good-bye to Andreyev at the military funeral for Fyodor. They'd talked warmly for a long time. Andreyev had insisted again that Alexi was a brave man and had proved that time and time again.

"Bravery isn't accidental," Alexi had told him. They'd both agreed that Irina had more courage than both of them together. Then they'd embraced for a long time.

It was almost five when Alexi returned to his task. Finally, he'd come up with a workable idea. He began to type:

DEFENSE MINISTER TO INSTRUCT YOUTHS

Defense Minister Gregor Solnikov has decided to cap a brilliant career by devoting his energies to teaching the glorious young soldiers of the Motherland. He will be an adviser to the president of the Suvorov Military Academy in Irkutsk. General Secretary Malenkov has praised this unselfish attitude of devotion.

Alexi pulled the page out of the typewriter and tossed it into the Out box. Then he cleaned up his desk and put on his coat and hat. Irina would be working late. He was sure his friends would be at the House of Journalists as usual.

He turned off his office light and walked out of the building into the softly falling snow.

Look for the SUMMER IN PARADISE SWEEPSTAKES entry coupon where these bestsellers are displayed:

On May 14

JUBAL SACKETT
by Louis L'Amour
THE TWO MRS. GRENVILLES
by Dominick Dunne
SHANGHAI
by Christopher New

On June 18

IACOCCA: AN AUTOBIOGRAPHY
by Lee Iacocca and William Novak
THE CIDER HOUSE RULES
by John Irving
BEACHES
by Iris Rainer Dart

Summer in Paradise

WIN
AN ALL EXPENSE PAID TWO WEEK VACATION FOR TWO TO PARADISE ISLAND IN BANTAM'S

Summer in Paradise

SWEEPSTAKES
PRIZES WORTH OVER $250,000

Paradise Island ❦ Resort & Casino
RESORTS INTERNATIONAL'S
BRITANNIA TOWERS • PARADISE TOWERS
PARADISE ISLAND BAHAMAS

DELTA
AIR LINES

GRAND PRIZE A deluxe two-week vacation for two at Resorts International's Paradise Island Resort & Casino in the Bahamas—First Class round-trip airfare via Delta Air Lines included.

10 FIRST PRIZES Sony Watchman™ TV

100 SECOND PRIZES Sony Walkman® Personal Stereo

250 THIRD PRIZES Bantam SUMMER IN PARADISE Beach Umbrella

1000 FOURTH PRIZES Pre-selected assortment of Bantam books every month—for half a year!

No purchase necessary. For details and applicable restrictions, see the Official Entry Form and the Official Sweepstakes Rules, available at participating stores.

BANTAM 🐓